BLIND RAGE

TERRI PERSONS

arrow books

Published in the United Kingdom by Arrow Books in 2009

1 3 5 7 9 10 8 6 4 2

First published in Great Britain in 2008 by
Century

Arrow Books
Random House, 20 Vauxhall Bridge Road,
London SW1V 2SA

www.rbooks.co.uk

Addresses for companies within The Random House Group Limited can be
found at: www.randomhouse.co.uk/offices.htm

The Random House Group Limited Reg. No. 954009

A CIP catalogue record for this book
is available from the British Library

ISBN 9780099504221

The Random House Group Limited supports The Forest Stewardship
Council (FSC), the leading international forest certification organisation. All
our titles that are printed on Greenpeace approved FSC certified paper carry
the FSC logo. Our paper procurement policy can be found at
www.rbooks.co.uk/environment

Mixed Sources
Product group from well-managed
forests and other controlled sources
www.fsc.org Cert no. TT-COC-2139
© 1996 Forest Stewardship Council
FSC

Printed in Great Britain by
CPI Bookmarque Ltd, Croydon, CR0 4TD

This book is dedicated to
my brother, Joseph,
his wife, Rita,
and their children,
Anthony, Robert, and Christina.

They have always been there for me and mine
with their love, faith, and sense of family.

Acknowledgments

My devoted husband, David, and our wonderful sons, Ryan and Patrick, keep me buoyant in this journey with their love and trust. I'm a blessed woman.

I continue to be awed by the excellent work of my agent, Esther Newberg, and my editor, Phyllis Grann.

I'm thankful for my supportive pals in the First Friday Club, a collection of cranky journalists and ex-journalists who meet once a month to gossip over soup and sandwiches. Where should we go for lunch next, guys?

To my buddy John Camp: Thank you for the ongoing advice and friendship.

Blind Rage

Prologue

THE HOUSE WAS FILLED WITH THE WARM AROMAS OF CHILI
powder and fried ground beef, the only leftovers from taco night. In
the white kitchen a boy sat at the table with his hands folded atop the
white linen as if immersed in a postmeal prayer. He was dressed in a
parochial school uniform: light blue oxford shirt, navy necktie, navy
slacks, thick-soled black shoes. Without being given any instructions,
he'd already wiped down the stovetop, cleared the table, scraped the
plates, and loaded the dishwasher. The racket of the rinse cycle rumbled under the counter, but it was the noise overhead that made his
eyes cloud with terror. The tub was running. In any other home, the
musical drum of water hitting the porcelain would mean it was bath
time. In this house the sound was a dirge.

Though his body was immobile with fear, his mind was convulsing
with questions and answers: *What did I do? I didn't do shit . . . Mid-
quarter grades are coming out. Did I get a B in anything? No fucking
way . . . Did the nuns bug Dad at the office over some bullshit, something I did during lunch or gym or mass? No. I'd know. School would
have hauled me into the office before calling him . . . Did Mom find
something in my room? Hell no. Nothing there to find . . . What is
it, then? What did I do?*

The rinse cycle lurched to a halt, leaving the running tub to a solo performance. He stared up at the ceiling and tried to kid himself: *Maybe Mom is taking one of her bubble baths. That must be it. All the worry for nothing.* The harsh voice of reality broke through: *Not this early. She'd miss her hospital show.*

Am I the one in trouble?

The yells rolling down the stairs from the second floor answered his question.

His father's booming voice: "Care to explain this?"

A teenager's rebellious response: "Weren't you listening? It's not mine!"

"Then whose is it? How did you end up with it?"

His mother, using a sweet singsong tone that was more frightening than his dad's loudest barks: "Answer your father. Tell the truth. We'll find out if you're lying. We always find out."

"It's not mine," the teen repeated.

The sugar voice again: "Come on now. How stupid do you think your parents are? It was in your backpack."

"I don't know how it got there. I swear to God. One of the kids at school must have put it in there."

"Who put it there?" bellowed his father. "When? How? Why would they?"

A litany of excuses: "None of them like me . . . Maybe they didn't want to get caught with it . . . They could have done it as a joke, while I was riding the bus . . . I don't know. I just know it's not mine."

"Fuck," the boy breathed to the ceiling. The reasons for his sibling's unworthiness scrolled through his head: *Can't even come up with a decent lie. Dummy deserves it. Always causing trouble. Always picking a fight with them.*

The tub faucet overhead squeaked to a stop, and all thought fled his mind in a panic.

Heavy footsteps took the stairs down slowly and purposefully. The boy lowered his eyes as his father stepped into the kitchen. He was tall, lean, and square-shouldered. Though his eyes were cool, his face retained the flush from the upstairs shouting match. His close-cropped hair echoed the military-like trim of his son's cut. He was still dressed for work, his only concession to being home was a slight loosening of his tie. Taking in the cleared table and countertop, he smiled. "Good job."

"Thank you, sir."

"Taco night's always fun, isn't it?"

"It is, sir."

"I need you to come upstairs now. You've got one more chore, and then you can hit the books. If you get done early, you can catch the second half of the Vikings."

The boy stayed seated, hoping to put off the inevitable.

"Now, son."

"Yes, sir." The boy bolted up from his seat, knocking his chair backward onto the white tile. He righted the chair while stumbling over an apology. "Sorry, sir . . . sorry."

"Don't worry about it, son. Accidents happen." The man checked his watch. "Now let's get moving. I have some calls to make before the game starts."

Trying to stall, the boy looked down at his polished shoes. "Shouldn't I . . . change first, sir? My school clothes might get . . ."

"A little water never hurt anything," said his father. He turned and walked out of the kitchen.

The boy followed wordlessly. Head bent, he slowly mounted the stairs after his father. Silently, he delivered a petition to God: *Please blind me. Don't make me watch this time.*

Chapter 1

MINNESOTA BRACED ITSELF FOR A WHITE HALLOWEEN. ONE of the wettest summers on record had been followed by a frigid fall, inviting speculation that there'd be snow on the ground by the end of October. Northland kids were accustomed to incorporating rain gear into their costumes, creating Spidermen in slickers and vampires armed with umbrellas. Being forced to add boots and mittens and down vests to their ensembles wouldn't be a huge leap; the show would go on.

In every neighborhood, picture windows were plastered with paper ghosts and Frankenstein monster heads, subtle declarations of war against the threatened early winter. Plastic tombstones were propped in front yards like protest signs. Bags of mini–candy bars were optimistically stockpiled in cupboards. Orange lights dripped from bushes and twined around tree limbs. Rubber skeletons dangled from porch ceilings while glowing skulls punched through the darkness.

The scariest thing about the Midwest that autumn, however, was the water.

Six college women had drowned in the Mississippi over a period of six months. Four had gone into the river at the University of Minnesota's Minneapolis campus, and two had perished around the

University of Wisconsin in La Crosse. Authorities determined that the women had killed themselves, but rumors of a serial killer and a cover-up persisted and grew. By that fall, the police and the public were at each other's throats.

Students demonstrated on both campuses, demanding the investigations into the deaths be reopened. During a press conference held in La Crosse, angry community members shouted down the cops and college administrators. The father of one of the Twin Cities victims took a swing at a university vice president in the middle of a regents' meeting. The mood was so volatile, professors on both sides of the border teamed up to issue an open letter to the cities asking for calm.

Bernadette Saint Clare, the FBI's lone agent in its downtown St. Paul office—a subterranean cell in the Warren E. Burger Federal Building—was not invited to the investigation. She sat at her desk late Monday morning, reading a *Star Tribune* story that rehashed the deaths.

The first drowning had taken place in April. No one witnessed the woman's plunge into the river, but University of Minnesota police found a note on the upper deck of the Washington Avenue Bridge. They called the death a suicide. The freshman's own parents agreed with the ruling, revealing that the girl had struggled with emotional problems and had been seeing psychiatrists off and on over the years.

"Sounds pretty cut and dried," Bernadette muttered, flipping to the next page of the news story.

The second drowning took place a month later, probably in the middle of the night. No one saw the jump, but authorities believed the graduate student could have gone off the same bridge. In place of a note, police found a telltale scarf left at the base of a lamppost. Another troubled young woman, they said. Another suicide. A drowning in June left investigators and university officials fearing a rash of copycat suicides. A flurry of press releases from health organizations followed, warning the public about the signs of depression.

Television news tapped assorted shrinks for interviews. Suicide help lines geared up for action.

For two months, there were no drownings at the University of Minnesota. Downriver was another story. During the summer session at the University of Wisconsin in La Crosse, two girls died, one of them in July and the other in August. In each case, the young woman had left a tavern on a Saturday night and turned up floating in the Mississippi days later. Autopsies determined the girls had been drinking. While neither had left a suicide note, both had been battling depression and eating disorders.

Come September, a medical student disappeared from the University of Minnesota campus after attending an evening seminar. Her high heels were found at the base of the rail lining the Washington Avenue Bridge, inspiring the editor of an underground student newspaper to dub the walkway "Murderer's Alley." Her body hadn't been found.

Reporters in both states connected the dots between the Twin Cities and La Crosse deaths, and the fists started flying.

Bernadette knew there were things going on behind the scenes that could serve to either placate the fearful public or inflame it further. The FBI's Milwaukee and Minneapolis offices were joining together to quietly review all the evidence in the deaths to see if local law enforcement had missed something. Were these drownings truly suicides, or were they the work of a serial killer?

"I could figure it out," Bernadette muttered to the newsprint.

She'd begged her immediate supervisor—Assistant Special Agent in Charge Tony Garcia—to let her pitch in. Garcia had instead assigned her to tracking down yet another bank robber, this one dubbed the Fishing Hat Bandit. She suspected her ASAC was holding her back from the bigger case because he feared she'd mess it up, especially if she tried utilizing *all* of her abilities.

She folded the newspaper and dropped it into the wastebasket next to her desk, one of three in her basement office. The other two were unoccupied, at least by living beings, and she used them as extra workspaces. They both contained dead computer monitors and were piled with paperwork.

Reluctantly, she reached for the manila file folder she'd kept pushed to the side of her desktop like a moldy sandwich. Flipping it open, she started to read. Overhead, she heard banging and sawing. They were renovating the building, a project that had started over the summer and promised to stretch well into the next calendar year. The sound of a jackhammer joined the chorus.

When her phone rang above the din, she was more than happy to drop the robber's file and pick up the receiver. "Agent Saint Clare!"

Garcia: "Why are you hollering at me?"

The racket stopped, and she glanced up at the ceiling. "Sorry. Construction noise is making me deaf."

"We've got another one, Cat."

Bernadette ran a hand through her short blond hair. "Which bank?"

"No. Another drowning victim. I need you at the scene."

She pushed the Fishing Hat file off to the side again. "What's changed? Why do you want me now?"

"This one turned up dead in her own bathtub."

She switched the phone to her other ear. "It can't be a suicide, then, right? This is something else."

"I don't know what it is. Just get over here."

Bernadette grabbed a pen and a pad. "Where am I going?"

"Dinkytown," Garcia said.

Dinkytown was a Minneapolis neighborhood immediately north of the University of Minnesota's east bank. "She lived in an apartment?"

"Shared a house with a bunch of other gals. It's off Fourth Street."

Bernadette scratched down the address and his directions. "I'll be there in twenty."

"Take a company car," he said. "Please."

Bernadette rolled her eyes. Garcia had been scolding her for continuing to drive her Ford pickup on the job. "All right. I'll take the damn Vicky. You happy?"

"Never," he said, and hung up.

She checked the holstered Glock tucked into her slacks, slipped her coat on over her blazer, and pulled on her leather gloves. It was cold out, but that's not why she shielded her hands. She didn't want any surprises this time. Even though it was a cloudy day, she plucked her sunglasses off her desk and dropped them in her pocket. Once she got to the scene, she didn't want to surprise anybody with her eyes.

SHE BUMPED OUT of the parking ramp and steered the Crown Vic to Wabasha Street. After a half mile of stop-and-go movement through the heart of downtown St. Paul, she turned onto Interstate 94 heading west. Traffic was heavy and got worse as she neared the Minneapolis border. Ever since she'd returned to her home state, she'd been struck by how congested the Twin Cities roads had become. She took the Huron Boulevard exit to the University of Minnesota. Huron Boulevard Southeast became Southeast Fourth Street.

Braking at a red light, she took in the storefront shops and restaurants lining the street. While she'd been born and raised on a farm, she had cousins who'd lived in town and attended the "Zoo of M," as they called it. They told her Minnesota native Bob Dylan wrote "Positively 4th Street" about this particular route and that he'd lived somewhere around Dinkytown. She'd visited the neighborhood a couple of times when she was a teenager. The Varsity Theater looked pretty much the way she remembered it, and so did many of the storefronts, but the students looked a little dressier. They seemed younger, too. Maybe that was because she was so much older than the last time she'd called the state home.

Adjusting the rearview mirror of the bureau car, she noted that the woman in the reflection was pale and tired looking—she rarely got a full night's sleep—but carried no lines on her face. When she dressed in jeans and sweatshirts (her preferred weekend attire), she could pass for a teenage boy. Was that a good thing or a bad thing for a thirty-eight-year-old woman? Frowning into the mirror, she took her sunglasses out of her coat and put them on. Now she looked like a teenage boy wearing shades.

The light turned green, and she accelerated.

Chapter 2

BERNADETTE DIDN'T NEED TO DOUBLE-CHECK THE ADDRESS
as she approached the house; the circus had to be visible from outer
space. A fleet of Minneapolis squad cars lined both sides of the narrow road. Parked on the street directly in front of the house were
an EMS ambulance and a medical examiner's wagon; only one of
the rigs would be leaving with a passenger. Uniformed officers and
plainclothes investigators milled around the walk leading up to the
home. Police tape stretched across the front yard and ran down each
side. The lawn was planted with cardboard tombstones. Television
crews were going to have a field day setting up with those props in
the background. She'd lay money at least one television reporter was
going to use the word *ironically* during a live shot.

What's that behind you, Angela?

*Ironically, Jeff, Halloween grave markers decorate the victim's
front yard.*

Bernadette cruised past the house and drove two blocks down to
the reporters' ghetto. She parked between two television news vans,
both plastered with propaganda claiming their station was number
one in breaking news. While she walked, she dug her ID wallet out
of her coat.

When she got to the sidewalk that ran in front of the home, she could make out the tombstones' inscriptions. *Here rests the Pillsbury Doughboy. He will rise again.* Another read: *RIP. Barry M. Deep.* The house was a two-story box covered in wood clapboard, with a sagging open porch running across the width of it. The front of the house was painted lemon yellow and the sides were lime green. She wondered which fruity clearance color decorated the back.

Two uniforms from Minneapolis PD stopped her the instant she stepped over the yellow tape. She held up her identification, and the bigger officer took it. She waited for him to ask her to remove her shades, but he didn't. He handed the ID back to her. "They're waiting for you."

Bernadette stuffed the wallet back in her pocket and navigated around the police officers clogging the walk.

A blob in a wrinkled suit stepped in front of her and blocked her way. He was Greg Thorsson, an agent from the bureau's Milwaukee office. He compensated for his diminutive stature with a gargantuan mouth. She'd worked with him years earlier when they were both posted in St. Louis. He started in with the insults as if they'd never parted ways. "What'd you do, stop for a latte?"

"Nice to see you, too, Greg." She veered around him. "Has your wife wised up yet and left you for another woman?"

He was on her heels as she started up the front steps. "Garcia must be desperate if he called in the witch doctor."

"Voodoo priestess," she said over her shoulder. "Get it right." As she weaved through the bodies crowding the porch, she felt the stares burning a hole in her back. As soon as she was inside, the cops would join Thorsson with the lame jokes. She'd heard it all before, behind her back and to her face. She could write the one-liners herself.

Where're her broom and crystal ball? . . . Maybe she can bring Hoover back from the dead . . . How about I dig my Ouija board outta the closet for backup?

Following her onto the porch, Thorsson continued the jabs. "Gonna cast an evil spell on me?"

She pivoted around and looked pointedly at his round belly. "I already have."

"You're not very Minnesota nice."

"Neither are you." She threw open the front door and went inside.

In the home's foyer, she spotted two men from the bureau's Minneapolis office yapping with a homicide detective. One of the agents gave her a nod and continued talking. The Minneapolis crew didn't know her well, and that was fine with Bernadette. While she'd initially wanted to work in the bureau's larger downtown Minneapolis office, she'd grown used to her basement digs in downtown St. Paul.

Garcia had instructed her to go to the second floor, and she started up the open staircase.

Someone yelled after her, "Hey!"

Thorsson had followed her inside. "Go away," she said without turning around. Looking to the top of the stairs, she could see her ASAC standing by himself, his black hair trimmed with Marine efficiency and his weight lifter's arms pushing out the sleeves of his trench coat. His back was to the stairs.

The pain in the ass jogged up next to her. "I heard you blew away a bad guy this spring. Any of that post-traumatic shit going on with you? You gonna snap on us?"

Thorsson was referring to a case she'd worked the previous May with Garcia. She and her boss had shot the killer dead. "If I snap, Greg, I promise to take you out first."

When the two agents reached the second floor, Garcia turned around and glared at Thorsson. "Don't you have someplace you need to be, Agent?"

Thorsson folded his stumpy arms in front of his bowling-ball body. "Sir. I thought Agent Saint Clare needed—"

"Agent Saint Clare doesn't need a damn thing," Garcia snapped.

Bernadette stifled a grin.

"Yes, sir," said Thorsson. He hesitated for a moment, seemingly unsure of where to go, then turned around and thumped down the stairs. He headed for a knot of police officers gathered at the bottom.

Garcia watched Thorsson with a frown and then looked at Bernadette. "Jesus. Did you fly here or what?"

She blinked, wondering for a moment if her boss was now taking shots at her, then realized she had indeed made the drive in record time despite the traffic. "How many did Milwaukee send?"

"Thorsson and another guy."

"So they sent one agent."

Garcia smiled. "Not bad, Cat."

She liked that her boss dropped the formalities when they were alone. She smiled and addressed him in kind. "Where are we going, Tony?"

With a tip of his head, he motioned her down the hallway. "This way."

While she followed him, Bernadette took off her sunglasses. She didn't need the camouflage with Garcia; he'd gotten used to her exotic eyes. "Crime lab here?"

"Come and gone."

She glanced around the second story. "How many bedrooms?"

"Three up. One on the main floor. Plus there's a bedroom under construction in the basement."

"Anyone hear anything? Who was actually inside the house?"

At the end of the long hallway, he stopped at a closed door. "Nobody was home all weekend except for the victim."

"That seems odd, with all the students living here."

"The other girls had gone home to Mom and Dad or were shacked up with boyfriends."

"I didn't think the U was such a suitcase college."

"For some it is. Depends on the kid, I suppose. Depends on the living arrangement. Whether the roommates get along." He snapped on a pair of gloves.

"So why wasn't she back home?"

"Home is—was—a bit of a longer drive. Chicago." He handed her a set of latex. "You're going to want these."

She held up her hands, clad in leather gloves. "These will work."

"You'll ruin them. Tub's only got a couple of inches of water left in it, but it's yucky water."

"I can guess why it's yucky." She took off her leather drivers, stuffed them in her coat pockets, and yanked on the latex. "What happened to the rest of the bathwater?"

"The tub's got one of those old-fashioned rubber cork deals on a chain. The kid who found her freaked, and his first instinct was to pull the stopper. It started to empty, and then the cork thing got sucked back into the drain."

"Give me the timing and all that. She was last seen by her house-mates—"

"Friday afternoon."

"She wasn't found until this morning?"

"Here's the deal. The basement, first-floor, and other second-floor apartments each have a small bathroom with a stool, sink, and shower. The other girls laid claim to them. Each chick got her own john, basically."

"As God and Mother Nature intended it."

"Our girl"—he fished a notebook out of his coat pocket, flipped it open, and read—"Shelby Hammond, age twenty and a junior ma-joring in psychology, was saddled with this goofy bedroom that's got a toilet stool in a tiny closet, and a bathtub sitting smack-dab in the middle of the room."

"Weird."

"The room is really a large bathroom," Garcia explained. "The owner added a bay window and a closet and called it a bedroom so he could squeeze in another student renter."

"Getting stuck with a tub would have annoyed me," said Berna-dette. "I have to have a shower. I hate baths."

"I'm not a tub fan either, and this didn't change my mind any." He flipped a page. "Minneapolis PD said one of the roommates' boy-friends found the body. He'd stopped by to pick his girlfriend up for class this morning and had to take a quick leak. All the other bath-rooms were tied up, of course."

"Of course."

"He thought our psychology major had left for class already and pushed open the bedroom door to use her closet toilet."

"They don't lock their doors around here?"

"Nope." Garcia opened the bedroom door.

"I'll bet they start locking them now," said Bernadette as the two of them faced the tub, one limb from the corpse draped over the side.

Chapter 3

THE TUB WAS ACROSS THE ROOM, SITUATED ALONGSIDE THE
bay window. A brass bed, a vanity with an attached mirror, and a tall
chest of drawers crowded the rest of the room. Pink shag carpeting
covered the floor, and matching pink fabric dressed the bed and the
bay window. Pink posters were tacked up on every wall, a pink Babe
on Board road sign hung from the wall over the bed, and fuzzy pink
dice dangled from the dresser mirror. The only things that weren't
overwhelmingly pink were the tub and its occupant.

From where Bernadette and Garcia stood just inside the threshold,
all that was visible over the top of the white tub was a white leg thrown
over the side. The porcelain and the flesh were identically pale, as if they
were part of the same modern sculpture. The toes of the white foot offered the only splash of color, with nails that were painted pink.

Bernadette walked over to the side of the tub, her shoes squishing
on the soggy carpet that surrounded it. "Why is it that all redheads
look like spitfires when they're alive . . ."

"And so damn dead when they're dead?" asked Garcia, coming up
next to her.

"Yeah. No one does dead like a redhead. It's like their skin turns
to wax or something. Why is that?"

"Maybe it's because they're so white to begin with," offered Garcia. "I'm sure there's a scientific reason."

The dead woman provided no opinion on the matter. With the one leg draped over the side and the other slightly bent at the knee, she was sprawled out on her back. Her arms were thrown up over her head and rested against the back of the tub. Her long hair fanned out in the shallow water and fell across her face, looking like the tendrils of some sort of orange sea plant. Her dead eyes—twin water bugs—peeked out from behind the hair.

Bruises dotted her legs and arms, showing she had flailed about. Constraint marks were visible around her shoulders, collarbone, and base of her neck. The water was murky; she'd defecated while she was struggling or her bowels had released after she'd succumbed. Bernadette hunkered down along the side of the tub. "She went kicking and fighting, the poor thing."

"Seems so."

She lifted one of the corpse's hands off the back of the tub and scrutinized the fingernails, painted the same shade of pink as the toenails. "I don't see any skin under her nails."

"If there was anything to be had, CSI got it."

"Right," she said, and set the hand back down.

Garcia bent over, plucked something off the carpet, and held it in front of his face. A rose petal. Pink. The crime scene crew hadn't bagged all of them. More were sprinkled in the dirty water. "What was this about?"

Bernadette picked a petal off the shag. "I'd say Miss Shelby Hammond was entertaining a gentleman."

"Couldn't a girl do that for herself? Sprinkle the water with flowers?"

"She could," said Bernadette, dropping the petal back on the floor and standing up. "But it'd be strange, even for a psychology major who likes pink. A bubble bath is one thing. Rose petals are quite another."

Garcia motioned toward the ledge that ran alongside the bay

window. It was filled with melted candles in various shades of pink. "What about candles?"

"Girl might light candles for herself. That is still borderline weird in my book, but not over the edge like rose petals."

"You're thinking she got the tub ready for a soak with Romeo. She went in first . . ."

"And then he turned on her." Bernadette walked around the tub to the windows and pushed aside the curtains. The miniblinds behind the curtains were folded shut. Spreading a pair of slats, she saw a duplex across the street. "What about the neighbors? Maybe they saw her with somebody over the weekend."

"Minneapolis PD is on top of it."

Bernadette went over to the vanity and studied the photos tucked into the frame of the mirror. They were all snapshots of Hammond with girlfriends.

"See any candidates for man of the year?" asked Garcia.

"Nope." Bernadette lifted each of the photos, checked the backs, and returned them. Nothing. Nothing. One—with Hammond and another girl—carried neat script on the back: "To my best friend. Have a blast at college." It made Bernadette sad and mad at the same time. "I really want to get this bastard."

Garcia was checking under the bed. "Me, too."

She took down another photo. A landscape shot. It had a red sticker on the back shaped like a stop sign, with a local phone number running across the middle. Underneath the number it said "Suicide Stop Line." Bernadette stared at it, then told herself it didn't matter if Hammond had contemplated taking her own life. This wasn't a suicide. She slipped the photo back under the frame.

"Anything?" asked Garcia, standing up.

"Nada." Bernadette started opening vanity drawers and poking around the clothing inside them. "Could have been a guy she picked up in a club. One-night-stand sort of thing."

"I don't see any obvious signs of sexual activity," he said, nodding at the perfectly made bed.

"Could be they did it on the floor because"—Bernadette's voice trailed off as she thought back to her college years—"Shelby's bed was noisy and she was afraid a roommate would come home and hear."

Garcia, while pressing down on the mattress with one hand and listening to the squeak, said, "Roommates told the police that Hammond wasn't into dating. Didn't go out to bars."

Bernadette held up a packaged condom. "Roommates don't know everything."

"Hmm."

She dropped the condom back in the drawer and closed it. "Did you tell your college roommates everything?"

"We didn't talk," said Garcia. "We drank and watched television."

"Nice."

Garcia said, "ME will let us know if he finds any evidence of sexual activity. Sexual assault."

Bernadette went over to the chest of drawers and started riffling through the contents. "Let's see what we've got here."

"Minneapolis PD has already been through here."

"Humor me," she said, closing one drawer and opening the one below it.

He watched as she continued to dig. "What do you think?"

"I think she had a lot of pink clothes. I thought redheads couldn't wear pink."

Garcia went over to a closet, opened it, and stared with wide eyes. "Wow."

Bernadette closed the drawer and looked over. The closet was jammed with pink dresses, blouses, shoes, and purses. "Was the *wow* for the pink or the mess?"

"Both," said Garcia, shutting the door before something tumbled out. "If I have kids, I hope they're all boys."

"Something's missing." She put her hands on her hips and ran her eyes around the room. "Where are her textbooks?"

"Downstairs," said Garcia. "Apparently the kitchen doubled as the study hall."

"Laptop?"

"Computer forensics took it."

"Cell?"

"Bagged. Cops are snagging phone records."

"I don't suppose they found anything juicy in her directory or on her redial."

"Nope."

Bernadette went back to the tub. Hammond was a small-breasted girl—her chest was as flat as a young boy's—and her arms and legs were like toothpicks. Her hip bones practically poked through her skin. She looked thin in the photos, too. "Was she ill?"

"Why?"

"My arms are bigger than her legs."

"And you're pretty slender."

"Thank you for not using the word *skinny*."

"When the ME does his deal, that should uncover any illnesses," said Garcia. "I know our people didn't mention anything regarding an illness. Maybe the cops heard something. But like you said, she might not have told the other girls."

"Have the parents been contacted?"

"They're in Europe. Minneapolis Homicide is trying to track them down."

Bernadette bent over the tub and brought her face close to that of the dead girl's. "Maybe she was anorexic or bulimic. That wouldn't be something she'd share with friends or family." She peeled down the bottom lip of the open mouth. "Her teeth look funky."

"From stomach acid?"

Bernadette stood straight. "The other victims, some of them had eating disorders, too."

"They had a lot of problems, which is why the suicide rulings weren't hard to swallow," said Garcia.

"The angry villagers aren't going to swallow this one," she said. "They're going to break out the torches."

"We're reviewing the earlier drownings," Garcia said defensively.

"We've got to step it up," she said. "People are going to freak. They're going to say we let a maniac run around unchecked."

"The police are taking action. We're taking action."

She walked back and forth along the side of the pink bed. "We're passing out Prozac and telling people to take the 'How to Tell You're Depressed' quiz."

"The others could still be suicides." He nodded toward the tub. "This could be completely unrelated."

"All the victims have been young college women with problems. All drowned. In every case, there were no witnesses. These can't be a string of coincidences. If that's not enough, look at the rate. Since April, it's been one a month. Clockwork."

"If we count La Crosse, it's one a month. If we don't count La Crosse—"

"We've got to count La Crosse." She leaned against the side of the bed.

"Do you think we've gone from the river to a tub?" asked Garcia.

"You know what that tells me? That tells me the killer needs a more intense experience, a more up-close-and-personal drowning. He could crank it up in other ways, too."

"How?"

"The next killing might not be spaced so far apart."

Garcia dragged his hand over his face. "What do you want from me?"

"What do *you* want from me?" she asked. "Minneapolis Homicide is all over it. Our Minneapolis office is all over it. Milwaukee sent an asshole and an agent. They're tripping over each other interviewing roommates."

"It's Minneapolis PD's case, first and foremost. I can't do shit about that. It doesn't become yours unless—"

"Unless I prove that we've got a serial killer."

"What do you need to do that?"

She got up from the side of the bed. "The files, going all the way back to the first one."

"The one in April? That was a suicide for sure."

"Why?"

"There was a note."

"I want the note. I want the file. Did notes come with any of the other 'suicides'?"

Garcia's brows knitted. "I think the second one . . . no . . . they found a scarf she'd dropped on the bridge. No note."

"That's right. I remember reading about the scarf. A convenient clue left for the cops. I want that scarf, too."

"What're you going to do with that thing? Think you might try using your—"

"I might."

"Flag me beforehand. I'd like to be there, if that's okay."

Garcia was unlike any of her previous supervisors. While the others didn't want to know exactly what she did or how she did it, Garcia wanted to watch. "I'll flag you," she assured him.

He stuck his head into the hallway and turned back to her. "Coast is clear. No one to bug you if you want to try a fast one right here."

She surveyed the pink room. Since the bed was neatly made—with a pile of pink pillows resting in an artful arrangement against the headboard—Garcia was probably right that Hammond and her visitor hadn't had sex on the mattress. Nothing to touch there. The woman had probably filled the tub herself. The killer had touched the porcelain at some point during the struggle, but after so many victims, she suspected he was clever enough to wear gloves. "I don't know, Tony. I hate quickies. Let me wait for the scarf. I'll bet the murderer left that scarf for the police to find."

"You really think those river drownings were murders staged to look like suicides?" His eyes traveled to the leg dangling over the side of the tub. "There was no attempt to make this look like a suicide."

"Could be he figures this is so outside his previous MO, we'd never tie it to the river deaths." She pointed a finger at Garcia. "Let's let him think that. Let him think we've made no connection between this and the river deaths. He'll get cocky and make a mistake. Plus it'll keep a lid on the rioting citizens. Tell the cops and the ME to talk like this thing is an isolated murder."

"That won't be hard. The police still don't buy the idea that the river deaths are anything but suicides."

"Doesn't sound like you believe they were murdered either."

"I'm waiting to see what you come up with."

"Fair enough." She started for the door. "Make sure the cops keep us out of it."

"Again, not hard. They love keeping us out of it."

"Our public information guy didn't blab to the media that we've got agents in this house?"

Garcia followed her out into the hallway. "We treat reporters like mushrooms. Feed 'em a load of shit and keep 'em in the dark."

"That's a line from a cop movie. A police detective says that's how he treats federal agents."

"That's *our* line. They pilfered it from the FBI and turned it against us. Bastards."

The two agents stepped to one side as a man and a woman from the Hennepin County ME's office clattered up the stairs and into the hallway with a stretcher carrying an empty body bag. They unfolded the gurney's legs, and then the woman reached over and unzipped the flat sack, preparing it for an occupant.

"Can we take her?" asked the man.

Garcia thumbed over his shoulder. "Last bedroom."

"One of your fellas downstairs told me he was going to be there for the autopsy," the woman said.

"Agent Thorsson?" Garcia asked.

"Yeah. He told me to tell you," said the woman.

"That's awfully nice of him to keep me updated," Garcia said with a tight smile.

"Thorsson," Bernadette said under her breath.

The two agents fell silent as they watched the grim pair wheel the hardware down the hallway. There were few sights as chillingly final as that of the medical examiner's gurney on its way to pick up a corpse.

BY THE TIME Garcia and Bernadette left the house, the sea of blue uniforms had thinned out considerably. The pair stood on the sidewalk in front of the house, taking in the epitaphs on the decorative tombstones. "I like that one," said Garcia, pointing to *See! I told you I was sick!*

Bernadette turned away from the yard and pushed her sunglasses tighter over the bridge of her nose. "I'll be in the cellar if you need—"

Garcia snagged her elbow. "Cat. Wait a minute."

She pivoted around to look at him. His face was knotted with worry. She pulled off her shades. "What's the problem?"

He glanced up and down the sidewalk to make sure they were alone, then said in a lowered voice, "As you were coming up the stairs, I caught the tail end of your conversation with Thorsson."

"For God's sake, I was just giving him grief. I'm not going to crack up and—"

Garcia raised his hand. "I know, I know."

She fingered her sunglasses. "It's been six months since the shooting, Tony. I'm over it."

"No one gets over it."

She squared her shoulders. "I'm handling it, then. Okay? Seriously, why bring it up now? Is it because Thorsson opened his big mouth?"

"Between that mess and this case and your own history—"

"My history?"

"It's just that—well, you seem so resistant to the possibility that the river deaths are suicides. It's like you're taking it personally."

Her mouth dropped open as she realized why Garcia had been hesitant to bring her into the drownings, and she didn't know if she should be angry or touched. Torn between the two emotions, she stumbled over a response. "I'm not . . . It's not personal."

"You sure this isn't dredging up some bad stuff? Want someone to talk to tonight?"

"The only reason I talked to a shrink after the shooting was because you made me," she said. "The last thing I need is to go back to one of those operators."

He gently squeezed her shoulder. "I was talking about me, Cat. You want me to come over?"

Before answering, she studied his face. She thought she saw something new there but wasn't certain. "I'm good, Tony."

"You sure about that?"

She nodded. "I'm sure."

"I'll check in tonight, with an ETA on those files."

"The scarf, too. Don't forget the scarf. I've got a feeling about it."

While Bernadette walked back to her car, she replayed the expression she'd seen on Garcia's face. Was it concern beyond that of a boss for an underling? Her eyes must have been playing tricks on her. She slipped her sunglasses back on her face.

Some days she despised her damn eyes.

With those damn eyes, Bernadette could see things. She could hold something touched by a murderer and watch through the killer's eyes. Problem was, her talent wasn't a science. She could be seeing through the murderer's eyes in real time or be observing something from recent history. An execution could pass before her eyes, or she could be saddled with mundane scenes of everyday life: A pair of hands scrambling eggs for breakfast. An old movie on a nondescript television set. The pages of a paperback book at bedtime.

If she landed in the murderer's eyes during his dreams, she saw bizarre images that would be no help at all to a case. She'd suffered through the visions of maniacs who were hallucinating because of their drunkenness or drug use or mental illness. Again, no use when it came to solving a crime. She could misinterpret what she saw (not hard to do since her vision was filmy when using her special sight) and lead an investigation in the wrong direction. Send the bureau running after the wrong person. Even in the most ideal settings (she often went to empty churches to help her concentration) she came up with blanks. Conversely, it could come on unexpectedly with a casual brush of her hand. Each time she used the sight, it sapped her of energy. Worst of all, it could put her in the same emotional state as the killer, leaving her furious or frightened or homicidal.

Certainly she'd had successes over the years—otherwise the bureau would have cut her loose a long time ago—but her missteps were what attracted the most attention from the front office. A transfer routinely followed the failures. She'd landed in Minnesota the previous May after getting shuffled around Louisiana, where her co-workers had nicknamed her "Cat" because she had weird eyes like the South's Catahoula leopard dogs. She had a brown right and a blue left.

Garcia liked calling her Cat, and she didn't complain. He'd asked for her when none of the other bosses wanted her. She was thrilled to be back in her home state, even though she had no close family left there. The farm had been plowed over by developers. Her parents and only sibling, a twin sister, were dead. So was her husband.

HEADING BACK downtown, Bernadette steered the Crown Vic onto the interstate. Halfway to St. Paul, the traffic slowed and then stopped. "I hate cars," she muttered, and tried to see around the minivan parked in front of her.

While waiting for the logjam to break, she struggled to keep her mind off of the skeletons that the drowning case was bringing to the surface. She punched on the radio and turned up the volume on an ancient Rolling Stones tune, hoping to blast away the memories filling her head. The last thing she needed was to relive that sunny September day, three years ago, when Michael hanged himself on the water with his own boat rigging.

Chapter 4

BERNADETTE WAS STUDYING THE DIRECTIONS ON THE BACK OF a frozen turkey dinner when she was interrupted by a knock.

"Cat. It's me."

She tossed the carton onto the counter and went to the door. Garcia was standing in the hallway with a pizza box in his hands. "Hope you don't mind. I slipped inside the building right after one of your neighbors went outside. The front door doesn't shut all the way unless you force it. You should tell the caretaker—it's dangerous and should be fixed."

"I'll add it to the list." She inhaled. "Sausage and green peppers and onions. Now *that's* dangerous."

He looked past her into the open loft. "I thought I heard someone else in here."

"I wish. Can't remember the last time I had a date." She pointed to the CD player. Sinatra was launching into another song. "You must have heard the Voice."

"Right." Garcia adjusted his grip on the box. "You didn't eat already, did you?"

"Nope."

"Let's tear into it before it gets cold."

She directed Garcia to the kitchen. "Set it down. I'll get the plates."

He dropped the box on the table. Dipping his hands into his trench pockets, he produced a wad of paper napkins. "We don't need plates."

"Beer, wine, or water?"

He peeled off his trench and blazer and draped them over the back of a kitchen chair. "Beer for me. A beer would be good."

"St. Pauli okay?" she asked as she headed to the refrigerator.

"Perfect." He spotted the carton on the counter and pointed at it. "Lean Cuisine's on the menu at my house at least once a week."

Embarrassed, she retrieved the turkey dinner and shoved it back in the freezer. "Cooking for one sucks. What can I say?"

"Aren't we a couple of pathetic singles?"

She pulled a beer and a bottle of Chardonnay out of the refrigerator. "You didn't have to make a house call. I told you I was fine."

"I know you're fine," he said, loosening his tie. "I was in the neighborhood. It was dinnertime."

"Right," she muttered, and popped the top off the St. Pauli.

AFTER POLISHING OFF the pizza, Bernadette took one end of the couch and Garcia sat on the other. He was working on his second St. Pauli while she held her second glass of white wine in her hand.

She propped her stocking feet up on the coffee table. "When do I get those files?"

"I've got to wrestle them away from Thorsson. He and his partner were digging into them tonight."

"Thorsson. You shouldn't let that moron anywhere near those files."

"I hate it when you kids fight." He kicked off his shoes and pushed them under the coffee table. "Can't we all just get along?"

She took a sip of Chardonnay. "Watch. He's going to hang on to them just to tick me off."

"I won't let him hang on to them." Garcia took a bump off his beer. "I'll get them off him first thing tomorrow."

"Should I swing over to Minneapolis and pick them up?"

"I'll come by the cellar with them. I've got a meeting over at the St. Paul cop shop."

"Don't forget the—"

"The scarf. I know, Mom. I'll remember."

"I caught the six o'clock news," she said. "Television played it just the way we wanted. There wasn't even a mention of the other drownings."

"That's enough work talk, okay?"

She took a sip of wine. "Fine with me."

Garcia pointed across the room, to a chrome and red Honda parked in a corner of her condo. "Your trail bike or motocross bike or whatever you call it. I swear to God I see dust on the seat."

"You do." Rather than leave the bike in the condo garage or on the street, she routinely sneaked it up in the elevator so she could keep it under her sight. It hadn't seen much action lately.

"When you gonna take the thing out for a ride? You should get some mud on it before the snow flies."

"You're right. Maybe this weekend, if the weather holds out."

"I wouldn't mind going with."

Surprised by his request, she paused before answering. "Sure."

With his beer bottle, he motioned toward her DVD collection. "Why don't we pop in a movie?"

She set her glass down on the table and went over to the rack. "What's your pleasure? Something scary? A comedy?" She took down a copy of *The Departed*. "How about a police flick?"

"I hate cops-and-robbers movies. They never get it right. Bunch of bullshit. Comedy sounds good." He polished off his St. Pauli and set the empty on the table. "I could use a laugh after what we saw today."

"I second that," she said, and started riffling through her Adam Sandler movies. "Help yourself to another beer."

"In a bit." Garcia yanked off his tie and tossed it on the table. "That's better. I hate those things."

She looked over and nodded to his chest. "You must hate your dress shirt, too. You've got sauce all over it."

He looked down. "This is my lucky shirt."

She went over to him with her hand out. "Give it to me, and I'll run some water over it, so the stain doesn't set."

He stood up and started unbuttoning. "Do you mind? My wife bought me . . ."

His voice trailed off, and she knew why. Garcia's wife was dead, her car run off the road by an unknown driver years ago. Bernadette preferred her own tragedy; at least she knew whom to blame for her spouse's death. The uncertainty continued to haunt Garcia. "Give it here. It'll just take a minute."

As he peeled off the shirt and passed it over to her, their eyes met. "Appreciate it."

"Not a problem," she said. Garcia wore a tank T-shirt under his oxford, and she couldn't help but notice the well-muscled arms and the six-pack rippling through the cotton. She went over to the sink, turned on the water, and held the fabric under the stream. "The stain's coming out."

"Great." Burying his hands in his pants pockets, he walked around her condo while she worked on his shirt. "So . . . any visitors recently?"

"Visitors?"

"You get what I mean."

Garcia knew she could see her dead neighbor, August Murrick, the former owner of the condo building. "Mr. Murrick hasn't made an appearance in quite some time," she said.

"Really?"

"Really." She wasn't lying.

"What happened? Why'd he hit the road?"

"I have no idea why he took off." *That* she was lying about. She'd never confided to Garcia that she and Augie had been intimate once, before she realized he was a ghost. For weeks, she rebuffed his efforts to get her back into bed. He finally got the message and disappeared for good over the summer. She prayed Augie had gone to a truer heaven than a converted warehouse on the banks of the Mississippi.

"He sounded like an interesting character," said Garcia, stopping to examine the movie titles.

"Oh, he wasn't all that interesting." She turned off the faucet, wrung out the wet shirt, and held it up over the sink. "Good as new. How lucky is that?"

"Thanks a bunch," said Garcia, coming up next to her.

She pivoted around and found his body inches from hers. "Glad to . . . do it," she stumbled, and felt her face heating up.

"Maybe we should forget the movie," he said evenly.

She nodded and said with the same careful lack of emotion, "I'll put this in a plastic sack for you."

While she dug under the sink for a bag and stuffed the wet shirt into it, he slipped his shoes back on and pulled on his blazer. "Thanks for the brew."

"Thanks for dinner." She handed him the bagged shirt.

He grabbed his trench coat and headed for the door. "I'll see you tomorrow, then."

"Wait," she said after him, retrieving his tie from the coffee table.

He turned around. "What, Cat?"

"You forgot your tie."

As he took it from her, his hand locked over hers. "I'm sorry I can't stay," he said hoarsely.

"You sure you can't?"

"More sure than I've ever been of anything." He released her hand, opened the door, and stepped into the hallway.

Bernadette watched his back as he headed for the elevators, putting his trench coat on as he went. She wished like hell he'd turn around and come back. At the same time, she knew that would be a huge mistake for both of them.

He glanced back, staring at her while she stared at him. Raising his hand in a small wave goodbye, he stepped into the elevator and disappeared.

She waved back to the empty corridor and closed the door. Resting her forehead against the wood, she cursed with frustration. "Shit, shit, shit."

THERE WAS a period after her husband's death when she'd lost the taste for sex. Then she found herself sleeping around too much, picking up strangers in hotel bars and going to their rooms. Since coming home, she'd struggled to find a middle ground between the nun and the slut. While her night with Augie had thrown her off balance, her relationship with Garcia was sending her into a tailspin. Far from being just a boss, he was becoming her friend, and buddies as hot as Garcia were hazardous.

Chapter 5

GARCIA HADN'T VISITED THE CELLAR IN A WHILE, AND BER-
nadette had slacked off in her filing. She went to work early Tuesday
to try to straighten the office before he showed up with the paperwork from the drowning cases.

She shrugged off her coat and tossed it over the back of a chair. As
she started lifting up layers of files from one of the spare desks, she
heard a familiar bass voice and felt a cold draft rolling in from the
hallway outside her office.

"Finally fixing up the place. Long overdue. It never looked this
bad when I worked here solo."

"Go away," she muttered without turning around. "And close the
door behind you, Ruben."

"It's 'Agent Creed' to you, missy. Keep it professional."

She heard the door shut but knew he was on the wrong side of
it. She pivoted around, a pile of folders in her arms. A tall, slender
African American man with short graying hair was sitting on the
office's ancient sofa, his ankle crossed over his bony knee. She'd been
using the couch to store old newspapers, and on one side of Creed
was a stack of *Star Tribune*s and on the other side was a *New York
Times* tower. The newspapers framed his figure like Roman columns

and made him appear even more cold and imposing. She especially resented the way he always strolled in impeccably attired as if ready for work, with his dark suit and dark tie and stiff white shirt. That hint of an accent—he was a native of the South—added to his air of superiority. "Whatever you have to say, make it quick," she told him. "I'm busy."

He propped one elbow on the *Times* pile and then had second thoughts. Lifting his arm, he brushed off his jacket sleeve and folded his hands on his lap. A saw buzzed overhead, and Creed frowned at the ceiling. "What in blazes is going on up there?"

She went over to a waist-high metal file cabinet, pulled the drawer open with the tip of her shoe, and dumped her armload of folders inside it. "They're renovating the building."

"It's about time," he said.

"I guess," she muttered, and picked up another stack of folders.

A jackhammer fired up, drowning out the saw. "How can you work with all this commotion?"

"Lots of Tylenol." She went back to the file cabinet, dropped the folders inside the drawer, and forced it closed.

"What kind of cockamamie filing system is that?"

"I'll straighten it out later."

"That's precisely the attitude that got you where you are today." He picked up a *Star Tribune* and waved it at her. "You know those people you read about in the paper, the ones with those garbage houses? That's how it starts with them. *I'll straighten it out later,* they think. *I'll do the laundry tomorrow.* Next thing you know—"

"Ruben . . . Agent Creed . . . I don't have time for you today." Her cell rang inside her coat pocket, but she didn't want to take a call in front of her visitor. "You'd better go for a hike."

He dropped the paper back on the stack and squared it. "You'd better answer that phone. It's our ASAC."

She plucked a collection of Starbucks cups off her desk and dropped them into the wastebasket. "*My* ASAC. He isn't your boss. Not anymore."

The cell stopped ringing. "You'd better pick up the next call. It'll be him again."

"How do you know? Are you God or something?"

"I know people who know people."

"Why don't you go visit those people and leave me alone?" The phone on her desk rang. She glared at Creed, but he wasn't budging. She sat down at her desk and picked up the receiver.

Garcia: "Why didn't you answer your cell just now?"

"Tony . . . uh—I—" She saw Creed grinning mischievously from his throne across the room. She turned her back to him and continued talking into the phone. "I had my hands full. I'm trying to get some office work done before you come by."

Garcia: "Relax. I won't be by the cellar until this afternoon, after my meeting at the cop shop."

Swiveling her chair around, she saw Creed still sitting on the couch with his smug grin. She spun the chair back so she wouldn't have to look at his mug. "You've got the files?"

"Got them."

"Great. See you later." She hung up.

"Are you going to brief your partner about the case to which we've been assigned?"

She got up from her chair and planted her hands on her hips. "Agent Creed, you are *not* my—" She stopped herself. If not partners, they were at least office mates, for better or worse. There was no harm in filling him in on the latest. Who was he going to tell? "You know all those college students who've been turning up dead in the river?"

"The ones who killed themselves?"

She wheeled a chair over to the couch and sat down across from him. "I don't think those deaths were suicides, at least not all of them."

"Keep talking."

"I went out to a murder scene yesterday. Another Minneapolis drowning."

"In the Mississippi?"

"A much smaller body of water," said Bernadette. "A bathtub."

"Why do you think it's related to the river deaths? If those were indeed homicides—"

"I know, I know. Killing people in their own tubs is a much different MO." She crossed one leg over the other and leaned forward. Surprisingly, she discovered she enjoyed hashing the case over with Creed. "Hear me out, though."

"I'm listening," he said.

"The victims have the same profile. They've all been white females attending the University of Minnesota or the University of Wisconsin. They've all had emotional problems . . ."

"Which would make it easier for a killer to pawn the murders off as suicides."

"Exactly," she said excitedly.

"Why the switch from the river to a tub?"

"Garcia and I discussed this," she said. "I think the murderer is seeking a deeper thrill, a more up-close-and-personal method of execution."

He got up from his throne and walked back and forth in front of the couch. "You're implying this is a sexual thing."

"What else would it be?"

"Have you researched this . . . what should we call it?"

"Water fetish. Drowning fetish."

"Yes." He stopped pacing and pointed at her. "What do you know about it?"

He seemed more alive than she'd ever seen him. It must be boring to be trapped in the world of the living, with nothing constructive to do, she thought. Maybe she could rope him into helping her. "I imagine there're things on the Internet. I suppose I could ask Thorsson to lend a hand."

"Thorsson. That idiot. What's he doing in town? Don't tell me Milwaukee dumped him on Minneapolis."

She grinned, pleased that Creed was equally disdainful of the agent. "Because two of the deaths were in La Crosse, Milwaukee sent Thorsson and another guy to Minneapolis when the girl turned up dead in the tub."

"In case there was a connection."

"Exactly."

"Leave Thorsson out of it. You don't need Thorsson." He planted himself at his old desk. Sitting in front of him was a dusty computer screen that hadn't seen any action for months. "What do you want me to do?"

She thought hard before answering. When she'd first arrived at the St. Paul office, Agent Creed was gone on a scuba-diving trip. He'd come back from the Cayman Islands in a body bag. Even though they'd never partnered together while he was alive, could they work together now without killing each other? Garcia said Creed loved St. Paul and had been happily doing his work in the cellar for years. Before she could give him something to do, she had to ask a delicate question. "What *can* you do?"

"I beg your pardon."

She got up and walked over to him. "Not to be insulting, but considering your current state . . ."

"My current state?" He reached over and punched on his monitor.

"You can use a computer?"

"I am not a caveman, missy."

She stood at his elbow and watched him log on. "Your password still works."

"I've been online since my untimely and utterly tragic demise."

"What do you do? Play solitaire?"

"Is that what *you* do with government equipment, Agent Saint Clare?"

"No. I look for deals on eBay."

He looked over his shoulder at her. "I sincerely hope you're pulling my leg."

She put her hand on the back of his chair. "I'd like to keep going on with my cockamamie housekeeping. While I'm doing that, how about you do some poking around online?"

"What am I looking for?"

"Fetish Web sites. Fetish clubs, especially local ones."

"Disgusting," he said. "I'm going to need a bath myself when I'm finished."

She went back to her own desk and sat down. "Dirty work, but somebody's got to do it, and I'd rather that somebody be you instead of me."

WHEN THEIR ASAC landed in the cellar with the files, Bernadette's partner vanished from his chair. Garcia deposited the armload of paperwork on Creed's desk and dropped down into the dead agent's seat. Bernadette stared at her boss.

"What?" asked Garcia, glaring back.

"Nothing," said Bernadette.

"Bullshit," he said. "You're looking at me like I have a juicy zit on the middle of my forehead."

"I am not," she said.

Garcia realized where he was sitting and jumped out of the chair. "Was he just here?"

"Who? What are you talking about?"

He walked over to her desk. "Has Ruben been around lately?"

She wasn't sure which Garcia would find more distasteful: that she'd tapped a dead dude for assistance, or that the research she was asking Creed to conduct involved porn. Both were rather unsavory, so she decided it was best to keep mum about the whole thing. "Agent Creed's been keeping a low profile," she said.

Garcia shoved his hands into his coat pockets. "Have you ever thought about, uh . . . getting rid of him permanently? I mean, having him hanging around here must creep you out."

She thought Garcia was the one who was spooked. "How would you suggest I send him into the light? An exorcism?"

"I don't think the bureau would appreciate a religious ceremony of that nature being conducted in a federal building." He glanced around the room. "Besides, I suppose we still need the strange bastard. There're some cases he left hanging. Have you ever asked him about those, by the way?"

She decided to bait her boss. "He said he won't help with dick until you pay him for the vacation time he still has on the books."

"He's dead. Why does he need vacation pay? Tell him to file a complaint with the ghost grievance committee."

"Maybe we should get back to matters of the recently deceased," she said. "Have you got the scarf?"

"I couldn't put my hands on it this morning. How about I drop it off at your place tonight?"

She wondered if he was fishing for a dinner invitation, even though the previous night had ended on a tense note. "I've got a couple of steaks in the fridge. We could cook them up and go over the files together."

He studied the stack he'd dumped on Creed's desk. "You might need an extra set of eyes to get through that mountain." His attention shifted to her face. "On the other hand, maybe you and I need to avoid after-hours—"

"A working dinner," she said quickly. "Strictly a working dinner."

He paused, then said slowly, "I'll get back to you on that. Depends on how the day goes for me."

"Let me know," she said, and got up to transfer the files over to her desk.

Garcia headed for the door. "I'll call you."

She gathered the folders in her arms. "The scarf?"

"Whatever else happens, I'll get the scarf to you," he said, and walked out of the office.

She set the files down on her desk and lowered herself back into her chair. "Whatever else happens," she grumbled.

"Strange bastard? Ghost grievance committee? Exorcism? Is that how you two talk about me when I'm not around, missy?" asked Creed, who'd reappeared at his computer.

"We didn't mean anything by it."

"What's this about a steak at your place tonight?"

"You heard what I told Tony. A working dinner."

"So now it's Tony." He peered at her over the top of his computer screen. "Be careful, Agent Saint Clare. Fraternization between supervisors and those under them is most definitely—"

She held up her hand to stop him. "I don't need a lecture, Ruben."

"And that nonsense about my wanting vacation pay! I never said that."

She plucked the top file off the pile and set it down in front of her. "I was having a little fun with Tony . . . Garcia."

"Make sure that's the *only* fun you have with him."

She flipped open the file. "Are you my partner or my dad?"

In place of an answer, he started typing furiously.

"Don't break the computer," she said without looking up from her reading. "That's government equipment, you know."

"Hilarious," he snarled from behind his screen, and continued banging on the keyboard.

The cellar was starting to feel crowded. She stood up and pulled on her coat. Started stacking the files. "You know what, Ruben— Agent Creed—I'm going to take this stuff home with me. If Garcia comes by my place—"

"I'm betting he won't."

"*When* Garcia comes by place, we can go over these together."

"Don't hold your breath, missy."

Behind his back, she flipped him the bird and took off for the day.

HE WAS RIGHT. Garcia didn't show. She fell asleep with the files.

Chapter 6

JUGGLING HER PURSE, AN ARMLOAD OF BOOKS, A CAN OF
diet pop, and the mangled remains of a Slim-Fast bar, the reed-thin
woman hustled up two flights of stairs and down a narrow hallway
with high ceilings. Just before she entered the classroom, she polished
off her drink, spotted a trash can, and tossed the empty into the re-
ceptacle. The clatter made her wince. The classroom door was wide
open, propped by an ancient copy of *The Living Webster Encyclopedic
Dictionary of the English Language*. The old building was stuffy, and
the prof kept the door open to prevent everyone from suffocating.

She slipped inside, zeroed in on an empty desk in the last row, and
dropped into it. She ran a hand through her short spiky hair, dyed
to match the color of black licorice, and checked her watch. As soon
as she was done with this class, she had to bolt for another appointment.

While she shrugged off her vest, she watched the professor scribbling on the board. In an attempt to blend in with their students,
some instructors wore jeans and T-shirts or the occasional flannel
shirt with the requisite frayed collar and cuffs. Some had beards or
other facial hair, and a few of the arty ones had long hair. This guy
looked the way college professors were portrayed in movies: Dress

slacks. Dress shirt. Necktie. Blazer. Loafers or wing tips. His belt always matched his shoes, a miracle for a single man who wasn't gay. Clean-shaven face. Short blond hair with a bit of curl on top and a smudge of gray on the sideburns.

When the school year started, he'd had a sunburned face and a tan on the back of his neck. During a hot spell that early September, he'd removed his blazer and rolled up his sleeves, revealing tanned, muscled arms covered with blond hair. She bet most of the girls in her class and a couple of the guys suffered a drop in grades that week.

Not surprisingly, his classes were popular with female students. His looks and the subject matter were both big draws, but they weren't the only ones. The professor listened to women when they spoke. It was a precious and rare commodity, a man who listened to the female voice instead of tuning it out.

Before opening her notebook, she reached around to the back cover and ran her index finger over the outline of the octagon. She'd seen the stickers before at student health fairs and the like but had been too self-conscious to pick one up. On the first day of class, the prof had distributed them to his students. Most of the kids waited until they were in the hallway and then tossed theirs in the trash can. A couple had made derisive remarks. She'd kept hers, plastering it to the back cover of the notebook. Just in case.

She opened the notebook to a clean page, clicked her pen, and emptied the last inch of Slim-Fast into her mouth.

The prof spun around and spotted her sitting in the back row, chewing. "Glad you could join us, Ms. Klein."

He called all the students by their names. Without assigning seats or checking a cheat sheet, he'd learned the first and last names of all twenty of them by the third day of class. Most of the students still didn't know one another's names. He went around the Formica-topped table that served as his desk and leaned his butt against it. She was glad she wasn't sitting in the front row; she'd be staring where she ought not. "Kyra, swallow your breakfast and read us anything by Dorothy Parker."

Kyra Klein cracked open *The Poetry & Short Stories of Dorothy Parker*, ran her tongue across her top front teeth to make sure she didn't have a nut wedged between them, and opened her mouth to launch into the poem.

"Wait," the professor said, holding up his palm like a traffic cop.

Klein glanced up from her book.

"Read us anything by Dorothy Parker as long as it isn't 'Résumé.'"

She looked back down and turned the page.

"Kyra. Don't tell me."

Grinning, she looked up. "It's my favorite."

"Fine," he said. "Torture me if you must. I've only heard the damn thing a million times."

She continued her page flipping. "I can find something else."

"While you're doing that, tell us why you picked Dorothy Parker for your paper in the first place."

She looked up from her book. "Actually, my first choice was Sylvia Plath, but you told us we couldn't do her."

He stood straight and ran his eyes around the room. "How many of you wanted Sylvia Plath?"

Nearly everyone raised his or her hand.

"Good God, people. Sylvia Plath?"

"What's wrong with Sylvia Plath?" asked a girl sitting to Klein's right.

"Cliché city," squeaked Jess, who always sat in the front row, smack-dab in the middle. Jess had a shaved head and was either a puffy guy with a Truman Capote voice or a puffy woman with the downy beginnings of an Ernest Hemingway beard. Out of sensitivity and without prior planning or discussion, the entire class avoided the minefield of transgender issues in literature while Jess was in their midst.

"I could fill the Metrodome with undergraduate papers on Sylvia Plath, and to a one, they would be wretched," said the professor. He went back to the board, scribbled madly, and stepped to one side.

He'd scrawled *Sylvia Plath*, drew a bell shape around the name, and then slashed a diagonal bar across it.

A young woman two seats in front of Klein raised her hand. "How can we take a class like this *without* Sylvia Plath?"

"I didn't say we'd do without her, Alisha." He went back around the Formica table and poked an index finger in his chest. "*I* shall discuss Sylvia Plath, and you shall listen."

He walked between the rows of desks, heading for Klein. Clasping his hands behind his back, he came up next to her. "Now tell us about number two on your hit parade."

He was wearing cologne. Did he have a date tonight? There were rumors he went out with students. Distracted by his closeness, she dropped her lashes and fumbled with the small volume under her hands. "Well . . . she . . . she had a hard life. Both her parents died. She lived in a boardinghouse for a while and played the piano to make money. She wrote fashion ads for *Vogue*."

"'Brevity is the soul of lingerie,'" he said.

She looked up with wide eyes. "What?"

He turned around and marched back to the front of the room. "That was one of her clever captions."

"She had a successful writing career. Poetry and short stories and scripts for Hollywood. But she wasn't always happy."

The professor leaned one hand against the table. "She tried to kill herself. More than once."

Klein nodded slowly.

"And that's what this class is all about, isn't it?" Returning to the board, he wrote something in large letters, underlined it three times, and stepped away so the class could read it. *Enough Rope*. "Who can explain what that means?"

A boy in a middle row raised his hand.

The professor pointed at him. "Jason?"

"It's part of an expression. Enough rope to hang yourself. It's like—I don't know . . . you do it to yourself."

Klein raised her hand.

"You'd better get this right, Kyra," the professor said.

"It's the title of one of Dorothy Parker's best-selling collections of poetry," she said.

"Excellent." He tipped his head toward her. "From that collection, please read the selection that you think best illuminates the creative and personal struggles of Mrs. Parker." He paused. "And, Kyra, if you really think your first selection does the job, then by all means, go right ahead."

Klein turned back to "Résumé," the oft-quoted poem about suicide, and began reading. " 'Razors pain you . . .' "

AFTER CLASS let out, she hung back while the other students surrounded him to ask questions about their papers and a quiz set for Friday. She'd wait and get him alone. While she leaned against the edge of a desk, she looked at her watch. Screw her doctor's appointment. Let him wait on her for a change.

After the room emptied of the other students, Klein approached him while he erased the board. There was that cologne again. "Professor, I'm having second thoughts about Mrs. Parker. I'm thinking I might do Anne Sexton instead."

He moved to the end of the board listing students' names alongside the writers they were set to profile. Before he erased "Dorothy Parker," he turned and asked Klein, "Why the change of heart?"

"It's—she . . . her life was a little too much like mine."

He looked at the clock on the wall. "There isn't another class in here for forty-five minutes. Let's sit."

She took a seat in the front row, he turned a desk around so it faced her, and they sat across from each other. While she talked, he listened and nodded and interrupted only to ask an occasional question. She was going to be really late for her appointment, and she didn't give a damn. This was better therapy.

Chapter 7

SIGHING, KLEIN TOSSED THE DOG-EARED COPY OF *WOMAN'S*
Day from two Thanksgivings ago onto the coffee table. She had
enough turkey pointers to write her own cookbook. She checked her
watch, looked at the wall clock hanging to the right of the receptionist's window, and sighed again, this time loudly and with more
feeling.

Taking the hint, the receptionist peeked over the counter and addressed the impatient patient. "I'm sorry about the delay. Wednesdays are always bad for some reason, and he had an emergency this
morning."

"I suppose my coming late didn't help," she said.

"Well . . . no," he said hesitantly. "But I'm sure you had a good
reason."

He was trying to be nice. She'd screwed herself. "Enough rope,"
she muttered.

"What?"

"Nothing. Never mind." Leaning over, she picked through the
other periodicals littering the table. The only magazines that were
current were the ones about golf.

Bored, she glanced through the window framing the man. He had his head down now and was pecking at a computer. Dressed in a polo shirt with a subtle designer logo embroidered on the sleeve, he appeared to be the type who would read golf magazines cover to cover. He looked like a younger version of that famous golf pro. What was his name? Jack something. Her eyes went to the cover of one of the golf magazines. No help. Everything was about Tiger Woods. She missed the grandmotherly receptionist who used to greet her with a sympathetic smile and offers of hot tea with sugar. This guy offered bad black coffee. At least he tried. He had a nice smile. A golf pro smile. Bright white.

He glanced up from his typing and caught her staring at him. "You could reschedule, Kyra," he offered.

She dropped her eyes and picked up a decorating magazine. "I wouldn't get to see him for weeks, and I need to talk now. You know what I mean?"

The golf pro head bobbed up and down in affirmation. "I understand completely. It shouldn't be that much longer. He just got your file and took it back with him."

Her file. Her masterpiece. Her version of *Enough Rope*. It was cleverly titled *Klein, Kyra A.*, and it started something like this:

Patient's biological mother, diagnosed with Bipolar I Disorder in early adulthood, committed suicide when the patient was ten years of age, leaving the juvenile in the care of her biological father . . . Father died of acute alcoholic hepatitis when the patient was twenty . . . Shortly afterward, the patient was diagnosed with depression, and was prescribed antidepressants.

That diagnosis turned out to be dead wrong and led to a really juicy plot twist in her opus.

On the patient's twenty-first birthday, she was hospitalized after ingesting a full bottle of an over-the-counter pain reliever/

sleep aid . . . During hospitalization, her mental status was re-assessed and she was diagnosed with Bipolar I Disorder.

She had to credit her current psychiatrist with that bull's-eye. The chapters that followed were downright mundane, thank God.

Patient has one sibling, a married older brother employed as a software designer in Seattle . . . Brother is assisting the patient financially so she can complete her studies. He communicates with her sporadically via phone and e-mail . . . Patient is currently taking undergraduate courses at the University of Minnesota–Twin Cities; she has not yet declared a field of study, but enjoys reading the American classics and writing poetry.

She was just another unemployed English major in the making, she thought as she flipped through the pages of an article giving tips on easy bathroom makeovers.

Patient is single and reports no steady "boyfriend," but has engaged in unprotected sex with multiple partners since the onset of puberty . . . Sexual activity increases during her manic episodes, as does her reckless driving and her excessive clothing purchases.

She'd once blown an entire paycheck on a pair of Manolo Blahniks and defiantly worn the stilettos to one of her appointments. Her psychiatrist had trouble taking his eyes off those heels, and she didn't blame him: black satin with crystal-studded ankle straps. Very expensive come-fuck-me shoes.

Patient works during the week as a part-time cashier at a grocery store near the Minneapolis campus and on weekends is employed selling hand lotion at kiosk located in the Mall of

America . . . Has stated that she enjoys her jobs and has twice received raises in her hourly pay as a cashier.

Patient is seeing a therapist, but reports that she is unhappy with this particular health professional . . . On more than one occasion, she has referred to the therapist as "the bullshit artist."

Patient states that the therapist "talks to hear himself talk" and "doesn't listen to a damn thing anyone else has to say." Patient has requested a list of recommended therapists/psychologists practicing in the university area.

Lithium has proven an effective maintenance treatment, although patient has complained about the "flat feeling" it causes.

That flat feeling seemed to be intensifying with every second she spent in that cell-like waiting room. Dropping "Breezy Bathrooms for Less" on the table, she looked at the clock again and double-checked its accuracy against her watch. Yup. Already noon. If she didn't get in soon, she was going to be late for her next class. She rested her elbows on her knees and dropped her chin in her palms.

She wasn't a new patient, nor was she very different from the hundreds of other cases this doctor had handled over the years, she suspected. She was just another nut job. He hated when she called herself that. *Nut job.* She told him it helped to laugh.

He didn't have a sense of humor, this doctor. He'd drum an eraser head on his desk while he reviewed the highlights of her masterpiece. He had high cheekbones and a prominent jawline, and when he read something that piqued his interest or disturbed his sensibilities, both facial features tensed almost indiscernibly. She could always tell when he got to the dirty parts of her little book: his face reddened. She loved it when that happened. At least she could tell he was human.

The blond head levitated from behind the counter and the receptionist cracked open the door leading to the bowels of the office. "The doctor will see you now."

"Great," said Klein, Kyra A. She got up with her purse and her books and followed the receptionist down the hall to the doctor's exam room. She scrutinized his bottom half as they went. Jack Something had a nice butt for a guy who sat at a computer all day. Why was she not surprised that he was wearing boring khaki slacks and geeky brown walking shoes?

"Miss Klein," he announced, pushing the door open for her.

"Thank you," she said, offering the receptionist a smile.

"You're quite welcome," he said, smiling back. He looked over at the man behind the desk. "Do you need anything, Doctor?"

"I'm good, Charles," the man said without looking up from his paperwork.

"Would you like some coffee, Miss Klein?" Charles asked her.

"No, thanks. I'm not a coffee drinker," she said.

Charles nodded and left. Klein stared at the closed door, feeling guilty about not accepting the damn drink.

The doctor looked up and nodded toward a chair parked across from his desk. "Please have a seat."

She headed to the leather couch planted against the wall. She tossed her purse and her books onto it and dropped down next to them. "I'm breaking in a new pair of boots, and my feet are killing me."

"Please make yourself comfortable," he said, pushing his chair back and standing up.

"I will." She started unzipping the knee-high boots, which were pulled over skintight jeans.

He pulled down on the sleeves of his blazer—his idea of making himself comfortable—and took the patient chair over to the couch. Sitting down across from her with his right ankle propped across his left knee, he opened the file up on his legs. He scrutinized her clothing—a fur vest over a cashmere sweater—and shot a look at her boots and Coach purse. "Did you go on another spending spree?" he asked in that judgmental tone of his. That assistant principal's voice.

"Don't worry," she said. "I'm not off my meds. My brother sent me a pile of money for my birthday."

"Happy birthday."

"It was last month, but thanks."

"How are you doing, Miss Klein?"

Now she was bent over her boots, pulling them off. "I'm as fat as a cow."

"Weight gain is a common side effect with lithium. So are tremors, diarrhea, nausea . . ."

"We discussed switching meds." She dropped her boots on the floor with a thud. "What about that?"

"Valproic acid has side effects as well."

"Such as?"

"Tremors, diarrhea, nausea, weight gain, hair loss."

"Dandy. I can be fat *and* bald. Let me think about it."

"How are you doing otherwise?"

"What do you think?"

He glanced down at her file. "Well, I can tell you that your blood tests—"

"Can we talk?" she asked.

Pulling his eyes off the file, he looked at her. "What's the problem?"

"This is hard for me." She folded her arms in front of her, crossed one leg over the other, and nervously jiggled her elevated stocking foot. "I don't know how to put this exactly."

"Let's hear it, Miss Klein."

"Kyra. The last time I was here, and the time before that, I asked you to call me—"

"Kyra. Yes. I remember now. What's wrong, Kyra?"

She chewed her bottom lip. "This isn't working out for me."

"What isn't working out?" He glanced down at the folder. "If you really want to switch medications, I'm sure we can find a more agreeable—"

"I want to find *me*. I want to talk about *me*."

"This *is* about you."

"It's the same thing every time I come in here. I get fifteen minutes with you. Twenty tops. You ask me how I'm doing, but you don't really listen to me. Half the time you're not even looking at me." She pointed to the folder. "Your face is buried in that crap."

"I apologize if you feel I've been—"

"You write me a new refill. I disappear for another month or two. I come back. Same thing. 'How're you doing? Your lab work looks good.' We never talk, and I need to talk. Really talk." Even as she said it, she knew it wasn't going to go anywhere. Psychiatrists hated when patients expected them to act like therapists. She could have predicted his response.

"You have someone for that aspect of your—"

"He's a royal dick." She raked the top of her spiky head with her fingers and waited for him to do his pencil drum.

Instead, he surprised her with a grin. "Well, yes, you've made your dissatisfaction known. We can provide a list of other capable—"

"I am so sick of getting shuffled around, shopping for doctors." She curled her legs up on his couch, sat back, and sighed. "I wish you could do it all."

He checked his watch. "Tell you what."

"My fifteen minutes can't be up already. You kept me waiting forever."

"I apologize for that," he said, drumming the pencil on her folder. "If you can come back later this afternoon . . ."

"I have class."

"What about the end of the business day? You can be my last patient. We can take a little longer."

"Will my insurance pay for two visits in one day?"

"I'll make it a freebie," he said.

She fingered her purse strap. "By the time we get through, it'll be dark out."

"I can give you a ride home, or Charles. Someone around here will be going your way."

"That sounds good." She pulled her legs down from the couch and put on her boots, suddenly energized by his offer. She was more than a file tab to him.

The door popped open, but this time it wasn't Charles. Another male head poked into the room. "You'll never guess who called me just now, out of the blue."

"It'll have to wait." The doctor closed her file and got up off the chair. "I'm busy with a patient."

The man in the doorway looked at Klein. "I'm sorry, miss. I didn't see you there."

"Don't worry about it. I'm on my way out." Klein sat up, stared at the man in the doorway, and looked back at her doctor. "This has *got* to be a relative of yours. You could pass for twins."

"He's my younger brother," her doctor said shortly. He went back to his desk and sat down.

"I wish my brother lived in town." Klein got up from the couch, plucked her purse off the cushions, and hiked the strap over her shoulder. She gathered her books in her arms and started for the door. "It's nice that you get to see each other."

The two men locked eyes, and the brother in the doorway laughed dryly. "Sometimes it's nice, Miss—"

She held out her hand and he took it. "Klein," she said.

He released her hand and opened the door wider so she could go through. "Have a good day, Miss Klein."

"Kyra," she said, smiling up at him as she stepped over the threshold. "Call me Kyra. I've been trying to get your brother to remember that."

He put his hand over his heart. "Kyra. I shall not forget."

Charles brushed past Klein and the brother.

"I'm sorry, Chaz," said the brother. "Didn't hear you coming."

Charles handed the doctor a file. "If you're finished with Miss Klein, we've got two other patients waiting."

Klein leaned back into the room and addressed the man behind the desk. "Almost forgot. What time exactly?"

He checked his wristwatch. "Is six o'clock too late?"

"Six o'clock is perfect." Charles gave her a curious look as he stood at the doctor's elbow with a file. She didn't want the golf pro to get the wrong idea about this after-hours session. She added: "Not too much later, though. I have a date tonight."

"Six sharp."

"See you at six." She gave a smile to the brother and the golf pro, turned back around, and went down the hall.

THE YOUNGER BROTHER turned to watch her go, a crooked smile lifting the right side of his mouth. "Kyra Klein," he repeated under his breath.

As he exited the doctor's office, Charles navigated around the grinning man and arched his eyebrows.

"What?" snapped the brother.

"I didn't say a word," Charles said.

"You were thinking it."

"How long have we known each other?" the receptionist asked over his shoulder, and headed back to the waiting room.

"I can look," the brother said defensively.

"Listen to Charles," the doctor yelled from the other side of the doorway, his head down while he flipped through another patient chart. "Leave her alone."

The brother shoved his hands into his pants pockets and groused, "I'm always being misjudged."

Chapter 8

MENTAL ILLNESS. EATING DISORDERS. ALCOHOL AND DRUG
addictions. Childhood rapes. Physically abusive boyfriends. Emotionally abusive parents.

Armed with a pen and a legal pad, Bernadette spent Wednesday in the cellar continuing the chore she'd started the night before at her kitchen table: immersing herself in the tumultuous lives of seven troubled women. As she plowed through the files taking more notes, the victims' stories started blending together, becoming indistinguishable from one another. It was as if she'd spent too long in a massive art gallery: her head hurt, her eyes felt dry, and everything looked the same.

"I gotta get organized," she muttered to herself, and pulled a pad of Post-its out of her desk drawer.

Going back over her notes, she transferred key points to the Post-its. Each victim got her own set of yellow squares listing name, age, date and place of death, college and field of study, emotional and health problems, and family issues.

When Bernadette was through with her transcription, she went over to the bare white wall on one side of her office door and started slapping yellow squares up on the Sheetrock. Each victim got a totem pole of notes, starting with her name and working down to the personal stuff at the base of the column. It wasn't an organizational method sanctioned by the bureau, but it had always worked well for her.

Like a student fretting over a blackboard math problem, she stepped back and studied the squares, first taking in each victim's story as she read from top to bottom, and then working across to compare each girl. Did they all share the same major? No, some hadn't even declared one. Did they go to the same clinic? No, some had never been treated.

"This is depressing," she said as she stood in front of the wall.

Creed peeked at her from behind his computer screen. "What are you doing?"

"Organizing my notes. Waiting for them to speak."

"So what do the Post-its say to you?" he asked.

She blinked. "They don't literally talk to me. You know that, right?"

He hesitated, then said unconvincingly, "Yeah. I know that."

"This time they don't tell me shit about shit," she said, more to herself than to Creed. She sat back down at her desk and picked up a single slip of paper, a photocopy of something the first victim had penned:

Dear Mr. Underwood: I hate you. I can't stand seeing your ugly face anymore. When you put on that stupid grin, it reminds me of the way you smiled while you were doing those sick things to me. All the crap you put me through, and I was just a little kid! Tell my mom thanks for looking the other way and doing nothing to help me. I'm leaving for good. When you drop dead, I'll come back to take a dump on your grave.

Corrine

Bernadette found no evidence in the file that Corrine had ever pursued charges against the man. The girl had probably doubted that anyone would take her seriously, especially with her history of emotional problems. In addition to being treated for depression at the time of her death, she'd been hospitalized twice for anorexia nervosa. A slew of different doctors and clinics.

Police had labeled the letter a suicide note, but Bernadette thought it read more like a goodbye letter fired off by an angry runaway.

She repeated the words out loud: "'When you drop dead, I'll come back to take a dump on your grave.'"

Across the room, Creed stopped his typing. "What're you reading?"

"A suicide note, supposedly."

"Sounds more like something one Mafioso would say to another."

"It was found resting under a bottle on the Washington Avenue Bridge after the body of the first victim was fished out of the river."

"What was the gal's name?"

"Corrine Underwood. No . . . wait . . ." She flipped to the front of the file. "Correction. Corrine *Randolph*. She hated her stepfather and never accepted his last name."

"His future burial spot was the one threatened with desecration?"

"Yeah. He'd sexually abused her as a child."

"Poor Corrine Randolph."

Bernadette got up from her desk and went back to the yellow notes. Seven vertical stripes representing seven unhappy women. She ticked them off by order of death. "Then in May we had poor Monica Taratino. June was poor Alice Bergerman. July, poor Judith Powers-Nelson over in Wisconsin. August, poor Laurel McArthur in Wisconsin again. Back to the Twin Cities in September with poor Heidi DeForeste."

"That's quite a roll call."

She stepped in front of the last column. "I don't have a full file on her yet, but let's not leave out poor Shelby Hammond. Miss October."

"The girl killed over the weekend, in the bathtub."

"The biggest oddball, really, because of *where* she drowned. Otherwise we've got seven women with similar, but not identical, profiles. All college students at one of two universities. All female. All messed up emotionally."

"All dead by drowning," said Creed.

She walked back and forth in front of the wall. "The two big connections are the colleges and their problems."

"So the killer is a college prof who's good at picking out fragile students."

"Except we're dealing with two different universities and students who run the gamut in terms of majors and years in school," she said. "Undergrads. Grad students. I rounded up their class schedules and haven't found any intersections. At no point were two of these girls in the same classroom at the same time. Nor did any of them share an instructor."

"A medical professional who treated them. A doctor. A therapist. A pharmacist. Hospital orderly even. They were *all* treated in some way, shape, or form, right?"

"Wrong." She ran her eyes over the columns as she paced. "Some of them, their files indicate their parents wanted them to get help for their head or health problems, and they refused, or just never got around to it."

"The ones who did have contact with a medical professional, was it the same clinic or hospital or whatever? Did the same doctor treat two different girls?"

"Not all the girls who got help had a doctor's name or clinic in their file. We'll have to get family members to cough up some medical info, if they even have it."

"Why wouldn't they?" he asked.

"Some of these ladies were not on good terms with their folks," she said.

"Of the ones that did mention a specific health provider . . ."

"None named the same shrink or clinic. I would have picked up on that immediately." She stopped pacing and turned to look at her office mate. "What if it's simply someone who favors troubled chicks, chicks who need to be saved, and he's got a talent for picking them out of a crowd? He talks to a lot of different people. Listens."

"A priest?" Creed offered.

"We've got a mix of religions and at least one atheist. Plus college kids aren't the biggest churchgoers. I think that theory goes out the window."

"A bartender?"

She smiled. "I like how you're thinking, partner, but not all of them were into the club scene. Plus, he'd have to be a traveling bartender. Remember we're dealing with drownings in two states."

"Whoever he is, he prefers troubled women. Why?"

"How about because they're easy to seduce or trick or overpower? Some of them had eating disorders. A lot easier to toss a skinny woman overboard than a chubby chick."

"Since we're on the subject of chubby, come over here and take a look at what I've come up with." He checked his computer's clock. "You missed lunch, I see, and that's a good thing."

"Forget about lunch," she said, eyeing the office wall clock. "It's almost time for dinner."

"I'd wait until after the show," he said, and tapped some keys. "This is not what I'd call good dinner theater."

She stood behind him and gawked at what was playing on his screen. A plump blond woman was on her knees on a cement floor, her hands tied behind her back, while a power spray alternated between pummeling her breasts and her face. "Nasty," said Bernadette.

"Revolting," contributed Creed.

"Do people really get off on this stuff?" she asked.

"Apparently so," he said as he called up yet another porn video.

A color image filled the computer screen. At first the only thing pictured was an outdoor hot tub with steam rising from the surface of the water. In the background were scraggly palm trees.

"Another fine art-house film from California," Creed commented.

A curvaceous brunette wrapped in a towel walked onto the wooden deck surrounding the tub, her back to the camera. She dropped the towel and stepped naked into the water. Turning around, she faced the camera. The cameraman closed in for a tighter shot, eliminating the background and showing the woman lowering herself into the water up to her breasts.

"Those aren't real, you know," said Bernadette.

"How do you know?"

"They're as round and overinflated as a couple of party balloons," she said. "If you took a pin, you could probably pop them."

A nude man stepped into the tub with the woman. He had a big gut and was hairy everywhere except for the top of his head.

"Now *that's* disgusting," said Creed.

Bernadette said, "The male leads all look like that, don't they?"

"How should I know?"

The furry fat man stood behind the woman, planted his hands on her shoulders, and dunked her straight down into the water. At first the only activity under the water was the woman's long hair floating over her head. Then she threw her hands up and waved them frantically, breaking the surface with her splashes.

"Not yet, baby," the man croaked to the woman struggling under his grip. He pushed harder and forced her down deeper.

"This is scary," said Bernadette.

Fat Man finally released the woman, and she popped up gasping for air, only to have the man dunk her again.

The video stopped abruptly.

"What happened?" asked Bernadette.

"That was a clip to tease you," said Creed. "You want more, you have to pay."

"I'll pass."

Creed punched on another clip. "This one is for the Houdini fans."

The video showed a nude woman bound in rope and hanging upside down above a tall, clear tank filled with water. Slowly, she was lowered into the tank. After showing a full body shot while the woman fought against the bonds, the camera closed in on her face to highlight the air bubbles escaping from her nostrils. Finally, she was lifted out of the tank, dripping and coughing and gasping for air.

"That's about all I can stomach for the day," said Creed, exiting the site.

Bernadette took her hand down from his chair. "How did you find this?"

"I went to a couple of general porn sites and clicked on specific fetishes."

"That would be—what . . . water sports?"

He laughed dryly and swiveled his chair around to face her. "No, I tried that phrase and discovered an entirely different fetish. Water sports has to do with—"

She raised her palm. "Is it relevant to what we're investigating?"

"Not particularly."

"Then I don't want to know."

He tipped his head back toward his computer screen. "These videos were listed under the heading of 'water bondage.' In addition to watching people trying to drown each other . . ."

"Do women also dunk men?"

"I've seen no evidence of that. Men do it to women, or females do it to each other while men watch."

"Lovely."

"In addition to that sick stuff, you can also view women wrestling in swimming pools. Women with their hands tied behind their backs and their faces held down in buckets of water. Women strapped into these medieval-looking torture chairs and repeatedly dunked backward into big tanks."

"Did you find any local links to this sort of thing? Clubs around town? Web sites we can trace to someone in the Twin Cities?"

"Not yet," he said. "That will require a little more digging. If you don't mind, I'd like to take a break before I go another round with this smut."

She wheeled over a chair and sat down across from him. "Am I right about this, Ruben? Are these drownings about sex?"

"Sex and violence. Violent sex."

"What if I'm wrong? What if these were—I don't know, something else? Robbery attempts gone sour or . . . I don't know." She looked at the yellow wall. "Maybe some of them *were* suicides. These women were screwed up."

"No," he said firmly. "You're on the right track, Bernadette. After watching those disturbing videos, I'm certain we're after someone who gets sexual satisfaction by drowning women."

"Watching the videos is one thing, but taking it all the way and *really* drowning someone . . . I don't get it. I don't get how someone would get his rocks off by doing something like that."

"Could be it started out as a game."

"A game?"

"Playacting. Fake drownings, like in the videos. To really get off, he graduated to the real deal."

"I guess that works. It's just that this water fetish thing is so—I don't know . . . I've never heard of it before."

Creed nodded at the computer screen. "This might be new, but horrifically violent sex offenders are not. Some of them blame the porn."

"Ted Bundy."

"Yup. Maybe we need to talk to some shrinks," said Creed. "Develop a profile of the sort of gentleman who would get his jollies by drowning women."

"Sounds like something for the folks in BSU," she said, referring to the Behavioral Science Unit at the FBI Academy in Quantico.

"We don't need those big shots," Creed snapped. "We can do it ourselves, Bernadette."

She smiled, pleased that they were finally on a first-name basis. "Touché. Did someone try for a spot in BSU and get turned down?"

"I never bothered applying; I figured I wasn't . . . different enough."

"You're different enough now." She checked her wristwatch.

"Waiting for a call?"

"Garcia." She wanted that scarf off him, and it looked like she wasn't going to get it until Thursday.

"He didn't show last night?"

"No. He got tied up, and he's running around today." She went back to the wall of yellow scraps. "There's got to be someone we missed. Someone they all trusted."

Creed looked at his screen again. "Someone who was into some really sick stuff."

Chapter 9

"BRACE YOURSELF," SHE SAID, CRACKING OPEN HER APART- ment door and flipping on a ceiling light.

He ran his eyes over the messy room. "I suppose it doesn't help if your roommates are sloppy."

"I live alone."

"Open mouth. Insert foot."

She sighed. "Don't worry about it."

"You sound tired," he said.

"Long day." She took off her vest and tossed it and her purse onto a chair. "Can I get you something?"

He took off his coat and draped it over the back of the chair. "Sit. I'll get *you* something."

"Seriously?"

"Seriously. Sit. I mean it."

She kicked away some empty Chinese takeout cartons, picked a cat off the sofa, and lowered herself onto the cushions. "The kitchen is bad."

"I'll manage."

"Be afraid. Be very afraid."

"I'm going to use your bathroom first."

"Down the hall," she said, pointing.

She bent to pull off her boots. Heard the toilet flush and the bathroom door pop open.

"How about I pour you a glass of wine?" he asked as he headed to the kitchen. "Do you have any?"

She chewed her bottom lip. "I really shouldn't, but I guess a little would be all right."

"After all," he said, "it is a special occasion."

"You're right. If you can find it, go for it." Because of her meds, she didn't react well to alcohol. She became dizzy and drowsy. She didn't want to think about her illness tonight, however, and told herself a single glass couldn't hurt. She heard him opening and closing drawers and hollered, "Corkscrew's in the drawer to the right of the sink!"

After a few minutes, he reappeared with a tall tumbler filled to the top with red wine. A paper towel was wrapped around it. "I filled it a little too full."

"Good thing I don't work until tomorrow afternoon," she said, taking the drink from him.

He went back into the kitchen. "Now I've got to find a second clean glass."

"Good luck with that," she said after him. She took a sip. She hadn't had booze in a while, and it tasted off to her. It was also flooding her body with warmth, however, and that couldn't be a bad thing. Putting the glass to her mouth, she tipped it back and swallowed hard.

SHE AWOKE on the floor, with him on top of her. Her jeans and sweater were off. How had that happened? She couldn't remember. She was dizzy and felt out of control—like one of her *up* days.

He reached around with both hands and cupped her buttocks under her panties. At the same time, he lifted his right knee and pressed it into her crotch. "Do you like that?"

"Oh, God," she moaned.

"Excellent." His mouth went to her breasts.

"That's good," she panted.

He rolled off her, reached down, clamped his hand over the waist of her panties, and ripped them down. "You won't need these."

"This is not how I expected things to go tonight," she said.

"Are you complaining?"

"Hell, no," she said, and gave a short, hysterical laugh.

"Stop talking," he said.

"Why?"

"You're ruining the moment."

She watched while he unrolled a condom over his erection. "You came prepared."

He crawled back on top of her. "Please stop talking, Kyra dear."

She gasped as he entered her and wrapped her legs around his hips. "You're a horse."

As he pumped, he cupped his hand over her nose and mouth. "I instructed you to stop talking."

Only after he climaxed did he remove his hand.

Shoving him off her, she panted a question to the ceiling. "Were you trying to suffocate me or what?"

"Who are you kidding?" he asked, sprawled out next to her. "You loved it."

She closed her eyes, trying to make the dizziness dissipate. "So what if I did?"

A cat walked across his legs, and he kicked at it, but it danced out of the way. "Cutting off oxygen at precisely the right moment during intercourse heightens the orgasm."

"I've read about that," she said, her eyes still shut. "People hang themselves. Autoerotic something."

"Autoerotic asphyxia."

"Yeah. I've always wanted to try that. It sounds so hot."

"It is hot."

She opened her eyes in time to see him reach down, remove the spent condom, and slip it inside the front pocket of his discarded pants. She found that behavior odd but didn't question him. "I've heard it's dangerous. People have accidentally died that way."

"There are lots of variations on that theme," he said.

She went onto her side to look at him. "What do you mean?"

He reached over and outlined her lips with his index finger. "How about a warm soak in the tub before we go another round?"

She locked her lips over his finger and sucked hard while he slowly withdrew it. "What have you got in mind?"

"A variation on a hot theme."

She hesitated. "I don't know."

With the tips of his fingers, he combed through her spiky hair. "You are so beautiful, Kyra."

"You are so full of shit." She grabbed his caressing hand and brought it to her mouth. She chewed on the heel of his palm.

"There's a lovely frailty about you that I find . . . arousing." He tipped her onto her back and went down on top of her. "Your life has been so—"

"I don't want to talk about my life," she said, her lashes lowered. "My life has been horseshit, but I'm getting it together."

"I didn't mean to bring up bad memories." He kissed her on the mouth. "Let me run a bath for you, beautiful."

She looked up at the face hovering over hers and was embarrassed by his attention. She couldn't stop herself from rambling. That out-of-control feeling again. "That tub's bigger and deeper than you'd think, and we could both fit. I've got scented oils in there. Bubbles, too, if you want to get real fancy. Don't use the lavender bath salts, though. They're in the jar with the purple ribbon around it. I keep them on the counter for decoration."

"No lavender bath salts. Got it."

She was glad she'd kept the bathroom clean and organized. "Candles," she said. "The matches are in the medicine cabinet."

"I hope I can remember all this."

"You're a smart man," she said. "You'll figure it out."

"You're right." He reached up, snatched an afghan off the couch, and draped it over her. He took down a throw pillow and slipped it under her head. "Don't exert yourself, unless it's to masturbate."

"Yes, sir," she said.

He got on his feet. "Think salacious thoughts while I draw you a bath."

"That won't be difficult." She rolled over onto her stomach and watched his muscled body move and flex as he went down the hall to her bathroom. The guy was a surprise. Under his clothes he was built like a professional athlete. She listened as the water started to drum the porcelain. A man had never before run a bath for her. She heard him opening and closing the medicine cabinet. He was going to go for the candles. Great. Maybe she could get him to shut off all the lights and make love by candlelight. Despite his flattering words, she felt as fat as a pig, and scrunching up in the tub wasn't going to make her gut look any prettier. She hoped like hell he opted for the bubbles. Every woman looked better buried in bubbles.

He came back into the front room and stood over her with his hands behind his back. He was unabashedly proud of his body, and he should be, she thought. "What do you need?" she asked.

"What do *you* need?"

"I can't think of a thing."

"More wine," he suggested, and went back into the kitchen.

"More wine!" she yelled after him, and laughed. She sat up, pulling the afghan over her midriff but continuing to expose her breasts. The best part of her, she figured. He returned with another overflowing glass. She accepted the tumbler and dropped the paper towel on the floor. "I'm starting to enjoy this."

"There's more to come," he said with a small smile.

"You'd better check on the tub. I don't want *that* filled to the brim."

"Right," he said, and headed back to the bathroom.

Her back propped against the couch, she sighed and took a drink of wine. Wondering what water recreation he had in store for her, she was anxious for the tub to fill.

She was half-asleep by the time he came for her, and she could barely hold her head up as he tore the afghan off her. "What took you so long? Is the water still hot?"

"The water is perfect," he said, wrapping an arm around her and lifting her to her feet.

The room started spinning. Her head flopped backward and she felt herself going down, falling into a black pit. "I'm tired."

"No wonder," he said, scooping her into his arms. "The meds you take, mixed in with all that wine, a dangerous cocktail. You trying to kill yourself or something?"

"No, no," she said. Her head was resting against his bare skin, and she liked it. He smelled like perspiration and the remnants of good cologne. His words were confusing her, though, and she told herself to stop listening to them. Stop remembering and replaying them.

"How about I pour you a glass of wine?"

"I filled it a little too full."

"You trying to kill yourself or something?"

A wave of nausea rolled over her as he carried her down the hall, and she groaned. "I don't feel so good."

"Don't get sick on me, Kyra," he said, stepping into the bathroom and adjusting his hold on her. "That would be very unladylike."

She blinked in the blinding whiteness of the walls and tile work. There were no candles lit, and all the lights were on. "Too bright," she said, and buried her face in his chest.

"Here we go," he said, carrying her over to the tub.

She turned her head and looked down into the water. The tub was filled to the top, just like the wine-filled tumbler. "Too full."

"Stop your complaining, Kyra."

She suddenly noticed his gloves. He was naked, except for his hands. Had he been wearing them all night? "You're going to wreck the leather," she mumbled.

"I suppose I am." He leaned over and dropped her into the water, sending waves splashing over the sides and onto the floor.

The water was cold, and even in her drunken, drugged stupor, she realized something was terribly wrong. She gasped one word— "No!"—and started to sit up, but he pushed her back down. Her torso was under water while her feet were sticking out and banging frantically against the faucet and the wall.

Eyes closed and holding her breath, she flailed her arms and kicked her legs, but the only object she was certain she struck was the unyielding hardware of the tub's taps. The water and the meds and the booze all worked to muffle her senses and weigh down her limbs. It was as if she were fighting and dying in slow motion. After a minute or two, she couldn't feel his hands on her anymore; all she sensed was something heavy pressing against her chest and keeping her from sitting up. Was he even there? She opened her eyes, but everything above her was blurry. The water rushed inside her mouth and nostrils. Was it real or a bad dream? She tasted something flowery. Her final thought: *Bastard used the lavender bath salts.*

Chapter 10

RETIRED HIGH SCHOOL SHOP TEACHER HUDSON BLACK
scratched his backside over his flannel boxers as he shuffled down
the hallway of his apartment. Eleven in the evening, it was the usual
hour for the first of his four late-night visits to the toilet. As was his
habit, he silently cursed his enlarged prostate and promised himself
he'd make a doctor's appointment in the near future to deal with the
problem.

He stepped into the bathroom and flipped the light switch up, but
nothing happened. "Fuck," he grumbled to the dark cell.

Whenever he sat on the john to get his stingy stream going, he
passed the time with a crossword puzzle. That required enough light
to read. He flicked the switch up and down four more times, each
time issuing a curse.

He reached around the doorway, fumbled along the wall, and
flipped on the hallway fixture. It didn't cast enough light for him to
work the crossword puzzle, but it did allow him to notice something
strange.

The bathroom's globe-shaped light fixture was so filled with water, it could pass for a fishbowl. The floor under the light was wet,

too. He glanced up at the ceiling and frowned while scratching his crotch. Crazy bitch upstairs was up to her old shenanigans again. He should have guessed something was amiss when earlier that night he'd looked out the window and caught a glimpse of her coming up the walk with a man. Then while he was using the facilities for one of his many postdinner pees, he'd heard them overhead banging and thumping and making all sorts of godawful racket. They were probably doing the dirty deed in the tub.

Because she was such a head case, he and the other tenants had grown accustomed to her crap the last couple of years and pretty much ignored it. When she was having one of her hyper episodes, she'd have the television and the stereo blaring. She'd be dancing and hopping around like someone had plugged her full of quarters. At two in the morning, she'd start running the vacuum and moving the furniture. Sometimes she'd bring home armloads of shopping bags filled with clothes and shoes and purses. Bringing boys home to bang was not out of the ordinary for her either. He swore he never saw her with the same one twice.

Her hyper episodes had made her down days seem almost pleasant. She'd be dragging her sorry butt around the building like it was the end of the world, but at least she was quiet. She did have that one day when she brought the cops to the building after swallowing a bottle of baby aspirin or some such shit. It was a weak-ass suicide attempt, but it seemed to get her the help she needed. Her up-and-down episodes weren't nearly as frequent after that.

This water damage told him she was up to her old tricks, however. Come sunrise, he was going to phone the super and complain.

Carefully avoiding the area directly under the dripping ceiling light, he padded over to the john. With a sigh, he dropped his boxers and lowered himself onto the stool. He grabbed the puzzle book and pencil off the top of the toilet tank. Holding the book open on his lap, he squinted in the weak light thrown into the bathroom from the hallway. There was enough light to make out the empty blocks but not nearly enough to read the clues. Still, he flipped through the pages once just out of habit, then put the book back on the toilet tank.

For lack of anything better to do while he sat, he counted the drips from the light fixture as they hit the puddle on the floor. It was going to be a long night, and it was that crazy bitch's fault. With any luck, the super was going to kick her nutty ass out onto the street by week's end.

Chapter 11

WHILE TALKING ON THE PHONE WITH GARCIA, BERNADETTE looked over at Creed, and he shook his head solemnly.

"Who found her? When?"

"Downstairs neighbor noticed water dripping from his bathroom ceiling last night and left a message for the building caretaker this morning. Caretaker goes upstairs this afternoon, knocks on the girl's door, doesn't get an answer, lets himself in. Finds her dead—faceup in her own bathtub."

Bernadette reached for a pen and a pad. "Same profile as the other victims?"

"Pretty much. Name was Kyra Klein."

"Kyra Klein," Bernadette repeated, looking at Creed. He scratched down the name.

"Early twenties," Garcia continued. "Undergrad student at the U of M. Lots of problems. Tried to off herself a couple of years ago by swallowing some pills. She's been seeing shrinks for . . ."

Bernadette heard some papers shuffling on Garcia's end. "Let me guess. Depression? Anorexia?"

"Here it is . . . bipolar disorder."

"Bipolar disorder," she repeated, so Creed could keep up with the conversation. "That's where people have big-time mood swings, right? They go from the highest high to the lowest low?"

"Something like that," he said. "She was being treated with lithium."

"Lithium, huh? I've heard of it." She looked over at Creed, and he shrugged. "But we're not . . . I'm not sure what that does exactly."

"It's serious shit. You don't want to take too much."

"Are you saying she overdosed?"

"Crime scene found an empty bottle in the medicine cabinet," he said.

Bernadette tapped her pen on the pad. "So this could be a suicide."

"There are restraint marks on her body and bruises on her legs, just like with the other bathtub victim," he said.

"The killer slipped her a mickey to make his job easier, but she still put up a fight."

"There was an empty glass with traces of wine in it," he said.

"I'll bet the lab finds traces of lithium, too." She clicked her pen. "I want to talk to the doc who prescribed the stuff. Got the bottle handy?"

Paper shuffling on Garcia's end. "I've got the name of her therapist."

"That won't do me any good," she said. "They can't prescribe drugs. I need the psychiatrist."

"I'll get his name off the police."

"Did anybody see anything? Hear anything?"

"The downstairs neighbor, the fellow with the place right below her place, heard banging last night. Figured she was up to her old manic 'bullshit,' as he put it. He did see her enter the building earlier with a man."

Bernadette looked over at Creed and said: "The neighbor saw her with someone? With a man?"

"Big blond man. That's all he can give us. All the neighbor basically saw was the top of the guy's head."

"A big blond dude in a state filled with big blond dudes," she said. "That'll get us far."

"Plus it was dark out, so who knows if he even got the blond part right."

"No one else heard or saw anything?"

"Police are doing their usual. Going door to door. So far, nothing. Apparently Miss Klein was the village eccentric, and folks stopped paying attention to her comings and goings. Her gentleman visitors. I've been told she had a lot of those."

"Was she hooking?"

"No. I think the sexcapades might have something to do with her manic spells."

"I *really* need that doctor's name." She clicked her pen a couple of times.

"I said I'll get it," said Garcia.

"How much of this is being released to the media?" she asked.

"Police are withholding her name until they can reach her brother. He lives out in Seattle."

"Her parents?"

"Both dead."

"What *is* being handed out to the press? What are we saying about this?"

"We aren't saying squat. Like I've been telling you—"

"This belongs to the Minneapolis cops. I know, I know. What are they telling the reporters?"

"Not much. Woman found dead in her home. Possible OD. That's it. They aren't even mentioning the tub. They know we need to keep a lid on these deaths until we know what's going on."

"Sounds like everything is under control," she said evenly. "What's left for me to do?"

"I'd like you to spend your time working this case in a way that the police and our agents can't."

Her eyes drifted over to her wall of yellow Post-its, but she knew that that wasn't what Garcia was talking about. Unlike her previous bosses, Garcia was blunt about asking for her sight, and she found that validating. Creed didn't approve of her ability, however, and she didn't want him to overhear. She swiveled her chair around so her back was to her office mate. "I need the scarf, unless there's something else we think the killer touched. Did he leave anything behind with this victim? Was there anything he obviously touched, something portable you can grab?"

"I don't know. Crime scene is still inside. I'm calling from my car."

She wondered if Garcia was embarrassed to have someone overhear his end of the conversation with her, and then told herself to stop being paranoid. "I'd like to join the mob. While I'm there, maybe I'll see something I can use."

He gave her the address. The apartment was on the west bank of the campus, while the previous victim's home had been on the east. "Make it quick," he said. "There's a lot of stuff here, and they're going to town with the bagging."

"What do you mean, a lot of stuff?"

"You'll see."

OPENED CAT FOOD cans and pop cans. Empty Kleenex boxes surrounded by wads of tissue. Half-spent rolls of toilet paper and paper towels. Empty cigarette packs. A coffee mug filled to overflowing with cigarette butts. Spilled bags of potato chips. Banana peels and orange peels. A bowl of shriveled grapes. Cans of whipped cream. A massive collection of Chinese takeout cartons. Unopened mail and rolled-up newspapers with the rubber bands still wrapped around them.

The odors—the strongest came from the cat waste and the rotten fruit—made Bernadette nauseous. Keeping her hand over her nose and mouth, she walked deeper inside. Even in the middle of the day, the drapes were drawn. With the lights out, it would have been as dark as a cave. As dark as Klein's mood, she imagined.

"Hi," she said to one of the crime scene crew.

"Want a mask?" one of them asked through his mask.

She shook her head and continued gawking at the mess. She was well aware that people with emotional and mental problems let their housekeeping go to hell, but this was stunning.

Weaving around the men and the garbage they were picking through, she went into the kitchen. Dirty dishes were mounded in both sinks and it stank like sour milk. Each of the stove's four burners was topped with a saucepan; she didn't have the intestinal fortitude to check what was inside them. The dishwasher was open and the bottom rack was pulled out. A lone plate covered in tomato sauce sat in wait. Was it a feeble attempt at starting the cleanup, or was it the last housekeeping chore the young woman managed before falling into some sort of emotional abyss?

When she went back into the living room, something brushed up against her shin. Looking down, she saw the furry source of the feline odors. "Cats," she grumbled, and pushed the animal away with the side of her shoe. It detoured over to the Chinese takeout cartons sitting under the coffee table and stuck its head inside one of the boxes.

"Want to take him home with you?" one of the crime scene guys asked.

"No, thanks," she said, snapping on her gloves. "Where's the body?"

He pointed across the room to a closed hallway door. "Help yourself. We got what we needed out of there. Bedroom is all clear, too."

"Anybody come up with any DNA goodies?" she asked through her hand.

"Nothing under her nails or anything easy like that." He sat back on his heels and sighed. "Maybe we can come up with some people hair buried in all this stinking cat hair."

She nodded and walked into the hallway. The instant she pushed the bathroom door open, a kitten scurried out. She was surprised to find the bathroom uncluttered and relatively clean, save for the smelly litter box tucked into a corner. Klein had allowed herself one tidy space. A refuge of sorts.

While pulling the gloves tight over her fingers, Bernadette ran her eyes around the compact bathroom. No signs of a struggle, but the floor was a lake. The guy in the apartment below must have gotten quite a shower. She went over to the side of the tub, a white rectangle that was built into the wall. It was short but deep. Deep enough to drown someone.

Klein wasn't quite as emaciated as the first girl, but she was close. Instead of long red hair, she had a cap of short black hair. Bruises on her body. Feces in the water. No rose petals this time, but something floral scented the water. Again, her evening had started out as something pleasant and morphed into murder.

Down the short hall to the bedroom. The twelve-by-twelve space smelled like the inside of a wet tennis shoe. Clothes littered the floor and the mattress. The dresser and nightstands were covered with more dirty laundry, as well as tampon boxes, tampon wrappers, cans of body spray, cotton balls smeared with makeup, and a pizza carton containing crusts. Every drawer was pulled open and had bras or panties or nylons hanging out, as if underwear thieves had rifled through the place.

"God Almighty," she said to the squalor. It was hard to believe someone actually slept in the room. Did homework there, too, apparently. A tower of texts and a shorter stack of notebooks sat on the nightstand next to the bed.

Bernadette went over to the books and examined the titles on the bindings. A volume on Dorothy Parker. An astronomy text. European history. Economics. Her eyes traveled to the notebook pile. Was there a personal journal buried in there? Carefully, she lifted one after the other. The notebook at the very bottom set off an alarm. On the cover, in black marker, a handwritten title: *SUICIDE*.

Garcia came up behind her, pulling on gloves. "Find something?"

"Maybe." Holding it by the edges, she lifted it so that Garcia could see it.

"Shit. What was that about?"

"It can't be a class." She opened it and a set of stapled papers fell out.

Garcia bent over and picked up the packet by the edges. "Syllabus."

"It *is* a class." Reading over Garcia's shoulder, she saw the full name of the course at the top: The Poetry of Suicide. Below the title was the name of the instructor. Professor Finlay Wakefielder. It was an unusual first name and she remembered seeing it before. "Hmmm."

Garcia looked over his shoulder at her. "Yeah?"

"It was a different class, but he was the instructor. I didn't think anything of the course title when I first saw it, but now . . ."

"What're you talking about?"

"One of the other victims took a class from this Professor Wakefielder. I think it was the June victim. Alice Bergerman."

Garcia lowered his arms, the syllabus still in his hand. "Coincidence? I mean, if you teach two hundred kids at a time in a big lecture hall, chances are . . ."

"Biology 101 is held in a big lecture hall, Tony. This sounds like a small lit seminar."

He raised the syllabus again and stared at it. "What was the other course called?"

"Madness in American Literature," she said.

"This guy has issues," Garcia said.

She turned the notebook over and noticed a sticker with a phone number for a suicide hotline. The girl had definitely been interested in the topic. She set the notebook down the way she'd found it. "I'll check him out tomorrow," she said. "Tonight I want to go a round with the scarf."

"You're pretty sure the killer planted it on the bridge?"

"I'm hoping he did."

"And that when he touched it, he did so with his bare hands," added Garcia.

"I can't guarantee anything, though. Even if he did put his naked mitts on it, I can't say my sight is going to feel like helping me out today."

"Should I bring it over to the St. Paul cathedral? I could meet you there."

It was a decent suggestion. Garcia had accompanied her to churches; the quiet and dimness of the cavernous spaces helped her sight. She eyed the clock on the dead woman's nightstand. "I'm pretty sure the cathedral has services during the week. Really, it's still early enough that any church might have stuff going on. Choir practice and whatnot."

"Meet me in your office, then. You could give it a go right there."

"No way is that going to work for my sight."

"There's no one else around, and if we turned off all the lights, it'd be dark enough."

Even if the construction racket was gone by the time they got there, Creed could be lurking about. "Cellar won't work," she said shortly.

"Then where?" he asked impatiently. "Someplace close. We need to do this pronto."

"Murrick Place has a basement, dark and empty. The walls are so thick, somebody could detonate a bomb outside and you'd never know it."

"Do you have a key?"

"We don't need one," she said, praying that was correct.

"After we're through here, I'll meet you at your loft with the scarf, and we'll go down together," he said. "Be ready to work."

Garcia had an edge to his voice. Bernadette figured he felt guilty he hadn't produced the scarf earlier in the week. Both of them were wondering the same thing: *Could her sight have helped them prevent this?*

Chapter 12

SPOOKED BY THE TWO VISITORS, THE STRAY CAT FLATTENED itself against the wall as it darted into a dark corner. The stink of degeneracy hung in the air, an acrid combination of booze and urine. In the middle of the large space, a lone bulb dangled from the ceiling on a frayed cord and swayed in a draft that seemed to rise up from the floor. A semi rumbled past on the road outside, the sound muffled by the density of the basement stonework. Anyone passing by wouldn't have given a glance to the dim light dancing against the basement's glass block, but something extraordinary was about to take place on the other side of those windows.

Rubbing her arms over her blazer, Bernadette walked the perimeter while Garcia stood at the bottom of the steps with his arms folded in front of him. They'd had no trouble gaining access to the space. The door to the basement was not only unlocked but also practically falling off its hinges. More maintenance the building's caretaker had been neglecting.

"What're we looking for?" Garcia asked.

"A place to sit and do this," she said distractedly. "A ledge or a chair."

"You're going to get dirty in this hole," he said. "You should have changed into your jeans."

"Too late for that now." Seeing nothing along the walls, she made her way to the middle of the basement and stood under the bulb. The light flickered for a moment, then held steady. She ran her eyes over the ceiling, a maze of joists and pipes laced with cobwebs. "Built like a brick shithouse."

Garcia wrinkled his nose. "Smells like one, too. Homeless folks must have used the basement as a toilet for years before the building was rescued."

"I think Kitty is still using it as a litter box," she said, lifting up her shoe and checking the bottom. "I've had my fill of cat shit today, I'll tell you."

Garcia checked his own shoe and scraped the bottom on the edge of the last step. "Let's hope this *is* from Kitty."

Her eyes widened. "Did you hear that?"

"What?"

"I heard some . . . I don't know—scraping."

"Are you trying to spook me?" he asked.

"No. I'm serious."

Slipping his hand past his coat and blazer, he touched his holstered gun. The basement was dotted with massive support pillars, and he peeked around them as he walked toward her. "I don't hear anything."

"Probably a mouse or another cat taking a poop," she said.

He stepped next to her. "Should I go upstairs and get you a folding chair? I could grab a blanket out of your condo."

"Don't forget the wine and bread and cheese."

He laughed gently. "Right."

"Actually, I can sit on the floor against the wall," she said.

"I don't want you to do that; it's filthy down here."

"No biggie," she said, and headed for a corner of the room.

"Wait." Following her, he took off his trench coat and spread it out on the floor.

She was both touched and amused by his gallant gesture. Looking down at the spot he'd prepared on the floor, she said, "I feel like I'm on a bad date. A really, really bad date that is about to get a lot worse."

"It's not too late for the wine. Bottle of Ripple would be about right."

"My daddy warned me about boys like you," she said, lowering herself onto the makeshift blanket. She stretched her legs out in front of her and leaned back against the wall.

"I'm really sorry about this," he said, gazing at her.

"In case you haven't noticed, I am not into high-end fashion." She patted her thighs. "I get all my suits from the junior department. Wash and wear."

"That doesn't make me feel any better." He reached inside his blazer and produced a plastic bag the size of a sandwich. He squatted down next to her and stretched out his hand. "Here you go."

She stared at the bag without making a move to take it. "I'm afraid."

"Of what you'll see?"

"That I won't see anything."

Fingering the plastic, he said, "We don't have to do this today. I put pressure on you because I didn't . . ."

She reached out and took it from him. "Give me a minute to get in the mood."

"Whatever you want."

Bernadette unsealed the bag and tipped it upside down. A scarf the length of her arm spilled out onto her lap. It was olive-colored silk. Monica Taratino had gone missing in May, and Bernadette thought the color was subtle for a spring scarf. What had the young woman been thinking about the moment she put it on? Probably not her own mortality. The fabric smelled vaguely of a woman's perfume. Had she dabbed it on to impress a particular man or to please herself? It was something spicy and Oriental and indulgent. "Opium," Bernadette murmured.

Garcia frowned. "Drugs are involved?"

"No. She wore Opium perfume." An elegant scent and a tasteful silk scarf. Despite her emotional problems, Monica Taratino had a touch of class. A sympathetic pang stabbed Bernadette's gut, and she stared at the puddle of perfumed fabric resting in her lap, at once anxious and afraid to touch it.

"What's wrong?" he asked.

"Nothing," she said, and scooped up the scarf.

She tightened her right fist around the silk, rested her hand in her lap, and closed her eyes. It was as quiet as an empty church. The only noise she heard was the sound of her own breathing and that of the man hunkered down inches from her. Inhaling deeply, she took in the basement's stench. Rather than fight the dankness, she embraced it. The pit became her own private dungeon, a hell to which she'd been rightfully banished for her offenses. Practicing or not, she remained a Catholic and had no trouble coming up with a list of sins: Lusting after the man sharing the basement with her, a friend and boss she couldn't and shouldn't have. Letting her husband die by failing to spot his depression. Recklessly wielding an unnatural gift that she only vaguely understood.

She exhaled slowly. Under her breath, she made her usual petition: "Lord, help me see clearly."

SHE OPENS HER eyes. The basement stonework melts away and is replaced by a wall of windows. Curtains cover the panes, but the fabric is so sheer she can see through them. It is night out, but a weak, white glow is seeping through the curtains. Is it moonlight? Streetlights? A yard light? Whatever it is, Bernadette wishes it was stronger. Between the poor illumination and her blurry sight, the room is a poorly focused black-and-white photo rather than a snapshot offering sharp details. The killer moves closer to the windows, and Bernadette prays he takes a peek outside so that she can get a clue about his location. Instead, he turns around.

He's standing by the side of a mattress. He glances across the bed—it's a big four-poster—and looks at a woman standing along the other side. She is slender and pale and has long brown hair that flows past her shoulders. The most striking thing about her, however, is the fact that she's nude. It's too early for bed, so they're obviously hopping in the sack for another reason. Is she going to be his next victim? Will he bed this one before he drowns her?

The murderer's eyes are locked on his partner, and all Bernadette can see of the room is what is beyond the woman's pale naked body: a single, massive piece of furniture. An armoire. This is either a very simple bedroom or a hotel room. There must be a mirror in the room. If only the murderer would step up to a mirror. Even though the room is dimly lit, a glimpse of his reflection would give her something. A verification of his size. His hair color. *Are you a big blond dude?*

He looks back to his side of the bed. There's a nightstand with a lamp on it. *Turn on the lamp!* He doesn't, of course, but he glances at a digital clock with large glowing numbers. This is real time. This is happening right now.

Reaching down, he tears back the bedspread. As he does so, Bernadette catches a glimpse of his right hand. It's white. He glances across the mattress, and the woman pulls down the covers on her side of the bed. She hops onto the mattress and pulls the covers over her body. She's wearing rings on the fingers of both hands, but Bernadette can't tell if there's a wedding band in the collection.

He climbs in next to her and reaches across her. Are those blond hairs on his arm? Too difficult to see for certain. He yanks the covers out of her hands; he wants to see her naked body. His right hand goes to her breasts. This isn't gentle fondling; he's kneading and squeezing. Her legs move restlessly as he touches her, but she makes no move to push him away. He crawls on top of the woman, and Bernadette wonders if he's already wearing a condom. She hopes not.

The murderer's mouth goes to her throat. Though his face is close to his partner's, Bernadette still fails to get a clear picture of her. In the dimness, all she sees is a white oval slashed with almond eyes.

The woman beneath the killer brings her arms up to hold him to her, but he doesn't want that. He grabs her wrists and brings them up over her head, pinning her arms against her pillow. Bernadette senses this is about to get rough, and she feels her own body tense. She wishes she could release the scarf and end the unsettling movie, but she must see this thing through. Bernadette needs to know if he kills the woman after having intercourse with her.

He releases her wrists. The woman rocks wildly under his thrusts and clutches the rails of the headboard in an attempt to brace herself. She opens her mouth. Is she crying out in pain or pleasure?

Suddenly it all goes black. The connection is severed.

BERNADETTE CLOSED her eyes and relaxed her fist, letting the scarf drop from her hand. Opening her eyes again, she saw only blackness. It was like having a sack pulled over her head.

"Tony," she said to the void.

"I'm here."

She turned her head toward his voice and blinked twice. Her regular vision cleared and she saw his face. Her breathing was rapid and shallow, and she struggled to speak. What escaped from her lips was a panted exclamation. "Oh my God."

He stood from his crouched position. "What did you see?"

"A woman."

"Not another victim."

"No . . . not yet, at least." The words came, but they were labored. She felt as if she were talking while running a race. "He was making love to her, but it wasn't tender. It was cruel . . . I could feel it . . . I can still feel it."

"What do you mean? What do you feel? What was he doing to her? Did he hit her? Choke her?"

"No, but . . . it was rough," she panted. "He was rough."

"Can you describe the woman or where they were? Their surroundings?"

Garcia sounded desperate, and she wanted to help him, but nothing she had seen could immediately lead them to a particular person or place. "I don't have specifics . . . I'm sorry."

"Can you give me *anything* we can use? Is there something I should be calling in right away?"

"No," she snapped. "I'm sorry. You know how this works." She scrambled to her feet and stumbled backward against the wall. "This was nothing but a waste of time. God, what if another one turns up dead tomorrow!"

"Take it easy," said Garcia, grabbing her by the shoulder to steady her.

"I'm fine." She pushed his hand down. In the next instant, she wanted to throw herself against him.

He took a step back. "What's wrong with you?"

She opened her mouth to retort and quickly closed it. The murderer's mood had become her own, and she had to regain control. "I need a second," she said, leaning her back against the wall.

"You've got it," he said.

Closing her eyes and concentrating, she worked to moderate her breathing and cool her temper. She inhaled deeply and released the air slowly. In and out. She was having a harder time clearing her system of the lust. Her genuine desire for Garcia was fueling the residual passion of the killer. Perhaps leaving the basement and putting some space between herself and her boss would help. Opening her eyes, she said, "Let's get out of here, Tony."

"Fine by me."

She felt something under her feet. She'd been standing on his coat. "I'm sorry," she said, and stepped off it.

Garcia retrieved the scarf and slipped it back inside the plastic bag. He picked up his trench, gave it a snap, and draped it over his arm. "I'm sure you got something we can use. Maybe if you sit down and think about it. Tell me what you saw."

"First let's crawl out of this sewer," she said, and headed for the stairs. She was light-headed and paused before placing her foot on the first step.

Garcia put his hand in the middle of her back. "You okay?"

His touch sent a hot, dizzying rush through her body, and she gripped the rail for support. "I'm good," she croaked, and started up.

Garcia thumped up the steps next to her, sniffing his coat as he went. "Should we just head to your loft?"

"Sounds like a plan," she said, while thinking it would be a huge mistake.

"I'm starving. How about you talk while I fry those steaks you promised me?"

She was famished, too. It had to be the killer's hunger. Watching through his eyes had roused more than one sort of appetite inside her. She pushed open the door to the first-floor hallway. "Steak sounds great."

Chapter 13

WHILE GARCIA FRIED THE STEAKS, SHE SAT AT THE KITCHEN table with a Post-it pad in front of her and a glass of Chianti in her hand. She'd hoped to organize her thoughts before recounting what she'd seen, but she was too unsettled to sort through it. Taking a sip of Chianti, she stole a peek at the chef. He was a big reason she remained flustered. He'd peeled off his jacket and tie and rolled up his shirtsleeves. She set down the wine, picked up a pen, and clicked it repeatedly.

Fork in one fist and a beer in the other, Garcia turned around and eyed the yellow pad on the table. "Not that goofy shit again. I don't know anyone else in the bureau who does it that way."

"Good. That means I'm special." She glanced over at the stove. "Getting a little smoky in here, Emeril."

He took a sip of beer and pointed the bottle at her. "You look like hell."

"Thanks."

"Don't mention it."

She rested her elbows on the table and dropped her face in her palms. "Fuck," she said through her fingers.

"What?"

She put her hands down. "The woman I watched. Suppose she's dead right now? I can't think of a single thing I saw that would help us. I'm sitting here, as useless as tits on a boar."

"I love it when you talk farm talk." He turned around, took another drink, and flipped the steaks. "Maybe you should kick back for the rest of the night. Relax and clear your head. We can hash it over in the morning."

"I want to talk about it while it's fresh in my mind."

He took a bump off his bottle. "Your call, but it's not as if you're the only one assigned to this."

She didn't like how this conversation was going and started clicking the pen again while glaring at his back. "Don't tell me you're relying on that moron Thorsson to work this."

"I'm relying on the cops. It's not a federal case yet, and you know it."

"Yes, *sir*," she said with mock stiffness.

"Stop with the sir crap." Pointing the greasy fork at her, he added, "And stop with the Thorsson bashing. You're not in competition."

"Yes, *sir*," she said, and took a sip of wine. "We're all on the same team, *sir*."

He bumped off his St. Pauli and stifled a burp. "That isn't even remotely funny."

She grinned. "I think it is."

"These are done," he declared, and shut off the stove. He carried the frying pan over to the table. "Got any steak sauce?"

"In the fridge."

He yanked open the door and stuck his head inside to rummage around. "I don't see it."

She suddenly became lost in watching his body as he bent and moved. *Snap out of it! He's splattered with grease and smells like fried meat.*

"Here it is." He came back to the table and sat down with the bottle. He speared the smaller steak with the fork and dropped it on her plate. Deposited the big T-bone on his.

"Want to hear about what I saw?"

"Once again, is there anything we can use right away?"

"No," she said.

He shook the steak sauce, unscrewed the cap, and poured a puddle on his plate. "Then let's save it for dessert. It'll still be fresh in your head after dinner, won't it?" He picked up his knife and fork and started sawing the meat.

He'd lost his edge and intensity, she thought. Garcia was relieved that her sight hadn't helped. As far as he was concerned, his delay in getting her the scarf had had no impact on the case. But what if he'd gotten the scarf to her sooner? What would she have seen then? Bringing it up now would only aggravate him. She picked up her fork and knife and started cutting into the steak. Maybe Garcia had given up on her sight, but she hadn't. She could always give it a try again later.

AFTER DINNER, she cleared off the table and started filling the sink with water.

"Why are you doing dishes the old-fashioned way?" he asked as he fished another beer out of the fridge. "Miss the farm?"

"I miss a working dishwasher."

"Can't the caretaker fix it?"

She squirted a stream of dish soap into the sink. "Maybe he could, if I could find him."

"This joint doesn't believe in maintenance, I take it. I mean, how long has that security door out front been busted?"

"Since I moved in."

He set his beer down on the counter and stood next to her, loading dishes into the sink. "Go put your feet up."

Garcia was too close, and she had to get out of the kitchen before she got the both of them in trouble. Drying her hands on a towel, she said, "I am not going to turn down an offer like that."

"What kind of cheesy renovation job did that August Murrick do on this building?" he asked as he dipped his hands into the suds.

Lowering herself onto the couch, she glanced around nervously. She was sure Augie was gone, but she didn't want to tempt fate. "Can we not talk about my dear departed neighbor?"

"Fine by me," Garcia said, scrubbing the frying pan. "He was your dead buddy, not mine."

She kicked off her shoes and set her feet on the coffee table. "I could get used to this treatment."

"I'll be sending you a bill."

She polished off her wine and raised her glass. "When you're through over there, I could use another one of these."

"Is that how you ask?"

"I could use another one of these, *sir*."

After he finished the dishes, he refilled her glass and dropped down onto the opposite end of the couch with his St. Pauli. "What did you see and when did you see it and why won't it help us?"

"I saw a room with a four-poster bed and an armoire."

"That's the complete description?"

"Sheer curtains on the windows."

"That could be—"

"A bedroom anywhere. A hotel or motel room. The honeymoon suite at a bed and breakfast. Hell. It could have been the set of a porn movie."

"By that you mean you saw them having sex?"

She took a sip of wine. She was still struggling to keep her libido in check, and this conversation wasn't making it any easier. "Remember my limited point of view," she said. "I saw what he saw."

"Which was?"

"His bedmate. A pale woman with long brown hair."

Garcia finished his beer and set the empty on the coffee table. "You said he was rough with her. What did you see him do . . . I mean, what did his partner do that indicated he was being rough?"

She put the wineglass to her lips, tipped it back, and drained it. "He grabbed her breasts and . . ."

Garcia raised his hand to stop her. "If this is making you uncomfortable—"

"No, no," she said, and set her wineglass on the table. "We're all adults here."

"What else? If you saw him fondling her, you must have gotten a look at his hands or arms. Tattoos? Scars?"

"Neither. He's white. I'm pretty sure there were blond hairs on his arms, but I can't be a hundred percent certain. They didn't have any lamps on, and the room was dark because it was nighttime. The sheers were allowing a little light inside from, I don't know, the moon or streetlights or something."

"Do you think it was nighttime *here*, in the Twin Cities?"

"I got a look at a bedside clock, and it was the same time as it was here. If they're not in town, they're at least in the same time zone."

"Wow. That nails it. A white male, maybe blond, in a bedroom or a motel room located somewhere in our time zone."

Ignoring his crack, she snatched her wineglass and his bottle off the table and took them into the kitchen. She opened the fridge. "You want another beer?"

"I don't know," he said, checking his watch. "Do you want to kick me out?"

She did, but not because she was tired. Telling herself she had enough self-control to keep her hands off him, she pulled out a St. Pauli and went over to hand it to him. "No. Stay. Stay."

"You sure?"

"I'm sure," she said, and returned to the kitchen to pour another glass of wine for herself. "Hey. Did you get that doctor's name? The one who prescribed lithium to Klein?"

"Almost forgot." He reached into his pants pocket and dropped a folded square of paper on her coffee table.

"Good," she said.

"Cops have already interviewed him, by the way."

"I've got my own set of questions."

"Gonna start with him in the morning?"

"The professor."

"Let's plug in a movie and forget about work for a couple of hours." He went over to her DVD rack.

They watched two movies, a Johnny Depp film about a writer wigging out and turning homicidal, followed by a Robert De Niro flick about a widower wigging out and turning homicidal. Garcia had made both picks. They sat together on the couch but remained firmly planted on opposite ends. She was going to suggest the Glenn Close–Michael Douglas classic about the jealous mistress wigging out and turning homicidal but decided there was too much rough sex in it and it might set her off again.

It was close to midnight by the time Garcia went home, but she was still too wound up to go to sleep. He'd left the bagged scarf on the coffee table next to the paper containing the doctor's name. Both objects seemed to be calling to her, but one more than the other, and she couldn't resist.

She ran upstairs to change into her rattiest jeans and a sweatshirt. She'd take the scarf for another round in the basement. While Garcia had disliked the hole, she'd been pleased with how quickly it had allowed her to connect with the killer.

Chapter 14

RETURNING TO THE SAME URINE-SCENTED CORNER OF THE
basement, she lowered herself to the floor and leaned her back against
the wall. The kitty had gone into hiding. Bernadette heard a scuffing
noise, however. It was cleaning up after a visit to the makeshift litter
box. She shifted uneasily, wondering if it had been a mistake to come
without some sort of barrier between her jeans and the disgusting
floor. Something else made her uneasy as well, but she tried to dismiss it as her earlier nerves acting up.

She set the bag on her lap and stared at the scarf inside it, wondering what it would bring to her at that late hour. Would he be sleeping
next to his lover or fleeing her home with her body left behind in the
tub? Would he linger, admiring her corpse in the water?

The scraping grew louder, and she knew it wasn't an animal. She
shoved the bag into her pocket and jumped to her feet.

A gravelly voice: "Hey, Blondie. What's the rush?"

Two long-haired men in jeans and tattered camo hunting jackets
were walking toward her. Had they been there all along, or had they
just come in off the street? Had they been there when she and Garcia
were down earlier? Didn't matter; the building's defective doors were
to blame. "Stop right there," she said.

The shortest of the scruffy pair froze, but his taller buddy—the one who'd addressed her—kept coming. He had an empty whiskey bottle in his right hand. He grinned, exposing a black gap where a row of front teeth had rotted away. "You got a tight little ass on you, Blondie."

She took a couple steps backward but kept her attention on the tall one. His eyes were buggy, and he reeked of liquor. She instinctively reached under her sweatshirt to the waist of her jeans and felt her heart sink. Her gun wasn't there; she'd left it upstairs after changing. Her eyes traveled beyond the men to the stairs behind them.

The tall one stopped a few yards away from her, threw his head back, and laughed, revealing a mouth filled with more rotting teeth. "You'll never make it, Blondie." He grabbed at his crotch with his grimy hand. "You're gonna have to do the both of us, and then maybe we'll let you out of here. Maybe."

Shorty found his courage and his tongue and came up next to his partner. He swayed and slurred and pointed a filthy finger at her. "Fuckin' right about that."

"Fellas," she said calmly, "you don't want to do this. I'm an FBI agent."

They were unimpressed. With a grunt, the taller man swung the whiskey bottle against the side of a pillar, knocking off the bottom. Brandishing the jagged half, he resumed his march toward her. "Gonna fuck you and cut you up good."

The short guy was hanging back again. Bernadette figured she could weave through them and reach the stairs. She made a dash for the hole between the two. Shorty stayed where he was, but his pal spun around and went after her.

She was halfway up the stairs when she felt a hand around her ankle. He pulled her down, and they both slipped and fell on their faces on the steps. Miraculously, he lost his grip on the bottle. She heard it clatter and land on the concrete below them. The guy let go of her for an instant but then snagged her ankle again—this time with both hands. She yanked her leg away and turned. From a sitting position on the steps, she raised her foot and smashed his face with the bottom of her sneaker.

He stayed on his knees on the stairs. "Bitch! I'm gonna kill you!" He crawled up a step and lunged for her. Fell on top of her.

"Get the fuck off!" Pushing against his chest with both hands, Bernadette struggled to raise his body off hers. He smelled of sweat and booze and mildew and urine. The stairwell of a dirty parking ramp. He felt like a bag of wet sand, damp and heavy and immobile. She slid out from under him and, still on her back, pushed herself up two steps.

He crawled after her. "I'm not done with you, cunt!"

She cranked her foot back and landed another blow to his face, hitting him square on the nose.

He tumbled down the stairs and landed at the bottom, flat on his back. "Bitch," he gurgled, holding his face with both hands. "You broke my nose!" He tried to get up and fell back with a confused look on his face.

She sat where she was for a moment, enjoying his pain. They were lucky she didn't have her gun.

She jumped up and darted up the steps, ran all the way back to her place, and called the police.

AMAZINGLY, THE two drunks were still in the basement when the police arrived.

A young female uniform met Bernadette at her loft and took a statement. Bernadette followed her downstairs and stood in the hallway watching through the front glass doors as the two interlopers were loaded into the squad car by a team of policemen.

The female officer, a slender African American woman, put her hand on Bernadette's shoulder. "You need me to call someone to stay with you tonight?"

Bernadette said, "I'm good. The bastards will be locked up. Was nice of them to stay put for you."

"We're not dealing with geniuses here. Plus they were both drunker than skunks. Maybe high, too. Talking crazy talk."

"Crazy talk?"

"Bogeymen in the basement." The policewoman closed her notebook and tucked it into her jacket.

"Appreciate the quick response," said Bernadette.

"We aim to please," said the officer, pivoting around and heading down the hallway.

"Thanks again," Bernadette said after her.

The policewoman opened the door to leave and said over her shoulder, "Someone will contact you for follow-up. They've both got outstanding warrants, so neither one is going anywhere anytime soon."

Harold Winston, the building's elusive caretaker, padded barefoot out of his first-floor condo and came up next to Bernadette. His massive gut hung over the elastic waistband of his sweatpants, and his curly white beard was so long that it met up with the fur poking out of his V-neck T-shirt. The snowy hair on his head was sticking straight up on top and matted on the sides. Even though he was still in his fifties, he looked ancient. Bernadette thought he could pass for a Santa Claus fallen on hard times. The only thing that gave away his younger age and strength were his thick arms. Santa never had a set of pipes on him like Harry's.

He tipped his head toward her and said in a low voice, "Cops banged on my door and told me what went down, that you ran into a couple of lowlifes in the basement. You okay, Miss Saint Clare?"

"Ducky," she said as she watched the red lights flashing outside.

"Really sorry about this." He paused and tugged on his beard. "But I gotta ask: What were you doing down there, and so late at night?"

She gave him the same lame excuse she'd given the police officer: "The bureau is looking for more office space downtown. I couldn't sleep and thought I'd check it out. See if it was something we could fix up and use."

"But it's one in the morning."

Wanting to get him off the subject, Bernadette pointed through the glass as the squad cars pulled away with their seedy passengers. "When you gonna fix that front door, Harry?"

"Well, as I was telling the officers . . ."

"This was a bad deal."

"I'm sorry, Miss Saint Clare," he said, tugging harder on his beard. "I'm really sorry."

"You keep saying that. Stop saying that, and let's talk about some changes around this joint." Hands balled at her sides, Bernadette realized she was starting to lose it with the caretaker. That rage she'd felt earlier in the evening was bubbling up again, and she willed herself to calm down.

"Changes?" Harry gave his beard a hard yank. "I can't afford no changes. I need this job; I got bills to pay. Besides, Mr. Murrick's will don't allow for no changes."

A former sports bookie and burglar (his clumsiness with numbers had doomed the first profession, and his weight had sabotaged the second), Harry had been a pro bono client of Augie's for years. The soft-hearted attorney had made a cushy arrangement for the failed felon in his estate: Harry could have the caretaker's job for as long as he wanted it and could stay in the condo indefinitely, free of charge.

"What I mean is, we need to get stuff done on a more timely basis," she said, trying to soften her tone. "That's all."

He nodded. "We're on the same page, Miss Saint Clare. I'm gonna get on that front door at first light. I swear to you."

"The basement?"

"Then I'm gonna fix *that* door and swab the stink hole with a case of Clorox. One thing at a time."

"That's what I mean," she said. "It doesn't have to be one thing at a time. I'm sure the association would approve subcontracting some of these repairs if they're too much for you to handle."

His posture straightened as he pulled himself up to his full height of five feet and a couple of inches. "I don't need no help. I can do the job just fine."

She sighed and put a hand on his shoulder. "Go get some sleep, Harry. You look beat."

"You okay by yourself tonight? You got a boyfriend who can come stay with you? Those scumbags must have scared the shit out of you."

"I'm good," she said. "You go on to bed yourself."

"All right, then." He turned and padded to his door. He took his collection of building keys out of his pants pocket and ran the mess through his fingers, looking for the key to his own door. He slipped one in the lock, turned to the left and right. Nothing. He pulled the key out and tried another.

Bernadette shook her head and went to the elevators. Pushed the Up button. While she waited for the door to open, she checked her watch. Dawn was hours away. Glancing down the hall, she saw Harry was still fiddling with his door. She yelled at him, "Need some help?"

He looked up from his keys. "Don't you worry about me none."

The elevator door opened. Bernadette put her foot on the threshold to keep the car open until she finally saw Harry get inside his condo. She stepped onto the elevator and punched her floor.

Closing her eyes, she leaned back against the elevator wall while the car went up. She wished for all the world that she did have someone to stay with her until daybreak. Opening her eyes, she checked her watch again and tried to imagine what Garcia would say if she gave him a call at this bizarre hour and asked him to come over. Why was Garcia the one she thought of tapping for such an intimate favor? Truth be told, she didn't have anyone else. Her boss was her best friend. Pathetic.

The car stopped and she stepped off. As she walked down the hall, she told herself that she didn't need Garcia or anyone else. She'd tough the night out by herself; she'd been doing that very thing for years.

Chapter 15

BERNADETTE PUSHED OPEN THE DOOR TO HER LOFT. SHE'D left it unlocked while she was running around the building; she'd no longer be so cavalier about her home's security. Closing the door tightly, she turned the deadbolt and slid the security chain into place. While she flipped on every light, she continued to mull over the idea of calling someone. She picked up her cell and studied it, as if the screen would tell her whom to call or what to do. Finding no answers, she hurled the phone onto the couch and marched into the bathroom.

She stripped and tossed her clothes into a corner. Come morning, she'd chuck the works straight into the trash chute, including her tennis shoes. Cranking the water as hot as she could stand it, she stood under the shower and scrubbed for twenty minutes. She went through two towels drying herself off, rubbing her skin red. She wondered if she could have picked up any fleas from the drunk. Should have gone back downstairs with her gun and finished the both of them, she told herself.

Wrapped in a robe, she walked out of the bathroom, picked up the television remote, and collapsed onto the couch. She surfed through every cable channel twice before stopping at an old black-and-white

Terri Persons

horror flick starring Boris Karloff. It was one Frankenstein movie or another: *Frankenstein. Bride of Frankenstein. Son of Frankenstein. Ghost of Frankenstein. House of Frankenstein.*

After five minutes of angry villagers, she decided she couldn't get into it and punched off the set. She changed into a nightshirt, brushed her teeth, and went upstairs to try to sleep.

Going down on her knees beside the mattress and propping her folded hands atop the bed, she launched into her nightly bedtime ritual. Though she'd been raised Catholic, she'd long ago stopped attending Sunday mass. The only time she set foot in a church was to use the tranquil physical space for her sight. She hadn't stopped believing in God, however, and every night said the only two prayers she remembered from childhood.

" 'Our Father, Who art in heaven, hallowed be Thy name . . .' "

Saying the words out loud muffled the commotion in her head more effectively than the loudest Frankenstein movie. By the end of the second prayer, the Hail Mary, her body was starting to surrender to exhaustion. She made the sign of the Cross, got up off her knees, and crawled between the covers.

THE MOB CHASED *her along the riverfront, their torches casting bright reflections in the nighttime waters of the Mississippi. Berna-dette could feel her heart pounding in her chest as she ran from the shouts. She didn't know why they were pursuing her. She couldn't understand what they were yelling at her. The only word she could make out was the name they'd given her.*

Monster.

She stopped running and turned to plead with them, ask them to spare her life. They froze fifty feet from where she stood. The hollering hushed. Bernadette looked into the crowd of men and women and children, their furious expressions illuminated and ani-mated by the dancing flames. She recognized two of the faces: they belonged to the bums from the basement.

"*Monster!*" *screamed a female voice in the crowd.*

"*Monster!*" *repeated a raspy male voice. One of the bums.*

Suddenly the entire throng was chanting the word. "*Mon-ster! Mon-ster! Mon-ster! Mon-ster!*"

"*Why?*" *she yelled at them.* "*Why am I a monster?*"

"*Mon-ster! Mon-ster! Mon-ster!*"

At her side, her fists clenched in rage. She reached into her jacket, pulled out her Glock, and aimed into the center of the crowd. "*FBI!*" *she hollered.* "*Drop your weapons!*"

The chanting grew louder and faster. "*Monster! Monster! Mon-ster!*"

She squeezed the trigger, and the crack of her gun silenced the throng. A small blond girl in a white dress and veil put her hands to her chest. A circle of blood appeared under her tiny fists. The stain widened and the girl's face contorted. Then the child fell facedown on the ground.

"*No!*" *Bernadette screamed, and threw her pistol and ran.*

She could hear the villagers closing in on her, their voices loud with a new chant.

"*Kill-er! Kill-er! Kill-er!*"

"*I'm not a killer,*" *Bernadette panted as she ran.* "*Not a killer. Not.*"

The chant changed. "*Kill her! Kill her! Kill her! Kill her!*"

She spotted a dock up ahead and thumped onto the boards. At the end of the dock was a houseboat. Bernadette ran up to the front door and pounded with her fists. She heard music on the other side of the door, but no one answered her knock. She screamed the name of the only person she trusted. "*Tony!*" *Bernadette yelled to the closed door.* "*Open up! Tony! Help me!*"

The mob drew closer. Leading the charge was the blond girl, her dress dripping with blood. Raising her torch in the air, the child led her followers in a new chant, "*Burn her! Burn her! Burn her!*"

Bernadette flattened her back against the houseboat door and yelled, "*No!*"

The girl touched the torch to the dock, and an army of spiders spilled out of the fire. They rolled toward Bernadette like a gray, greasy wave. She collapsed against the houseboat door, closed her eyes, and curled her knees to her chest. Shuddering with horror, she felt the creatures enveloping her body. Biting her. A million tiny needles pricking her flesh. She took a final breath, and they invaded her nostrils, suffocating her.

HER EYES flying open, Bernadette bolted upright in bed. She'd kicked off her covers in her sleep. Though her loft was cool, her body was warm and covered with perspiration. She peeled off her wet night-shirt and tossed it onto the floor. Her heart was pounding like crazy, and she was panting as if she'd just finished a long run. She took a deep breath and let it out. Inhaled again, and let it out slowly. She swore she could smell something burning inside her condo. Had she left the oven on?

She slid off the mattress and took the stairs, hanging tightly onto the rails as she spiraled down. She flipped on the kitchen lights and checked the stovetop. No flame had been left burning on the range. She pulled open the oven door. Empty and cold. She slammed the door shut. Nothing had been left on during the night. She took down a tumbler, turned on the tap, and got a cold drink. It took three glasses of water to quench her thirst.

Exhausted but too tense to go back to bed right away, she stood at the counter and ran her fingers through her damp hair. She pressed her cheek with the back of her hand. Her face was feverish. "I'm losing my mind," she said aloud.

Chapter 16

CREED FAILED TO MAKE AN APPEARANCE IN THE CELLAR
Friday morning, and the construction noise had subsided. The jack-hammer crew must have slept in. Enjoying the serenity, Bernadette sat at her computer to plug into government and other databases.

Professor Finlay Wakefielder had no criminal record. One speeding ticket three years ago. Married and divorced twice. No kids, or at least none that he claimed. Drove an eight-year-old Saab sedan. Lived in the Grove, an exclusive faculty neighborhood next to the university's St. Paul campus. Ph.D. from Harvard University. Before coming to the University of Minnesota, served as an assistant professor in the department of English at Princeton. Scored numerous prizes and fellowships. Dissertation Writing Fellowship. Prize for Excellence in Teaching. Prize for Excellence in the Humanities. English Prize Fellowship. Published two books, one a history of poetry in the Midwest, the other a biography of the poet John Berryman.

The book about Berryman gave her pause. She remembered something about the famous poet and a bridge. She typed in Berryman's name and read an online bio. In 1972 Berryman ended his life by leaping from the Washington Avenue Bridge—the same bridge from which the four Minnesota drowning victims had supposedly jumped.

She went to the university's Web site and looked up the work phone number and address for the professor. Wakefielder's office in Lind Hall, home to the University of Minnesota's department of English, was barely a block from the bridge.

Next, research on the bridge itself. Even before the spate of coed drownings, the bridge was fraught with weird mojo. Despite cosmetic makeovers—the most recent being a coat of paint in the school colors of maroon and gold—the campus community complained that the structure had an indefinable bleakness about it. Certainly the girls weren't the first to go over its railings. Students venturing on the bridge late at night reported hearing phantom footsteps behind them, supposedly the ghosts of those who had leaped or fallen from the bridge in years past.

"I wonder if Creed knows any of them," she said out loud, and continued with her research.

SHE DROVE TO the east bank of the Minneapolis campus and parked the Crown Vic in the Church Street Garage, an underground ramp that was north of the university's mall area. Before dropping in on the professor, she wanted to check out the bridge, which was at the south end of the mall.

She walked past Northrop Memorial Auditorium, a massive concert and dance venue that anchored the north end of the mall. Its wide steps led up to a front entrance lined with tall columns. Bernadette found it reminiscent of a Roman bathhouse on steroids. Other buildings on the mall echoed the design on a smaller scale, their fronts boasting tall columns, tall windows, and wide steps. She had no idea who the mall buildings were named for, but they all sounded sturdy and unassuming: Johnston Hall. Smith Hall. Walter Library.

The sidewalks of the grassy, tree-lined square were teeming with students lugging backpacks and books. Even in the bitter cold, some kids were tossing Frisbees on the grass or sitting outside with their morning coffee and Cokes.

The bridge itself was crowded, too. It crossed the Mississippi, connecting the east and west banks of the university, and was used primarily by students and faculty. The top was for walkers and bikers, and the bottom was for cars. The girls would have gone off the top, which was railed and dotted with globe light poles. A long roofed and walled structure with windows ran down the middle of the walkway. It served as a windbreak for walkers in the winter.

The walkway railing was about waist-high, and as Bernadette stood against it, she judged it wouldn't take much to toss a small person over it. As she leaned over and stared down into the water below, a bicyclist dressed in fatigues zoomed past her. He turned his head and gave her a long stare while pedaling to the west bank end of the bridge. Two boys hiking across also gave her a funny look. She stepped away from the railing. The students were on high alert after the drownings. She didn't need someone calling the campus cops on her because they thought she was a jumper.

She moved off the bridge and headed for Wakefielder's office.

LIND HALL was an older, four-story brick building on Church Street, just off Washington Avenue. Bernadette glanced up at its tall windows as she mounted the steps leading to the Church Street entrance. Wakefielder's office and classroom were both on the third floor. She hadn't made an appointment with him but had uncovered his teaching schedule and office hours by poking around the university's Web site. She'd timed it so she could catch the tail end of the class that Kyra Klein had attended Mondays, Wednesdays, and Fridays.

The classroom door was wide open, and Bernadette saw a few empty desks in the last row. The professor's back was turned, and she sat down without drawing his attention. Students around her gave her a quick look and then went back to their papers. They were taking a test.

While Wakefielder wrote on the board—he was assigning reading—Bernadette studied his hands. No scratches or bruises. That didn't mean anything; no skin had been recovered from Klein's nails. Under his blazer, he seemed to be of average build. Stood six feet or better. Blond hair like the guy Klein's neighbor had seen. Yes, this man was a solid candidate.

A female student got up, went over to the prof, and handed him her paper. She whispered something. To hear her, he bent to one side. Ever so lightly, he placed a hand in the middle of her back.

Definitely in the running, this Wakefielder.

Bernadette unbuttoned her trench coat and the blazer underneath. Holstered under the waist of her slacks was her Glock.

ONE BY ONE, the students quietly put their tests on Wakefielder's desk and filed out the door with their books and bags. The professor was so immersed in his writing on the board, he didn't see a stranger in the room. When a girl to Bernadette's right turned in her paper and exited the room, Bernadette went after her. She waited until the girl was at the other end of the hall. She didn't want Wakefielder to overhear.

"Miss," Bernadette said.

The girl was hunched over a drinking fountain. She stood straight and wiped her mouth with the back of her hand. She was a tall, slender African American girl with almond-shaped eyes and a head of braids tied back from her face. "Yes?"

Bernadette hesitated. College students tended to distrust anything federal, but she went for her ID wallet anyway. Held it up. "I'm with the FBI."

The girl blinked. "Yes?"

"We're investigating the deaths of some female students."

She took a step back from Bernadette. "The bridge murders?"

"There's a student from your class. She may have been another victim."

Her eyes got big. "Jeez. Really? Who?"

"Kyra Klein."

The girl tightened her hold on her books, clutching them to her chest like a shield. "She's dead? Someone from my class is dead? When did she die? She went off the bridge?"

"You knew her?"

Chewing her bottom lip, the girl hedged. "Not really. I mean . . . I've heard Professor Wakefielder call on her. I think I know who she is. Sits behind me. Blond."

"Short black hair."

"Oh, her. Real skinny, right?"

"It's a small class," said Bernadette. "Don't you all know each other?"

"Not really. We've only been in session about a month. We meet three times a week for like fifty minutes, if that. It's not like we hang out together."

"What if somebody is absent? Does anyone notice?"

"People skip out. It's not like the teacher takes roll. Bunch were gone today, even though we had a quiz. Fridays are good for that. People turn it into a three-day weekend by cutting class."

So that the girl wouldn't think every male in the class was a sociopath, Bernadette worded her next question carefully. "Did Kyra mention to you that she was having problems with anyone inside or outside of school?"

The girl shook her head. "Never really talked to her. No one in our group talks to each other. After class lets out, everybody takes off."

Bernadette dug into her coat and pulled out a card. "If you think of something—what's your name?"

The girl took the card and examined it. "Alisha."

"Look, Alisha, if you think of something, call me."

"Now I feel bad that I didn't talk to her." She looked toward the open classroom. "Do you think whoever did it might come after the rest of us?"

"No, I don't think that's what—"

"Has it been in the papers yet? Wait until I tell my boyfriend at the *Daily*."

"Do *not* tell anyone we had this conversation," Bernadette said firmly. "It's part of an ongoing investigation. A federal matter. You could get in big trouble."

Alisha said, "But—"

"I mean it, young lady." Bernadette couldn't believe she had just called someone *young lady*. She was getting old.

"Yes, ma'am," Alisha said.

Bernadette tried to lighten her voice. "So . . . that's an interesting course you're taking, The Poetry of Suicide. What's the big attraction? The subject matter or the professor?"

"Both, I guess. At least it isn't the same old, same old. Who wants to suffer through more Shakespeare, right?"

"Right."

"Professor Wakefielder, well . . . I like him. He's different."

Still keeping her voice light, Bernadette asked, "Why is he different?"

"He gets it. He's a guy, but he gets it. It's like—I don't know—he knows what it's like to be . . ." Her voice trailed off.

"Female?"

"Yeah. That sounds sick, doesn't it?"

"He's a caring, sensitive male," Bernadette said pleasantly. She made the zipper sign across her mouth. "Remember, Alisha."

"Yes, ma'am."

Bernadette turned and went back to the classroom. She didn't want the professor to get away from her. While she walked, she looked around. The hallway was empty. She quickly transferred her gun to the pocket of her trench coat. Those caring, sensitive males could be dangerous when cornered.

THE STUDENTS had all disappeared from the classroom. Alisha was right; they weren't a social group. Wakefielder was bent over the desk, squaring the stack of tests. Bernadette went up to the opposite side of the table. "Professor Wakefielder?"

He set down the papers. "I'll bet you're the student who called about my class on—"

"I'm with the FBI," she said.

Glancing up, he gave her a nervous smile. "What fresh hell is this?"

Bernadette paused, her attention darting to the board for an instant. She extended her ID. "Agent Bernadette Saint Clare."

His eyes went to the badge and then back to her face. "What can I do for you?"

"May we talk in your office, Professor Wakefielder?"

"I'm . . . down the hall," he said hesitantly.

He led the way. Bernadette followed a step behind him, saying nothing. He was scared, and at the same time she swore he was baiting her. Bernadette knew the "fresh hell" crack was Dorothy Parker's signature greeting, and the dead girl had picked that writer for her paper.

THREE WALLS of his office were lined with floor-to-ceiling shelves crammed with books of all sorts, organized in no sane fashion. George Orwell's *Animal Farm* and *Homage to Catalonia* both rested atop a row of Stephen King paperbacks. *The Stranger* by Albert Camus was crammed between a collection of Anne Rice's vampire novels. *The Time Machine*, *The Maltese Falcon*, and *Fahrenheit 451* were followed by the Harry Potter books, which were followed by a fat book titled *Library of World Poetry*. More books by and about poets were wedged between other volumes and were used in stacks as bookends to hold up other books. Bernadette recognized the most famous names of the lot: Longfellow, Shelley, Wordsworth, Tennyson, Keats, Blake, Emerson. Finally, there were textbooks with titles like *The Role of Confessional Poetry in Contemporary American Literature*.

The only wall without books—the one with the door—was plastered with posters and other pop art. Psychedelic Pink Floyd poster from a London Concert. Ad announcing a Metropolitan Opera visit to Northrop Auditorium. Muhammad Ali/Joe Frazier boxing poster. Tin street sign that said "Fenway Park." Poster of Winston Churchill with a plane-filled sky behind him and the words *LET US GO FORWARD TOGETHER*.

As she stood in the doorway—the door itself was propped open with a phone book—he lifted some books and papers off a folding chair. "Excuse the mess."

"You should see my office." She walked inside and lowered herself into the seat. She didn't spot a computer. He had to have a laptop buried somewhere under the mess, she thought. She'd love to get her mitts on it.

He went around and sat down behind his desk, a metal clunker piled high with more papers and books. He folded his hands in his lap and leaned back in his chair, a cushy leather piece with arms. It was the only modern furnishing in the office. He smiled nervously. "I assume you're here about the suicides."

Bernadette didn't answer immediately; she was stunned he'd gotten right to it. "How did you know?"

"I teach a university class called the Poetry of Suicide, and most of my students are young women. Young university women have been committing suicide by leaping off the Washington Avenue Bridge." He leaned across the top of his desk and dropped his folded hands on a stack of papers. "I was waiting for someone to come to me for a consult."

"A consult?"

"As a footnote, you should know I was one of the faculty who helped draft the open letter to the community pleading for peace." He smiled. " 'Restrain the passions' lawless riot.' That was one of my contributions. It's from Horace Smith's 'Moral Cosmetics.' Not a particularly fun poem. 'Ye who would have your features florid'—"

"Two of your students are dead, sir," she interrupted. "What do you know about—"

"Two?" He took his hands off his desk and sat up stiffly in his chair. It squeaked with the sudden movement. "Who—"

"Kyra Klein."

"She . . . I just spoke with her after class on Wednesday . . . She's not—she can't be . . . When?" He dragged his hand across his forehead as if scraping off sweat, but Bernadette could see none. "Don't tell me she jumped from the—"

"Before her, there was the student in your class on madness," said Bernadette, emphasizing the last word to prod him.

"Alice Bergerman dropped out after the first day of class. She wasn't really one of my students. I spent two seconds talking to her after she decided to—"

"For someone you knew for two seconds, her name came to you pretty quickly."

His face blanched, and he swallowed hard before answering. "The police talked to me over the phone to see if she'd demonstrated any despondency in class. When they found out that she'd dropped my course, they didn't even bother to—"

"Where were you Wednesday night?"

"What?"

"Two of your students have died under mysterious circumstances."

"Alice killed herself. The police said so. What happened to Kyra? Did she—"

"Why do you suppose two of your students have died? That can't be pure coincidence. Even if they were both suicides—and I don't believe they were—why would two of your students kill themselves?"

"I . . . My classes attract young women who are . . . tortured. Emotionally . . . tortured."

" 'Tortured?' " Bernadette repeated. She didn't like his use of the word.

"Look at the course titles. Madness in American Literature. The

Poetry of Suicide. Sometimes they talk to me. I listen. They think because I teach the class, I know something about the mental illnesses themselves. I have *some* insight, certainly. I thought that's why you were here."

"That was a smokescreen on your part, or maybe wishful thinking," she snapped.

He stood up and slammed his hands on his desk, knocking off a mound of papers. She reached inside her coat and put her hand on her gun. He had a temper, the caring, sensitive male.

"I want a lawyer. I am not talking to you any longer without a lawyer present."

She could smell the sweat on him now, pushing through the cologne. She bet that under the nice blazer, his dress shirt sported armpit stains the size of dinner plates. Even though there was no record of the other bathtub victim having been one of his students, Bernadette tossed her name at him. "Shelby Hammond. What about her?"

"Never heard of her," he said, coming around his desk and motioning with his hand toward the door. "Please."

"You haven't been arrested or charged with anything, Professor. I just need you to answer a few questions." She stood up. "If another girl turns up missing or dead, your lack of cooperation could look bad."

"I've done nothing wrong." He walked to the door and continued to motion with his hand. "Please leave. Please."

She stayed standing in the middle of the office, one hand on her gun and the other on a business card. "Look, Professor. It's obvious the kids like you."

He shook his head back and forth. "Don't try to—"

"You may know something that would help. Maybe one of the dead girls said something telling, something that you wouldn't recognize as valuable." She set a card on top of *Flannery O'Connor—Collected Works.* "Think about it."

He walked into the hallway and turned around, waiting for her to leave. "You should think about talking to these girls' health care providers. Some of these young women were really disturbed. *Tortured.*"

He used that word a little too frequently, thought Bernadette. She wondered what putting the word *water* in front of it would do for him.

SHE WALKED OUT of his office and felt his eyes on her until she went down the stairwell. When she got outside, she called Garcia. "I want to pull together a surveillance of this Professor Wakefielder. Tonight."

Garcia said, "You sure?"

"I just left his office. He was sweating bullets. Pulled the lawyer card on me and clammed up."

"That sure as hell isn't enough to get a judge to bless a wiretap."

"I'm not asking for one. Besides, I don't want to deal with TSS," she said, referring to the Technical Support Squad. They were nicknamed the Tough Shit Squad, because that's what they said when turning down the many requests for their tech talent.

"So what do you want?"

"A vehicle parked out front." She saw Wakefielder exit Lind Hall and ducked behind a tree to continue watching him. He had a lunch sack in his hand and was headed for the student union across the street. "If he drags a body out of the house over the weekend, it might make for a nice Kodak moment."

"You really don't have—"

"Two of the dead girls were his students. *Two.*"

"I'll work on it," he said. "I suppose Thorsson and his partner could use a little *us* time in the front seat of a car."

That made her smile. "Sounds good."

"What're you doing now?"

She pulled out the square of paper Garcia had given her. "I made an appointment to see a Luke VonHader. He's in the neighborhood."

Chapter 17

THE MAN'S ATTENTION SHIFTED BACK AND FORTH BETWEEN
the agent's blue left eye and brown right eye. "I should have asked if
you wanted cream or sugar."

Bernadette accepted the mug from the receptionist—he'd introduced himself as Charles—and lowered herself into a chair. "Black
is fine."

"Are you sure you don't want me to take your coat?"

She cupped the mug between her gloved hands. "I'm still trying to
warm up."

"It is cold out there," he said. "I wouldn't be surprised if we got
snow before Halloween."

"That's Minnesota for you," she said, offering the gold-standard
response to any weather report.

He left her side to dote on two girls, twins, who, along with their
mother, were sharing the waiting room with her. The girls couldn't
have been more than ten or twelve. Bernadette wondered why such
young things needed a psychiatrist.

"I've got a treat for you," he said, and reached into his shirt pocket
to withdraw a pair of lollipops. The girls snatched the suckers. Their
mother looked up from her magazine and smiled at Charles. He led

the twins and their mother into one room and came back and took Bernadette to another.

"Are they identical?" said Bernadette, trying to make conversation during the walk down the hall.

"I think so," he said as he opened the doctor's office door for her. "Twins are so . . . special."

"They are," she said, remembering her own twin. She went over to the couch, sat down, and patted the seat next to her. "Is this where all the action takes place?"

His blond brows arched like startled caterpillars. "Action?"

Bernadette smiled pleasantly. "Do the patients actually recline on this while talking to the doctor, like in the movies?"

"Sometimes, if they've had a really bad week." He nodded toward a straight-backed chair facing the doctor's desk. "But most patients sit over there."

She nodded but didn't say anything to extend the conversation. She wanted the candy man to take off.

He cleared his throat. "Can I get you anything else? Another cup of coffee?"

She shook her head.

"Well . . . if you'll excuse me, I have some calls to make."

"Go right ahead," Bernadette said. "Don't worry about me. I'll be fine by myself."

As soon as Charles closed the door, Bernadette got up to snoop. Her first stop was VonHader's desk, but the top was bare except for a telephone, an ink blotter, and a black-and-white family portrait. "A neat desk is a sign of a sick mind," she muttered to herself.

She picked up the framed photo and examined it. A handsome man, obviously the doctor, was resting on his side on a beach with one leg stretched out and the other bent. An attractive woman in a wide-brimmed sunhat was seated cross-legged in front of his bent knee, cradling a baby. Behind the couple, a toddler girl stood with an arm draped over her mother's shoulder. They were all in jeans, including the baby, but the man nevertheless seemed stiff and formal. While the others topped their outfits with T-shirts, he was in a dress shirt with buttoned cuffs. The group was smiling into the camera, but the man's grin appeared forced. Almost pained. Bernadette got the distinct impression that Dr. Luke VonHader needed to lighten up.

She set down the photo and tried pulling open his desk drawers. They were all locked. "Figures."

She went over to the bookshelves that took up the entire wall behind his desk. Taking down one volume tucked into the middle of the library, she examined the cover. *Diagnostic and Statistical Manual of Mental Disorders.* "Riveting," she said to herself, and put it back. She took down another book. *Homicide: A Psychiatric Perspective.* Finding the title more interesting, she flipped through its pages and put it back.

She went over to a wall on one side of the desk and took in the collection of certificates and awards. A framed cover from the *Harvard Review of Psychiatry* caught her attention, and she examined it closely. He'd authored one of the main articles in that issue. It had to do with distinguishing borderline personality disorder from bipolar spectrum disorder. His degree was from Harvard Medical School.

"Another Harvard man," she muttered.

He had awards from the National Alliance for the Mentally Ill and the American Psychiatric Association.

The brag wall didn't provide her with much more than she already had on the guy. After researching Wakefielder and the Washington Avenue Bridge that morning, she'd gathered a bit of background on the psychiatrist. Medical professionals didn't easily surrender information about patients, and shrinks were especially skittish about privacy. She'd wanted some leverage should this doctor put up a fight.

The office door popped open, and a man wearing a mop of blond hair leaned inside. "Are you in the right room, miss?"

Her eyes shot back to the desktop photo, but she still couldn't tell if this was the doctor addressing her. Outfitted in rumpled slacks and a long-sleeved rugby shirt, he looked more casual and relaxed than the stiff in the portrait. The face and the hair were similar, however. She went over to him. "Dr. VonHader?"

He stepped inside. "No, I'm Matt."

Charles came in behind him. "This is your brother's appointment."

Smiling broadly, Matthew flashed a set of white teeth and pointed a finger at her. "I'll bet you're the new drug rep from—"

"She's from the FBI," Charles blurted.

Still smiling, Matthew folded his arms in front of him. "Is that right?"

Bernadette had a feeling she'd get more out of this guy than she ever would out of his brother. He looked younger and wore no wedding band. His leering grin had *player* written all over it. She extended her gloved fingers. "Agent Bernadette Saint Clare."

"Nice to meet you," he said, accepting her hand. "What's this about?"

"Can you tell me anything about Kyra Klein?" Bernadette asked.

"Not really," he said with a shrug. "Sad story, though."

The doctor had been sharing with his brother. "Maybe you can answer a few general questions about—"

Charles put his hand on Matthew's back. "Can I see you for a moment—alone?"

"Excuse me, Agent Saint Clare," Matthew said, and turned to follow the receptionist out the door.

"I'd like to speak with you later," Bernadette said to his back.

"Sure," he said over his shoulder, and disappeared into the hallway.

Candy Man's large fingers reached into the office and closed the door after them. Bernadette put her ear to the wood but heard nothing. Charles had probably taken Matthew into another room for a stern lecture about talking to strange women.

As she returned to her inventory of the senior VonHader's office, the door opened again. This time she knew it was her man. Wearing a somber suit and expression, he looked as lighthearted as a veteran IRS agent.

Wasting no time with pleasantries, he walked briskly inside and stepped behind his desk. "Agent Saint Clare?" he asked, dropping a briefcase.

She moved toward him with an extended arm. "Dr. Luke Von-Hader?"

"Yes." He clasped her hand briefly and released it. He nodded at the chair parked in front of his desk. "Please have a seat."

"Thank you," she said, and lowered herself into the chair.

"I assume you're here about Kyra Klein," he said, while pulling folders out of his briefcase and setting them on his desk.

"Yes, I am."

"I'm confused," he said, snapping the briefcase closed and shoving it to one side of his desk.

"About?"

He sat down behind his desk. "How is her death a federal matter?"

"I can't answer that question," she said. "This is an open case and I'm unable to release any details about it."

"You realize I've already spoken with the Minneapolis police."

"Their investigation is entirely separate from the bureau's."

"Also keep in mind that I was her *psychiatrist*, not her psychologist or therapist."

"I'm aware of the difference."

"Are you?" He picked up one of the folders and tapped the bottom of it on his desk. "The police seemed to need an education on the subject."

"You're a professional who has completed both medical school and training in psychiatry. You diagnose and treat mental illness. You prescribe meds. Psychologists and therapists are more into the touchy-feely stuff."

"You get an A plus." He set the folder down in front of him and checked his watch. "I don't have much time, so if we could get to it."

She took out her pen and notebook. "For starters, tell me about—"

"Keep in mind that patient privacy regulations prevent me from saying anything about Miss Klein's medical issues and treatment."

"She's dead."

"That doesn't change the fact that she was my patient," he said.

"I'm sure you're aware that law enforcement may have access," she said.

"My understanding is that medical records may be subpoenaed for court cases, but even that has been challenged," he said. "For example, there was that Supreme Court ruling that federal courts must allow mental health professionals to refuse to disclose patient records in judicial proceedings."

"This isn't a courtroom," she said.

He held up his palms defensively. "I'm not trying to be an obstructionist, Agent Saint Clare. I'm trying to honor my patient's privacy."

"Kyra Klein doesn't care what you tell me. She's dead."

"She has a family."

"What *do* you feel comfortable giving me?"

"Information about mental health matters in general. Descriptions of various disorders and how they're treated. Side effects of drugs. Anything beyond that—well . . . I'd have to consult with my attorney before talking to you."

Another helpful citizen trying to trump her with the lawyer card. Bernadette decided to hurl her bluntest questions and observe his reaction: "Did Kyra Klein commit suicide?"

He didn't flinch or hesitate in his answer. "I suggest you ask that of the Hennepin County medical examiner. He must make that determination."

"She may have overdosed on the lithium you prescribed for her. Doesn't that concern you?"

He flipped open the file in front of him and trained his eyes on it. "The welfare of all my patients and their medication use concerns me."

"There's also the possibility that a murderer laced her wine with the lithium to make her easier to subdue. Wouldn't it bother you to know that a bottle with your name on it was used to dope your patient and facilitate her homicide? Doesn't that make you want to help find her killer?"

"The fact that Miss Klein is dead troubles me greatly." He looked up from the folder. "But this theory that she was the victim of murder . . ."

She leaned forward. "I'm listening."

"Without commenting on the specifics of Miss Klein's case, let me say this. Mood disorders are by far the most commonly diagnosed mental illness in suicide deaths, and patients with bipolar disorders are at a particularly high risk. In fact, a quarter to one-half of all patients with bipolar disorder attempt suicide at least once."

"There are things about Miss Klein's death that indicate it was something other than suicide," said Bernadette.

"What *things*?"

"If she was murdered, who did it? Who wanted her dead? She must have told you if she was having problems with someone in her life."

"Agent Saint Clare—"

"I just want to know what you think. Who should we be looking at for this?" She dropped her pen and pad back into her pocket and held up her empty hands. "Look. No notes."

"No notes?" He offered her a tight smile. "I'm an educated man, Agent Saint Clare. Do you really think I'm that naïve?"

"I think you're hiding something or protecting someone," she said. "That's what I think."

"I'm trying to protect my practice."

"Protect it from what?"

"Let's say for a moment that her death is indeed ruled a suicide. I am not saying that it was or wasn't. But let's say, for the sake of argument, that's what the medical examiner determines." He folded his hands atop his desk. "Who might be blamed for that suicide? In this litigious society, who might end up drawn into a protracted and expensive legal battle?"

She leaned back in her chair. "That's what this is really about, isn't it, Doctor? You don't give a damn about patient privacy. You're covering your rear end in case her family comes after you."

He checked his watch again. "I've got to get some paperwork done before my afternoon patients."

She picked up the family portrait and studied it. "Pretty girls."

"Thank you."

"Emily and Melissa, right?"

His posture stiffened in his chair. "If you're finished, I need to get back to my—"

"Pretty wife, too. Elizabeth, isn't it?"

"Yes."

"She and the kiddies are in Arizona right now, isn't that correct? Where was your vacation home again? Scottsdale? How's the golf game these days?"

"How do you know where my family is and—"

"You've got it all, haven't you?" She set the photo back down on the desk and spun it around so it faced the psychiatrist. "Picture-perfect family. Successful practice. Kudos from your colleagues hanging up on the wall."

"I'm not liking your tone, Agent Saint Clare."

"Big fancy house in Scottsdale. Big fancy house on Summit Avenue. Nice cars. Did you drive the Lexus today or the good old Volvo wagon? Actually, it's not old, is it? It's brand spanking new. It'd be a shame to lose all that nifty stuff."

His jaw tensed and his eyes became slits. "How do you know where I live and what I drive?"

"You *are* naïve, Doctor," she said.

He stood up. "Are you attempting to intimidate me?"

"Not at all," she said evenly. "I'm just trying to figure out why someone with so much to lose would refuse to cooperate with his government."

"My government has no business trying to force me to—"

Someone tapped.

"Yes!" VonHader barked.

Charles opened the door. "Do you two need coffee or anything?"

"I need you to see Miss Saint Clare to the exit."

"Certainly, Doctor." The receptionist opened the door wide and held it for the agent.

Bernadette sat frozen for a moment, staring at Luke VonHader from across the desk. She stood up, pulled a business card out of her trench coat, and slapped it down on the corner of his desk. "In case you change your mind."

"I won't," the doctor said.

"This way, please," said the Candy Man.

"I know the way out," said Bernadette, walking through the door.

Chapter 18

"THAT COULD HAVE GONE A LOT BETTER," SAID BERNADETTE,
stomping into the cellar and throwing her notebook on her desk.

Creed was there and he looked up from his computer. "Now what?"

She took off her coat and tossed it over the back of her chair. "I met with Kyra Klein's prof this morning and her psychiatrist over lunch. Neither one would tell me anything."

"I'm not surprised about the shrink. Patient privacy laws are a pain."

"He's just covering his rear," she said, dropping into her seat. "He's afraid of getting sued for wrongful death. That's what this is really about. Hind End Covering 101. They teach it in med school. It's a required class."

"The prof, though. Why wouldn't he want to help?"

"Klein is the second of his students to be found floating."

"The second?"

"The other was the June victim. Alice Bergerman."

"Damn. You're on to something." He nodded toward his computer screen. "But what about—"

"Don't worry. I'm not bailing on the idea that these murders could be the result of some sort of water bondage thing. In fact, he kept using the word *tortured*. Some of his female students have these *tortured* souls."

"Sounds like he was dangling it in front of you. Waiting for you to bite."

"My thoughts exactly. I'm putting together a surveillance of him over the weekend. I want his ass watched."

"Since we've latched on to the scintillating subject of butts"—he pointed at his monitor—"I've got something for you."

"More porn? Are you becoming addicted to the stuff or what?" She got up from her chair and went over to his desk. "Am I going to have to organize an intervention?"

"You're killing me," he said.

Instead of dripping naked bodies, she saw a completed form for MapQuest. The Starting Location was the address for the cellar. She didn't recognize the address of the Ending Location. She put her hand on the back of his chair and frowned at the screen. "Where are you sending me, Ruben?"

"To a studio across town." He put his cursor over Get Directions and clicked his mouse. "The Land of Ten Thousand Lakes is home to a major producer of these aquatic films and other fetish adventures. Visceral Motion Pictures."

She took her hand off his chair and stepped back. "You're kidding me."

"I kid you not." He hit Print, and the office clunker started cranking out a copy of the directions.

"I can't believe this is your harebrained scheme and not mine," she said.

"You'll have to dress more appropriately, of course."

"What do you mean?" she asked indignantly.

"Trade in the bureau uniform."

She was used to going undercover in jeans. Otherwise, her suits were nearly the only clothing she had in her closet. She looked down at her navy pantsuit and white blouse. "This isn't so obvious. I could be a . . . banker."

He swiveled his chair around. "The second you walked onto the set, the actors and actresses would pull the sheets over their heads."

"Are there sheets?" she asked.

"Good question." He tapped his keys, and a video came up on his screen. "Here's one of their earlier films."

"How early?"

"Last month. The critics gave it four out of five penises."

"I don't see any sheets," she said, leaning in to get a look. "All I see are big boobs and lots of water."

"These people are at the commercial epicenter of this fetish," Creed said. "They should be able to give you the names of the big players. Maybe there's a local person known for pushing the envelope. Perhaps there's a whole club or cult that takes it to the limit and beyond. Could be your prof is a charter member."

"What's my story?"

"Here's what I told them."

She stepped around to face him. "You . . . called them?"

"Don't be ridiculous."

"So how did you contact them?"

"We exchanged e-mails."

"Oh. Right. That makes sense."

"I told them I represented some venture capitalists who were interested in investing in their operation."

She slowly nodded. "I suppose that works."

"You sound disappointed."

"No. That's a good yarn. I can work with that."

He folded his arms in front of him. "Don't tell me you want to waltz in and pass yourself off as an actress."

"Ruben . . . no," she sputtered.

He threw his head back and laughed. "You do! That's what you want to do! You want to play porn star!"

"Not porn *star*. I know I have modest . . . acting abilities." She crossed her arms in front of her chest. "I just figured I could go in as an extra. That way I could keep my clothes on."

"First off, these films don't have extras," he said. "Either you're naked or you're not on-screen. Are you willing to get naked for this case?"

Her arms tightened around her body. "No."

"Secondly, at the ripe old age of . . ." He squinted at her. "How old are you?"

"Thirty-eight."

"Really? You don't look that old. You could pass for thirty."

"Thanks. I guess. You were saying?"

"They like them in their early twenties, so you're too old to be answering a casting call for a porn film."

"Thanks again," she said.

"You're a venture capitalist." He nodded toward her dark suit. "A venture capitalist in something other than an FBI uniform."

"Fine, fine. I'll put on a colored blouse."

"For accessories, I'd suggest a Glock."

"I never leave home without it." She went over to the office printer and retrieved the directions to the studio.

"Do you think you should take someone with you?"

She read the directions. The studio was just outside Eden Prairie, a second-ring suburb southwest of Minneapolis. The area was punctuated by parks, green space, and rolling hills overlooking the Minnesota River. "This isn't exactly a rough neighborhood."

"But it can be a rough business."

She gave him a dismissive wave of her hand. "I'll be fine."

"Don't get sloppy, missy," he warned. "It's gotten you in trouble before."

Was that a veiled reference to the basement mess? How would he know about that? She let it go. "I'll be careful."

"Want me to accompany you and cover your back?" he asked.

He couldn't do that. Could he? Again, she didn't want to know.

"Keep working the case from here. See if you can come up with any other local links. You made more progress today than your partner. All I did was piss off a prof, then aggravate somebody's shrink and get thrown out of his office by his receptionist."

"I'll keep at it," Creed said.

"What time are they expecting me at this studio?"

"They're shooting all day, so it's pretty wide open."

"Did you give them a name? What's our company's name?"

"Capital City Venture Group."

"My name?"

"I didn't know if you'd be going alone or what you had for ID, so I left that and a whole lot of other particulars up in the air."

"And they were okay with that?"

"They want our money."

"If they ask for ID, I've got something I can whip out."

"I figured as much. But just in case . . ." He opened the top drawer of his desk and fished out a handful of business cards. "Feel free to use these."

She took them and read: *Capital City Venture Group*. "From an old undercover assignment?"

"Real old."

She eyed the name on the card. "Chris Udahl. That's a good gender-neutral name. Works for me. But what about the phone number?"

"Rings to one of the cells in my desk. My voice mail will pick it up."

"Still works?"

"Far as I know. If it doesn't, who cares? This is a one-time-only visit to the set, right?"

"I sure as hell hope so. This whole water porn thing is . . ." She searched for the right word.

"Icky," he offered.

She took her coat off the back of her chair and stuffed the business cards inside the pocket. "I'll go home and change and drive over there right now. Get it over with."

"Take a bureau car," he said.

"Jeez," she said, slipping her coat on. "You're starting to sound just like Garcia."

"Since you brought up his name . . . Aren't you going to get permission from our ASAC for this little expedition to the nether-world?"

She still hadn't briefed Garcia on the bums-in-the-basement fiasco. She'd save that treat for later. "I'll give him a holler while I'm on the move."

BERNADETTE CALLED Garcia on her cell while walking to her loft.

"How'd the visit with the shrink go?" he asked.

"He wouldn't give me a thing."

"No surprise. Patient privacy, right?"

"I think he's more worried about getting sued by Klein's family," she said. "I left him my card, in case he changed his mind."

She told him where she was headed next and why, and briefed him on the story she was using to gain access to the studio. Because she was afraid it would freak him out, she omitted the fact that Creed had actually set it up. Garcia was surprisingly receptive and offered to join her.

"Aren't you busy pulling together the surveillance?" she asked.

"Everything's set," he said. "You've got the second shift. Since he'd recognize you, I figured late would be better. He should be all tucked in."

"Who drew the short straw in partnering with me?"

"I did."

She wasn't sure if that was a good thing or not. "Great," she said evenly.

"I'll meet you at this porn place," he said. "We'll say I'm another one of the players in this . . . What's it called again?"

"Capital City Venture Group."

"Why does that sound familiar?"

"Uh . . ."

"How did you come up with it?"

"Yeah—uh . . . I found some old cards in Creed's desk."

"Creed. I remember that sting." Silence on his end. Then: "Did he—"

"Here's the address," she interrupted. "Oh, and don't dress like a fed, Tony."

SHE FOUND a forest-green suit in the back of her closet and tried it on with a cream-colored silk blouse and black pumps. The short skirt exposed more leg than she liked and the low-cut blouse revealed some cleavage, but the ensemble did make her appear less federal. To complete the nongovernmental look, she ran a bead of bronze gloss over her lips, dusted her cheeks with blush, and put on a gold chain. When she slipped back into her coat and leather gloves, however, she realized her clothing change had been for naught. Her outerwear screamed FBI. The Crown Vic would do the same.

She steered her Ford Ranger onto Shepard Road and glanced at the Mississippi River on her left, taking in the citrus-colored fall landscape while she had the chance. Autumn in Minnesota came and went in a heartbeat. In a couple of weeks everything would be brown and gray. Then winter would settle in for its interminable stay. She didn't mind. She'd lived long enough in states that seemed to have minimal change from one season to the next.

After five miles of moderate traffic, she merged onto Minnesota 5 going west and took that to 494 heading west. The interstate was a parking lot, and it wasn't even rush hour yet. She slowed behind a semi and then came to a dead stop behind the wall of metal. Punching on the radio, she was just in time to catch a news report on the latest drowning.

"*. . . this afternoon identified the dead woman as twenty-three-*

year-old Kyra Klein, a student at the University of Minnesota. She was the second university coed found dead in her home this week. On Monday, the body of twenty-year-old Shelby Hammond was discovered by her housemates. The Hennepin County medical examiner is conducting autopsies to determine how the young women died."

Bernadette turned up the volume and held her breath, waiting for the report to mention that bathtubs figured in each of the deaths.

"Authorities refused to comment on whether the two deaths are related. A source within the Minneapolis Police Department said that at least one of the women could have died from an accidental overdose of prescription medication but declined to release further information."

"Feed 'em shit and keep 'em in the dark," Bernadette said to the radio. She was pleased the police had kept the details under wraps.

"Student leaders and university officials are holding a joint press conference in Morrill Hall this afternoon to address student safety concerns. University police have already announced additional patrols."

"Like that's going to do any good," Bernadette muttered.

"The two deaths come on the heels of a series of suicides that rocked the university and sent demonstrators into the streets. Since April, four young women have drowned in the Mississippi River at the Minneapolis campus. Claiming a serial killer may have murdered the young women, students and relatives of the victims demanded that the investigations into those deaths be reopened. There is no word yet on whether authorities plan to do that."

Bernadette waited for the report to raise the possibility that the two most recent deaths were linked to the ones in the river.

"In sports, the Minnesota Wild have a—"

Relieved, Bernadette reached over and punched off the radio. The truck in front of her rolled ahead, and she did the same. She plucked the directions off the seat and glanced at them. Her exit was about a mile up. The studio wasn't far from the freeway.

———

THE DIRECTIONS LANDED her in a parking lot adjacent to a building that resembled one of those windowless, big-box wholesale clubs. The only thing missing was the cart corral. She saw no signs, but the address stenciled on the glass double doors matched the one on the printout. She pulled into a parking spot between a silver Mercedes sedan and a black BMW convertible. She got out and leaned against the back bumper of the truck, waiting for her business associate.

Minutes later Garcia pulled in with his heap and parked in a far corner of the lot. She was glad he hadn't driven a bureau car. As he walked toward her, she saw he'd ditched his trench and was wearing a white shirt without a tie. The dark slacks and blazer were still government issue, but they worked.

He came up next to her with his hands in his pants pockets. "I didn't have time to change, so I did some editing. What do you think?"

She looked around the lot and saw no video cameras. She reached behind her neck and undid her chain. "Turn around."

"I'm gonna look like a lizard," he whined as she clasped the necklace behind him.

"That's what we're after," she said. "Unbutton another button, too. Show a little chest hair."

He did as he was told. "Now how do I look?"

"Like a g-man wearing jewelry."

As they walked up to the entrance, they passed more luxury vehicles. Garcia looked longingly at a white Hummer that was as big as a house. "If this FBI gig doesn't work out, maybe we should seriously invest in the porn industry," he said.

"Probably has better fringe benefits," she said.

Passing through the glass doors, they immediately stepped into a compact lobby furnished with black leather furniture, fake palm trees, and glass-topped tables. She eyed the magazines scattered on a coffee table, expecting to find copies of *Playboy* and *Penthouse*.

Instead, she saw *Bowhunting World* and the latest Cabela's catalog. Were they in the right building?

As they approached the long, glossy reception desk at the back of the lobby, however, she was reassured. The woman behind the desk wore a fuzzy fuchsia sweater over breasts the size and shape of musk-melons. Her long feathered hair was silver-blond, and her earrings were loops as big as bracelets. Bernadette cast a sideways glance at Garcia and decided he looked a little too happy about this assignment.

Bernadette took off her trench, draped it over her arm, and went up to the counter with a smile stretched across her face. Garcia stayed back, taking in the mountainous scenery. "Hello. We're with Capital City Venture Group."

"Oh, yes. They're expecting you." The woman jiggled out from behind the desk, displaying long legs barely contained by a short black spandex skirt and fuchsia stilettos. "Follow me to the set."

Bernadette felt like a midget librarian in her green suit as she jogged to keep pace with the twenty-something woman. Garcia continued to bring up the rear, and Bernadette knew why.

The trio went down a long hall lined with framed poster-size photos of young women posing like vintage pinups. Busty blonde on ice skates, falling on her butt. Busty blonde hanging upside down on a trapeze, her short skirt flying. Two busty blondes having a pillow fight. Busty blonde cowgirl wielding a six-shooter. Busty blonde Mrs. Santa in furry red boots. Busty blonde in a stars-and-stripes bikini bottom, tossing a sailor's cap in the air. Bernadette bet that in the original posters, however, the girls weren't wearing nipple rings.

"Uh . . . no brunettes," noted Garcia, struggling to come up with a neutral comment about the artwork.

"I never noticed," said the busty blonde in the tight sweater.

"Actually, they all look like you. Is that you?" Bernadette asked.

The young woman giggled. "I wish. Someday maybe. I've got to work on my look."

"You're gorgeous," said Bernadette, and she meant it.

"I need a nose job, and I've got to drop ten," she said. "My ass is as wide as the back of a school bus."

"That sounds like a jerk boyfriend talking," said Garcia as they walked.

"Yeah . . . well . . . it is." She pushed open one side of a metal double door and held it for the two visitors. "My boyfriend is the director."

"Which one is he?" asked Bernadette, looking toward a brightly illuminated cluster of people and equipment moving around in back of the warehouselike space.

"I don't see him right now," said the woman. "Ask anyone and they can point him out. Skip Masterman. He looks like that model on the cover of all the romance books. Muscles and long hair. Big nose. What's that hunk's name?"

"Fabio," Garcia volunteered.

She nodded. "That guy. Skip looks like that guy."

While they talked, Bernadette kept her eyes on the commotion across the cavernous space. She saw men and women in jeans clambering around cameras, lights, and other equipment. They were all facing a pool of light. That was where the action was taking place. "If he's that hunky, what's your boyfriend doing *behind* the camera?" Bernadette asked distractedly.

"He's been in adult films," she said. "But the real money is in the directing and producing. He came home to do that."

"He's from Minnesota?" asked Garcia.

"Straight off the soybean field." She paused. "But don't get me wrong. Skip isn't a Jethro. He's smart. He has a degree in philosophy."

So that's what philosophy majors did after college: direct porn. "How is the money?" asked Bernadette.

"It's coming," said the young woman. "Some of his old high school buds are backing him on these fetish films."

Bernadette was intrigued. A clique of country boys was interested enough in water porn to pour money into it. She turned to the fuchsia sweater. "We're good if you need to get back to the desk."

"You sure? I can take you over there," she said, casting an interested glance at Garcia.

"We're not shy." Bernadette looked across the room. "We'll find Skip and introduce ourselves."

"Okay." She jiggled out of the room, closing the door behind her.

"How do you know who Fabio is?" Bernadette whispered to Garcia.

He grinned. "Just shut up about it."

"Let's go into the light," Bernadette said, and they made a straight line for the knot of activity.

Chapter 19

THE JERK'S GIRLFRIEND WASN'T EXAGGERATING. SKIP MASTER-
man could pass for Fabio—until he opened his mouth. He had long
yellow teeth with a gap between the top set, scary choppers that gave
him a wolflike appearance. Like everyone else, he was dressed in
jeans and a T. The front of his shirt had a movie camera on it, and
the words "I'm Famous in Europe." A diamond studded his left lobe;
the rock was the size of a thumbtack.

Standing at the elbow of a stocky woman armed with a tiara and
a hand mirror, Masterman directed the positioning of a huge water
tank that was being wheeled in front of the cameras and lights. Unlike the tanks Bernadette had viewed over the Internet, this one was
horizontal. It resembled a giant aquarium.

"Right here," he said, pointing with a pencil to an X chalked on
the concrete floor. "Center it right here."

The three men wheeling the tank missed the mark, positioning the
tank to the right of the X.

Masterman marched over to the X and repeatedly stomped his
foot on top of it. "Here! Here! Here!"

"This thing keeps . . . getting away from us," said one of the crewmen, panting as he pushed the tank left toward the mark. The front of his jeans was wet from water splashing over the sides.

"The floor is sloped or something," panted another of the trio.

Where was the diving diva? Scanning the crowd, Bernadette's eyes landed on a large-breasted blonde wrapped in a bathrobe. The young woman didn't seem the least bit nervous about the prospect of getting dunked naked into a tank of water. She was busy puffing on a cigarette, flicking the ash onto the floor as she watched the three struggling crewmen. "That must be the star," Bernadette whispered to Garcia.

"Must be," he said, his eyes locked and loaded.

"So you recognize her?"

"Yeah. No. I mean—" He saw her smirking. "Funny."

Masterman stepped off the X and watched the trio again miss the mark, this time wheeling the tank too far to the left. "Jesus H. Christmas," he spat. "Why is this so difficult?"

"Is the water still warm?" the robed woman asked no one in particular.

"It's perfect, Tiff," Masterman answered without tearing his eyes off the X.

"It was cold yesterday," she said, and flicked another ash onto the floor. "I froze my ass off."

"You'll feel like you're back in the womb," said a guy with a clipboard.

Masterman looked over at the clipboard guy with a grin. That's when the director spotted Bernadette and Garcia. He tucked the pencil behind his ear and walked over with an outstretched hand. "Hello."

"Nice to meet you, Mr. Masterman." Bernadette accepted his big mitt while trying to imagine all the places it had been during the course of his career. She was glad she'd kept her leather gloves on her hands. "My partners e-mailed you earlier today."

"Capital City Venture," he said, shaking Garcia's hand vigorously. "I've heard of your group. Impressive projects."

Garcia fired back with a similar line of bullshit. "Your films are what's impressive."

Masterman turned around and addressed his crew. "Take ten, kids."

The trio struggling with the tank started to walk away, digging their smokes out of their pockets.

"Not you, bozos," Masterman yelled. "Keep working on positioning that water. X marks the spot."

"I hate that X," one of them groused, and the three of them returned to muscling the tank into place.

Masterman turned back to his visitors. "Which one is your favorite?"

Bernadette frowned. "What?"

"Which of my films is your favorite?"

Recognizing a lose-lose situation, Garcia kept his mouth shut. Bernadette thought back to the clip Creed had shown her. "The one with the fire hoses. The critics gave it four out of five, right?"

Masterman thumbed over his shoulder to the scene behind him. "This one is going to take the top prize. I'm sure of it."

She wondered what the top prize was called. The Platinum Penis? "Good to hear," she said.

"I didn't catch your name," he said.

"Chris Udahl." She dug Creed's business card out of her coat and passed it to him. "This is another partner . . . Mr. Richard Ricardo."

Garcia smiled pleasantly.

Masterman stuffed the card in the front pocket of his jeans without looking at it. "Questions? Comments?"

"I understand you have another Minnesota group financing your films at the moment," said Garcia.

"You've done your research," he said, crossing his arms and tucking his hands under his armpits. "They want to keep a low profile, however, so I'm unable to discuss the particulars."

Bernadette said, "I was hoping to talk to them about their experience, what they know about the industry, whether this would be a wise—"

"Their experience is limited to writing out the checks," the director interrupted. "They've never expressed an interest in visiting a set or meeting any of the talent. All they care about is whether I turn a profit, which I do."

Garcia asked, "They don't care about the subject matter?"

Masterman said, "I could be doing a Civil War documentary."

"You seem to be carving out a niche for yourself in the fetish area, water fetishes in particular. What's the market like for those sorts of specialty films? What sort of person watches them?" asked Bernadette, thinking about the professor.

"Everyone watches them," Masterman said. "Fetish films, Web sites, and magazines—they're all growing like gangbusters."

"What's fueling the interest?" asked Garcia. "Are people practicing this stuff more and more in their own bedrooms?"

"I think they watch when they aren't getting action at home," the director said. "This is the only thing left, the only turn-on besides hookers." He paused, then declared with a straight face: "We're performing a public service."

Garcia said, "Keeping them off the streets, huh?"

"Yeah."

Bernadette eyed the crew wrestling with the water tank. "But why do some men get turned on by certain fetishes? Why drowning, for example?"

Masterman launched into a speech Bernadette suspected he'd given before: "Why do some men get turned on by tits while others like legs? Why do some like to spank and others want to get spanked? There are dudes who like to watch and those who want to be watched. Why? Were they breast-fed as babies? Were they spanked? Did they take baths with Mom? Did Dad leave copies of *Penthouse* sitting around? Did they peek when Big Sister was getting dressed? Did they try on Big Sister's dress?"

"It's all about how males are raised," said Bernadette.

"We can only be domesticated to a point, right, Richard?" said Masterman, throwing an arm around the taller man. Garcia gave him the eye, and the director took his arm away. "At our core we're all feral. As Plato put it so eloquently: 'Of all the animals, the boy is the most unmanageable.' " He nodded toward the tank. "*This* is an attempt to placate the savage."

"By *this*, you mean the water films," said Garcia.

"*This* can be anything," Masterman said. "I don't care what *this* is. I don't give a damn what turns their crank or why, as long as I can get them to open their wallets and plunk down their dollar bills."

Garcia said, "So if next month the latest fetish involves slathering big toes with chocolate syrup—"

"I'm slathering big toes with chocolate syrup. Pass the nuts and whipped cream." Masterman shrugged. "It's not my fault popular tastes have declined. 'The people that had once bestowed commands, consulships, legions and all else, now longs eagerly for just two things: bread and circus games.' I'm the circus."

The philosopher-pornographer and his people weren't dedicated practitioners. For them, the drowning films were less about satisfying their personal libidos and more about meeting current market demands. Bernadette realized she'd get no leads for the case through Visceral Motion Pictures, but she'd gained some insight. "I think we've seen enough of your operation."

The talent dipped her fingers into the tank and whined. "Skippy, the water's getting cold."

"It's fine, Tiff!" he yelled.

"I'm gonna freeze my ass again." Tiff flicked her cigarette butt onto the floor and stepped on it.

For the first time Bernadette took note of the sagging sweat socks and worn house slippers on the star's feet. The tank sat in front of a fake wall slapped with beige paint. Bordering each side of the tank were plastic palm trees identical to the ones Bernadette had seen out in the lobby. Otherwise the set was bereft of furnishings. Suddenly the whole production seemed depressingly low-rent and tired, and she wanted to get out of there fast. "We'll let you get back to work. I'm sure every minute you spend talking to us is costing you money."

"Since you're already here, stay and observe," Masterman said cheerily.

She checked her watch. "I don't know."

"This is a key scene," he said. "It summarizes the entire movie."

"We can stay," Garcia said quickly.

Bernadette gave Garcia the eye and asked, "Where do you want us to stand?"

The director put a paw on her back and guided her to the director's chair, positioned a few yards from the tank. He seemed to have forgotten about Mr. Ricardo. "Front-row seat for you."

She was close enough to get wet if the water play got out of hand. Lowering herself into the chair, she clutched her coat in front of her. "Great."

Garcia came up and pointedly inserted himself between Bernadette and Masterman.

"Can we get started?" asked Tiff, kicking off her slippers and bending over to pull off her socks.

"Where's Doug?" asked Masterman, stepping up to the tank.

A tall, ripped man pushed through the jungle of plastic palms and stood next to the leading lady. Sporting a black ponytail, tight jeans, and a yellow rain slicker pulled over a bare chest, the guy looked like the Chippendale version of a lobsterman. "Ready to rumble," he announced, slapping his flat gut.

"Then let's get rolling," said Masterman. He turned around and addressed the crew. "We have to do this in one take, so get it right."

The director went over to Bernadette, saw Garcia planted on one side of her chair, and took the opposite side. Tiff dropped her robe and handed it to Clipboard Guy. Mirror Lady passed Tiff the tiara and held the mirror up so the nude actress could position the crown on her head.

Masterman leaned against the arm of Bernadette's chair and brought his mouth close to her ear. "Tiff's an outcast mermaid princess stripped of her fins and banished to a life on dry land. Doug is trying to restore her to her throne."

"Your subject matter seems over the top even for an adult video," Garcia said.

"It's too risky for our group," added Bernadette. "Maybe if you returned to more conventional fare."

"I can show you our books. We're highly profitable."

"We don't need to see your books," Garcia said.

Bernadette said, "We know our people, and they won't go for this drowning business. Hoses are one thing, but that tank is scary."

"I guess I screwed myself when I insisted that you stay and watch."

"Better to find out at this early juncture," she said, pulling her gloves tighter over her fingers.

"What can I do to change your mind?" Masterman laughed dryly. "I really want your money."

"As Mick Jagger penned, 'You can't always get what you want,'" said Garcia.

She extended her hand. "We'll call you."

Masterman trapped her small hand between the two of his and flashed the wolf grin again. "If you ever want to meet outside of work and discuss it further over drinks . . ." Garcia glared at Masterman, and the director released Bernadette's hand. "Or not."

The two agents headed for the exit, letting the heavy door slam behind them.

"How did it go?" asked the fuchsia sweater as the pair hurried past the lobby desk.

"Swimmingly," said Garcia, punching a plastic palm as they made their way to the glass doors.

THEY DECOMPRESSED while standing together in the parking lot behind her truck. "Well, that was illuminating," said Bernadette.

"Right," said Garcia, fumbling behind him to try to undo her necklace.

"Here, let me," she said, and he turned around and scrunched down so she could unfasten the chain.

"Is the professor still on your short list?"

"This didn't change anything," she said. "He's our main suspect."

"Motive?"

She looked toward the building they'd just exited. "Some sort of sexual perversion involving drowning."

Garcia watched while she put the necklace back on. "I hope you're ready to see more sick shit. You and I have second shift tonight."

She wrapped her coat tight around her. "At least that gives me time to go home and shower. I really feel like I need a shower."

BERNADETTE KEPT the windows rolled down as she navigated the truck back to St. Paul. The cold autumn air roared into the cab and slapped her face hard, knocking the image of the drowning tank to the back of her head.

Masterman's explanation for why men latched onto certain fetishes wasn't a revelation. She knew that the way people were raised influenced their adult habits. As an FBI agent, she'd witnessed the criminal behaviors passed from one generation to the next in a troubled family. Molestation victims became molesters. The children of thieves grew up to make their living by cheating and stealing. Kids raised by drunks became drunks themselves. Hearing a pornographer's spin on childhood influences, however, pushed the idea to the forefront of her thinking. Had Professor Wakefielder suffered some sort of water-related trauma? It could be basic: he'd nearly drowned as a child or watched a playmate go under.

Chapter 20

IT WAS GOOD TO BE HOME. IT HAD BEEN A TOUGH DAY, BUT IT was going to be a fine night. He sipped and savored the lava flowing to his gut, joining the fire that was always there. As he set the Scotch down on the bathroom vanity, he took stock of the reflection in the mirror. Fair hair and brightly colored eyes. Properly sized nose for the face. No real wrinkles and a minimal number of lines. Mouth a little too full and feminine, perhaps. Overall, it was a handsome face when viewed in the right light.

It was an amiable face that betrayed nothing of the tumult beneath the surface.

He reached down and scratched himself through the robe. Performing the music of Giuseppe Verdi, the voice of Andrea Bocelli washed from the master bedroom into the tiled cubicle. He dropped the bathrobe onto the floor and stepped into the stall. He closed the glass door and activated the hot water. A rain-shower spray needled his scalp.

While he lathered, he thought about the little blonde he'd met that day. So small he could hold her under with one hand.

Closing his eyes, he tilted his face up to the spray and imagined what it would be like not only to hold her under but to wrestle with her in the water. She would writhe and roll and push against his body. Scream and scratch and kick. The two of them would become a single entity, a multilimbed monster churning the waters in a magnificent death thrall.

While a heavy aria from *Ernani* provided the background, he reached down, wrapped his hand around himself, and worked his imaginings into an erection. He didn't take it to completion; he needed to reserve himself for the woman waiting for him in the next room. He would do her differently from the rest; he would keep her around for a while. An extended courtship.

HIS CLOTHES SAT in a heap in a corner of the dim bedroom, the only light coming from the open door of the bathroom. Curled in another corner was what appeared to be a second mound of clothing.

The mound moaned.

He'd stuffed an oily rag in her mouth and twined her wrists together in front of her with fat, coarse rope that burned and scratched her skin every time she moved against it. She couldn't see her ankles, but they felt bound together in the same fashion. To make her more cooperative, he'd shot her up with something that had caused her to pass out. When she awoke, she found herself bound and naked, curled up on her side in a fetal position. The blanket thrown over her body reeked of urine and feces. Was it her waste or someone else's? As limp as a rag doll, she couldn't lift her head or roll onto her back. Music floated over her and around her. She didn't recognize it. An opera? She hated classical music.

Bastard was in the shower; she could hear the water running and the son-of-a-bitch humming. He was happy as hell. She wished he'd slip and fall and crack his crazy skull open. She prayed to hear the thud. Closing her eyes, she practiced the positive-thinking techniques that one of her therapists had taught her. She visualized a SWAT team in black bursting through the door, their guns drawn. She visualized his body riddled with bullets, oozing blood like a sieve. She visualized walking out of this place. *Stupid cow,* she told herself, and opened her eyes to her dark reality.

The worst part was that she'd come to him willingly. Eagerly! She should have guessed there was something wrong with him. His love-making had been too intense. Angry. Really, he'd seemed off to her from the moment they met, but she'd been desperate to have a man, especially one who seemed interested in listening. Now her desperation was going to get her killed. Most pathetic was that no one would notice her absence, at least not soon enough to do her any good. That was her fault, too. Having perfected her bridge-burning skills, she'd isolated herself from anyone who ever gave a damn about her personally. When it came to work and school, her boss and her classmates had grown accustomed to her spotty attendance. They'd write off her disappearance as yet another one of her psycho episodes.

The shower lurched to a stop, and the rag doll shuddered. He'd be back in the bedroom soon.

HE CAME OUT with a towel wrapped around his waist, his chest glistening with water. "You're awake," he said flatly.

Eyes narrowing into dark razors, she visualized a knife going into his back, stabbing him again and again. *Die, you crazy fucker! Die right now!* She flinched as he neared her corner, expecting him to pounce. Instead, he sat down cross-legged on the floor across from her.

"Do you know why you're here?" He reached out and caressed her cheek with the back of his hand.

She shuddered but didn't have the strength to pull away. She felt her eyes start to close; she was going to pass out again.

He clapped his hands in front of her. "Are you listening?"

Her eyes snapped open, and she moaned a response. She visualized his head exploding in front of her. Gray matter flying. Hitting and sticking to the walls of his bedroom.

He trapped her chin in his hands. "Do you know why you're here?"

She moaned and managed a small movement, a shake of her head. More a protest than a response.

"Not yet, though," he said, uncrossing his legs and getting to his feet. He looked down at her. "We must get to know each other . . . intimately."

She shook her head again.

He crouched down in front of her and wrinkled his nose. "First order of business is a bath."

She grunted loudly in protest.

"A shower, then. Would you prefer a shower?" He smiled. "I'll take your silence as acquiescence." Using two fingers, he plucked the blanket off her and deposited it on the floor. He hooked his hand over the ropes tying her wrists together and started to drag her on her back across the wooden floor toward the bathroom.

Mustering all her strength, she thumped her heels on the floor and squeaked a muffled scream beneath the gag.

"That's enough," he said.

When he dragged her past a floor lamp, she kicked at the base with the bottom of her feet and toppled it.

He dropped the rope and grabbed a fistful of hair from the top of her head. "We'll do it the hard way, then."

While she continued screaming, he dragged her into the bathroom by the hair and backed into the shower stall with her. He released her head, letting it crack against the tile floor, and stepped around her body. Her legs were still sticking out. He picked them up and folded them into the stall. Reaching inside, he adjusted the showerhead so that it was aimed at her face and turned on the cold water.

"I'll be back in a bit," he said, and snapped the shower door shut.

She gurgled a scream to the glass.

His response was to turn up the volume on his CD player.

On her back with her legs bent up, she shivered and moaned under the icy spray. Her head throbbed. Her wrists and ankles ached from the bindings. The gag in her mouth was collecting water. Instead of turning her face away from the shower, she closed her eyes and visualized herself dead in the stall before he got back. She started to drift off, and her head tipped to one side. The cold water continued to hammer her face while her ears drowned in a booming aria from an Italian opera.

Chapter 21

ABOUT HALF A MILE LONG AND A COUPLE OF BLOCKS WIDE,
University Grove was a swath of land huddled next to the University of Minnesota's St. Paul campus, bucolic and agriculture-themed, noted more for livestock studies than for student demonstrations. The hundred or so single-family homes gracing the Grove's curving, oak-lined streets were built specifically for university professors and administrators, which meant the compact community contained a good chunk of the state's intelligentsia. Chemists. Economists. Physicists. Architects. Anthropologists. An economic adviser to Presidents Kennedy and Johnson had lived in the Grove, as had a member of the team that developed the atomic bomb.

Bernadette had learned about the neighborhood during her research on Professor Wakefielder. While waiting for this particular member of the intelligentsia to drag a body past a window—preferably one with open blinds and excellent backlighting—she gave Garcia an architecture lesson.

"Modern functionalism," she said, pointing to a blocky home on their side of the street. "I also detect the strong influence of the Bauhaus."

"What does that mean?"

"Hell if I know."

Garcia looked across the street at the handsome homes on either side of the surveillance subject's well-kept Tudor. They all had generous lots, offering plenty of room between neighbors. "I'd love to own here."

"Actually the U owns the land," she said. "The profs buy the houses and pay rent for the land."

"What happens when they want to sell?" asked Garcia.

"It can't be to Joe Six-Pack. It has to be to another university faculty member or staffer."

"So you and I couldn't live here," he said.

"Even if they sold to regular slugs, we couldn't afford it," she said.

He grinned. "Hey. Maybe *you* couldn't, but I—"

"Don't go there," she said.

"I suppose we're not brilliant enough," he said. "We'd feel out of place."

"I always feel out of place," she said cheerfully.

Dressed in jeans and jackets, the pair sat in the front seat of an undercover beater that looked remarkably like Garcia's personal beater. Their heap did not look out of place. It was parked between two other junkers, one a weathered Toyota sedan and the other an old VW "hippie van," as Garcia called it. It seemed the profs on this block did not put their money into their rides.

Garcia shifted the driver's seat back and stretched out his legs. "Does anything suck more than a stakeout?"

"You're the boss. You didn't have to suffer through this."

"Nothing else to do."

"A Friday night, and you had nothing else to do?"

He looked through the driver's side at the two lighted rectangles on the second floor of the house. Every once in a while, Wakefielder got close enough to the windows to reveal a shadow of movement. "Yeah, well . . . sometimes these things can get highly . . . entertaining."

"You've been watching too many mermaid movies." She looked through Garcia's side. She couldn't tell if the windows were dressed with sheer curtains, like the bedroom windows she'd observed through her sight. The blinds were down. Had been down since they'd relieved the first shift at eleven o'clock.

The agents they'd replaced—two buddies from the Minneapolis office who had plans to leave for pheasant hunting early the next morning—said they'd spotted the subject several times downstairs, through windows with blinds at half-mast.

"Traipsing around in his boxers, scratching his balls, having a cocktail," one reported, adding: "My plans precisely when I get home."

They had nothing more to relate other than the time the downstairs lights went off and the upstairs went on: "Twenty-two hundred hours on the nuts."

It was now two on the nuts.

She yawned and shifted in her seat. "When is he going to go to bed?"

"I could call him up and ask."

"Tell him to run us out a snack first. Cheese and crackers would be lovely."

"There's still half a pizza left," he said.

"It'd make me thirsty."

"I have pop."

"Then I'd have to pee."

"You girls do have it rough in that department. Guys can go in pop bottles."

"Please. Who does that?"

"That's what you do in a deer stand. Whiz in a bottle and put a cap on it so the odor doesn't alert Bambi."

"You'd better not plan on doing that while—"

"Car," said Garcia, looking in the rearview mirror.

They ducked down as a cab cruised down the street and turned into the Tudor's driveway. A long-haired woman got out, leaving the back passenger door open, and walked up the steps leading to the Tudor's front door. She had a big purse slung over her shoulder. At first it appeared she wore a short skirt under her pea coat. When the woman raised her arm to ring the doorbell, Garcia and Bernadette realized that that wasn't the case.

"Nice panties," observed Garcia.

"I'm not big on animal prints," said Bernadette.

"It's a look, especially with those flip-flops."

"What sort of gal would arrive by taxi at this hour, dressed like that?"

"Call girl?" Garcia volunteered.

"This is Minnesota. Even our hookers dress sensibly."

The woman started attacking the door with both fists. Bernadette sat up to get a better look. She was young enough and slight enough to fit the physical profile of the fragile drowning victims. Her state of undress, combined with the hysterical way she was beating the door, fit the emotional profile of the unstable girls.

Garcia pulled Bernadette back down. "Sit tight. She's fine. Let this thing play itself out."

The cab was still in the driveway, the motor running. The woman turned as she stood on the stoop and looked at the driver.

"There's stuff all over her coat," noted Garcia. "What is that?"

After more banging and ringing, the Tudor's downstairs lights flicked on and the storm door popped open. Wakefielder stood on one side of the screen door. He'd pulled on some sweats, but his chest was bare. For a guy in his early forties, he was pumped.

He opened the screen door, put a hand on the young woman's shoulder, and pulled her inside, slamming the screen door but leaving the storm door wide open. Bernadette and Garcia sat up and peered into the house. The prof and the woman were standing nose to nose. The woman fell against him, and he put his arms around her.

"This is juicy," whispered Bernadette.

"You think she's a girlfriend? A student? His ex?"

"His wives are older than that. I'm laying money it's a combination of those first two."

The professor eased the girl off him, took his wallet off a foyer table, and went outside. Garcia and Bernadette sank down again while Wakefielder padded over to the driver's side of the taxi. He and the cabbie talked through the driver's window. The prof looked in the backseat of the sedan, shook his head, and reached inside. Extracted a skirt, holding it by two fingers, and slammed the passenger door.

"There's her bottom half," said Garcia. "Covered in puke."

"Drunk or stoned or acting out some sort of bulimic behavior," said Bernadette.

The prof handed the cabbie a couple of bills. The taxi pulled away, and Wakefielder padded up the steps, went inside, and shut both doors. The agents sat straight.

"Show's over," said Bernadette.

"Not necessarily," said Garcia.

Through the half-open blinds lining the home's front-room windows, they could see the leopard print creeping up on the sweat pants. Close. Closer. The next instant, Wakefielder peeled away from his guest and approached the windows. The blinds dropped down all the way.

"Crap," said Garcia.

Ten minutes later all the lights in the house went dark.

The two agents stared at the black windows. "I'm not liking this," Bernadette said.

"Neither am I." Garcia reached into his jacket, pulled out a stocking cap, and yanked it on over his head. Then he turned around and snatched the pizza box off the backseat.

"Tony . . ."

He opened the glove compartment and rummaged around. Pulled out a pen.

"This is a neighborhood of rocket scientists. Literally. This isn't going to work," she said.

He checked the Tudor's address and scribbled a number on the box that was ten higher. "It's never failed me before."

"You're not serious."

He popped open the driver's side. "Watch me."

"I intend to." She opened the passenger door.

"Meet you at the end of the alley," he whispered.

They quietly closed their doors, looked up and down the street, and dashed across the road to the house. While he went up the steps, she slipped between two evergreen bushes growing under the front-room windows. When she heard the doorbell, she unsnapped her holster, took out her gun, and crouched down. Garcia shot her a quick glance from his post on the stoop.

Another ring, followed by Garcia's "Pizza."

The lights in the front-room windows flashed back on, and the storm door cracked open. A young woman's voice through the screen: "One sec . . . I don't have any money on me."

The girl disappeared for a minute. Garcia shuffled his feet and angled his head, trying to see inside through the screen door. Bernadette could hear the heavy thump of a man coming down the stairs. Wakefielder had apparently gone up for the night while his guest had stayed on the first floor.

Their man was at the door. "Jesus Christ! It's two in the morning!"

"You didn't order this?" asked Garcia, raising the box.

Scrutinizing the carton's address through the screen, Wakefielder grumbled: "That's at the end of the block."

Playing dumb, Garcia scratched his head through the stocking cap. "Shit. I'm an idiot. Hope I didn't—"

The door slammed in his face, and Bernadette could hear the deadbolt turn.

Casting a look over his shoulder as he went, Garcia took his time returning to the car. By the time he got behind the wheel, the lights on both floors were out. He started the engine, piloted the heap out of the parking spot, and rolled toward the end of the block.

Bernadette scooted around to the back of the house, crossed the prof's backyard, and stepped into the alley. She looked up at the Tudor's back windows. All dark. She jogged to the end of the alley, where Garcia picked her up. He steered to the next block.

"He's got her camped out on the couch," Garcia said as he hung a left and steered down the road that ran parallel with Wakefielder's street. "She came to the door wrapped in an afghan."

"Surprises the shit out of me," said Bernadette.

"You thought he'd take advantage. Go for a roll in the sack."

"And *then* kill her. Yeah. Why didn't he take her upstairs?"

"Maybe he isn't such a bad guy."

"Maybe he just doesn't want Animal Print Girl throwing up on his bed."

"She *did* stink like vomit. I could smell it through the screen."

Bernadette wrinkled her nose. "What else did you notice about her?"

"Wrists like twigs. Eyes the color of a strawberry margarita."

"From bawling or puking or a hangover?"

"All of the above, I would say."

"Should we go back and park?" she asked.

"He might have seen me get in the car," Garcia said. "Besides, they're both tucked in for the night."

"This whole thing . . . semihysterical, half-naked girl banging on his door in the middle of the night . . . the fact that he let her in and let her stay . . . how the chick fits the profile of the dead girls . . . I don't like any of it," she said. "Plus, when I used my sight, the woman I saw with the killer had long brown hair like Animal Print Girl. This could be that woman and that maniac."

"You're saying—"

"I'm saying I want the house watched all weekend."

"You're not going to be very popular around the office," Garcia said as he navigated the car out of the neighborhood and headed for the highway.

She smiled tightly. "Tell me something new."

Chapter 22

HELL ISN'T RED; IT'S BLUE.

The first thing she saw after coming to wasn't a person or an object but a color. Blue. Blue everywhere. Blue on the walls. Blue on the bed. Blue hovering over her and around her. Blanketing her. She blinked twice and tried to bend her legs but couldn't. They were tied spread-eagled and anchored to the posts at the foot of the bed. Her head was heavy and hot and sore, but her body was so light and detached she wondered why it didn't float away to freedom, leaving only her skull behind on the pillow. When she opened her mouth to ask the blue void why her head hurt, she felt something constricting her mouth. She tried to move her hand to her face and couldn't. Her wrists were tethered to the posts at the head of the bed.

The questions washed over her, blue words roaring into her mind one after the other like waves crashing against rocks: *Where am I? Why am I tied up? Who did this to me? Am I dead? Is this hell? Why was I sent to hell? What did I do that was so wrong? Why do I deserve this?*

She heard footsteps and a soothing voice.

"We're the Twin Cities' classical radio station, providing more music and less commercial interruption. That was Mozart's Sinfo-

*nia in B Flat performed by the New Zealand Chamber Orchestra.
For your listening pleasure this chilly Saturday morning, we have a
selection from . . ."*

The voice would come if she hollered. She struggled to speak and
wasn't certain if she said the word or imagined she said it: *Help*. She
closed her eyes and visualized herself adrift in this blue, the only
survivor of a shipwreck. *Help*. She'd managed to climb aboard a life
raft while the others had perished. All she had to do was hang on
and wait for rescue. *Help*. The waters were calm and flat. There was
music on this ocean. Violins. Flutes. Footsteps. *Help*. She opened her
eyes, and the blue sea parted for a man. Big blond man. This had to
be her savior, the body belonging to the soothing voice.

The man floated to her side, his face coming down to hers. "Awake
already? You were dead to the world when I carried you to bed this
morning."

No savior, this man. She blinked back tears, fully remembering
where she was and how she got there. The bastard had doped her and
trussed her up good. A stupid cow ready for the slaughterhouse.

He brought his mouth close to her ear: "You fell asleep in the
shower, and I didn't have the heart to disturb you. I let you spend the
night there."

More than anything, she wanted to tell him. She wanted to say
three words. Were she free, she would clamp his skull between her
hands and beat the back of his head against the floor while she
screamed the words over and over. *I hate you! I hate you! I hate you!*
Then she would spit in his face and bang some more. Bang and bang
until his head cracked open and his brains spilled out.

He hooked his hand over the blue sheet covering her and ripped it
off. It floated away like a blue ghost. "You won't see me for quite a
while, and I apologize for that. I have things I need to do. Will you be
all right without me?"

Leave, she pleaded in her mind. *Please leave.*

He cupped her breasts with his hands and squeezed. "I'd like to
leave you with a smile on your face."

No! She strained against the ropes, pulling all four limbs toward her body while lifting her head off the pillow.

He picked a damp curl off her forehead. "You know it's futile. You're expending all that energy for naught, and if you perspire, I'll have to send you back to the shower."

Her legs and arms and head collapsed back against the mattress with a dull thud. The words thundered inside her head. How could he not hear them? *I hate you! I hate you! I hate you!*

Leaning closer to her, he cooed: "That's a good girl. Relax. Just . . . relax."

He reeked of soap and aftershave, and the sweet stink made her nauseous. Something sour snaked up her throat, and she wondered if she was going to drown in her own bile.

He sat down on the edge of the bed and said in a conspiratorial whisper, "Before I go, let me tell you a story about the first one, the one I . . . encouraged after a phone conversation." He crossed one leg over the other. "It was a cold night in April, late even for college students. I knew there'd be no one on the bridge."

I don't care about the fucking bridge. Let me go. Shut up and let me go.

"I headed to the east bank and parked behind the auditorium. If she went with my suggestions regarding the hour and the place, I had plenty of time. If she didn't show, well . . . I had the benefit of a nighttime stroll. The campus had an almost ethereal shine from the lights lining its streets and sidewalks, but I saw no signs of life except for a student at the opposite side of the mall, hurrying with his backpack.

"The moment I set my feet on the bridge, I saw her planted at the midway point. She hadn't let me down. Then things moved quickly—too quickly, really. She hopped up, put one leg over the rail, then the other. For a few seconds, she stood facing the river, her hands behind her back and locked over the railing. She let go, tipped forward, and sailed down. Disappeared into the blackness."

You sick puppy, she thought. *You didn't try to stop her.*

"I ran up to the railing. Had she survived the fall? It had to be a hundred-foot drop. Did she know how to swim? I couldn't find her right away. Even with the waterfront lights, the river was like ink. I finally spotted her paddling clumsily. She was trying to save herself while the Mississippi swirled and churned around her. The sight of her struggling . . ."

His voice trailed off, and he reached down between his legs. She snapped her head to one side so she didn't have to watch.

"A gust swept across the deck of the bridge . . . Was it wishful thinking, or could I really hear her cries carried along by the wind? What was she screaming? What were her final words? Did she call out someone's name while the river dragged her? I watched while she went under, resurfaced, and went under again . . . I imagined it was . . . my beloved suffering, her mouth and nostrils filling with icy water. The river would enter her lungs, and she would sink . . . drown."

The more graphic his story became, the faster his breath came. She closed her eyes. She wished she could close her ears.

"The familiar, guilty thrill sent a wave of pleasure washing over me, and I . . ."

She felt him relax against the bed, the panting gone. Twisted bastard.

". . . I backed away from the rail. My foot bumped something, and I looked down. She'd left a note under an empty bottle of liquor. I put on my gloves, picked up the note, and gave it a read. I didn't much care now that she was gone. I put the note back so the police could read it.

"At the far end of the bridge, a couple of pedestrians were starting their hike from the west bank. Would they see her letter, or would a hundred people go by before it was noticed? It wasn't a blatant suicide note, but it showed her mental state. I wondered how long it would take for her body to turn up. I headed back to the car. At least she was no longer suffering."

He turned on the mattress and dragged the tips of his fingers from between her breasts down to her navel. "I'll end your suffering soon."

She snapped her head and tried to hide in the blue of the pillows while he climbed on top of her. His body felt heavy and damp.

He trapped her chin in his hand and forced her to face him. "Look at me," he ordered.

She closed her eyes tight and tried to concentrate on the soothing radio voice, her only friend in the blue hell.

"This offering is by Aleksandr Borodin. Nocturne for String Orchestra. It was recorded by the St. Louis Symphony Orchestra, conducted by Leonard Slatkin. The venue: Powell Symphony Hall in St. Louis. Listen carefully and you'll hear . . ."

"Open your eyes."

Drop dead, she thought, closing her lids tighter. Her eyes were the only things she could control, and she was damned if she'd surrender them.

"Open them." He squeezed her chin hard. "I could staple them open. Would you like that? I have a stapler right here in this nightstand."

Her eyes snapped open and stayed wide with fear. He smiled at her and caressed her cheek with the back of his hand. "Much better."

As he sprawled on top of her, the bile from her own stomach crawled all the way up her throat and filled her mouth with acid. She swallowed hard, wishing the sour fluid were poison.

"I prefer my partners thin. No food for you, just plenty of . . . fluids."

While he moved his mouth down to her breasts, she stared up at the blue ceiling, wishing it would crash down on him and kill him.

"I've always loved you, Ruth," he muttered.

Chapter 23

EARLY SATURDAY MORNING, THE DOOR TO THE PROFESSOR'S attached garage lifted with a metallic groan, causing Thorsson and his partner to bolt upright in the front seat of their van. Peering into the bowels of the garage from their parking spot across the street, the agents saw a young woman in a pea coat and baggy jeans exit through a service door and slide into the front passenger seat of a Saab sedan. A purse was slung over her shoulder, and a paper grocery bag was in her arms. Ten seconds later, Wakefielder walked out of the service door, went over to the driver's side of the sedan, and got behind the wheel. The Saab started up with a smoky cough and backed out of the garage. After a stall in the middle of the street—during which the two agents flattened themselves on the bench of the dry cleaner's van—the Saab restarted and chugged south down the street.

Thorsson called Garcia at home while his partner—a young, freckled redhead who always looked startled—turned on the van's engine and steered out of their parking spot.

"He's on the move," Thorsson said into his cell. "The woman's with him. She's carrying something in a sack."

"Probably the puke clothes," Garcia said. "Where are they right now? In what direction are they headed?"

A pause while Thorsson got his bearings. "They just turned onto Cleveland. Heading south."

"Keep me apprised. Any big moves, give me a call immediately. Need help tailing them?"

Thorsson said, "Red and I have it under control, sir."

"The kid's behind the wheel?"

"He's from these parts, sir."

"I know. Good. That's good."

Thorsson, with great reluctance in his voice, asked, "Should I give Agent Saint Clare the heads-up?"

"I'll do it," said Garcia. "You two just keep your eyes on the prize."

Thorsson closed his phone and snarled, "That Breast Fed is leading Garcia around by the short hairs."

As he navigated the dry-cleaning van, Red kept the Saab at a distance of about a block. "Why do you say that?"

"She's got him convinced that there's a serial killer running around. What a bunch of bullshit. I hope she falls on her ass on this one. Right on her bony ass."

"I think she's got a nice ass, actually," said Red.

"I'm not talking to you for the rest of the day," said Thorsson.

BERNADETTE FLOPPED onto her stomach, reached over to her nightstand, and knocked the ringing object to the floor. She felt as if she'd just fallen asleep. Stretching her arm down, she fumbled around on the floor until her fingers found the phone. "What?" she croaked into the cell.

"Wakefielder and the girl are on the move. Thorsson just called it in."

Kicking off the covers, Bernadette jumped out of bed and scooped her jeans off the floor. "Where're they headed?"

"South on Cleveland."

She danced into her jeans while cradling the phone between her ear and her shoulder. "Could be they're going to the Minneapolis campus. If she's a student, she might live around there."

"Aren't they taking a roundabout way?"

She stepped into her sneakers. "Yes and no. They'd go from Cleveland to Raymond to University Avenue. It works, especially if she lives close to the St. Paul border."

"What do you want to do?"

She picked a sweatshirt up off the floor, grabbed her gun, and started spiraling down the stairs. "Did you say Thorsson is doing the tailing?"

"The kid is driving."

"There's some hope we won't lose them, then."

"Yeah. My thoughts."

"I'm going to tool on over to the east bank," she said. "I might luck out and get in on the fun."

"Stay in contact."

BERNADETTE HAD GUESSED the professor's path exactly. The Saab went along Cleveland Avenue and followed the fork onto Raymond Avenue. The tree-lined residential area gave way to a stretch of neighborhood storefront businesses. Thorsson ogled a coffee shop as they rolled past it and ran his tongue over his top lip. "I'd love a cup of java."

"Then you'd have to pee," said Red.

"I got an empty pop bottle in back."

Wakefielder, in the right lane, braked at a red light at University. A Saturn compact in the right lane separated the van from its target. When the Saab's turn signal started flashing, Thorsson called Garcia. "We're on Raymond at University, and he's preparing to take a right."

"The east bank of the U is a couple of miles from there," Garcia told him. "Saint Clare's thinking that's where they're headed. She's on her way over."

Silence on Thorsson's end. Then: "We'll be glad for the help, sir."

The light turned green, and the Saab hung a right. The Saturn did the same, and the van followed. "Here we go. We're on University heading toward the Minneapolis border."

"I'm gonna call Saint Clare and update her," said Garcia.

"You do that, sir." Thorsson closed his phone and growled, "That little witch."

Red gave his partner a quick sideways glance and kept driving. For a Saturday morning, traffic was heavy. At a red light, Red propped his elbow on the van's door and rested the side of his head in his hand. "I'm starving."

"Me, too. I could go for a Whopper. Let's hit a Burger King after we turn over the baby-sitting duties."

Red checked his watch. "That's hours away."

"Christ. I feel like we've been on the road for a week." Thorsson glared past the Saturn at the Saab. "What has he been doing? Ten under the limit?"

"He's had traffic in front of him," said Red.

After the light turned green, the Saab, the Saturn, and the van paraded through the intersection. The Saturn swerved into the left lane and hung a left, vanishing down a side street. Trying to keep his distance, the agent slowed to a crawl. An Audi pulling out of an office building's parking lot slipped between the Saab and the van. To be safe, Red hung back a little more and let another car join the motorcade.

"Careful," cautioned Thorsson.

"I know what I'm doing," said his partner.

A couple of blocks to the Minneapolis border, the agents saw the Saab ease to the curb and stop in front of a duplex. "Now what?" wondered Thorsson.

Hanging back half a block, the van pulled to the curb. There were no other vehicles parked between them and the Saab. Red fished a clipboard out from under the driver's seat while his partner reached behind and grabbed a shirt encased in dry cleaner's plastic.

Red asked, "Should we call Garcia back so he can call Saint Clare?"

Thorsson said, "We don't need her holding our dicks for us."

"I guess we could wait and see what's up first."

The Saab's front passenger and driver's doors popped open in unison. Wakefielder got out, went around the car, and offered his hand to the girl. Ignoring his gesture, she got out of the car and headed for the front door of the duplex, weaving a bit while she walked. The professor reached inside the Saab, took out the paper bag, and followed the girl, standing at her elbow while she foraged in her purse. She dropped the purse, and the professor picked it up. She snatched it out of his hand and resumed her digging, swaying while she did so.

"Is she drunk or what?" asked Red.

"Fucking early for that shit," said Thorsson.

She finally produced a key, worked the lock and knob, and pushed the door open. She ripped the bag from the professor's hand, went inside, and slammed the door in his face.

Even from half a block away, the agents could see the tension. "Trouble in paradise," said Thorsson.

Red craned his neck while scratching on the clipboard. "I got the address."

"Good," said Thorsson.

Wakefielder got back into the Saab and started it up.

"Do we stay with her or go after him?" asked Red.

"We call the boss," said Thorsson, tossing the dry cleaning behind him and picking up his phone.

"He's pulling away," said Red.

"Don't move," said Thorsson, punching his cell.

Wakefielder did a U-turn in the middle of University Avenue, cutting in front of two eastbound cars. The drivers laid on the horns. Red didn't like the aggressive move. "Do you think he saw us?"

"He didn't see shit. He just drives like a putz."

"What if we lose him?" Red asked worriedly.

"We can catch up."

Garcia answered after one ring. "What?"

"Girl got dropped off at home." Thorsson took the clipboard out of his partner's hand and gave Garcia the address. "This might be a good time to pump her for information."

"What makes you say that?" asked Garcia.

Thorsson said authoritatively: "She had a fight with the man. Slammed the door in his face. On top of that, she might have had a couple. Tongue should be good and loose."

Garcia asked, "Booze this early? You sure?"

"She was swaying and dropping her belongings." Thorsson cleared his throat. "Uh . . . I'd be willing to go inside and talk to her."

"Saint Clare's in the neighborhood, and I'm thinking she's going to want to visit with the young lady. Besides, you're tailing the professor." Garcia paused. "You *are* still on him, aren't you?"

"Like white on rice, sir." Thorsson looked at his partner and thumbed over his shoulder.

Shaking his head with worry, Red checked his rearview mirror and looked through his windshield. He pulled out of their parking spot and did his own U-turn in the middle of University Avenue. He looked up ahead. Lots of traffic but no Saab.

Seeing what his partner was seeing, Thorsson ran a hand over the top of his head. "Pardon me for asking, sir, but are you sure we should bother with surveillance the whole weekend? How certain are we that this is the right guy? That's a lot of man-hours based on a hunch."

"Agent Saint Clare's got more than a hunch, Agent Thorsson," Garcia said brusquely.

"Yes, sir," said Thorsson, his face knotted with anxiety.

"Well, nice work, Greg," said Garcia. "Pass it on to Red. I know it wasn't the most exciting assignment."

Thorsson rubbed his face with his free hand. "Yes, sir."

Garcia said, "Hang in there. Your relief should be showing up at noon."

Thorsson closed his phone and turned on his partner. "Fuck! How did you lose him?"

Red came up on a minivan in the left lane and stopped at a light. He veered into the right lane and blew through the intersection, barely missing a station wagon crossing in front of him. A cacophony of horns followed. "It's your fault. You told me to wait."

"You know what you're doing, right? That's what you told me, you little shit."

Weaving in and out of traffic, the frenetic delivery van finally reached Raymond, where it took a screeching left. "He's gotta be back home."

"He'd better be home," snarled Thorsson.

"What if he's not?" squeaked Red.

"Then you're fucked, my friend."

SPEEDING BACK to University Grove, the two agents didn't hear the wails of a police car and a paramedic rig coming down University Avenue from the west.

The squad and the rig took a hard left and screeched into the duplex's driveway. Ten seconds later, Bernadette pulled up in front of the building. They'd all arrived too late. Animal Print Girl—Zoe Cameron to her family and friends—was already dead.

Chapter 24

"WHAT'S HE DOING RIGHT NOW? FIND OUT!"

"Calm down, Cat. You're going to pop a vein." Garcia punched a number into his phone. "You know, Greg and the kid have been on top of him the entire time. They've been real good about calling in."

"Find out."

Garcia held up his hand to silence her while he spoke into his cell. "Give me the latest on Wakefielder . . . Good . . . Good . . . Don't let him out of your sight." Garcia closed his phone.

"Well?"

"Raking leaves in his front yard."

"Of course he's raking leaves." She motioned toward the house with a chop of her hand. "This is the last thing he'd do if he were guilty. The last thing!"

The pair stood on the front lawn of the duplex. Behind them, Minneapolis cops moved in and out of the house like a blue swarm. Not a single reporter or photographer pestered them. When private citizens in private homes commit certain acts, they don't make the news.

"He just had a federal agent harass him at work," she said. "So why would a smart man—a Harvard guy, for chrissake—turn around and kill someone the very next day?"

"Because it's the last thing you'd expect him to do?" Garcia offered.

"He wasn't even in the city limits." She flapped an arm toward the east. "He was in St. Paul, with an agent and a half watching his ass."

"Perfect alibi," said Garcia.

She nodded. "Brilliant."

"So how does he do it from across the city line?"

Bernadette threw up her hands. "I don't know. Talks her into it and gives her something to take. Maybe he slips her something before driving her home."

"ME will do a tox screen, but you saw her. She was literally starving herself. She had a death wish."

"If it turns out she completely did it to herself, then he's still culpable," said Bernadette. "He should have taken her to a hospital instead of dumping her at the door. Even that moron Thorsson noticed she was falling down. Wakefielder should have forced her into treatment."

"You heard the roommate. Been there. Done that. Didn't stick."

The roommate, a red-eyed young man sitting in the back of one of the squads, was hugging his knees up to his chest and rocking. He told Bernadette that he'd been in the bathroom getting ready for his job at a shoe store when he'd heard a door open and someone moving around inside the duplex. Figuring it was Cameron, he left the bathroom to touch base. The girl's bedroom door was closed. When he hollered and knocked and got no response, he pushed inside and found Cameron on her back on the floor.

Bernadette watched while a crew from the Hennepin County ME's office carried a gurney topped by a body bag out of the house. "This makes me sick."

"Let's think this through," said Garcia, walking back and forth in front of her with his hands buried in the pockets of his trench. "Alice

Bergerman signs up for his Madness in Lit, drops after the first day of class, goes into the river the same month, making her our third victim. Our June drowning."

Bernadette said, "Kyra Klein is in his Poetry of Suicide course for a month or so. She's found dead in her own tub Thursday morning. Probably killed Wednesday night. Victim eight."

Garcia tipped his head toward the ME wagon. "Number nine never had him in class. They went out a couple of times, according to the roomie."

"So three murder victims with ties to Wakefielder."

"One murder victim," corrected Garcia. "Bergerman was ruled a suicide and—"

"It wasn't a suicide, and you know it."

Garcia pulled his hands out of his pockets and folded his arms in front of him.

"And today's death is looking like it was caused by an accidental or intentional OD, or possibly by the eating disorder of the month."

"These are murders made to look like suicides," she said as the wagon's door slammed after the body bag was loaded. "And this last one . . . God . . . this is evil genius."

"It's entirely possible he's simply guilty of surrounding himself with attractive train wrecks. Stupid, but not criminal."

"To have your young, pretty, skinny ex-girlfriend croak the day after a federal agent questions you about the murders of young, pretty, skinny girls is . . ."

"Really bad luck?"

"Wakefielder or someone around him is doing this. There's an . . . intersection or a—a connection that we're missing."

A crime scene investigator for the Minneapolis PD came up to the two agents with an armload of pill bottles. He held up the evidence bags. "Found these in her purse. Some empty, some half-empty."

Bernadette tore the bags out of his hands.

"Whose meds?" asked Garcia while Bernadette examined the labels through the plastic.

"A bunch are hers, and a couple she pilfered from the roommate."

Garcia asked, "If this is what did it, when would she have downed them?"

"Thing is, you don't swallow a handful of pills and then immediately keel over dead."

"I realize that," said Garcia. "Ballpark it."

"Depends on the dosage and the meds and a whole lot of other factors. I see some psychiatric meds in there. Potent stuff. They were prescribed by a—

"Dr. Luke VonHader," said Bernadette, looking up from the bags.

"Whoa," said Garcia.

"There's an interesting intersection." She handed the bottles back to the crime scene guy. "Thanks."

"Sure." The guy frowned and finished the trek to his van.

Garcia smiled grimly at Bernadette. "Are they working in tandem? How do they know each other?"

"They both went to Harvard."

"So did a lot of evil geniuses."

"There's a connection of some sort. I've gotta get one of them to start talking."

"Whose balls you gonna bust first?"

"The shrink is way too cool, but Wakefielder was nervous when I questioned him yesterday."

"Need some help?"

"I'd love some," she said. "This case is making my head hurt."

Garcia's cell rang, and he pulled it out of his trench. "Yeah?"

Bernadette scrutinized his face. It was turning a color she'd never before seen on a human being. Not quite purple. Eggplant?

Garcia switched the phone to his other ear. "You have got to be kidding me! How? When? For how long? Why did you wait so long before telling me?"

Bernadette didn't like the sound of that.

"It *does* matter!" Garcia's ears were starting to match his face. "It sure as hell could have been long enough!"

"Oh, no," Bernadette breathed. An agent and a half hadn't been on the professor's ass the entire time after all, and now Thorsson was calling to fess up.

A pause while Garcia listened to excuses. Then: "I don't care to hear it right now, Agent Thorsson. Save it for your report." Garcia checked his watch. "Your relief is on the way. Try not to lose him before they get there."

He closed his phone and drew his arm back but had second thoughts about hurling it. He calmly dropped the cell in to his trench and sighed. "Our men lost Wakefielder right after he dropped her off. They caught up with him at his house as he was pulling back into the garage."

"That wasn't a lot of time."

"They had to wait a bit before he got home."

She took a deep breath, let it out, and tried to be generous—more for the kid's benefit than the moron's. "No signs of a struggle in the duplex. No forced entry. She probably did OD like you said."

Garcia wasn't in a charitable mood. "Roommate said the back door was unlocked. Wakefielder could have circled back around to the alley, slipped inside, suffocated her, and left."

"No one has suggested suffocation at all. There was no visible trauma to the body. No pillow found near the body. Roommate would have heard."

"You said it yourself. The guy is smart."

"I don't think the fact that Greg and Red lost him for a few minutes makes a damn bit of difference."

Garcia asked through clenched teeth: "Why are you defending these idiots?"

"The kid deserves a chance," she said.

"Red was the driver."

"I don't care. Thorsson is somehow responsible."

Garcia watched glumly as the ME wagon backed out of the driveway. "Maybe I am, too."

"How so?"

"Thorsson volunteered to go inside and talk to her after the prof dropped her off. That's why he lost the guy. He was thinking I'd want him to question her. Maybe if I had let him go that route . . ." His voice trailed off.

"Greg would have gotten inside just in time to give mouth-to-mouth to a dead woman."

Garcia dragged his hand down his face. "My head is spinning."

"You need some exercise." She put her hand on his arm. "Let's go see if the prof needs some help with the yard work."

"He's going to recognize me as Pizza Man and realize we've had him under surveillance."

"That should jar the truth out of him."

THE INSTANT Wakefielder spotted Bernadette stepping out of her truck, he dropped his rake. Instead of dashing into his own home, however, he calmly walked across his neighbor's yard, went up the front steps, and knocked. Garcia met up with Bernadette and both stood on the sidewalk eyeing the neighbor's house.

"Classic colonial," Bernadette observed. "Nice."

The neighbor's door popped open and the professor went inside.

"Where does he think he's going?" Garcia asked.

"Maybe he's gonna get someone to beat us up."

"Should we go after him?" Garcia wondered.

"I'd rather get inside *his* house."

"What if he stays inside the neighbor's place?"

Before she could respond, they saw the professor exit the classic colonial and thump down the steps. A tall, gaunt, bearded man was right behind him. Both wore L. L. Bean's version of weekend work duds: corduroy pants and earth-toned turtlenecks under cable-knit cardigans. Wakefielder wore a barn coat over his sweater while his neighbor finished his ensemble with a plaid wool vest.

Wakefielder walked back to the leaf pile in the center of his yard and stood facing the agents, his feet planted square with his shoulders. His plaid pal stood next to him, burying his hands in the front pockets of the vest.

"Good afternoon, Mr. Wakefielder," Bernadette said, as she and Garcia walked into the yard. "I've brought Assistant Special Agent in Charge Anthony Garcia."

Wakefielder turned his head to his neighbor. "And I've brought Professor Nathaniel C. Selwyn. He's an expert in criminal law, criminal procedure, and criminal evidence."

"I'm familiar," Garcia said tightly as he and Selwyn exchanged hard stares.

Bernadette said, "We'd like to talk about Zoe."

"How do you know Zoe?" asked Wakefielder. "What does she—"

"Don't say another word, Finlay," said the law prof, putting his hand on Wakefielder's shoulder.

"She's dead," said Garcia. "Died this morning, shortly after you dropped her at home."

"No, that's not . . . I just saw her," Wakefielder stammered. He looked from Garcia to Bernadette, as if seeking confirmation from her.

Bernadette nodded. "Her roommate found her dead. Do you know anything about that?"

"Don't answer that!" Selwyn barked.

Wakefielder zeroed in on Garcia's face. "Nate, this gentleman came to my door at two o'clock this morning—*two o'clock*—under the pretense of delivering a pizza."

"I'm not surprised," said Selwyn. "The Minneapolis Division has a reputation for such . . ."

"Such what?" snapped Garcia, who took a step toward Selwyn.

"Professor Wakefielder, aren't you hearing us?" asked Bernadette. "Your former girlfriend is dead."

"This is another ruse, Finlay," said the law prof, pulling Wakefielder backward by the elbow. "Don't respond. Let's go in the house."

With Selwyn in the lead, the two neighbors turned their backs on the agents, marched across the yard, and went up the Tudor's front steps. The men disappeared inside, the door slamming hard after them.

"Fuck," Garcia spat, his eyes burning a hole in the Tudor's front door. "Of all the people for him to hide behind."

"You've crossed swords with Selwyn, I take it."

Garcia turned and started back for the cars. "Let's go."

"That's it?" she asked, going after him.

"Let's get some lunch," he grumbled.

OVER SOUP and sandwiches at a café in the neighborhood, Garcia told her about Selwyn.

"The bastard conducts seminars for other attorneys so they can beat us." Garcia picked up his roast beef on a Kaiser, chomped it into a half moon, chewed twice, and swallowed.

"He teaches them how to successfully defend someone against federal charges." Bernadette snipped off the corner of her grilled cheese sandwich and chewed.

Garcia raised his sandwich to his mouth. "Yeah."

"Good for him." She lifted her spoon and sipped some tomato soup.

"Not good for him." He took another bite of his roast beef.

Bernadette dabbed at the corners of her mouth with a napkin. "Citizens have a right to—"

"I was a speaker at one of his bullshit seminars," said Garcia. "Afterward I took questions."

"What'd they do, rip you a new one?" she asked, and took another bite of grilled cheese.

"It was a feeding frenzy," he said. "They took off on me about the fingerprint screwup in that Portland terrorist case and the legality of that Russian computer crimes sting."

"Old news," she said, and took a sip of water.

"They went on and on about warrantless wiretapping."

"That's to be expected."

"They even bitched about the IRS," he said.

"They heard the word *federal* and went after you."

"Like a pack of dogs."

"Selwyn didn't warn you?"

"He told me to expect questions about—I don't know—the increase in bank robberies across the Midwest or something."

"He set you up."

Garcia nodded and shoved the last wedge of roast beef into his mouth.

"What about the surveillance?" she asked.

He swallowed and wiped his mouth. "Now he knows we're watching him, so it won't do any good. Plus with that Selwyn on his side and living right next door—"

"We'd better think of another way to get at Wakefielder."

"What did you think of Wakefielder's reaction, or lack thereof, to the news his ex was dead?"

"I don't know," she said. "If he did do it, you'd think he'd be smart enough to act grief-stricken."

"Could be he's not good with the dramatics and decided he couldn't pull them off," Garcia suggested. "Pretending he didn't believe us was more in his range."

They heard ringing coming from the coats piled next to her on the restaurant bench. She set down her spoon, went into her jacket pocket, and produced her cell. Opened it.

"Agent Saint Clare? This is Matthew VonHader."

She frowned for a moment, and then her eyes widened as she remembered Dr. Luke VonHader's younger brother. "What can I do for you, Mr. VonHader?"

Garcia set down his glass and leaned across the table.

"What can *I* do for you?" Matthew responded.

She had only been on the phone for a few seconds with this operator, and she was already losing patience. "Look, if you're calling to—"

Matthew: "I have some . . . information I'd like to share."

"What sort of information?" she asked while smiling at Garcia.

Matthew said, "Over dinner."

"What sort of information?" she repeated.

"Dinner tonight. Seven o'clock," said Matthew.

"Dinner? I'd like to know what this is about first." She watched Garcia. He looked ready to jump out of the booth.

Matthew said, "Dinner, or I'm hanging up."

He sounded like a brat threatening to hold his breath. She rolled her eyes and asked, "Where?"

"Downtown St. Paul," he said, and gave her the name and address of the restaurant.

The trendy eatery was in walking distance from her office. She'd passed it a hundred times but had never set foot inside. "I know the place."

"Seven o'clock," Matthew repeated.

"Right." Shaking her head with wonder, she closed the phone.

"The shrink?" Garcia asked.

"His younger brother, Matt. I met him at the doc's office. He wants me to meet him for dinner downtown. Seven tonight. He has 'information.'"

The waitress came by with the check, and Garcia picked it up. Dug out his wallet and opened it. "Want me to go with you?"

"You might scare him off."

He set some bills on the table. "I could sit at the bar and keep an eye on you."

Now Garcia was sounding weird. "What is he going to do, attack me with the pepper mill?"

"I really think I should—"

"Let me deal with this," she said, sliding from the bench with their outerwear in her arms. Garcia got out, and she handed him his coat.

"What good is the little brother?"

"Could be he knows about Luke's relationship with Wakefielder, or maybe he can tell me something about Klein and Cameron. He's real talkative. The receptionist whisked him away before his mouth really got going yesterday."

"This Matt isn't hitting on you, is he? That wouldn't be too smart."

"I don't think he's a Harvard man. He strikes me as a *mimbo*."

Garcia's brows knitted with confusion.

"That's a male bimbo."

"Nice. Well, call me when you're done with him."

"I'll call you," she said, and they both headed for the door.

Chapter 25

WAITERS AND BUSBOYS AND CUSTOMERS DRESSED IN BLACK.
An effusive menu that read like a romance novel. A wine list as thick
as an issue of *National Geographic*. Tables set with crystal, candles,
and white linen. Floor-to-ceiling windows draped in sheer white curtains.

Matthew VonHader looked as trendy as the restaurant he'd selected. He'd eschewed the unofficial dress uniform for Minnesota
men—khaki pants and a blue oxford shirt—and had shown up in a
sophisticated black turtleneck, black blazer, and black slacks. Bernadette felt like a slouch for wearing one of her work suits.

She'd spent part of the afternoon on her home laptop, trying
to research the accomplishments of the younger VonHader. There
weren't many. The older sibling was the overachiever. She'd found
scant background, good or bad, on Matthew. Unless hanging out at
his brother's office qualified as a career, he seemed to have no job. He
was unmarried and had an appetite for expensive cars and a thirst for
expensive booze. She got a glimpse of the Cabernet Sauvignon he'd
pointed out to the waiter, and the wine list priced it at two hundred
dollars a bottle.

Their twenty-something server—a skinny kid with spiked hair

who'd earlier introduced himself as Clive—came up to their table with pad and pen in hand. "Have we decided yet, or would we like a few more minutes?"

Bernadette flipped the pages of the menu. She'd initially intended to stick with a quick salad but decided to stretch out the meeting to increase her chances of getting dirt on the doc. "I'm debating between the pineapple teriyaki salmon and the Moroccan chicken with chickpeas," she said, glancing up at Clive for guidance.

"Are you in a stew mood?" he asked.

"Not particularly," she said.

"The Moroccan dish is a tagine of sorts, a stew," said Clive. "So if you're not in a stew mood, I'd suggest the salmon."

She closed her menu and handed it to him. "The salmon it is."

Clive turned to Matthew. "For the gentleman?"

"I'm not in a stew mood either, but Moroccan sounds good." Matthew pointed to his menu. "The Moroccan swordfish with yogurt sauce."

"Excellent choice," said the waiter, scribbling. He nodded toward the half-empty wine bottle. "If you would like something with your fish, I could recommend—"

"The Cab is fine," interrupted Matthew.

"Very well, sir." Clive took their menus and disappeared into the kitchen.

Matthew looked across the table at Bernadette. "The wine police are going to slam me for pairing red with fish, but screw 'em. I'm sick of all whites, especially the Pinot Grigios everybody's drinking. They've been so overproduced and rushed, they're practically tasteless. The light beer of white wine."

"What I know about wine you could fit on the back of a postage stamp," she said, taking a sip of water.

"Are you sure you won't have a glass with me?" he asked, refilling his own.

Bernadette didn't want him getting plastered. So to keep him from guzzling it all, she pushed her glass toward him. "I'll have one."

"That's the spirit," he said, filling hers to the top.

"That's more than enough. Thank you." She'd have to pick up her own tab and tried to calculate the cost of a single glass of two-hundred-dollar wine. Garcia was going to have a fit when he saw her expense account.

He took a sip of wine. "Were you surprised that I called you?"

"I was curious," she said, fingering the stem of her wineglass. "How'd you get my number? Did you steal my card off your brother's desk?"

"I rescued it from Chaz," he said. "He was about to deposit it in the circular file."

"Chaz?"

"Charles, my brother's manservant." He took a sip of wine.

"Chaz . . . yeah—he hustled you out of there before we could talk at the office," said Bernadette. "Did Luke tell him to do that? What was your brother afraid of? What didn't he want you to say to me?"

Matthew dodged her questions by rambling on and on about Charles. "Luke was going to hire a woman after Rosemary retired, but then Chaz called for a job. One of the old neighborhood gang. He's more my brother's friend than mine. I don't like him. He's so—I don't know—smarmy. Don't you think it's odd to have a male receptionist? He makes shit coffee. A pretty young woman would be so much more—"

"What are you intending to tell me or give me?"

"My brother said you were interested in lithium."

"I am," she said.

"Lithium is one of the oldest and most frequently prescribed drugs for the treatment of bipolar disorder. There's nothing criminal in the fact that a bottle of lithium was found in Kyra Klein's home."

"What if I told you Klein could have been murdered with the help of those meds? Would you classify that as criminal?"

He polished off his glass of wine. "You may not be privy to the fact that Miss Klein's own mother was diagnosed with bipolar disorder and committed suicide when Kyra was a child."

"How would I know that? Your brother is sitting on her file."

"You should also be made aware that Miss Klein attempted to kill herself a couple of years ago."

Big brother had no qualms about sharing with his younger sibling. So much for patient privacy, thought Bernadette. "Sounds like Luke was having trouble helping his patient manage her illness."

Matthew emptied the remainder of the bottle into his glass. "Her suicide attempt was while she was under the care of another physician. She'd been improperly diagnosed as having depression and was on medication that made her bipolar disorder worse."

"So your brother rescued her."

"My brother made the correct diagnosis and got her going on the proper medication."

"And she died anyway."

He shrugged. "It happens."

"Is that going to be your brother's defense if Kyra Klein's family drags him into court? Death happens?"

"I really doubt her family is going to sue," he said.

"Your brother is worried about it," she said. "That's why he won't talk to me."

He took a long drink of wine. "He's protective of his patients and their privacy, as he should be."

"I'll tell you what I told him: Kyra Klein is dead!"

Diners a table away stopped talking and looked over at them. "You're scaring the children," Matthew said with a smirk.

She leaned forward and said in a lower voice, "He needs to give me those files."

"The police didn't ask for them."

"We're approaching this case from different angles."

"Can we please get off the subject of Miss Klein?"

"Fine." She took a drink of water. "What can you tell me about Zoe Cameron?"

He sipped his wine. "Never heard of her."

She didn't believe him. "You seem to know a lot about your brother's business. Have you got one of your own? What do you do for a living?"

"I'm in between jobs." He eyed her untouched wineglass. "Is there something wrong with the Cab?"

She picked up her glass and took a small sip. "No. It's fine."

He grinned. "Oh, I get it. The wily FBI agent gets the dummy drunk so he spills his proverbial guts."

"Now, Matt, if I did that, I couldn't trust or use what you gave me." She took another sip of wine to appease him. "Besides, I'm not the one who called this meeting. In fact, I'm a little mystified as to why you even bothered. This is your brother's problem."

"Problem? Is he in trouble for declining to answer your questions?"

His concern for his brother sounded genuine, and she played off it. "His lack of cooperation doesn't look good. He seems more interested in covering his backside than in getting to the bottom of what happened."

"He's following federal patient privacy guidelines."

"Baloney," she said. "He's got a lot of wiggle room when it comes to those regs. He could help us more."

"Has he done anything illegal?"

"Maybe not illegal, but certainly unethical."

"My brother is not only one of the top psychiatrists in the country but also an honorable and generous man. On his own time and at his own expense, he developed a school-based program that screens teens for mental illness. He's worked hard to increase the public's understanding of brain disorders through free educational seminars. He goes to bat for patients who are discriminated against on the job. He started a suicide help line that is still up and running and saving lives today." He took a deep drink, nearly finishing his wine, and pointed a finger at her. "You'd be hard-pressed to find a more ethical and giving man than Luke."

"He needs to give to me. When a patient dies—"

"It's tragic, but it happens." He drained his glass. "People with mental illness are at great risk for—"

She held up her hand to stop him. "I already heard the company line."

"It's not a line," he shot back. He ran his eyes around the restaurant. Catching the waiter's attention, he pointed to the empty bottle.

She took a sip of water and checked her watch. She regretted ordering dinner. The conversation was moving in circles, and he was getting drunk. "Why am I here?"

"You're here because you're hoping I'll say something inflammatory that you can use against my brother. Get him to turn over those patient files."

Staring at him, she wondered if he was one of those rare individuals who actually got smarter as they got drunker. "Fair enough. Why are *you* here?"

He grinned. "I wanted to have dinner with a beautiful, interesting woman."

"Spare me."

His smile flattened. "I wanted to see why you were focusing on my brother. He doesn't make a very good first impression, and I wanted to . . ."

"Do a little PR work for him?"

He shifted in his seat. "Don't you have any siblings, Bernadette? Someone you feel protective of?"

She noticed a catch in his voice. Had he somehow found out that she'd lost a sister years ago? Rather than answer his question, she said evenly, "Your brother is a smart man. He doesn't need your help." She took a sip of wine. "He went to Harvard, I noticed. Saw the degree on his office wall. Did you go there, too?"

Matthew barked a laugh.

"I'll take that as a no," she said with a small smile.

"It's a difficult school to get into," said Matthew, trying to recover a little dignity. "I don't know any other people in our circle who went there."

"I just met a professor at the U. Wakefielder. He went to Harvard. He's about Luke's age."

"Don't know him," said Matthew. "Is he at the medical school?"

"Literature professor," she said.

"The liberal arts," he said somberly. "Good stuff."

"You're sure you don't know him? Luke wouldn't know him?"

"Sorry." He perked up as he saw Clive approach. The waiter showed Matthew the label, uncorked the bottle, and poured a small amount. Matthew tasted it and nodded. "Very good."

"Matt, I'm only good for the one glass," she interjected.

"That's fine," he said. "I'm good for more than one."

A lot more, thought Bernadette. Watching Clive refill Matthew's wineglass, she hoped she wouldn't have to give her dining companion a ride home. As far as she was concerned, she'd wasted enough time with this man. "Will our food be much longer?" she asked as the waiter set down the bottle.

"I'll check," said Clive.

Matthew took a drink of wine. "What's the rush? It's a Saturday night."

"Believe it or not, I still have work to do," she said.

"Now you sound like my brother."

"He's a taskmaster?"

"Taskmaster. Perfectionist. Always on the job."

"What do his patients think of him?"

"They like him." He took another drink. "No. Wait. *Like* isn't the correct word. They respect him. I doubt any of them actually like him. For all his good works, he's not a likable man. I don't think his own wife *likes* him. She loves him, I'm sure. But she doesn't *like* him."

If not enlightening, the conversation was at least getting interesting. She wondered what a third bottle would do for him. "Why is Luke unlikable? Does he have a temper?"

He retrieved his goblet and used it to motion toward her. "You're trying to get me to say something incriminating about Luke, and I refuse to do it. As I said, he's a saint."

"An *unlikable* saint."

"Like our father," he said, and downed his glass of wine. "Strict. Disciplined. Very moral. Very Catholic."

"Hence Matthew and Luke," she said.

"Exactly. My parents were very fond of biblical names." He tipped his empty wineglass toward her. "Not that Bernadette is a slouch name when it comes to holiness."

"What do your parents do for a living?"

"Mother was a homemaker. That's the politically correct term, isn't it? Father was a psychiatrist."

"*Was.* He's retired?"

He shook his head. "Deceased. Both my parents are deceased. And you?"

"My parents are dead, too," she said. "Heart stuff."

"That's what did my mother in," he said sympathetically. "Bad ticker."

"Your father?"

"He had a lot of health problems. He was older. They were both older parents. At least they never had to be in a nursing home." He sighed and asked wearily, "So . . . no husband? No Mr. Saint Clare?"

This conversation was depressing her. She held up her barren left hand. "What about you?"

"Unattached," he said, sighing again.

Mercifully, the waiter materialized with their dinners, setting a steaming plate down in front of each of them. Clive noticed Matthew's wineglass was nearly empty and refilled it. "Is there anything else I can get for the two of you?"

"I'm good," said Bernadette, her hands folded in her lap.

"I'll check back in a few minutes," said Clive, moving on to the next table.

"This looks divine," Matthew said, picking up his fork.

She waited for him to resume the melancholy Q and A, but he'd put his head down and was poking at his fish. She tried to keep her voice light. "How large of a family did you come from, Matt?"

Rather than answer he took a drink of water. "Would you please pass the bread?"

She handed him the basket. His eyes were down as he fiddled with a pat of butter. He'd gone from a painfully personal discussion to a quiet fascination with hard-crust rolls. The wine must have loosened his tongue too much and now he was reining it back in. Maybe if she gave him an opening, he'd resume the proverbial gut-spillage. "I came from a small family, especially by farm standards."

"Came?"

She pushed a cube of pineapple around with her fork. "I had a twin sister. She died when we were in high school."

He looked up from his food. "I'm sorry. An illness or . . . an accident?"

"Drunk driver."

He nodded. "It must have been hard. Did they get the fiend?"

"Slap on the wrist," she said.

"Do you have any others in your family?"

"Cousins," she said. "Otherwise—"

"You're all alone."

"Yes," she said, although she didn't like hearing someone say it out loud.

"How does that make you feel?" he asked somberly.

"I'm okay with it," she said hesitantly.

"I suppose your work helps."

She popped a wedge of fish into her mouth and waited for him to say something, but he returned to his meal in silence. She washed the salmon down with a drink of water. "Your turn to share."

He glanced up. "My turn?"

"What about your family? Besides your parents, anyone else? Any other siblings?"

"There's just the two of us."

"You and Luke and that's it?"

He nodded and looked away.

Something is wrong there, she thought.

AS THEY STOOD under a streetlamp outside the restaurant, the October wind buffeted their backs and sent crumpled McDonald's bags flying past their ankles. Urban tumbleweeds. She waited patiently while the swaying man searched for his buttonholes. She couldn't remember the last time she'd seen a man in St. Paul wearing fur. It wasn't something moderately rustic, like a raccoon jacket or a beaver bomber. It was a full-length black mink coat with wide lapels.

"I wish you had let me pay," he said, finally unearthing the holes and buttoning up. "Going Dutch with a woman is so junior high."

"I'll tell you what," she said, pulling on her leather gloves. "Let me hail you a cab and you can pay for that."

"I don't need a ride," he said, pulling on his gloves.

"You can leave your car in the ramp," she said. "It'll be fine."

They both stepped to one side. A Wild hockey game had just let out, and a wave of green jerseys was rolling down the sidewalks. A couple of the female fans eyed the mink as they passed Matthew.

"I walked here and I can walk back," he said.

"Where do you live?"

He thumbed over his shoulder, toward the Mississippi River. "Across the bridge. I'll be home before your car warms up."

"That's convenient."

He buried his hands in his pockets and hunched his shoulders against the gale. "Are you in the ramp? I can at least walk you to your car."

She didn't want him to know she lived downtown and had walked to the restaurant. "Don't worry about it. I'm close. Parked on the street."

"You sure? I don't mind a little walk."

"I'm good." She held out her hand. "Thank you. It was interesting."

"*Interesting,*" he repeated as he shook her hand.

"No. Seriously. It was . . . nice."

He stood staring at her for a moment, his weight shifting from one foot to the other. A teenage boy trying to put closure on a disastrous first date. "Well, good night," he said with a tip of his head, and turned his back to leave.

"Matt?"

He pivoted around, a pained expression on his face. His escape had been delayed. "Yes?"

"Ask your brother to think about the files," she said.

"I'll talk to him," he said dully.

As she watched him go down the sidewalk, she wondered if his unsteadiness was from the wind or the wine. The mink bumped shoulders with a hockey jersey going the opposite way on the sidewalk. It was the wine.

She waited until he was a block away before she started to follow him.

Chapter 26

DEFTLY WEAVING THROUGH THE PEOPLE CROWDING THE DOWN-
town sidewalks, Bernadette kept Matthew at a distance but within
eyeshot. While she'd easily found a home address for Luke, she'd
been stumped when trying to track down the younger brother's residence. Did he live in his Jag?

When he stepped onto the west side of the Wabasha Bridge and
continued south over the river, she slowed her pace. There were few
pedestrians on the bridge, and she didn't want to risk being spotted
by her quarry. The walk was ten feet wide, and the side bordering the
road was dotted with fat concrete pedestals topped by streetlights.
She hugged that side of the walk, moving from pedestal to pedestal.
Burying her hands in her coat pockets, she felt the comforting outline of her gun tucked under all the clothing.

About a third of the way across, Matthew stopped to look out
over the river. Afraid he'd spot her, she stepped onto one of the over-
looks that jutted out from the bridge like concrete balconies. The
apron was surrounded by a cagelike structure that camouflaged her
but still allowed her to keep him in her sights.

While the river side of the walk was bordered by railing as high as
Matthew's shoulders, Bernadette was still nervous at seeing him lean

against the bars and stare into the water. Nighttime on the river was always the most dangerous. The downtown lights became a string of pearls cast against black velvet, making the Mississippi appear deceptively safe and beautiful. Alluring. More than one person had jumped off that bridge at night on a stupid dare. Some were saved. Others died in the black water.

She sidled next to one of the light poles that lined the overlook and continued to watch him. What was he doing there all by himself, half in the bag from four hundred dollars' worth of wine? Was he frustrated he hadn't charmed the FBI bitch into backing off? Were his thoughts even darker? Perhaps he was wondering what it would be like to drop into the river, sink to the bottom. She could almost understand that sort of fantasy.

A frigid wind rolled down the deck of the bridge. A man and a woman, both dressed in jeans and flannel shirts with puffy down vests zipped up over them, hustled past Bernadette without giving her a glance. They wore matching Minnesota Wild stocking caps pulled over their heads. They'd been to the hockey game and parked on the outskirts of downtown to save money. As they moved past Matthew, they shot a quick look at his back. They were probably wondering what a guy in a mink coat was doing walking.

Shivering, she pulled her gloves tighter over her fingers and told herself that she'd picked the wrong night to chase after someone out of curiosity. What would she do once he got home? Knock on his door?

FINALLY, MATTHEW moved off the railing, buried his hands in his pockets, and resumed his walk. She hesitated, telling herself it would be more sensible to abandon this foolish hunt and go home. Her gut had other ideas.

As she trailed him south on the bridge, she tried to guess where he was leading her. Anchoring the south end was Harriet Island, a groomed park directly across the river from downtown. It had picnic tables, a pavilion, and a playground. Tied up along its shoreline were a floating dinner theater, a floating restaurant, and massive paddle-boats. To its west was Lilydale Regional Park, a long, narrow tangle of woods and marshes that ran along the river. The area immediately south of the parks was mostly commercial, with a gas station, a health clinic, office buildings, and assorted factories. Beyond that, overlooking downtown and the river, were bluffs dotted with trees. Atop the bluffs were homes. If that was where Matthew lived, she had a long hike ahead of her.

After the bridge, however, he hooked to the right and jogged down a set of steps that led to Harriet Island. Strange, she thought. Even the homeless folks would avoid hanging out in that park on such a frigid night.

There was a small parking area near the entrance to the island, and Bernadette figured Matthew was going there to collect his car. He passed the parking lot, however, and crossed the street to a chain-link fence that followed the banks of the river. He stopped at a gate in the middle of the fencing and dug into his coat pockets. He pulled a key out of his pocket and dropped it on the sidewalk. "Fuck!" he said, loud enough for her to hear. He bent over, retrieved the key, and inserted it in the gate's lock. After some fiddling and more cursing, he pushed the gate open and stepped through. It clanged shut behind him.

Leaving her hiding spot, Bernadette jogged over to the gate and hunkered behind some bushes planted on either side of it. There was enough light cast by the streetlamps for Bernadette to read the small signs posted on the gate. One read "Slips Available" and listed a phone number. The other read "St. Paul Yacht Club, Gate G, Lower Harbor, 100 Yacht Club Road."

Peeking through the bushes, she saw that behind the fence were steps leading down to the docks. Matthew was thumping along the wooden boards, heading for one of the few houseboats still tucked into the slips.

During the summer months, the popular yacht club was crowded with watercraft. As the cold weather settled in, however, only a handful of winterized houseboats remained. Their owners, called "liveaboards," resided there permanently. Was this his home or just his crash pad when he partied too hard downtown?

She could see there were some luxurious year-round crafts—one floating mansion had to be more than sixty feet long—and some tiny boxes that appeared to be the equivalent of efficiency apartments. Every other one had interior lights on, and almost all of them had bright floodlights shining against their exteriors. It could have been a well-lit street on any block, except for the fact that the river was everyone's backyard.

Matthew stopped at a houseboat near the end of the dock. He'd left the boat's interior lights on, as well as an outside floodlight mounted near the door. The cabin was about forty feet long and had modest decks at each end. The suburban rambler of the neighborhood. The craft's flat top was railed and littered with lawn chairs. In the summer, sunbathing women probably populated that upper level. Matthew's party palace.

He dropped his keys while standing next to his boat. When he bent over to pick them up, his door popped open. Bernadette could see a long-haired woman standing in the doorway. Was her hair brown, like the woman she'd observed through her sight? Bernadette couldn't tell. The woman was clothed in a short black nightgown, and the interior lights of the boat shined through the flimsy fabric, leaving little to the imagination. She had a glass in her hand.

Bernadette strained to listen. The woman's words were indecipherable, but Matthew bellowed loudly enough to be understood.

"What are you doing here?" he asked, standing up with his keys. "How in the hell did you get inside? I told you, we're through!"

The woman extended the drink to him.

"You're not staying. I've got commitments tonight. Places to go."

Like detox, thought Bernadette.

Matthew snatched the glass out of the woman's hand and stumbled inside the houseboat, the door slamming behind him.

Bernadette stood up and tried yanking on the gate. Locked tight. The fence was about six feet tall. Not a big obstacle, but she wished she were in jeans and sneakers instead of a suit. Wedging the toes of her shoes through the chain link, she climbed to the top of the fence, threw her legs over, and jumped down. She was grateful she'd worn flats.

There was a smaller houseboat moored next to Matthew's. Even though its interior and exterior were unlighted, she could read its name by the light of the neighboring boats. *Good Enuf,* it said across the transom. It had a deck at each end, and neither one of them was railed. She hopped onto the closest, grimacing while the boat rocked and groaned. Dropping behind a large planter filled with dead flowers, she peered into Matthew's lighted windows.

Matthew and the woman were in the houseboat's galley; Bernadette could see kitchen cupboards, granite counters, and a stainless-steel refrigerator. The place wasn't huge, but it was outfitted beautifully. He was pacing back and forth with the glass the woman had given him, but he wasn't drinking from it. Maybe Matthew finally figured out he'd had enough liquor for the night. He set the drink down and peeled off his fur and his blazer. The woman went up to him and twined her arms around his neck. Now Bernadette could clearly see her hair was brown. Was she the one Bernadette had watched in bed, getting the rough treatment during sex? Had Bernadette been seeing through Matthew's eyes?

He seemed in no mood to touch this woman, let alone hop into the sack with her. He pulled her arms down, turned his back to her, and marched to the other end of the boat. Bernadette followed, sliding down a narrow walkway that ran along the side of the *Good Enuf.* When she got to the far deck, she didn't bother trying to hunker down; there was nothing to hide behind. Matthew's craft was nearly twice the length of the *Good Enuf,* extending much farther into the river. Even posted at the very end of the shorter craft's deck, Bernadette had trouble observing everything that was going on next door. She was gambling that the feuding couple couldn't see her standing outside, especially with all the lights on inside their houseboat.

Looking into the last window, Bernadette saw clothes flying. She spotted a corner of a headboard and figured she was spying into the master bedroom. More clothes sailed through the air. Was Matthew stripping? No. He was tossing the woman's own garments at her. The woman stepped in front of the window and was catching each article as he hurled it. Black bra. Black panties. Black sweater. *She likes black.* Both of their mouths were moving like crazy. Bernadette wished she could hear what was being said, but the boat was too well insulated. At least that meant they couldn't hear her thumping around on the neighbor's deck.

Matthew pivoted and tried to walk away from the woman, but she threw herself at him, wrapping her arms around him from behind and molding the front of her body against his back.

"Have some pride, lady," Bernadette muttered under her breath.

Matthew pushed the woman's arms off him and spun around. He grabbed her by the shoulders and held her at a distance while saying something to her. Surprisingly, his expression was calm. Patient. It was not the face of an out-of-control killer.

The pair moved away from the window.

"Dammit," mumbled Bernadette, bobbing her head and shuffling along the end of the deck in an attempt to locate the couple. "Where are you?"

They suddenly slid into view in a middle window positioned directly across from her. Nervous about being spotted, she dropped to her knees and sat back on her heels to watch. They were standing a foot or two apart, their mouths still going. While Matthew's expression remained relaxed, the woman's face was red and distorted with rage.

Suddenly the woman rushed at Matthew, her arms raised. He caught her wrists and held them over her head. She pulled away from him and lunged again, her nails ripping his face. Looking up at his bloody face, Bernadette contemplated barging in to help. Then Matthew pushed the crazy woman off him again and she fell back against the windows. The *crack* made Bernadette start. Matthew could take care of himself.

They moved out of view, with Matthew heading toward the far end of the houseboat. The woman was on his heels, her brown hair and her black nightgown flying behind her like a witch's cape.

Bernadette waited a minute to make sure they didn't rematerialize in the window across from her, then stood up. She went to the very end of the deck and leaned over as far as she could to scan the bedroom window at the end of Matthew's boat. No one popped into view. She looked back at the window directly across from her. Still nothing. She scaled the ledge to the other deck and studied the kitchen windows. No action there. They had to be in that bedroom, she thought, and skated back to the far deck.

Standing on the end of the *Good Enuf*'s deck, she locked her eyes on the window and waited. The lights stayed on, but nothing moved. All she saw was the corner of that headboard against a white wall. With each passing moment, the knot in her gut tightened. What if the crazy killed him? Bernadette wasn't sure whether to go for her cell or her gun. Eyes glued to the bedroom window, she started to unbutton her trench coat when a creak behind her sent a rush of ice water shooting through her veins. She spun around and looked behind her. No one there. She darted from one corner of the small deck to the other, checking the ledges along the sides of the boat. Nothing. She reached past her blazer, put her hand on the butt of her gun, and waited. A loud groan vibrated the small boat. The *Good Enuf* was like an old house settling.

Satisfied that no one was there, she took her hand out of her coat and turned around. The woman was standing in the bedroom window, staring out at the river, and slowly running a hand through her hair. The expression on her face was unsettling. It was flat. Blank. How could someone go from zero to ninety and back to zero that quickly? Where was Matthew? Bernadette didn't like it and once again reached inside her trench coat. Her fingers landed on the butt of her gun, but she never had a chance to unsnap her holster or even look behind her.

WINDING UP LIKE a batter, he brought the paddle around and slammed it against her back. The splash her body made as it hit the river gave him some satisfaction, but he was disappointed she hadn't uttered a word. A scream would have been rewarding. Standing on the edge of the deck with the paddle still locked in his hands, he looked into the water with hopeful anticipation. If she resurfaced, he would push her back down. If it got real ugly, he might have to drop his weapon and use his hands to hold her under. Perhaps he'd have to go in himself. The water would be cold, but it would be worth it to get rid of her. She was going to ruin everything.

The rumble of a car pulling into the yacht club's parking lot made him glance nervously over his shoulder. He gave a last look to the smooth, black surface and told himself she was gone for good. Taking the paddle with him, he shuffled off the *Good Enuf* and went to the end of the dock. He cranked his arm back and flung his weapon into the water. The thing would be far downriver in no time. With any luck, so would her body.

Chapter 27

IT SEEMED TO TAKE FOREVER TO FIGHT HER WAY TO THE surface. When Bernadette finally bobbed up, she was gasping and coughing up putrid water. She didn't holler for help; it took every bit of energy to stay afloat. Her back and her lungs ached. Splashing madly with her arms, she made no progress in any direction; all she did was tread the cold water. Her limbs were starting to lose sensation, and she forced herself to stop thrashing around. Kicking her legs like a frog, she did a sloppy breaststroke to the edge of the small houseboat. Panting and shivering, she hung on to the wood trim of the *Good Enuf* while trying to throw her right leg up onto the deck.

"Hell," she wheezed, her leg slipping off the edge and falling back into the water. Spasms of pain radiated across her back. Low to the river while she was standing on top of it, the deck now seemed insurmountably high. She felt as if she were trying to clamber up the sheer sides of a cruise ship. Something beneath the surface of the water brushed past her body, and she tried not to think about what it could be.

When she got to the deck on the other end of the boat, her fingers bumped up against a narrow horizontal bar. She locked her fist over it and brought her other hand around to pull her body in front of the ladder. It took every ounce of her remaining energy to set her feet on the ladder and climb up one rung and then another. Her numb foot slipped on the third rung, and she nearly fell backward into the river. Slowly, she returned her foot to the third rung and stepped hard, propelling herself up and out of the water. The impact of her body against the boards sent another ripple of pain across her back.

Dripping and cold, she stayed facedown on the *Good Enuf*. A wind blew across the deck, and she groaned into the wood. Shivering uncontrollably, she got on her knees and crawled to the patio doors of the houseboat. She reached up with one hand and pulled on the handle. Locked. She used the handle to pull herself to her feet. While she rested her forehead against the glass door, she thought about the walk back across the bridge. Between her sore back and her wet clothes, she'd never make it. She dipped her trembling hand into her soggy coat pocket and felt nothing. Her cell had been lost during her tumble into the water. It wouldn't have worked anyway.

Another gust whipped across the deck of the boat, and she twined her arms around her shivering body. She wondered if she should peel off some of the wet clothing, then told herself that was a bad idea. She remembered something from a survival class taught at Quantico. *Paradoxical undressing.* That's what they called it when hypothermia victims removed clothing even as they were freezing to death. She'd be damned if they were going to find her dead *and* naked.

Lifting her face off the patio door, she looked to the lighted windows of Matthew's boat. She couldn't go there for help. He was most likely the one who'd batted her into the river. What had he used to hit her? It felt like a concrete block.

She scanned the water's edge for safer options. On the other side of the *Good Enuf* was a medium-size craft with two levels, both of them lit. Beyond that were two smaller boats that looked dark and vacant.

Hugging herself, she hobbled across the deck of the *Good Enuf* and stepped onto the dock. With the greatest of effort, she put one foot in front of the other and made it over to the double-decker houseboat, the *Three-Hour Tour*. Lighted plastic pumpkins stood sentry, one on each side of the entrance, and the door itself was plastered with cardboard cutouts of tarantulas. As she raised her fist to knock, she remembered her nightmare about spiders crawling over her while she beat against the door of a houseboat. Did that mean this was the wrong place to go for sanctuary? *Screw the dream,* she thought, and brought her fist down on the wood. She knocked again and yelled, "Hello? Is anyone home?" She heard a deadbolt being turned on the other side.

The door opened a crack. Long bangs and a big nose peeked out at her from the other side of a security chain. Gilligan's double. "Holy crap," he sputtered, taking in her wet figure.

"I f-fell in," she chattered.

He took down the security chain and opened the door wide. "Get inside."

"Thank you." As she stepped over his threshold, she glanced down at her feet and realized that her shoes were gone.

He closed the door after her and ran over to his couch. He snatched a purple Minnesota Vikings throw off the cushions and draped it over her shoulders. "I'm gonna call an ambulance."

She shook her head. "No. I just gotta get out of these c-clothes."

Taking a couple of steps back from her, he ran a hand through his dark mop. "Maybe I should call the cops."

"No," she said, and felt herself start to totter.

"What's your name?" he asked, crossing his arms as if he were the one who was cold. "What're you doing out here at night?"

"Is it the pizza?" a young woman yelled from another room.

"No!" he yelled back, nervously tucking his hands into the front pockets of his jeans. "She fell in. Someone fell in. Get in here, Lor."

A petite brunette dressed in yellow pajama bottoms and a Sponge-Bob T-shirt thumped into the room. She took one look at the visitor huddled near the door, a throw hanging from her shoulders, and blurted, "Holy crap. Who're you?"

"I'm . . . I fell in," Bernadette said, holding the throw tight around her body.

The woman went over to Bernadette and put an arm around her. "You look ready to pass out."

The guy seemed relieved to have the woman on the scene. "Get her outta those clothes, Lor."

Lor started steering Bernadette to a door at the side of the living room. "Bathroom's this way. You can take this stuff off while I get you some sweats."

"What happened? How'd you fall in?" the man asked her.

"I . . . had this really bad blind date."

"I'll bet it was Jason down at the end," the man said as the two women walked side by side.

"I don't want to get into it," Bernadette said.

"It was Jason, all right."

Lor stopped and snapped over her shoulder, "Wally! Give the Jason crap a rest, would you?"

"I left in a hurry," Bernadette continued. "I got all turned around and thought I was walking to shore. I stepped right off the dock and into the water. I don't know how it happened. I got so flustered."

"Jason does that to women," said Lor, pushing open the door to the bathroom. "He's such an asshole. I can't believe someone fixed you up with him."

Bernadette felt guilty about tarnishing some innocent person's reputation. "It wasn't Jason," she said as she stepped into the bathroom.

"Do you want me to phone someone for you?" Wally asked from the living room.

Bernadette knew who would come get her, but she didn't want her hosts to make the call or overhear it. "There's . . . this other fella," she said through the door. "It's kind of awkward."

Lor got the hint and came back to the bathroom with a cell. She hesitated, studying Bernadette's face. "Don't call China or any shit like that, okay?"

"Promise," said Bernadette, taking the phone and closing the door. Though she was beginning to warm up, she remained wobbly and sore. She dropped the toilet lid and sat down on it. After punching in his number, she held the phone to her ear with one hand and crossed her fingers with the other.

He picked up after five rings. "Garcia."

She was never so relieved to hear his voice. "Tony. Thank God."

"What's going on? Where are you?"

The swampy taste of the river climbed up her throat, and she felt nauseous. Bending over, she whispered into the phone, "I'm at the St. Paul Yacht Club, on Harriet Island."

"I know where it is, but what—"

"The boat is called the *Three-Hour Tour*. I'll have them unlock the gate for you. It's Gate G. The lower harbor."

"What are you doing on a boat? What happened to dinner with the brother?"

"I'll fill you in when you get here."

"What did you do?"

Bernadette heard a knock at the bathroom door. "One second," she said into the phone, and set the cell on the bathroom counter. She got up off the toilet lid, wincing from the back pain, and shuffled over to the door while clutching the throw around her. She felt like an old lady. She opened the door and took an armload of clothing from Lor.

"Keep the works," said the young woman. "It was all headed to Goodwill."

"Thanks."

"The ex-boyfriend coming to the rescue?"

Bernadette paused, amused by the role assigned to Garcia. She smiled. "Yeah. He's on his way. I told him the name of your boat. If you could unlock the gate for him."

"I'll send Wally," said the young woman. "You need anything else?"

Bernadette adjusted the clothes in her arms. "No. This is great. I really appreciate it."

"Oh, wait," said Lor, bending over to retrieve something from the floor. She passed a plastic garbage bag to Bernadette. "For your wet clothes."

"Thanks again."

"I'll let you get dressed," she said, and closed the bathroom door.

Bernadette sat back down on the toilet lid with the phone. "Are you there?"

"I'm the ex-boyfriend, am I?"

"This is a really long story," Bernadette whispered into the cell.

"I'm in my boxers, so it better be a good one."

"It is," she said, and hung up.

Bernadette dressed quickly. The gray sweats felt warm, dry, and comfortably baggy. The woman had even included a pair of wool socks, some well-worn running shoes, and an old ski jacket. While Bernadette stuffed her wet clothes into the garbage bag, she eyed the gun and holster she'd set on the bathroom counter. She'd heard the Glock could survive getting run over by a tank. A dip in the river should be nothing.

Lor tapped on the bathroom door. "How're you doing in there?"

"Give me one minute," Bernadette said while tucking the damp holster and gun into the bottomless pockets of the sweatpants. These people had been more than generous, and Bernadette decided to meet Garcia at the gate rather than impose upon them any further. She pulled on the ski jacket and was glad to see it hid the bulge of her gun.

The door popped open and Lor stuck her head inside. "Want me to toss your clothes for you, or are you gonna try to salvage them?"

Bernadette had removed her ID and her wallet. As far as she was concerned, the rest of it, even the coat, was a loss. She never wanted to set eyes on the stuff again. She handed the heavy bag to Lor. "Trash it."

"That's what I figured," said the young woman.

BERNADETTE MANAGED to get off of the *Three-Hour Tour* without giving Wally and Lor a name, real or fabricated. She figured they were thrilled to rid themselves of the nighttime drama as quickly as possible. As she thumped down the dock, she adjusted her grip on her gun. If her assailant showed up for another try, she wanted to put a bullet in the sneaky bastard. Before she started up the steps that would take her back to the park, she stole a quick look at Matthew's houseboat. All the lights were off now. He and the woman either had gone to bed or had left while she was inside the *Three-Hour Tour*.

In her mind, she went back and forth over whether Matthew was indeed the villain. He could have seen her and slipped outside to push her into the river, but what excuse would he have given the woman for leaving the boat? *Pardon me a minute while I drown an FBI agent, and please freshen up my drink while I'm gone.*

Garcia was just pulling into the parking lot in his Pontiac Grand Am. Spotting her standing in front of the fence, he navigated his heap over to the sidewalk. "Hey, lady, need a lift?" His face darkened when he saw the gun in her hand.

She dropped her gun in the ski jacket's pocket, opened the passenger door, and hopped inside. Slamming the door hard, she said: "Let's get the hell out of here."

Garcia turned out of the park. "Why did you have your piece out? Why are you dressed like a bum?"

She reached over and turned up the heat. Looking through the windshield, she noticed the crack was gone. "I see you finally fixed the—"

"Let's hear it." He turned the car north onto the Wabasha Bridge and headed for downtown. "Let's hear it, Cat. Spill it."

"Not yet." She looked through the passenger window. The nighttime river would never again seem beautiful and mysterious. She'd tasted it. Nearly drowned in it. A bit of it still clogged her ears and clung to her body. The romance was gone. "I need some time."

"Time for what?"

"How about we wait until we're inside?" she asked. "Can we save it until my place?"

"You'd better have beer," he said, bumping off the bridge and heading for her loft.

"I have beer," she said, using her index finger to work water out of her ear.

He braked at a red light and wrinkled his nose. "It smells like a swamp in here."

"Maybe you need to put up one of those air fresheners," she said.

Chapter 28

WHILE SHE SHOWERED OFF THE STINK OF THE RIVER, GARCIA sat on her couch with the remote in one hand and a beer in the other. The instant she cracked open the bathroom door, he punched off the television and looked expectantly in her direction.

"Keep your shirt on," she said as she tightened the belt around her bathrobe and headed for the kitchen.

He punched the set back on and started surfing the channels. "You're walking like a grandma."

"Thanks. You want another beer?"

"I'm good." He stopped at a program about insects.

"Ants communicate primarily through chemicals called phero-mones."

He dropped the remote on the couch. "Ever wonder how they get those close-ups? I mean, how do they get right into the ant hole—right into the ants' faces—without disturbing the little turds?"

"What is it about males and nature shows?" she asked, frowning at his selection. "It's either that or the History Channel."

"We like war and bugs." He leaned forward with his elbows on his knees.

"Eureka! This hardworking forager has found a supply of food, a wedge of apple discarded by picnickers."

She went to the cupboards to check her store of hard liquor and saw a dusty bottle of Jack Daniel's hidden behind some ancient vodka. "Eureka! The hardworking agent has found a supply of good booze." She took down the bottle and a shot glass. "Will you be pissed if I call in drunk the rest of the month?"

"She leaves a pheromone trail along the ground as she makes her way home. Before long, the other ants are following this very same pheromone route. Returning home, they reinforce this same path. This in turn attracts more ants."

"What did you say?" he asked.

"Never mind," she said, pouring a shot.

"A new obstacle—a fallen twig—blocks the established route to the food supply, so the foragers deviate from the path to find a new trail. If successful, the victorious returning explorer leaves a new trail marking the shortest detour."

Glancing into the kitchen, he saw her down a shot while she was standing at the counter. "Are you getting lit?"

"The trail is no longer reinforced and slowly dissipates once the food supply is completely exhausted."

"I'm drinking until the liquor supply is completely exhausted," she said, and held the bottle up to study the level of whiskey.

He aimed the remote at the bugs and shut off the set. "What happened to you tonight, Cat?"

She poured a second shot and took the glass and the bottle over to the coffee table. She dropped down next to him on the couch. "Someone tried to drown me."

"What? Who? How'd you end up down by the river in the first place?"

She tipped back another shot and shuddered. The heat of the whiskey sent a pleasant warmth rippling through her body. She set down the glass and rewound to the beginning of her story. "Matt and

I had dinner at that fancy restaurant, the one on Wabasha Street with the tall windows and the froufrou curtains."

"Nice place."

"You'll see how nice when I turn in my expense account," she said.

Garcia sat back against the cushions. "Sounds like he was he trying to soften you up."

"He wanted me to lay off his big brother and his big files," she said. "He went on and on about what a great human being Luke is, how he started this suicide hotline and that clinic. While he's giving me this sales pitch, Little Brother is getting bombed on high-end vino."

"What about you? Did you drink with him?"

She paused, feeling insulted by the question. "I had a sip or two of wine."

He glanced at the whiskey bottle.

"Seriously," she said. "Two sips."

"I believe you." He set his St. Pauli on the coffee table. "Did he tell you if the doc knows Wakefielder?"

"Matt claimed not to know the guy. I'm not sure I believe him."

"Did he give you anything on the dead girls?"

"He said Klein's mother killed herself and Klein tried to kill herself before his brother took her on as a patient. He said he never heard of Zoe Cameron. Again, I don't know if I believe that."

"Did you get *anything* useful off him?"

She rubbed her hands together. "I—I got a sense that something isn't right in that family. Something between Matt and Luke. Something . . . strange."

"Where does the yacht club fit into this strangeness?"

"It's coming," she said. "After dinner, I was worried that he couldn't drive and suggested he take a cab. He told me he lived in walking distance."

"So you walked him home."

"Followed him home, to his houseboat. He lives on a houseboat, or at least crashes there after partying."

"He didn't see you tailing him?"

"I'm sure he didn't," she said. "I was careful."

He rubbed his face with his hand. "God, Cat. Why did you tail him? Based on a feeling?"

She ignored his questions and kept going. "I was standing on a neighbor's boat—don't worry, they weren't home—and I saw him arguing with a woman who'd busted into his place. Old girlfriend or something."

"Back up," said Garcia. "You *saw* him? How did you see him? Were they arguing outside?"

"I was watching through the window. They had the shades up and the lights on inside, and it was hard not to see."

He slapped his hand over his eyes. "Christ."

"How was it different from any other surveillance? How was it different from the stakeout of the prof's house? We tap people's phones and we keep tabs on their—"

"Okay, okay," he said, holding up his hand to halt her diatribe.

"Anyway, they both suddenly disappeared from the window," she said. "After a while, she popped back up, but I didn't see him. I got worried."

"Why?"

"She—the girlfriend—practically scratched his eyes out when they were fighting. I literally saw blood. His face was bloody."

"If you were that worried, maybe you should have intervened or called the police."

"I thought about that." She looked down at her hands. "But I didn't have the chance. While I was standing there watching, someone came up behind me and whacked me on the back with a shovel or something. I went in. Went under."

"Shit."

She grabbed the Jack Daniel's, poured a third shot, and laughed nervously. "I'm telling you, Tony, it was cold."

He rubbed her shoulder through her robe. "Are you okay?"

"My back is still sore, but otherwise I'm fine."

"I want you to go see a doctor."

She gave the idea a dismissive wave, tipped back the third shot, and swallowed hard. "I crawled onto the neighbor's boat. Practically crawled down the dock. Found a houseboat with the lights on. Banged on the door. I made up some story about accidentally walking off the dock. Didn't give them my name or anything. They gave me a change of clothes and let me use their phone." She paused. "I need a new cell, by the way."

"Who hit you? Did you get a look?"

"I don't know," she said, cupping the empty whiskey glass between her hands. "They were gone by the time I came up for air. It could have been Matthew. Maybe he saw me through the window and sneaked off his houseboat. Came after me. That's why I couldn't see him in the windows. On the other hand, it could have just as easily been a neighbor who'd had too many break-ins already and thought I was another burglar. Or maybe it was another bum."

"*Another* bum?"

Rolling the glass between her palms, she fumbled an explanation. She hadn't intended to tell him about the basement fiasco yet. "Something happened downstairs."

"What happened? Downstairs where?"

"The basement here." She felt a knot in her gut as she remembered the scumbag's body on top of her own. "These two tramps came after me. One of them jumped me."

"Shit. When?"

"Late Thursday night, after you left. I went back down to try another round with the scarf." She felt guilty seeing his stressed face. "But I'm okay. They were drunks. I kicked the crap out of the one who tried to grab me. The cops came and hauled them away."

"Who were they?"

"Nobody. Bums. Drunk bums. They got in through that busted front door."

"Great. When were you going to tell me about it? Were you going to let me find out from my cousin at the cop shop?"

"I'm telling you now."

"Christ Almighty." He got up off the couch and paced back and forth in front of the coffee table. "You've been physically assaulted twice in a forty-eight-hour period. Do you really think you should be going in to work Monday morning? You need some time off."

"So I can sit at home and feel sorry for myself?" She picked up the whiskey bottle to pour a fourth shot, had second thoughts, and set it down. "If you're worried that I'm going to get all wiggy and go postal at the office, think about it. Who am I going to shoot? Creed's already dead."

"Funny." He stopped pacing and stood in front of her with his arms folded. "I want you to see a doctor first thing in the morning. Urgent care or the ER or whatever."

"I'm fine."

"You complained about a sore back."

"I'm on the verge of something with these drownings," she said. "I am not going to put the investigation on hold so I can put my feet up."

He pushed the Jack Daniel's bottle off to the side and sat down on the edge of her coffee table to face her. "I got an update from the ME today."

"What did he say?" She pointed at him. "What about the lithium? Did he find lithium in Klein's wineglass and in her system?"

"He did."

"Crime scene crew. What about them?"

"Hairs and fibers from Klein's and Hammond's. It'll take the usual eternity to do the DNA deal."

"What *color* hair?"

"Blond." Garcia's eyes narrowed. "I didn't even ask before. Is Matthew VonHader—"

"A towhead? You betcha. So is Luke VonHader."

"Hmmm. With the prof, that makes three blonds."

"What about prints?" she asked.

"They're thinking the killer used gloves."

"Evidence of sexual assault?"

Garcia shook his head.

"He used a condom, then. Or he drowned them, dried his hands off, and left to have sex elsewhere." She chewed her bottom lip. "What is Minneapolis PD releasing to the media?"

"They're going to issue a statement saying the tub deaths were homicides. Period. No mention of the river deaths and certainly no mention of Zoe Cameron. If reporters ask whether the tub deaths are related to each other . . ."

"They have already asked; they're not that obtuse."

". . . Minneapolis is going to say that possibility is being investigated, which is the truth."

"Have the cops or our folks mentioned Klein's neighbor to the media yet? Has anyone hinted to the press that he gave us a description—albeit a crappy one—of Klein's late-night date?"

"No. That's still being held under wraps."

"Let's keep it that way." She stood up, crossed the living room, and went over to the windows facing the riverfront. "I've got an idea."

Garcia got up and joined her at the windows. "I'm not going to like this, am I?"

The sight of the Mississippi made her shudder. She buried her hands in the pockets of her robe, turned away from the water, and rested her back against the glass. "Ask them to hold off on releasing the description."

"I might be able to get them to do that. It's so general—big blond dude—it's useless."

"If word gets out that we have a witness who saw Klein with someone the night of her death, it could put one of our blonds on the move. If the newspapers and TV run a description of the suspected killer—even a vague one—it could really light a fire under someone to get out of town. I want people to think we're all clueless. I want Wakefielder to think we've backed off."

"Lots of these serial killers get angry if they don't get some sort of ink. They live to string law enforcement along and read about it in the papers."

"That's not what this maniac is after. He's not into it for the glory. It's all about his sexual gratification."

"I've seen some freaky stuff in all my years of law enforcement. Torture and sex. Cannibalism and sex. Satanic worship and sex. Rottweilers and sex." He shook his head. "But this water and sex . . ."

"It's not just water and sex. It's about *drowning* and sex." She felt her skin crawl under the terry cloth. Almost unconsciously, she pulled her robe tighter around her body. "Really, if you think about it, that old nautical tale about those sirens or whatever they were. They lured sailors to their deaths. Isn't that about drowning and sex? This is the flip side of that."

"A man luring women into the water." Garcia turned and looked at the river through the tall windows. "I hate to ask."

"Go ahead."

"If Matt did it, do you think he bumped you into the river to get off on it?"

Her upper lip curled. "I wish you hadn't asked, but I don't think so."

"Why not?"

"He didn't stay around to watch. I think he knocked me in to get rid of me, or because he was furious with me. Both."

His brow furrowed. "You really think he's the one who knocked you in?"

"The more we talk about him, the more I want time to find out," she said. "I haven't ruled out the prof or the shrink as players in this. But I want to surprise little brother at his boat and check out his reaction. He may have tried to steer me away from Luke because I was getting too close to home."

He walked into the middle of the living room and turned around. "The water thing. Besides the fact that he hangs out on the river, which is fascinating as hell in light of your theory, any other indications he's got some kind of water fetish? Drowning fetish?"

She remembered the way Matthew had stood along the rails that night, staring out onto the water for a long time. It had seemed such an odd thing for a man out walking alone to do. Garcia would pencil in that observation under the "feelings" column, however, and summarily dismiss it. She left her resting spot against the windows and walked over to him. "Just get the cops to sit on that stuff about the witness and his description."

"For how long?"

"Until I can pay a visit to my favorite drinking buddy. Ask him if he wants to go for a swim. Maybe he'll make me breakfast on the river tomorrow."

"Take your gun."

"You think the Glock is okay after going into the river with me?"

"Hell, yes. I'll put in for a new one if you want, but shit. People fire it under water, which is a real dumb-ass idea. I heard about this one dude who put his Glock in a bucket of Drano, just to see what would happen. It came out good as new. He ran a hundred rounds of ammo coated with Gorilla Glue and had no failures."

"Give me a break. I read about that online."

"You don't believe it?"

"The part about the Drano maybe, but not the Gorilla Glue." She lifted his wrist and checked his watch. "Time for you to go home, unless you plan on sleeping here."

"Best offer I've had today," he said.

Feeling her face heat up, she let go of his wrist. "I was joking."

"Seriously, are you okay by yourself tonight? You've been through the wringer. I could——" His eyes fell on her sofa.

"Oh. Right. Great idea." She took a step back from him. "I can't imagine anything more distracting than having you right downstairs. I'd never get any sleep."

His brows arched. "Distracting?"

"You probably snore. You look like the type that snores."

He took a step toward her. "You're right. I do snore."

They stood inches apart, staring at each other for several seconds. Bernadette finally broke the silence. "Well . . ."

"Yeah." He took his coat off the kitchen chair and put it on.

They walked to the door together. "Thanks for pulling my backside out of the hot coals. Again."

"That's what I'm here for."

As soon as the door snapped shut behind him, she made a beeline for the whiskey bottle to pour one last shot before bed. For a lot of reasons, it was going to be a long and sleepless night.

Chapter 29

DISGUSTED WITH HERSELF FOR HER JD BINGE, BERNADETTE stood under the shower for a good twenty minutes while the hot water pummeled her scalp. The top of her head felt ready to erupt, and her mouth tasted like swamp swill with a whiskey chaser. She had to shake it off. Since Matthew was undoubtedly not a morning person, she wanted to barge in on him while it was early and catch him off guard. Hopefully the out-of-control girlfriend was still at his place; the woman might blurt something useful in front of Bernadette.

Even though she was nauseous, Bernadette forced herself to choke down some toast with her coffee. While she longed to throw on a pair of comfortable jeans, she pulled on one of her usual dark suits and a stiff white blouse. This assignment required that she dress every bit the part of an FBI agent. If he was the one who'd tried to kill her, Matthew needed to know whom he'd targeted: an officer of the goddamn federal government.

The holster was dry enough to use. Snapping in her Glock, she wished she had time to take it to the range and try it out. Nevertheless, she was confident the gun would work. She found her backup trench in the closet, with a pair of gloves inside a pocket. She slipped on her sunglasses; this morning the shades were needed to camouflage her hangover as much as her mismatched eyes.

SHE HESITATED for an instant before turning her Ranger onto the bridge. Crossing the Mississippi felt like getting back on a horse that had thrown her and then kicked her in the head. The river wasn't the enemy; Matthew was probably the one to blame for her dunking.

The sky was gray, but the wind wasn't blowing as it had been the night before. She spotted a rowing crew taking advantage of the calm to break out their longboat. It used to be that when she saw boats gliding along the Mississippi, she'd try to imagine what it would be like to tip and go into the water on a cold day. Having had the experience for real, she now fought to push tipping thoughts from her mind.

Her personal cell rang. "Yeah," she croaked.

Garcia said, "Cat?"

"You've got the right number."

"Are you still in bed?" he asked.

"Funny."

"Seriously, where are you right now?"

"Heading for my diving coach's house."

"Wait for me in the parking lot."

"I don't need any backup," she said, turning onto Harriet Island. "I can handle it solo."

"That was not a request, Agent Saint Clare."

"Yes, sir."

"Stay in your vehicle until I get there."

She rolled into the St. Paul Yacht Club parking lot and slowed as she went by Matthew's gleaming Jag. "I'd like to go down to the houseboat by myself."

"I don't have a problem with that," he said. "I'll stay out of sight."

She pulled in between two sedans, slammed on the brakes, and put the Ford in park. "Why didn't we discuss this earlier?"

"I had a chance to sleep on it. Besides, last night didn't seem a good time to start a fight. You were two sheets to the wind."

She turned off the engine and fingered her keys. "I was not. Anyway, how long will you be?"

"Ten minutes tops."

True to his word, Garcia pulled into the lot ten minutes later. He cruised past her truck and parked at the opposite end of the tar rectangle. She waited until he was at her door before getting out of the pickup. Bernadette kept her eyes on the gate. "How do you want to do this?" she asked.

"You tell me," he said. "It's your show."

"Let's get down to the dock and scope it out. I'm thinking you can cover me from the deck of a neighbor's boat."

"What if he invites you inside? Then what?"

"I'll stand by a window. His boat has a lot of windows, and he doesn't seem to care about closing the blinds."

"And if he makes a move you don't like—"

"I'll signal you. I'll look out the window like I'm taking in the scenery."

"This is stupid and dangerous," Garcia groused. "We should have stopped at the office and got you wired."

"I'm not worried about him," she said. "He's a soft rich boy."

"A soft rich boy who might have tried to drown you last night."

"He got lucky," she said. "Today I've got someone watching my back."

"Damn straight." Garcia reached inside his coat, took out his Glock, and pocketed it. "I suppose we're going to have to hop the fence," he grumbled.

"Pretty much."

The two of them jogged across the street and were almost to the gate when a man and a woman exited. Bernadette caught the gate before it closed shut. The couple didn't give a glance to the man and woman in trench coats. Bernadette waited until she and Garcia were going down the steps before she said anything. "They didn't recognize me."

"Who?"

"The couple leaving through the gate—they were the ones who took me in last night. Lor and Wally. Nice folks." She pointed to their houseboat. "That's their place. The *Three-Hour Tour*."

"Cute name."

"I can't believe they didn't recognize me."

"You did look pretty scary last night. In fact, your skin still has a toxic sort of glow this morning. A greenish vibe. Is it the river or the Jack Daniel's?"

"I don't care to talk about it."

As they stepped onto the boards, Garcia ran his eyes over the moored boats. "Which one?"

"Matthew's is near the end of the dock," she said in a low voice. "It's the one with the lawn chairs topside."

"The *Ruth*?"

She'd missed the name of the craft last night. "Yeah. The *Ruth*."

"Must be the name of a girlfriend."

"Not last night's girlfriend. That boat would be called the *Harpy*." She stopped and stared at the *Good Enuf*. It was dark, and she saw no signs of activity inside. Its window shades were in the same position as the night before. "This was where I was camped out last night, until Matt or another asshole pushed me overboard."

"No rails around the deck," observed Garcia. "You were an easy mark."

She nodded toward the massive planter sitting on the *Good Enuf*. "Want to crouch down behind that?"

"That wouldn't hide one of my butt cheeks." He stepped onto the small houseboat. "I'll hide along the far side of this tub's cabin and watch from around the corner."

"That side walkway is pretty narrow, and it isn't railed either," she warned. "Watch your footing."

"Same to you." He took his place at the far corner of the smaller houseboat's cabin and nodded. She walked up to the *Ruth* and turned her ear to the door. She couldn't hear a thing, but she wasn't surprised. Even during the wild domestic spat, the boat had remained soundproof. She tapped twice while glancing over at Garcia. After waiting a minute or so, she knocked harder. No answer. She banged on the door with her fist.

The door popped open, and she stepped back. Matthew was standing in the doorway barefoot and in a bathrobe. "Agent Saint Clare," he said, running a hand through his wet hair. "To what do I owe this unexpected pleasure?"

"Sorry to get you out of the shower," she said.

He tightened the belt around his robe. "It seems like we saw each other just twelve hours ago."

"You got home all right, obviously."

He folded his arms in front of him and said indignantly, "I wasn't *that* intoxicated."

"I was afraid you were going to fall in, and the river this time of year is so cold," she said evenly, and watched for his reaction.

He didn't bat an eye. "How did you figure out where I . . . Oh, never mind. Stupid question. You're the FBI. You know everything."

His door was wide open, and she could look into his kitchen, but she didn't see anything except stainless steel and granite. "May I come in?"

He buried his hands in the pockets of his robe. "Not that it's any of your business, but I have someone staying with me and my guest is asleep."

"I'll keep my voice down," she said.

"If this is about my brother's files, I haven't even had a chance to talk to him about them yet. I promise I'll badger him later today."

"This isn't about Luke. I have a few questions for you."

"Kyra Klein was my brother's patient. I only know about her through Luke. I am so sorry I volunteered even that bit of information. Let's not forget who called whom."

"That was damage control done on your brother's behalf." She brought her fingers up to her cheek. "What happened to you?"

He put his hand over the large bandage slapped across his face. "I . . . cut myself . . . shaving," he mumbled.

"What did you do? Use a machete?"

"Are you always this charming so early in the day?"

She heard a thump and looked past him into the houseboat. "I'd really like to have a cup of coffee and talk. I've never seen the inside of one of these."

Reaching behind him, he grabbed the doorknob and pulled the door closer. "What is this really about, Agent Saint Clare?"

"What did you do after you walked home last night?"

His brows came together. "What in the world does that have to do with Kyra Klein?"

"Please answer the question."

"I had a nightcap and went to bed."

"That's it?"

"That's it." A motorboat sped by on the river, gently rocking the houseboat. Behind him, the door swung open.

"What about your guest? The girlfriend? Didn't you have to stay up and entertain her?"

"I never said my guest was female, now did I?" He smiled. "It's a good assumption, though."

Bernadette heard another bang from inside the houseboat, and music playing. "It sounds like she's awake. If I could speak with her a minute and get her to vouch for you . . ."

"Leave her out of this." He turned around and snapped the door closed. "She's not feeling well this morning and I can't imagine how talking to an FBI agent is going to improve her disposition."

"What are you hiding, Matthew?"

"Hiding? Give me a break." He pulled the collar of his robe tighter. "You come banging on my door at the crack of dawn on a Sunday, rousing me from the shower. I have a hangover. I have a guest I need to expel. I apologize if I'm not prepared to ask you inside and make you a plate of waffles."

"This won't take long."

"I'll talk to my brother about the files today. If you want something more from me, call me at a more civilized hour. I'd be happy to meet for drinks. I'm just not ready for you at present." Dripping blond bangs fell across his forehead, and he combed them back. "Believe it or not, I am not a creature of the daylight."

"Matthew—"

"We're finished," he said, turning around and opening the door.

"I don't have your phone number," she said after him.

"Right," he said dryly. He disappeared inside, slamming the door in her face.

She went down the dock, meeting Garcia as he hopped off the deck of the *Good Enuf*. "What did he say?" asked Garcia.

The two of them walked side by side. "Not much. The crazy girl-friend is still there. I heard her thumping around. He didn't want to let me in."

"You think he hurt her?"

Bernadette grinned crookedly. "I think she beat him up."

"Think he's the one who pushed you in?"

They stepped off the dock and headed up the stairs. "He didn't flinch once. Didn't seem shocked or pissed to see me alive. He was aggravated to be bothered so early in the morning. He had a hang-over, but so do I."

"Did he lawyer up?"

"Hardly. He said I could call him later for drinks."

Garcia opened the gate and held it for her. "Was he making a pass at you?"

She stood on the sidewalk while Garcia closed the gate. "I think Matthew is one of those men who can't help himself. He probably flirts while he's at church. Stands too close to women while riding the elevator. Peeks down blouses. It's like breathing to him."

They crossed the street and walked toward the parking lot. "Is the serial flirt a serial killer?"

"I'm not sure anymore. I'm not sure he's the one who knocked me in. Not sure he's the murderer." They stopped and stood in front of her truck. As she rubbed her throbbing forehead with the tips of her fingers, an idea pushed past the hangover. "I just thought of something."

"What?"

"Matthew got my number after snatching my card from his brother's receptionist. What if the receptionist told Luke that his little brother was having dinner with me?"

"The doc goes to the restaurant to stop Matthew from flapping his lips. He gets there just in time to see Little Brother leave. Watches you tail Little Brother . . ."

"Damn," she said, leaning against the side of her truck. "I'm going to head on over to the doc's house right now."

"Want some company?"

"He doesn't hang out on the river. He lives in a nice house on Summit. He has neighbors all around him, and it's a Sunday morning. I'll be fine," she said. "Besides, don't you have something better to do?"

He checked his watch. "Actually, I could still make morning mass. Care to—"

"Say a prayer for me." She turned and opened her truck door.

Chapter 30

SUMMIT AVENUE, ONE OF THE MOST CELEBRATED STREETS IN
the Twin Cities. The boulevard extended nearly five miles, anchored
at the east end by the towering copper dome of the Cathedral of St.
Paul and at the west end by the University of St. Thomas. In between
the two Catholic institutions ran the longest remaining stretch of
residential Victorian architecture in the country. The massive homes
had wraparound porches, expansive lawns, carriage houses instead
of garages, ballrooms in addition to family rooms, swimming pools
in their basements, and gazebos in their backyards. The wealthy and
the powerful—lumber barons and railroad tycoons and bankers and
judges—had built these homes. Early on in his writing career, F. Scott
Fitzgerald had lived on the street in a brownstone row house. The
Minnesota governor's residence was on Summit, as was the opulent
mansion built by James J. Hill, founder of the Great Northern Railroad.

Bernadette's head snapped back and forth as she took in the scenery while driving west along the avenue. She braked at a red light
and used the stop as an opportunity to double-check the address.
Glancing up from the note, she saw that it was starting to drizzle and
clicked on the truck's wipers. Even through the rain and with a lot of

the leaves already down, the tree-lined street was stunning in the fall. The oranges and yellows and reds seemed more vibrant when serving as a backdrop to the magnificent homes.

The light turned green, and she accelerated, driving another mile. She hung a right, drove a block, and pulled over to the curb to leave the Ranger on the side street. The doc's house was a couple of blocks away. Through the windshield, she looked up at the gray sky. She reached under the driver's seat and took out her umbrella.

Hopping out of the truck, Bernadette paused to inhale the chilly autumn air. Someone was burning wood in a fireplace. Opening her umbrella, she began her short hike. She stopped at the corner and waited for a break in the traffic. While she crossed, a gust blew against her back and almost took the umbrella out of her hands. Tightening her hold on the handle, she quickened her pace.

THROUGH THE DOWNPOUR, Bernadette squinted at the address over the front door. She looked down at the slip of paper again. This was the right place.

She didn't know the psychiatric profession could be so lucrative. The mansion had a screened porch that extended across the front and wrapped around one side. A black wrought-iron fence twice her height surrounded the place, giving it the air of a fortress. The home itself was constructed of red sandstone, each rugged block the size of the hood of a Volkswagen Beetle. On each side of the wide steps leading up to the front door was a marble lion, sitting at attention like a guard dog.

Stuffing the scrap of paper in her coat pocket, Bernadette pushed open the front gate. The porch was crowded with statues, probably placed inside for storage before winter. There were robed women—with one or both breasts exposed—and a muscular man in a toga. A terracotta Buddha was biding his time next to a painted statue of the Virgin Mary. All the VonHaders had to do was put out a bowl of candy and the porch would be a perfect haunted house for Halloween.

Urns filled with topiaries stood on each side of the entrance to the house, and a wreath of dried flowers dotted with minipumpkins hung from the door itself. To the left of the door, mounted up high near the ceiling, was a camera. If the VonHaders were like most homeowners, they'd installed a security system but stopped using it after the first month or two. She scrutinized the tall windows looking out onto the porch and was disappointed that they were hung with lace curtains dense enough to keep her from seeing inside. She closed her umbrella, stepped up to the door, and pressed the doorbell. She waited and pushed it again.

Hearing a deadbolt being turned on the other side of the door, she braced herself. He was going to be furious that she'd come to his home, and on a Sunday morning to boot.

He opened the door, his figure blocking the entire entryway. He was dressed in a gray jogging suit and coordinating sneakers. The outfit probably cost more than her work suit, she thought ruefully. The doctor looked past her at the rain coming down in sheets. "Guess I'll have to postpone my run."

He opened the door wider and took a step back. "Come inside, Agent Saint Clare."

She propped her umbrella against the porch wall. "Matt told you to look out for me."

"Yes, he did."

As she stepped over the threshold, Bernadette glanced up at him. He was tall and trim, with a runner's physique. She hadn't noticed that in the office, under his stuffy suit.

"Cold?" he asked, closing the door behind her.

Her attention went back to the door as she heard him activate the deadbolt. "A little."

"Let's sit in the parlor," he said. "I have a decent fire going this morning."

"Thank you for seeing me without an appointment," she said dryly.

"I didn't think I had a choice," he said.

She trailed after him as he led her down the long foyer. She saw an open staircase leading to the second story. "Beautiful home."

"My parents left it to me."

"Lucky you." As she followed him to a room on the left, an Oriental carpet cushioned her feet. Walking deeper inside, she got a full view of all the pricey-looking furniture.

"Please," he said, motioning toward a couch parked on one side of the fireplace.

She lowered herself onto the sofa. "Thank you."

He extended his hands. "I could take your wrap and gloves."

"Maybe after I warm up."

"May I bring you something to drink?"

He was acting way too civilly. That bastard Matthew's call had given his brother just enough time to prepare for her. "I'm fine," she said shortly.

"I just put on a pot of fresh coffee."

She folded her hands on her lap. "Sure. Coffee would be good."

"Cream or sugar?"

"Black, if you please."

"I'll be right back," he said.

Bernadette watched him leave the room, stood up and went to the fireplace, and held her gloved hands in front of the blaze. The fireplace opening was large enough to roast a pig. The mantel was lined with a row of old oil lamps, many with fluid in the base. Her parents had left her a pair of those lanterns. Never thinking of them as collectibles, she hung on to them for a utilitarian purpose—in case the power went out.

Turning around, she ran her eyes over the large room filled with antiques. Tall chests with brass handles lined the walls. In addition to the couches situated on either side of the fireplace with a coffee table between them, she saw two other sofas across the room, both covered in some sort of maroon velvet. A forest of small tables took up floor space. They had marble tops and wooden tops and were round and square and rectangular. One of the tables had a silver tea set arranged on top of it. A large oak library table was pushed into a corner. She recognized the clean lines as mission style and speculated that it was an original Stickley piece. She was familiar with that furniture maker because her mother had taken her to a farm auction where some of Gustav Stickley's pieces were up for bids.

The walls of the room were as crowded as the floor, with framed pieces of art from miniature portraits to massive landscapes. She went over to the gallery and studied a set of First Communion photos hanging side by side. The blond, dark-suited boys posing with folded hands, rosaries twined around their fingers, had to be Luke and Matthew. Bernadette's eyes drifted to the right of the boys' photos, where she saw a rectangle of bright wallpaper. A photo had hung there for a long time. Whose photograph had been removed?

She pulled her eyes off the gallery and continued her self-guided tour of the museum. Wandering over to a table, she picked up an enamel vase and speculated about how much it cost. "If you have to ask," she muttered.

"That's a highly important signed Norwegian vase, circa 1900."

She turned around with the piece in her hands. "What makes it so important? The signed part, the Norwegian part, or the circa 1900 part?"

Luke set down a silver tray loaded with a silver coffeepot, silver creamer, and porcelain cups and saucers. "Actually, that's a very good question. I would have to say that all three together classify it as highly important."

Trying to imagine the price tag attached to "highly important," Bernadette scrutinized the vase. It looked like an overgrown champagne flute and was decorated with small, dark red flowers set against light blue glass. She thought it was hideous.

"What do you think of it?" he asked as he poured a cup of coffee.

As she set the vase back down, Bernadette employed the word all Minnesotans used when trying to be nice. "It's *different*."

He handed her a cup and saucer. "Yes," he said tiredly, "I think it's ugly, too."

She nodded toward the fireplace mantel. "I like the lanterns."

"I light them at night to entertain the girls. We pretend we're camping."

She smiled, genuinely touched by the idea. "That's neat."

"Mother would be horrified. Her things were for show, not actual use."

She sat down on one of the sofas and pretended to sip. Anyone brazen enough to try to drown an FBI agent could also try to poison one. "I wouldn't keep things I couldn't use."

"As the oldest, I inherited the good and the bad—my parents' wise moves and their mistakes—and I have to take care of all of it." He sat across from her and took a sip of coffee. "It's their legacy to me."

"What about Matt? Is taking care of him part of the deal?"

"I didn't appreciate the way you took advantage of his weaknesses. Getting him drunk."

"He got himself drunk. He doesn't need help from anyone in the boozing department." She decided to bait him. "How do you know we had dinner, by the way?"

He took another sip of coffee before he answered. "He told me."

"Or do you know because you followed us around last night?"

"Ridiculous. I have better things to do with my time than trail after my brother while he's having one of his misadventures."

His calm demeanor was aggravating, and she blurted her accusation. "You followed me and pushed me into the river."

He froze with his cup halfway to his mouth. "What?"

"You heard me."

"How? Why would I . . . ? Where were you that I would have . . . ?" He set the cup down with a clatter. "You followed my brother down to the river after dinner, didn't you? You got him drunk, and when that didn't get you anywhere, you decided to spy on him."

"I had him under surveillance."

"Surveillance. A government euphemism for a sleazy activity."

"While I had him under surveillance, you shoved me into the river."

"What do you want from us, Agent Saint Clare?"

"Where were you that night?"

He stood up. "I was going to give you those damn files this week."

"Why the sudden change of heart?"

"I had a chance to speak with my attorney, and he advised me to give them to you."

"Did he also advise you to try to drown me?"

"You're crazy," he sputtered.

"Is that your expert medical opinion, Doctor? If I were you, I'd refrain from making—"

"Get out of my house," he interrupted.

She stood up. "Trying to kill an agent of the government is a big crime, Dr. VonHader. Big crimes get big time behind bars."

"I'm calling my lawyer."

"Don't you think it'd be wiser to cooperate? Isn't that what he advised you to do?"

"He didn't know you were going to accuse me of attempted murder." He pointed toward the front door.

"I can find my way," she said.

He followed and pulled the door open. "Any additional communication to me, my brother, or my office staff must come through my attorney. There'll be no more drunken dinner dates behind my back."

She spun around and faced him. "What are you hiding, Doctor? Was Kyra Klein's death the result of your malpractice, or were you involved more directly?"

His eyes widened. "What?"

"Did you murder Kyra Klein?"

"No!"

"Does the name Zoe Cameron mean anything?"

"She's another one of my patients."

"I guess the police haven't contacted you yet. That's okay. You probably already know that she died yesterday, and that in her purse they found a bottle of meds with your name on it."

He took a step back. "I don't believe you."

"What about Shelby Hammond?"

"Who? That girl in the news? No! I had nothing to do with . . . What are you insinuating?"

"Do you like to take baths or showers, Luke?" She ran her eyes up and down his figure. "I'd say you're a tub man. Did I peg you right?"

His face whitened, and he stood motionless with his hand on the open door.

She decided to toss one last hand grenade at him, looking for an answer to a question that her gut told her had something to do with the case. She pointed to the room they'd just left. "What's the story on the missing portrait? Whose picture did you take down? Who's the black sheep?"

Dr. Luke VonHader—family man, respected psychiatrist, and winner of numerous professional and civic awards—looked ready to puke on the shoes of his departing guest. He opened the door wider and said hoarsely, "Get out."

Bernadette walked through the door and felt the breeze against her back as it slammed behind her.

THE RAIN had stopped. Maybe she'd take the rest of Sunday off and hit it hard on Monday. Checking her watch, she figured that Garcia would be back home. She felt guilty about cutting him off when he had suggested mass. She fished out her phone and called him.

"How was church?" she asked cheerfully.

"Good," he said. "How'd it go with the doc?"

She told him about it and her plans to pick it up on Monday with more research into the doctor's family.

"What are you doing the rest of the day?" he asked.

"Crashing with a heating pad on my back."

"Want me to bring over some lunch?"

"I'm not up for company, Tony. My back is really sore."

A long silence on his end. "Take care of yourself . . . Check in tomorrow."

He hung up, and she closed the phone.

Chapter 31

"WHAT'S UP?" ASKED CREED.

"Jeez," she said, slapping her hand over her heart. He hadn't been there when she'd first walked into the office on Monday morning, and his sudden presence at his desk startled her. "Can't you give me some warning before you pop in?"

"What kind of warning?"

"I don't know. Beep like one of those vans backing up or something."

"Beep, beep, beep."

"Oh, shut up," she said, and turned on her computer.

"I have to ask. Did Alice have a crappy time in Naked Land last week? Was it helpful at all?"

"Not really. I'd rather not talk about it."

"What about our ASAC? Did he enjoy himself?"

"I don't think so," she said, starting to peck at her keyboard. "VonHader, VonHader, VonHader."

"That only works if you say it into a bathroom mirror at midnight," Creed volunteered.

"What?"

"You summon someone by saying his name three times into a mirror."

"You say 'Bloody Mary' three times, and she comes out and kills you. I think that's how it works. I'm not a hundred percent certain. I've never been to a pajama party."

"No friends?" he asked.

"I had to get up early and help with the cows." She stopped typing for a moment and put her hand on her lower back.

"How are you feeling after that bad date and impromptu dip in the water?"

Blinking, she cranked her chair around to stare at Creed.

He stared back at her from across the room. "What's wrong?"

"I didn't tell you about going out to dinner with Matt or getting knocked into the river."

"Nor did you inform me about the close call you had in the basement with those reprobates." He folded his arms in front of him. "You've been holding back on your partner, and I don't appreciate it."

"How do you know about all that?"

"Phone conversation between you and Garcia."

She hadn't picked up the phone yet that morning. "Ruben—"

"I need to be briefed on these things and not via eavesdropping." He leaned back in his chair. "Tell me about this VonHader."

"I visited Dr. VonHader at home yesterday."

"The guy who was the shrink for a couple of these dead girls," Creed said. "Your bad date's brother."

"Yeah. Right." She paused, confused about what she'd actually told him versus what he was gleaning some other way. "I—I saw a blank space up on the wall where a picture must have hung. When I asked about it, the doctor flipped out."

"You think the missing picture has something to do with the case?"

"At the very least, it has something to do with how the brothers turned out, all screwed up and such. That's the only lesson I took away from my visit to porn central: how boys are raised determines their sexual habits."

"'Of all the animals, the boy is the most unmanageable.'"

"Plato," she said numbly, remembering the quote.

"Very good."

"What did you think of the surveillance at the professor's house?" she asked evenly.

"Thorsson did his usual to screw things up. Too bad about that Cameron girl. Are you sure her death is connected to these drownings? It seems a separate incident entirely."

Working hard to keep her voice calm, she said, "You've been following me around."

"I have not," he said.

"You've been following me around, and I want it to stop."

"I'm looking out for my partner. Doing my job."

She twined her arms around herself. "Have you been going home with me? Where have you been? What have you seen?"

He stood up and went around to the front of his desk. "I apologize if you feel violated."

"Don't do it anymore. Please."

His eyes went to her computer. "Need some help?"

"No," she snapped. Then in a softer tone: "No, thank you."

"Would you work more efficiently if I left for the day?"

She knew how much he enjoyed getting back into the job, but he was rattling the hell out of her. "Would you mind?" she asked.

"I have other things I can do," he said.

"Thank you." She returned to her typing. A minute later she glanced toward his desk, and he was gone. She exhaled with relief and got back to her research.

Abandoning her usual government databases, Bernadette started surfing the Internet. A Google search using the words *Luke VonHader* turned up screen after screen listing awards, research projects, and articles in professional journals. They all involved the doctor's stellar career, and she'd read enough about that. She wanted to get to his family life.

She tried using the brothers' names together, and one article came up: a brief story that had run in a neighborhood newspaper about a donation they'd made to a health care facility, Sunny Park Nursing Home.

She remembered Matthew's comment during the morose, drunken dinner conversation about dead parents.

At least they never had to be in a nursing home.

So why did they dump so much money there? The article didn't say. She tried plugging in just the last name—*VonHader*—and the name of the nursing home. In addition to the donation story, one other Web offering came up. It was the page from an electronic memory book maintained by St. Paul's daily newspaper, the *Pioneer Press*. The entries—mostly from nursing home workers expressing their regret for the family's loss—were about someone named Ruth.

Ruth. That was the name painted on Matthew's boat.

Bernadette read the entries carefully.

I'm so sorry for your loss. I was Ruth's night aide for ten years. Even though she couldn't thank anyone herself, I know she appreciated everything we tried to do to make her time at Sunny Park enjoyable. Be comforted knowing she is now resting peacefully with the angels.

—Respectfully, Cecelia O.

Ruth was a beautiful soul who suffered silently for so many years. She has surely earned her place in heaven. I will include her and all of you in my prayers.
—From the Rev. Stephen Whitrockner, nursing home chaplain

I am truly sorry for your loss. Ruth must have been a lovely girl when she was a teenager. You could still see that beauty in her face, especially in her pretty eyes. I will keep her family in my thoughts as you struggle to get through what must be a difficult time. All my sympathies.

—Tamara, the first-floor medication nurse

"Depressing as hell," Bernadette muttered. She was grateful to arrive at the final entry, a brief one that gave her pause:

Still waters.

—Love, C.A.

Who was C.A., and was that water reference a coincidence? She filed the question away.

The deceased had to be an elderly relative of the VonHader boys. An aunt or a grandmother. None of the entries indicated when Ruth had died.

A return to government databases didn't come up with a death record for a Ruth VonHader, but that didn't surprise her. There were hiccups in the system. How many dead people were still receiving Social Security checks? She couldn't find anything else in those databases about this Ruth. Still, there had to be a paid obituary notice containing this matriarch's story. She went to the *Pioneer Press* Web site and dove into its electronic archives.

There it was, a life summarized in two lines:

VonHader, Ruth A. Died at Sunny Park Nursing Home, St. Paul. Private services and interment.

No age, survivors, day of death, or cause was listed. From the date of the archived obituary, however, she could surmise the month of death—and it made Bernadette's heart race. The woman had died that April, the same month bodies started turning up in the Mississippi River.

To find out more about Ruth VonHader's life, Bernadette would start with her place of death. She couldn't find a Web site for Sunny Park Nursing Home, so she turned to the phone book. The facility was in St. Paul just off Lexington Parkway, a major road that crossed Summit Avenue—the street where the doctor lived.

She picked up the phone and told Garcia what she'd uncovered and said that she was going to visit the place where the woman had died.

"I guess you don't need someone covering your back at a nursing home," he said. "How *is* your back?"

"Good," she said, lying.

"I've got some news on the news front," he said. "Cops are holding a press conference in time for the six o'clock broadcasts. They're going to issue a description. They aren't releasing the name of Klein's neighbor, but they're going to say someone saw her with a fellow the night she was murdered."

"Well, they couldn't sit on it forever. We'll see what this does."

"Call me," he said, and hung up.

IMPATIENTLY NAVIGATING around other vehicles, Bernadette plowed her Ranger down Wabasha Street through the heart of downtown. It was the start of the lunchtime rush hour, and the streets were congested with cars and trucks and delivery vans. As she sat in traffic, she thought about the woman who'd been put to rest some six months earlier. What was it about her life and death that could have driven someone to commit murder?

Chapter 32

ON THE OUTSIDE, THERE WAS LITTLE SUNNY OR PARKLIKE ABOUT
Sunny Park Nursing Home. It was a flat-roofed, one-story brick
building pocked with foggy windows. Overgrown juniper bushes and
massive pine trees had taken over the front lawn, leaving little room
for grass. Expecting the pattern of neglect to continue, Bernadette
braced herself for the odor of urine and feces as she entered.

Once inside, she was surprised to smell nothing more ominous
than roast beef and mashed potatoes. Nevertheless, she felt squea-
mish about touching anything in the place and pulled her gloves
tighter over her fingers. She saw no one stationed at the reception
desk. A guest book was open and a basket of visitor badges sat next
to it, but she didn't bother with either.

Past the desk, the hallway divided into a T. Glancing to her left,
she saw a short corridor that led to a door labeled "Memory Care
Unit." That would be locked tight. She hung a right and went down a
hall that spilled out into an airy, open room. The carpeted floor was
dotted with plush couches and chairs, and the walls were covered
with striped paper in calming shades of cream and taupe. At one end
of the long space was a massive lighted aquarium teeming with trop-

ical fish, and at the other end was a large-screen television set tuned to *The Andy Griffith Show*. The room had everything but seniors.

"May I help you?"

"Where did everyone go?" asked Bernadette, turning to address the woman at her elbow.

"To the dining room for lunch," said the woman, a husky brunette stuffed into tight slacks and a tight sweater. Her plastic name tag identified her as Hannah.

Bernadette nodded. "Smells good."

"Do you need help finding someone?"

"I'm trying to nail down a place for my mom," said Bernadette, unbuttoning her trench coat. "I've been told good things about Sunny Park."

"That's nice to hear." She waved a hand around the dayroom. "This is all new, courtesy of a generous donor."

"I'd like to see the rest of the home," Bernadette said.

Hannah took in Bernadette's figure and apparently found a small woman in a suit no threat to the elderly. "Feel free to look around. I can't give you a formal tour right now; mealtimes are very busy. Plus I work in the Memory Care Unit. Does your mom have Alzheimer's?"

"No."

"Then I'm not the one to give you a tour anyway." She pointed down a hallway that skirted past the large dayroom. "Ask for Sheila at the nurses' station. Go past the dining room, head down the hall, and go to the very end."

"Sheila," Bernadette repeated. "Thanks."

Bernadette followed her nose down to the dining room. The linoleum floor was crowded with seniors, some of them piloting their own wheelchairs and walkers while others were getting wheeled or walked by aides. She wished she could question a few of the diners about Ruth VonHader, but she didn't want to be overheard by a staff member. They might tell the VonHaders she'd been snooping.

Past the dining room was a wall covered by brass rectangles the size of license plates, the entire collection headed by a sign: "Our Generous Donors." It was a plaque near the top containing a biblical quotation that drew her attention:

> THE VONHADER FAMILY,
> IN LOVING MEMORY OF RUTH.
> "WHITHER THOU GOEST, I WILL GO;
> AND WHERE THOU LODGEST, I WILL LODGE."

As Bernadette stood staring at the wall, a phlegmatic cough echoed down the hallway. An elderly man in a wheelchair was trying to get by her. "Excuse me," she said, moving to one side. "I'm right in the way, aren't I?"

"Don't worry about it," he said, and hacked again.

No one else was in the corridor. Bernadette trotted next to him. "Sir?"

In a hurry to get to his meal, he kept wheeling toward the dining hall while giving Bernadette a sideways glance. "What is it?" he grumbled.

She had to walk briskly to keep up. "Did you know Ruth Von-Hader?"

"Room 153," he said.

"But did you know her?"

"Room 153," he repeated. "She's got a big mouth. Been here the longest of anybody. Knows everybody."

Bernadette watched as he continued down the hall. She turned around and jogged toward the end of the corridor. Patient rooms lined both sides. All of the doors were open, and every room appeared empty. Finally she hit a room containing a patient. Eating alone, she was sitting in a wheelchair with a hospital tray in front of her. According to the plaques to the right of the door, the woman was either Inez or Gladys.

Bernadette checked the number posted over the names. Room 153. She tapped twice on the open door. "Hello."

The woman looked up, fork in her hand, and motioned Bernadette to come inside. "Are you lost, *chère*?"

"A little." Bernadette walked into the room.

The slight woman was dressed in a velour sweatsuit and sneakers. The skin on her face was olive-colored and leathery. The halo of white hair surrounding her head was as fine and fragile as a dead dandelion. She peered at Bernadette through thick bifocals, but her eyes looked clear and lively. "I had a dog like you. Blue left and brown right."

"Catahoula leopard dog?"

"How'd you guess?"

"I spent some time in Louisiana. The breed is big down there."

"My people are from the parish of East Baton Rouge," the elderly woman said proudly. "I still got folks down there."

"I thought I detected a little accent. *Parlez-vous Creole*?"

The elderly woman beamed. "*Oui, oui. Je parle Creole. Et vous?*"

"*Je connais un peu de Creole,*" replied Bernadette, holding up her thumb and index finger together to show a small amount. "Did I say that right?"

"Right enough for me, *chère*." The woman pointed at her bed with the fork. "Sit."

"Thank you." Hoping she wasn't about to sit down on dried urine, Bernadette gingerly plopped down on the edge of the old woman's mattress.

With a blue-veined hand, the woman extended a dinner roll. "Eat."

"I already ate," said Bernadette. "But thanks anyway. Is it Gladys?"

"Inez. Gladys passed away last week. Died in her sleep." She forked some mashed potatoes into her mouth.

"I'm sorry."

"What are you gonna do?" Inez sawed her roast beef with a butter knife.

Bernadette glanced around the room. The half belonging to Inez was filled with family photos, and her bed was covered in a colorful quilt. Stuffed toys were lined up along the windowsill. "You like teddy bears."

"My grandnephews keep giving them to me, and I don't want to hurt their feelings." She pointed the butter knife at the collection. "I don't know what got them thinking Auntie Inez likes them mangy things."

Perfect segue, thought Bernadette. "A friend of a friend had an auntie here."

"I know everybody." She popped a sliver of meat into her mouth and chewed. "Been here forever and a day."

"She died back in April."

"We had four of them pass away in April," Inez said, pushing some peas around the plate. "Bad month."

"Ruth was her name."

Inez took a sip of milk and nodded. "Brain damage. Had to be fed through a tube in her tummy."

"She couldn't eat?"

"Couldn't eat. Couldn't sit up. Couldn't toilet herself. She could see, but she couldn't talk. Couldn't move nothin' but her pointer finger, and that was on a good day. Skinny as a toothpick, but she hung on for years and years. She was my roommate for a bit. I been here so damn long, I've had everyone in the place as a roommate at one time or another."

"Did she have visitors?" Bernadette asked.

"Mark." The elderly woman took a sip of water. "No, wait. That isn't right. Matthew. Matthew and Luke. That's it. One of them was a doctor. The other one, I don't know what he did for a living. He seemed to have plenty of time on his hands. They were real good to Ruthie, especially the older one. He read to her. Massaged her feet. Brought her enough flowers every week to fill a funeral parlor."

"That's nice," Bernadette said stiffly.

"They'd chat it up with the other residents, too. Got real chummy with the aides and kept in touch with them after she passed. I think they even helped a couple of them find better jobs."

Bernadette didn't want to hear any more about the brothers' good deeds. "How did Ruth become brain damaged in the first place?"

"*That* was a touchy subject with the VonHader clan. The official explanation was 'household accident.'"

"What kind of household accident causes brain damage?"

"Exactly."

"What do you think happened?"

The elderly woman shrugged her narrow shoulders and resumed sawing into her meat. "Who knows? Families got secrets."

"Did Ruth ever communicate with you in some way? Try to tell you what happened to her?"

"Like I said, poor thing couldn't talk."

"But did she . . . I don't know—signal somehow? Did she indicate she was afraid of Matthew and Luke?"

"No, no. She loved those boys. I could tell. She looked forward to their visits. Her eyes would light up like sparklers." Inez paused with a sliver of meat halfway to her mouth. "There was this one time, though."

"What?"

"The older one, the doctor, this one time he treated the both of us to hairdos in the salon here. Three chairs. Looks like a real salon, only it's open one day a week." She dabbed at the corners of her mouth with a napkin. "So we're in there, me and Ruthie, and we're getting our hair washed in one of those sinks. You know, the ones with the curve in them so you can rest your neck more comfortable. They're spraying our heads with warm water and something must have gone haywire with the water temp or something. Maybe she just didn't want someone touching her hair."

"Ruthie freaked out?"

"I looked over at her, and that one finger was twitching like crazy."

Bernadette got up from the mattress. A horrific conclusion was forming in her head: someone had put Auntie Ruth in the nursing home via a near drowning. If it wasn't the brothers, it had to be another relative.

Inez scooped up a spoonful of pudding and held it out to her visitor. "Tapioca. They do a real nice job with it. You should give it a try."

"No, thanks," mumbled Bernadette, sitting back down.

"Skinny thing. You should eat more dessert." Inez shoveled the pudding into her mouth.

"What about other visitors? Did Ruthie have any other regulars?"

"Not many. And when they did, well . . . I don't think Ruthie liked her daddy all that much. Her eyes got all buggy when he walked through the door."

Bernadette blinked. "Did you say her *daddy* came by? How old was her father?"

"He's dead now. Died shortly after his wife. He had a stroke. Took a bad fall. Lucky bastard. Not like Ruthie." The old woman scraped one last spoonful of pudding from the bottom of her dish. "Pneumonia got her. I suppose there are worse ways to check out."

"They call it the old people's friend," said Bernadette.

"Not that she was that old."

Bernadette frowned. "How old was she?"

"Forty or so by the time she died." Inez licked the spoon clean. "But she was a girl when she got here. I still think of her as a girl."

"What?" Bernadette got up off the bed.

"Ruthie was but a teenager when she came here." Inez dropped her spoon on the tray and stared at her visitor's ashen face. "Are you all right, *chère*? You look like you just seen a ghost."

RUTH. THAT'S whose portrait was missing in the First Communion gallery. Ruth was the pretty blond girl in Bernadette's dream.

While she drove, Bernadette came up with a sickening theory: Ruth VonHader became brain damaged when her father tried to drown her. Her brothers knew about it, or even watched helplessly while it happened. Upon their sister's death, one of them started repeating the heinous act again and again—with coeds filling in for Ruth.

Whither thou goest, I will go . . .

SHE WAS WALKING into the cellar when her desk phone rang. It was Wakefielder, and what he had to tell her made her sink into her chair.

"Agent Saint Clare, I wanted you to know before I came under suspicion. One of my students is missing."

Was this for real, or was it some sort of ploy to make himself look good? She grabbed a pen. "Since when?"

"Nathaniel advised against calling you, but if she's in trouble . . ."

"What's her name, and how long has she been missing?"

"I mean . . . I don't know what happened to Zoe. You have to believe me. She was fine when I dropped her off at—"

"Professor. The girl's name. Please."

"Regina Ordstruman. She's been gone since, well, at least since class on Friday. We don't have class on Thursday."

"Did you try her at home?"

He didn't answer.

"Professor, I don't care about your extracurriculars."

"I tried her at home and got no response."

"Her parents?"

"They're not close. Haven't been for some time." He sounded genuinely concerned.

"Is it possible she's just taking a long weekend?"

"We had a big test today, and she wouldn't have missed it unless . . ." His voice trailed off.

"Professor, was she being treated for psychological problems? Did she have a shrink?"

"If by that you mean a psychiatrist, no. I tried to get her to go in, but she refused. I did give her some tools, in case she ever needed them in an emergency. I give all my students tools. My courses tend to draw a fair number of . . ."

"Train wrecks," Bernadette finished.

He paused. "That's putting it crudely, but yes."

"What sorts of tools are we talking about? Do you recommend specific doctors or clinics?"

"Nothing like that. I give them phone numbers. There's a suicide hotline. I've even got stickers I distribute."

He has suicidal girls signing up for his classes, and he gives them stickers. She decided to cut to the chase. "Do you know Dr. Luke VonHader?"

"That name sounds familiar."

"He was Zoe's psychiatrist. He was also Kyra Klein's doctor."

"What are you saying? Do you think one of their health care providers is involved?"

"Professor, three girls connected to you have died. Two of them went to the same doctor. Help me. There is some link between you, this doctor, and their deaths."

She heard a voice in the background. It was the pit bull butting in on the call. "Agent Saint Clare, we're getting into dangerous territory here," said Wakefielder. "I'm going to have to hang up. If you need anything else, please call Nathaniel Selwyn."

"Wait. I need more on Regina. A description. Her address. The names of her—"

"I've given you all I can," he said, and hung up.

"Dammit!" She snapped her pencil. If Regina Ordstruman was real and had been missing since Thursday, she could be the woman Bernadette had witnessed having intercourse with the killer.

She looked at the office clock. The first hours of a missing persons case were vital, and this girl had been gone for days. Bernadette needed a shortcut, and her sight would have to provide it. She only hoped it would be a short cut to a live girl and not another corpse.

She called Garcia and told him to meet her at her loft.

Chapter 33

HELL HAD SWITCHED COLORS; NOW IT WAS WHITE.

He came and went. He periodically removed the gag, let her drink tepid water or juice, and sealed her mouth back up. She didn't know how long he'd kept her in the blue bedroom, tied to the posts. Days?

Then he shot her up with something that knocked her out again. When she came to, she found herself flat on her face on his bathroom floor. The odors that had nauseated her during the assaults also permeated the snowy tile beneath her. Wanting to get her face away from the stink of his soap and cologne, she rolled onto her side and curled her knees up to her chest.

While she was unconscious, he'd changed her binds and gag. Now a strip of duct tape covered her mouth like a giant bandage. More of the stuff twined her wrists together so that her hands looked like those of a silver mummy, palms locked together in permanent prayer. The bastard knew what he was doing; she couldn't use her fingernails as tools. She didn't look down, but it felt as if her legs were just as thoroughly bound. Why had he bothered to untie the ropes and take her off the bed, only to rebind her with tape and dump her in the john? Maybe he got a rise out of finding new ways to subdue her, the sick bastard. Perhaps it was because she'd been emptying her bladder on the bed, forcing him to change the sheets. Too bad she had nothing in her bowels. Her stomach rumbled and she ignored it. Being hungry was at the bottom of her tally of woes.

Number one on the list was the large white object sitting on the floor beside her. The tub. He'd been talking about it, what he'd do to her once he dropped her in it. The thing towered over her like a menacing iceberg. Was it filled with water? She tried not to think about it.

The bathroom door was closed. She heard no sounds coming from the other side, not even the soothing radio voice, her invisible companion in this blue and white hell. Finding her position uncomfortable, she started to lie on her back, but felt something preventing her. A loose corner of the duct tape from her mouth was stuck to the tiles. Maybe she could keep working it and peel off the tape. She pressed the side of her face into the floor so the tape really caught and then rolled her head down onto the tiles. She could feel the tape peeling away. Throwing her whole body into it, she rolled until she was face-down on the floor again, and kept rolling.

She found herself on her back again, this time free of the gag. Closing her eyes, she caught her breath. The effort had left her nude body covered in perspiration but rejuvenated. She'd removed the tape over her mouth. With time, she could free her hands and legs. How long was he going to be away? She visualized him dead in a car crash, his body slumped against the steering wheel, broken and bleeding. The image energized her further.

Raising her hands to her mouth, she hooked her teeth over the tape and tried to create a tear in the wrap. There were too many layers, and her teeth weren't sharp enough. She dropped her hands and ran her eyes around the cell, searching for something she could use to slice the tape. He'd been careful, her jailer. There was nothing sitting on the floor itself, not even a wastebasket or toilet plunger. Even if she could get on her feet to reach for something, there was no medicine chest in the room, only a mirror hung over the sink. The top of the toilet tank was loaded with colognes and aftershaves;

the creepy fucker had more perfume than a woman. If she knocked down a bottle, she could use the broken glass to cut her bindings, like in the movies. *Forget it*. He'd probably hear the clatter and come running.

The shower door was closed, but she knew there was nothing useful in the stall. While the water pummeled her during her first trip to his bathroom, she'd had plenty of time to study the cubicle and its contents. One bar of Ivory in the wall-mounted soap dish. Two washrags hanging from the neck of the showerhead. A small window made of glass block positioned high up on the wall, near the ceiling.

Perhaps the metal edge of the glass shower door would work. She rolled onto her side, grimacing when the wad of tape pulled at her hair. Rather than traveling with her, it stayed stuck to the floor. She braced her feet against the base of the tub and used it for leverage to propel her body toward the shower. She curled her legs under her and rolled onto her knees. Slowly, she raised her torso so that she was in a kneeling position in front of the shower.

Sweat streamed down between her breasts, collected under her armpits, and beaded her upper lip. What would he do if he found her like this? Would he kill her right then and there?

After a couple of minutes, she mustered enough courage to slide her taped hands up the glass and over to the door handle. She'd have to open it carefully, or she'd end up falling backward onto the floor. The handle was the size and shape of a toilet paper tube, sliced in half lengthwise. She inserted her taped fingers into the curve of metal and slowly pulled toward her. The pop of the door unlatching echoed in the tiled chamber, and she froze. No devil materialized, and she mouthed a silent *Thank you, God*.

She opened the door a little wider and slipped her fingers out of the handle. She pressed the outside edge of her taped hands against the edge of the shower door as if she were pleading for mercy—in a real sense, she was—and started to move her hands up and down in short, quick strokes. She concentrated on the edge of the binds.

If she pulled her hands apart as hard as she could, she found she could create a small gap between her wrists. The tape that stretched between the gap was a good place to rub, a weak spot, and she could see the very beginnings of a tear.

As she worked, she kept an ear tuned to the bathroom door. If she heard him thumping around in the bedroom, she'd lower herself onto her belly to keep him from seeing her hands or her mouth. He'd assume she was still out and perhaps leave her alone, giving her time to finish the job. Once free, she'd kill him. She didn't know how. Maybe she'd come up behind him and strangle him with his own belt. If she could find the crap he'd been shooting into her body, she'd use it to knock him on his ass. She'd fill the tub and dump him in, do him the way he planned to do her. He'd be the one the cops would find floating.

Chapter 34

STEPPING OFF THE ELEVATOR, BERNADETTE WAS STARTLED to see Garcia standing in front of her condo talking to her caretaker. The shaggy-haired Harold Winston was in his usual workday outfit of bib overalls while crew-cut Garcia was in his dark suit, white shirt, and conservative tie. A study in contrasts. She wondered what in the world the two men had to talk about, and then it occurred to her: Harry was gossiping with Garcia about the bums in the basement. Her boss didn't need to be reminded of that mess, and she quickened her pace. She got to her door as Harry was piling on the excuses for the busted front door.

"So then I told the association folks that all the hardware around here is shit, the doors are shit, the windows are shit, and they'd better start looking at replacing—" Harry halted his diatribe as she came up to the pair.

She looked at Harry and smiled a tight smile. "What about my dishwasher, Harry? Is that shit, too? When you gonna fix that?"

He tugged on his beard. "Just waiting on the parts, Miss Saint Clare."

"Sure you are."

Harry pointed to Garcia. "This gentleman showed me his badge and asked me to let him inside. Hope that's okay, Miss Saint Clare. Since he works for the feds same as you, I figured—"

"That's fine," she interrupted.

Harry said, "I escorted him up, to make sure he knew where to go."

"He's been here before," she said.

Harry looked at Garcia and winked. "Is that right?"

Bernadette looked at Garcia and asked flatly, "Shall we take this inside . . . sir?"

"Sounds good." Garcia smacked Harry on the back. "Don't let them work you too hard, old-timer."

Rolling her eyes, Bernadette closed the door hard behind them. "Old-timer. Give me a break. That lazy, overpaid turd."

"He seems like a decent enough fella."

She shrugged off her coat and tossed it over a kitchen chair. "He's getting paid a lot and is doing absolutely nothing while the place is falling apart."

"It's not his fault that Murrick did a cut-rate renovation job."

"August spent a ton of time and money fixing this place."

Garcia followed her into the kitchen. "Awfully touchy about him, aren't you?"

"It isn't nice to speak ill of the dead."

He took off his coat and dropped it over the back of a kitchen chair. "What did you get from the nursing home?"

She leaned her back against the kitchen island. "Ruth was only a few years older than we are when she died. She'd been in the home since she was a teen. Her parents put her there after she became brain damaged. She was injured in a 'household accident.' That's the official line, at least. But I think . . ." She paused, unsure of whether she should unveil her theory.

"You think what?"

"I think her father tried to drown her, causing the brain damage. I think the brothers witnessed it. I think one of them went wiggy as a result and is drowning young women."

"Why now? If the girl was injured years ago—"

"Remember. She died in April, the same month the first victim was found floating in the river."

Garcia walked back and forth between the table and the island. "If you're correct—"

"I am."

"How did you get all this?"

"I talked to one of her former roommates at the home."

"Why are all the victims college women, especially ones with emotional problems?"

"I don't know. Could be the first victim happened to be a screwed-up coed and he decided to stick with a known quantity. That's the sort of girl he would have grown accustomed to through the practice. Skinny, emotionally vulnerable women. Easy pickings. Maybe it has to do with the fact that Ruth was injured in the years before she would have started college."

He stopped pacing and faced her, propping his butt against the edge of the kitchen table. "Which one, though? Which brother?"

"I came home to try to figure that out."

"You're going to use your sight."

"That's the plan. I've still got the scarf. All I need is the venue."

He loosened his tie. "The urinal downstairs again, or should we find a church?"

"The basement's good. I want to do this quick."

Garcia took off his blazer and rolled up his shirtsleeves. "Let's get to it."

"One more thing: I got a call at the office."

"Yeah?"

"Professor said he's got a student missing."

"Is he up to something?"

"I think I believe him. He said her name is Regina Ordstruman. Gone since Friday. Maybe since Thursday."

"He volunteered that information?"

"That's about all I could get out of him before his lawyer friend made him hang up the phone."

Garcia yanked off his tie. "Fucking lawyer."

"Forget about him. We might have a missing girl, and my sight could find her."

He threw his tie on the table. "Right. That's right."

"I've got to run upstairs and get the scarf." She headed for the steps spiraling up to her sleeping loft. "Mind if I quickly throw on some jeans while I'm at it?"

"Go ahead," he said. "Wish you had a pair that fit me."

While she changed, she heard him opening her refrigerator. Bernadette liked that he felt at home in her condo. It took her only a couple of minutes to change, but he was finished with his sandwich by the time she came down. "Superb salami."

She held up the bagged scarf. "Ready?"

He pushed his chair back from the table and stood up. "Let's rock."

Chapter 35

THE DUCT TAPE WAS A BITCH.

While the stretch of tape at her wrists developed a small tear, she'd made little additional progress in her bid to free herself. The stuff kept sticking to the shower door's edging, forcing her to stop and start again. Her knees ached, and at the same time her taped ankles were losing sensation, making it difficult to keep her balance. She'd gone from perspiring to shivering as the sweat coated and cooled her body. The lack of food was making her light-headed. As her concentration wavered, so did her determination to escape.

She repeatedly rested her forehead against the edge of the shower door. Was she in the middle of a bad dream? Of all the rotten men in her life, why had she picked this bastard to star in her nightmare?

THE BASTARD was in the kitchen making a sandwich to settle his nervous stomach. There was something comforting in the mechanical assembly of layers. Bread. Mayo. Cheese. Meat. Tomato. Lettuce. Bread. On the counter, between the jar of mayo and the bag of sliced whole wheat, was a handgun. He'd brought it out of storage for reassurance.

He'd been startled by the information on the six o'clock news. While the suspect sketch was vague, the very fact that there was a description told him there was a witness to worry about. Switching from station to station, he'd waited for a name, but the police were holding that card close. Thankfully, no one had connected the most recent incidents to the earlier ones—not publicly at least. The diminutive FBI agent was the only one near to getting it right.

As always, he'd selected his prey carefully. With her frail form and fragile psyche, she'd been easy to manipulate and overpower. No one in her life cared enough about her to register her absence immediately. Those who did notice would dismiss her disappearance as a continuation of her pattern of unstable behavior. He had plenty of time to play with her before releasing her into the water.

Admittedly, with each woman he was feeling less and less satisfied. Rather than increasing his pleasure, pacing them closer together had frustrated him. He'd have to see if keeping one around before finishing her intensified his satisfaction.

Feeling generous, he fished two more slices of bread out of the bag and worked on assembling his guest a ham and Swiss. She'd need to keep her energy up for what he had planned. While he worked, he eyed the gun. Silly to take it out. Everything was fine. He'd put it back in the drawer before going upstairs.

BY THE TIME she heard him, it was too late for her to play possum. He stepped into the bathroom and gaped at his captive kneeling in front of the stall. He dropped the plate and in two strides was on top of her. She opened her mouth to scream, but all that escaped was a squeak. He slapped a hand over her open mouth, wrapped his arm around her nude body, and yanked her to her feet. "You've made a serious mistake," he hissed into her ear as he held her body to his.

She felt his erection through his pants, pressing into her back. It terrified her, and she bit down hard on his palm.

He pulled his hand off her mouth. "Bitch!"

"Help!" she screamed, her voice bouncing off the walls of the tiled cubicle. "Help me!"

"Go ahead! There's nobody close enough to hear you." Hooking his hand over her throat, he growled, "If I strangled you right now, nobody would care. You're of value to no one."

"Fuck you," she breathed.

His hand closed around her throat. "I could snap that skinny chicken neck like a matchstick."

"Please . . . don't," she wheezed. "I—promise . . . I—"

"What do you promise? Hmmm? Tell me."

"I'll give you—"

"Give me what? What can you possibly offer that I haven't already taken?" He cupped one hand over her breast and bunched the mound of flesh. "This is the only appealing thing about you, and even *that* is beginning to bore me."

"Please," she panted. She spotted her own reflection in the bathroom mirror and saw a pitiful stranger, her face red and contorted and her eyes wide with terror. Spittle dribbled down her chin. Her hair was a tangled bird's nest.

He caught her looking at herself in the mirror. "You used to be such a pretty, classy girl. Now look at you. You've let yourself go, darling." He released her, letting her fall forward on her face with a thud. "What was I thinking? You're nothing like her."

She moaned on the floor. A puddle of red was forming on the tile beneath her. She'd broken a tooth or her nose or both. Her entire face throbbed, and she wondered why the fall hadn't mercifully knocked her unconscious. As she turned her head to one side, she felt the blood smear across her cheek. The bastard was standing over her, examining his bitten hand. She wished she could have taken a chunk out of his testicles. "Let me go," she slurred, spraying blood along with the words. Eyeing the food spilled on the floor, she licked the blood off her lips and said, "I'm hungry."

"Good. I made you a light supper." He kicked the plate, smashing it against the wall.

She cringed as the stoneware shards ricocheted around. "Please. I'll eat it."

He stepped on the bread and meat, grinding it into the floor with the bottom of his shoe. "*Bon appétit*, ungrateful bitch."

She rolled onto her back and coiled her bound legs back, preparing to deliver a kick. "Fucker!"

"That's quite enough theatrics." He stepped into the shower stall and returned with the bar of soap, dotted with his pubic hair. He held it over her face.

"No," she said.

"Yes," he said, trapping her chin with one hand and stuffing the soap in her mouth with the other. "Eat that instead of the sandwich."

The feel of his hair in her mouth repulsed her more than the taste of the soap. She gagged and coughed out the soap, sending it bouncing across the tiles. The white bar was streaked with red.

He stepped over her to get to the tub. "You need a bath."

"Why?" she groaned, and closed her eyes tight. The question was addressed not to the man brutalizing her but to God. "Why?"

"I told you why," said her captor. "Weren't you listening, or are you too obtuse to comprehend?"

She heard the water start to pound the bottom of the tub. What had she done to deserve this? Was this some sort of retribution for the harm she'd done to her own body and soul? Was this her penance? "I'm sorry," she whispered to the heavens. "Forgive me."

"Too late for that," he said. "Save your breath. You're going to need it."

He actually thought she was apologizing to him, the sick bastard. She stayed still.

"Open your eyes," he said, and kicked her side. "Look at me."

She grimaced but didn't open her lids. She wouldn't give him the satisfaction.

Again and again, he kicked her. Each time he did it, it was accompanied by an order: "Open your eyes . . . Open your eyes, bitch . . . Look at me."

She'd win this round, even if it killed her.

"Stupid," he said, giving her one last kick.

Her side throbbed, but she felt a small victory. Then something splashed in her face, and her lids snapped open. Her face and eyes were searing with pain. He was emptying a bottle of aftershave on her. "Stop it," she sputtered, shaking her head back and forth.

"It lives," he said, continuing to pour.

"Don't." She shut her eyes and turned her head to one side. "Why are you doing this?"

"Doing what?" he asked, setting the empty bottle on the toilet tank.

"Let me go."

He loosened his tie, took it off, and draped it over the towel bar. He started to unbutton his shirt. "I'd hoped we could have a pleasant evening at home, the two of us."

"Let me go. I won't tell anyone. I promise."

"Some music. A little wine. More lovemaking." He peeled off his shirt and hung it from a hook on the back of the bathroom door.

"They're looking for me," she said. "The police. My friends. Everyone."

He laughed dryly. "Don't kid yourself."

She wished she'd black out and never regain consciousness. She sensed him moving around the bathroom and heard the squeak of the taps being closed.

"I think that's sufficiently deep," he said cheerfully.

The background music—the running water—was gone, and the silence made her gut churn. She felt his hands under her, lifting her off the floor. *This is it. He's going to drown me.* A sense of surrender washed over her, and she rested her head against his bare chest.

"You're finally behaving. Good girl," he purred into her ear. "Relax."

"Yes," she mumbled.

"Let me know if the water isn't hot enough," he said.

She felt him lowering her into the water and found it was pleasantly warm and scented. "Flowers," she murmured.

"Lavender," he said. "From an old girlfriend."

She felt his hands locking on her shoulders. He was preparing to push her under.

From an old girlfriend.

She remembered what he'd called her while he was raping her. She tipped her head backward and through blurry eyes saw his face suspended over her. She whispered three words she hoped would buy her time: "Ruth loved you."

His hands froze. "What did you say?"

She trained her eyes forward and repeated the words without emotion, to make them more believable. "Ruth loved you."

He took his hands off her shoulders. "You don't know anything about—"

"Yes, I do," she said calmly. "I know . . . everything."

"How?"

"We were friends."

His hands returned to her body. "That would have been years ago."

"I visited her. We stayed in touch."

Tightening his hold on her shoulders, he growled, "What did she look like?"

Hope started to clear her head. Her mind raced. Was Ruth a student? His childhood sweetheart? A slut he picked up in a bar six months ago? *What was I thinking? You're nothing like her.* She took a deep breath and told him what she figured he wanted to hear. "She was skinny like me, but prettier. Much prettier. Classy. Liked . . . classical music. Older than me." She braced herself, waiting for the hands to push her down into the water.

"Tell me more," he said, his voice and grip softening.

He wanted to believe her. *Good.* "She never stopped caring about you, but her father was—"

"He was a fiend."

"A regular bastard." She needed to get free before she ran out of bullshit or he snapped out of his delusional state. She held her arms up out of the water. "This tape hurts like hell."

A long silence behind her. His hands dropped from her shoulders. "I'll get some scissors."

"Thank you," she said, silently releasing a breath of relief.

"I'll untie you and dry you off and get you dressed. We can have a lovely conversation about our mutual friend. Our *Ruth*." He reached into the shower stall and returned with a washcloth in his hand.

Her body tensed. He wasn't quite finished with her, the sadistic son-of-a-bitch.

"But before I get the scissors, let me take the liberty of cleaning you up."

She sat up stiffly. "No, that's okay. I can do—"

"Sit back," he said firmly. "Open your legs."

She did as she was told, opening her legs as wide as she could with the tape binding her ankles and calves. Staring straight ahead, she feigned indifference while his hands and the washcloth traveled up her thighs. She concentrated on a particular tile across the room. It was cracked, with a spiderweb of damage spreading across it from the center to the edges.

"Am I making you uncomfortable?" he asked with a small smile.

She didn't know what would please him more, a yes or a no. She said nothing and returned her concentration to the spiderweb. She tried to visualize herself out of the water and on the web. She would be the spider, not the trapped fly.

He wrung out the cloth, lifted it up to her throat, and tied it around her neck from behind. "Ruth enjoyed the way I bathed her. Did she ever tell you?"

"No . . . she didn't," she stammered, feeling the cloth tighten around her throat.

He removed the threatening bandanna and dropped the cloth down to her breasts. "I find it hard to believe she didn't even mention it."

"Maybe she did." She kept her eyes ahead.

He left her breasts, bringing the rag to her face. "Open," he said.

She opened wide, and he fisted the cloth past her battered lips. She stifled one gag after another as he drove it deeper, grinding it into her mouth while he leered at her. The cloth tasted of mildew and soap.

"That should take care of that lying tongue." He finally pulled the cloth out of her mouth, and she released a whimper of relief.

"I'm not lying," she said weakly.

"Nonsense." He reached between her open legs to immerse the washcloth. "I know you're lying, but I'm going to take pity on you and let you live a little longer." He draped the cloth over the side of the tub, leaned close to her ear, and dropped his voice to a whisper. "You behaved so nicely during your bath, I'm going to cut your hands free and let you scrub yourself—under my direction. For my entertainment."

When he left her side to retrieve the scissors, locking the door after him, she slouched against the back of the tub and swallowed a sob.

Chapter 36

THE KILLER IS MOVING DOWN A DARK, NARROW SPACE. A HALL-
way. Pictures line both walls, but Bernadette's sight doesn't allow her
to make out their details. They're smears of color corralled inside
a series of tall rectangles. They could be priceless works of art or
framed beer posters.

He enters a bedroom and walks through it so quickly, she hardly
has time to take it in. Is it the bedroom she visited during her first
round with the scarf? She can't tell. He comes up to a door and in-
serts a key in the lock. He turns the knob and pushes the door open.
Closes it behind him.

White walls. White floor. White ceiling. A glass shower door. A
toilet and a pedestal sink. It's a bathroom. Why would he keep a
bathroom locked? There's a mirror over the sink, and Bernadette
wills the killer to step in front of it. He doesn't, of course.

He goes down beside the tub, and Bernadette's heart sinks. Water
doesn't mix well with this guy. It's an old claw-foot like her own;
she'd recognize the sleighlike shape anywhere. Someone is reclining
against the tub's sloped back. Long brown hair. Small oval face. The
bather is a woman. She's motionless. Is she dead? Did he get another

one while Bernadette was changing clothes and Garcia was eating a salami sandwich?

The bather sits up and raises her hands out of the water. He's got her tied. The bastard has a girl locked in the bathroom, tied in the tub. Bernadette braces herself, waiting to witness a drowning. Instead, she sees the killer's hands reaching for his prisoner's. Something flashes, a glint of steel. A knife? Is he slashing them now before he submerges them? Why isn't the woman fighting back? Has he drugged her?

He's cutting her binds, hacking at them. The prisoner helps, unraveling whatever is wrapped around her wrists. The stuff is gray. Must be duct tape, endorsed by homicidal maniacs everywhere.

She rubs her wrists while he watches and then points across the room, to the toilet. He hesitates, standing frozen with the blade in his hand. Then the girl leans back against the tub while he dips the knife in the water. He's working at slicing something at her feet. More duct tape. She raises the leg closest to him, and he unravels her binds. Drops them on the floor. She sits forward and does the other leg, extracting more gray matter from the water and dropping it on the floor.

Grabbing the edge of the tub for support, she raises herself out of the water. Wobbling, she uses a hand to steady herself against the bathroom wall. The woman is grossly thin, her milky figure lost against the white wall. Either she's one of the anorexic chicks this psycho favors or her captor has starved her to fit the part.

The psycho stands and offers her his free hand. She takes it and steps out of the tub. He turns to take a towel off a bar, lowering his knife hand as he does so. He spins back around.

Stick Woman is standing with the blade in her hand; she's snatched it! Bernadette fears for this girl; she's obviously too weak and slight to take this bastard. He doesn't move while the girl backs away from him, inching toward the door. Still facing him, she puts her hand behind her, feeling for the knob. Is the door locked? No. She pulls the door open and slips through while still holding the knife in front of her. She's gone. He starts after her. The door slams in his face. He throws it open and runs after his loose prey.

Bernadette sees the pale figure bounding through the bedroom and escaping out the door. Down the dark hall, bony arms and legs flapping madly. An animated Halloween skeleton. As she runs, she looks behind her. Big mistake. She stumbles into a hallway table, knocks it over, and nearly goes down. Rights herself and keeps going.

He's on her heels. Reaching out, he snags her hair. Her head snaps back. She spins around with the blade in her hand. He halts and holds his palms up in a gesture of surrender, taking a step back from her.

She turns her back to him and starts down the stairs. He goes after her. It's a long open staircase that takes a turn at a landing. The woman makes it to the landing but stumbles into a potted plant. Falls to her knees. The knife. What happened to the knife?

He's standing over her now. As she's scrambling to her feet, he plants his shoe on her lower back. She pitches forward and tumbles down the steps. Landing at the bottom with arms and legs splayed, she resembles a splatter of white paint against the wooden floor.

Bastard is taking his time coming after her. She must be so badly hurt, he's confident she can't run off. As he makes his way down the stairs, he looks past the pale, prone figure. What he sees sickens Bernadette: his captive has almost made it to the door.

He comes up next to Stick Woman and pokes her in the hip with the tip of his shoe. She stirs. Good. She's alive.

Slowly, she gathers her arms and legs under her and crawls to her feet. She looks him in the face. Her mouth is red, and it isn't lipstick. As she stands before him, she starts to totter and stagger backward. He steps toward her, catches her by the shoulder. Holding her up with one hand, he cranks back the other and punches her in the stomach. As she folds, he knees her in the face. She flips onto her back and curls into a tight, white ball. He kicks her again and reaches for something on the floor.

The knife.

BERNADETTE INHALED sharply and instinctively opened her hand, dropping the scarf and inadvertently severing the connection. She retrieved the fabric and closed her fist around it again. "Return to me, return to me."

Garcia hovered over her, saying nothing.

"I lost it." She bunched the scarf in her hand and hurled it down.

"What did you see?"

The murderer's emotions were rising inside Bernadette, and this time no passion tempered the anger. It took every ounce of self-control for her to swallow back the rage and answer Garcia civilly. "He's got another victim. I saw him running her down."

"What do you mean?"

"She was tied up and sitting in a tub. He cut her loose, and she bolted. He caught up with her and shoved her down the stairs."

"Christ."

"As if that wasn't enough, he's beating her. This skinny, naked chick. He's punching the crap out of her." Holding out her hand, she saw that she was trembling—either from the shock of what she'd witnessed or the extreme effort it was taking to rein in her emotions.

"Is she dead?"

"I don't know. If she isn't now, she soon will be. We have to find her."

"Is this happening right now, or did it happen earlier?"

"I think it's now." She checked her watch. "I get the sense this is real time."

"What did she look like? Can you give any kind of description?"

He knew her sight was usually too foggy for details. "She was white. Skinny as a bird. Long brown hair. The prof didn't give me a description of this Regina Ordstruman, but it's gotta be her."

"So Wakefielder wasn't lying."

She picked up the evidence bag and dropped the scarf back inside it. She extended her hand to him. "We gotta move on this thing."

BY THE TIME they got back to her loft, the killer's anger had dissipated, but Bernadette remained dizzy. She went into the bathroom and splashed cold water on her face. "Let's go over to the house!" she yelled through the open door.

"Which one? Was he chasing her around a houseboat or a mansion?"

She thought about it and ruled out the houseboat; it didn't have a second floor. Also, Matthew's girlfriend would have seen it if her boy was holding another woman. "Let's go to the doctor's place," Bernadette said, blotting her face with a towel. "We can look for blood."

Garcia came up behind her and stood in the bathroom doorway. "Blood? The beating was that bad?"

"That bad." She wobbled past him and headed to the kitchen.

"You look like hell," he said, following her.

She took her jean jacket off the back of a chair and slipped it on. "Let's get going."

He put on his trench. "Should we call for backup?"

She checked her Glock. "When we're sure we have the right house."

"Is he alone?"

She pulled on her gloves. "I didn't see anyone except the victim."

"Is he armed?"

She started for the door. "Didn't see a gun. He had a knife."

Garcia was right behind her. "He was getting ready to cut her?"

"Yeah," she said, and pulled the door open.

THEY TOOK Garcia's car. She knew the Grand Am was up for the race; Garcia had won the loaded heap at a police auction. It was tempting to give him grief about not taking a company car, but by the glow of the dashboard she could see his face was tense. He was in no mood for giving or receiving any crap as he piloted the Pontiac through downtown.

"What if he won't let us in?" she asked. "We really don't have enough to—"

"He'll let us in." With a squeal, he steered around a slow-moving sedan.

"What leverage have we got?"

He turned onto Interstate 94 heading west. "The sister. What was her name again?"

"Ruth."

"I'll tell him we're opening an investigation into her death. If what you said is true, that isn't a line of bullshit. You can chime in with tidbits you picked up at the nursing home. Make it sound like we know what we're talking about."

She eyed the speedometer and was impressed. The sled had wings. "He could refer us to his lawyers and slam the door in our faces."

"Or he'll be so upset at the mere mention of the dead sister, he'll soil his trousers and let us inside." He slowed behind a taxi and swerved around it.

"You're being optimistic," she said.

"If by some miracle we get through the front door, where was most of the action taking place?"

"It started in an upstairs bathroom and ended on the first floor, at the bottom of the stairs. I couldn't tell if they were Luke Von-Hader's stairs, though. There was a landing at the killer's house. I don't remember if there was one at the doc's. The wood was the same. Dark banisters and floor." She balled her fists in her lap and glanced out the passenger's window. "I wish my sight could be more precise."

"Me, too," he said shortly.

The drove in silence after that, until he muscled the Grand Am onto the exit ramp. "Reach under your seat," he told her.

She bent over and retrieved a flashlight. "What do we need this for?"

"We'll scope out the place before we knock," he said, turning left and heading south toward Summit Avenue. "We might see something that would justify busting down the door."

She clicked the flashlight on and off and dropped it into her jacket pocket. "Like a body in the foyer?"

"A body in the foyer would do it."

Chapter 37

AS THEY ENTERED THE DOCTOR'S PROPERTY THROUGH THE back gate, they saw that the windows at the rear of the house were dark. Crouching down and hugging the side of the building, the two agents circled the stone mansion once and returned to the backyard. The entire place appeared devoid of light and movement.

Pulling the flashlight out of her jacket pocket, she went over to the garage—an old carriage house—and shined the beam through one of the windows. The light bounced off a sea of silver surfaces. Lexus. Volvo. Jag. "That's interesting," she muttered.

"What?" whispered Garcia, standing behind her and sharing her view through the window.

"The sedan and the wagon belong to Luke."

"So he's home."

Training the beam on the sports car, she said, "But that silver bullet is Little Brother's ride."

"They're both here."

She clicked off the light and looked over her shoulder at Garcia. "Which means if there's a body in the foyer, they're both culpable."

While the carriage house had no outside lighting, the neighbors on both sides had bright lights mounted on their garages, making it easy to read the concern on Garcia's face. "Time to call for backup," he said, slipping his hand inside his trench coat.

"Not yet. Let's keep looking around."

He paused. "Fine."

Reaching inside her jacket, she unsnapped her holster and took out her Glock. "You stay here in case they try to slip out the back."

Nodding in agreement, he took out his weapon.

She left Garcia in the backyard and went around to the side of the house. Bernadette ran her eyes up and down the sidewalk and street that ran past the front of the house. There were a few parked vehicles on both sides of the street, but no traffic from cars or pedestrians. It was a quiet residential neighborhood that wouldn't see any action until dawn. That was good. She had a feeling this saga wasn't going to have a tidy ending.

She entered the front yard and squatted behind one of the marble lions. Looking up, she noticed a light in a second-story window over the porch. Had they missed it? Didn't matter. Someone was up and about. Bernadette wanted to confront whoever it was before Garcia called the cavalry. As she was contemplating her next move, her cell vibrated. She fished it out. "What?" she whispered.

Garcia said, "I see a light upstairs."

"Me, too."

"Now what?"

A light downstairs flicked on.

After a long silence on his end, Garcia said, "Someone's in the kitchen. I can see their silhouette through the curtains. I think it's a guy. Big guy."

She hoped they stayed there for a while. "I'm going onto the front porch. Call if the kitchen light goes off or you see him leave the room."

"Careful."

"Right," she said, readjusting her grip on her gun. She closed the phone and dropped it into her pocket. Leaving the lions, she tiptoed up the front steps and put her hand on the porch door. It was unlocked. She went inside, closing the door carefully. She eyed the statues crowding the floor space. The collection of stone figures reminded her of a New Orleans cemetery, with its aboveground tombs. "Cities of the Dead," the graveyards were called. The VonHaders had a Porch of the Dead. She paid no mind to the camera, confident the thing was as dead as during her previous visit.

She went over to the windows and peeked inside. There was a fire going in the fireplace. A man in a robe was bending down in front of the blaze; Bernadette couldn't make out his face. She went back to the door and tried to peer inside through the small window but couldn't see a thing. She put her gun in her jacket and raised her fist to knock. The porch light flicked on; the security camera had been working after all.

Bernadette felt her phone vibrate again. She quickly took it out, flipped it open, shut it off, and dropped it back in her pocket. Hands folded demurely in front of her, she stood before the door waiting for someone to appear. Behind her, the screen door creaked open. She spun around and saw Garcia. His eyes went to the porch light above her head, then to the security camera mounted on the wall. Taking his cue from her, he pocketed his gun and stood next to her, facing the door.

They heard a deadbolt crack and then the door opened.

Standing shoulder to shoulder were the two brothers, the younger one dressed in a bathrobe. His hair was damp, and he had a glass of whiskey in his hand. His eyes were bloodshot. "We need to talk," she said to the pair.

"This was a long time coming," said the older man. He stepped back and opened the door wider for the two agents.

Garcia extended his hand to the doctor, who was dressed in khakis and a sweater but had slippers on his feet. "Assistant Special Agent in Charge Anthony Garcia."

Luke VonHader gave Garcia a firm handshake and turned around. "Let's take this into the kitchen."

While Garcia and the brothers went ahead, Bernadette stalled to scrutinize the foyer and the base of the stairs. The wooden floors were spotless, with no signs of blood. She eyed the staircase leading to the second floor. It was long, wide, and ornate, with carved spindles and a glossy banister. It was similar to what she'd observed with her sight, but the doctor's staircase seemed to have no landing. She needed to be sure. "May I use the restroom?" she asked as she trailed behind the three men.

Matthew set his glass on a foyer table. "Go on ahead, gentlemen. I'll show the lady to the facilities."

Garcia and Luke disappeared into the back of the house. Being separated from her boss gave Bernadette a twinge of discomfort. The doctor was taller than both his drunken sibling and Garcia, and he was stone sober. She reassured herself that Garcia was more muscular than either man and carried a big gun.

Matthew headed for the stairs. "This way, Agent Scully."

She gave one last glance to the lighted room in back of the house and followed the tipsy smartass up the steps. "If you point me in the right direction, I'm sure I can find it all by my lonesome," she said to his back.

Without turning around, he responded, "That would leave you free to snoop around, wouldn't it?"

"Exactly," she said as she scouted the steps for blood.

He hiccupped a laugh. "At least you're being honest this time."

She took notice of the artwork lining the staircase wall. The signature on the rendition of a dusty cowboy ranch looked familiar. "Is that an authentic Remington?"

"Frederic Remington, James Edward Buttersworth, George Henry Durrie," he said, waving his arm. He could have been ticking off the cereal selection in his kitchen cupboard.

Though Bernadette had snoozed through most of college art history, she recognized those names as important American painters. "Your brother is quite a collector."

"My parents were the collectors," he said as they reached the second-floor hallway. "My brother and I are stuck being the curators."

She remembered that Luke had had a similar complaint. "Most people would kill to inherit such treasures," she said.

"In a sense, we did," he said ominously.

Her eyes widened. "Is there something you want to tell me?"

More art hung from the hallway walls, and he ignored her question to point out the pieces. "Here we have a hand-signed print by Marc Chagall. That's hand-colored lithography by Currier and Ives. Those are all numbered and signed artist proofs by Norman Rockwell. A little too Main Street for my palate, but Mother and Father liked that sort of thing. They were all about the wholesome American family."

His voice carried a bitterness that alarmed her. "Matt, maybe we could talk. Just the two of us."

He stopped in front of a door in the middle of the hall and pushed it open. "I'll leave you to whatever it is you want to do up here. Wash your hands. Powder your nose. Dust for prints. I'll be downstairs with the menfolk."

She watched him head down the hall, his shoulders sagging, his gait unsteady. She found him more pathetic than menacing.

Scanning the second floor, she saw it wasn't anything like what she'd observed through her sight. The entire upstairs was ringed by railing, allowing all the rooms to look down onto the first floor. The corridor traveled by the killer had solid walls on both sides.

She walked into the hallway bathroom. She knew it wouldn't be the one she'd observed. For starters, the bathroom from which the young woman had fled had emptied into a bedroom, not a hall. Instead of a claw-foot tub, the doctor had a modern Jacuzzi. Instead of white walls, Luke VonHader had ornate wallpaper hung with framed art. She scanned the bottom of the tub, but found nothing more suspicious than a collection of children's toys: headless Barbie dolls, beach buckets, sand shovels, rubber ducks. The surface of the tub looked bone dry. She went over to a stall with a glass door—the only feature even remotely similar to what she'd conjured through her sight—and popped it open. The floor was wet. Not a surprise.

The robed Matthew had probably just used the shower. Was there a chance he'd been washing off blood? She studied the tiles on the floor and the grout between them and found no stains.

Bernadette opened the medicine cabinet and surveyed the contents. Tylenol and sinus tablets and bars of soap and shaving cream and a disposable razor. A few of the wife's cosmetics and perfumes. She took down the sole prescription bottle: amoxicillin, for the girls' ear infections. She put the bottle back and closed the cabinet, another fixture that wasn't in the killer's bathroom. He'd had only an oval mirror over the sink. Encased in dry cleaner's plastic, a set of the doctor's shirts hung from the back of the bathroom door. This was a messy family bathroom, not a murder site.

She quickly made the circuit around the second floor, poking her head inside one bedroom after another. None of them matched the sparsely furnished one Bernadette had seen during her first round with the scarf. The sleeping quarters were filled with dressers and nightstands and blanket chests. Armoires and tallboys and lowboys and vanities. Perched atop the tables and chests and dressers were vases and statues and linens and quilts.

The only things distinguishing the little girls' room from the other antique parlors were the mermaid spreads on the matching twin beds. Shuddering, she tried to imagine a childhood spent suffocating in this sea of old stuff. It all felt like a heavy weight pressing down on her, and she was only a visitor. She was starting to understand the brothers' resentment toward their parents.

The largest bedroom—it had to be the master—was the most jammed of all. Two veneered chests stood next to each other. A dark old armchair was parked in front of a cherrywood dressing table. On each side of the bed was a marble-topped nightstand. Nearly every inch of wall space was plastered with framed art. Taking up the center of one wall was a massive fireplace, its mantel crowded with old oil lanterns like the fireplace mantel downstairs.

Poking her head inside the master bathroom, she spotted another Jacuzzi tub, plus a marble-topped vanity with two modern sinks.

Satisfied that the doctor's home wasn't the killing ground, Bernadette started for the stairs, wondering how much she'd gotten wrong over the past week. But a woman had been kidnapped, and they had to find her.

When she walked into the kitchen, she saw Luke and Matthew VonHader seated on the same side of the table. The brothers were in handcuffs. Her boss stood across from them, holding his gun on the pair.

"Call the police, Agent Saint Clare," said Garcia.

"Yes, sir." Bernadette retrieved her cell with one hand and took her gun out of her pocket with the other.

While she punched the numbers on her phone, Bernadette's eyes went from one brother to the other. The expressions on their faces were calm, almost relieved. While she spoke into the cell, the room was silent. She noticed it was a small but bright kitchen, so unlike the rest of the house.

When she was finished with the dispatcher, she closed the phone and asked the question she'd been asking herself from the minute she stepped inside. "Where's the body?"

"In the ground," Garcia said grimly.

"So they killed—"

"Their father," said Garcia.

Chapter 38

THE BROTHERS TOOK TURNS RECOUNTING THE STORY. IT WAS a smooth retelling, almost practiced. Bernadette wondered how many times one had talked the other out of going to the authorities with it.

"Our parents were good people," said Luke VonHader, his voice a monotone and his eyes fixed at some invisible target beyond the agents. "They went to church. Made sure we went."

"Ten o'clock mass every Sunday," said Matthew, his lids lowered as if he were nodding off.

"They put us in Catholic school," Luke continued. "We had golf lessons. Tennis lessons. Piano. Growing up, we had everything."

"All three of us, nothing but the best," said Matthew.

"Someplace warm during Christmas break," said the doctor. "Come the summer, a big family vacation. France. Scotland. Denmark. We went to Ireland three times."

"Four times," his younger brother corrected him. He looked from one agent to the other. "Can I have a drink? I could really use a drink."

Garcia shook his head and addressed the doctor. "What went wrong?"

"Time. There was just no time," said Luke, dragging his hand across his face. "My parents were busy. Father worked sixty hours a week. Mother had her volunteer work. Her charities and antiquing. They didn't have time for traditional discipline. They were older and less patient, I suppose. They'd waited to have a family. With three high-spirited children, they took the quickest, most effective route to taming them. It was humane, in a sense. It left no marks. The worst you could accuse them of is—I don't know—lazy parenting."

"They weren't sane," said Matthew. "You of all people should be able to see that now."

"Shut the hell up," snapped the doctor.

Matthew turned to Bernadette. "Why would two otherwise fine people resort to water torture as a form of child discipline? They had to be *crazy*." He looked at his brother with that last word, a term a psychiatrist would find vulgar, and repeated it with a smirk. "*Crazy.*"

"How did your parents do it?" asked Garcia.

"It was very civilized," Luke said flatly. "Everyone had their role. Mother would fill the tub with cold water. Why waste hot water, right? Father was the judge, jury, and executioner. He determined who would receive the dunking and who of the other children would witness it."

"Witness it?" Garcia asked. "Why a witness?"

Matthew shrugged. "I suppose to lend some sort of validity to it, a modicum of ceremony and propriety."

"We offenders would put our hands behind us and lean over the side of the tub," Luke continued. "Our sister usually tied her hair back herself, when she was the one being punished. Then Father would hold our heads under. The length of time we were held, the number of dunkings—all of that was up to Father. The more serious the offense, the worse the punishment. When we were toddlers, I imagine the length of time we were held in the water was minimal. As we got older—"

"Everyone was okay with this?" Garcia interrupted. "I can't believe your mother went along."

"Mother had experienced this sort of discipline at the hands of her parents," said Luke. "She had no lasting physical damage and saw nothing wrong with using it on her own children."

"You kids didn't fight back?" asked Bernadette. "Why didn't you run away or tell someone? You could have gone to a teacher. Another relative. A neighbor."

Matthew sighed. "It had been a part of the fabric of our family for so long, we thought it was normal. We tolerated the dunkings the way other children accepted spankings or time-outs or getting grounded."

Bernadette's eyes narrowed as she addressed her next question to the doctor. "Have you used this on your kids?"

"Never," he shot back. "I now recognize it as perverted. Abusive."

"That revelation comes too late to help your sister," said Garcia.

"You think we don't beat ourselves up with that thought every day?" Matthew asked.

"Every minute of every day," said Luke, his voice cracking. He dropped his head and his shoulders started vibrating.

Bernadette ripped a paper towel off a roll and tossed it to the weeping man.

"Save the boohoos for the jury," said Garcia.

Bernadette shot a curious look at her boss.

"They're leaving something out of this sob story." Garcia tipped his head toward the doctor. "Tell her. Go ahead."

Luke stayed silent.

"One of them killed their father," Garcia explained. "Pushed him down the stairs. Told the cops the old guy fell."

Bernadette, leaning her back against the counter, kept her gun on the pair. "Which one did it?"

Luke wiped his eyes while his younger sibling slouched in his seat. Neither man volunteered an answer.

"They're fighting over who gets credit," said Garcia.

She smiled tightly. "Sibling rivalry."

"I did it," Matthew blurted.

"He's lying," said his older brother, bunching the paper towel between his cuffed hands. "It was my call. He'd had a stroke . . . and I . . . wanted to put him out of his misery."

Garcia said, "Who are you kidding? You hated his guts."

Bernadette walked back and forth between the counter and the table. "Who raised his hand first?"

"Matthew confessed first," said Garcia.

Bernadette studied the younger brother's face. He'd never expressed the understanding of his parents' behavior that his older brother had voiced. "Matthew did it, and the doc stepped in after Little Brother blabbed."

Luke shook his head. "You're wrong."

"We'll see who passes the polygraph and who doesn't down at the police station," said Garcia.

"That brotherly love thing again," she said. "It's serving them well—all the way to the jailhouse."

"Speak of the devil," said Garcia, seeing lights flashing across the kitchen windows.

Bernadette dropped her gun into her jacket pocket, went to the back door, and opened it. She held up her ID for two uniformed officers planted on the back stoop. "Can you give us a few minutes before you load them?"

The bigger cop looked into the kitchen and saw the two handcuffed men seated at the kitchen table. "Sure. This is your deal." He glanced over at Garcia and said, "Hey."

"Hey," said Garcia.

"You're Ed's cousin, right?" asked the cop. "Ed in Homicide?"

"You betcha," said Garcia. "Tell him I'm sending him a package."

The officer gave Garcia a crooked grin. "We'll hang out on the back steps."

"Appreciate it," said Bernadette, closing the kitchen door.

Seeing the officers jolted Matthew awake, and he was suddenly twitching in his seat. "Kyra Klein and the drownings in the river, we had nothing to do with those." He nodded toward Garcia. "He says we did, but we didn't."

The horrific family history that the brothers had recounted at the kitchen table, paired with the April death of their sister, had to have some association with the murders. There was too much to be a co-incidence. "Even if you didn't do it, you know who did," Bernadette told Matthew.

While the younger brother had touched back down to reality, his older sibling was drifting off. Drumming his fingers on top of the kitchen table, the doctor said in an eerily mechanical voice, "This is an early Victorian mahogany dining table. The piece is supported on beautifully proportioned fluted legs and came with two extra leaves, allowing it to extend to a length of nearly ten feet. It came with eight matching chairs, all but one with the original upholstery. I remember the day she picked up the set, at a well-attended auction outside of Chicago."

"Your mother?" asked Garcia.

"The instant she laid her eyes on it, she had to have it. She called home so excited. She beat out two other bidders." Luke meshed his fingers together, as if praying. "That same day my sister suffered a fall at the nursing home. Someone had dropped her during a bed transfer, breaking both her legs. When we told our mother, she acted as if we'd bothered her with some minor annoyance. We'd chipped a vase. The neighbor's dog had excavated one of her rosebushes."

"Doctor, please," said Bernadette. "We need your help."

"How?" asked Matthew. "How can he help? Tell us."

The younger brother sounded sincere. Bernadette pulled out a chair and sat down across the table from the pair. "I believe someone close to your sister snapped when she died. He's drowning these girls as some sort of—I don't know—reenactment or something."

"An old boyfriend?" asked Garcia.

Luke shook his head.

"Could I have a drink . . . of water at least," Matthew croaked.

Bernadette got up, took down a glass from a cupboard, and went to the refrigerator. As she pressed the glass into the water dispenser, she scrutinized the Catholic mosaic decorating the front of the refrigerator. Handmade magnets in the shapes of crosses and flowers, undoubtedly produced by the doctor's young daughters, held up church bulletins, fall fest raffle tickets, and Sunday school artwork.

Bernadette eyed one of the rare magnets not fabricated by a child's fingers. "What's this number?"

"What?" asked Luke.

She pulled the glass out of the dispenser and plucked the red octagon off the fridge. She set the water in front of Matthew and the magnet in front of his brother.

"My Suicide Stop Line," Luke mumbled.

"You call if you have thoughts of suicide?" she asked.

"Yes." He lifted his head. "Why?"

"Professor Wakefielder has been passing similar stickers out. A couple of the dead girls had this number. There's the intersection between the prof and Dr. VonHader." She walked around the kitchen table. "Who staffs the hotline?"

"Volunteers," Matthew answered. "I've done it a few times."

"Who else?"

"A slew of people," answered Luke.

Garcia asked, "Where are you going with this?"

Bernadette said, "Do any of the volunteers also work in your office?"

"Several," said Luke, his eyes wide and unblinking.

"Do any know the real story behind your sister's institutionalization?"

"What?" Matthew blurted.

"It would have to be someone who knew how she first landed in the nursing home," said Bernadette. "Who else knew about the . . . water discipline?"

"No one else," said Matthew. "She was taking a bath by herself. Somehow went under. That was the story. We stuck to it all those years, even after Mother and Father passed away. Sometimes I wondered if it wasn't the truth, we'd been saying it for so long."

"You never told anyone else?" asked Garcia.

"We confided in no one," Luke offered. "We trusted no one. It was only the two of us, and . . . Ruth."

Bernadette noticed it was the first time anyone in the kitchen had uttered the dead woman's name, and the word seemed to hang in the air like a cloud left behind by a smoker. *Ruth*. She was dead, as were so many other women. Shelby. Kyra. Corrine. Monica. Alice. Judith. Laurel. Heidi. She had no idea if Zoe belonged on the same list. Now another one was out there, waiting to be rescued—or buried. Regina.

"Think," Bernadette said impatiently. "Perhaps someone overheard the two of you talking about Ruth. Someone at your office who also worked on the help line. Maybe you didn't know they heard, but this person took a sudden interest in your sister. Asked questions. Even started visiting her in the nursing home."

"Oh, God," blurted Luke.

"What?" Garcia and Bernadette asked in unison.

"He had a crush on her," Luke said. "Always had a crush on her, since they were kids."

"Who?" Bernadette asked.

"But he never saw or heard anything," Matthew said to his older brother.

Luke, his voice tremulous, added: "I caught him in the hall once, after one of her punishments. A bad one. He'd come into the kitchen and wandered upstairs. I didn't think he saw anything. But his face, it was euphoric."

"Is that when he started coming over more?" Matthew asked him.

"Yes," Luke said numbly.

Garcia frowned at Bernadette. "Who are they—"

She held up her hand to silence her boss. The brothers were immersed in a trancelike exchange with each other. An outsider interrupting with a question might break the spell. Make them clam up.

Matthew, nodding slowly, said, "I remember. Suddenly, he was hanging around more. Our new best friend. Always walking in like he owned the place."

Luke replied, "Mother and Father didn't mind because both his parents were patients. Some sort of post-loss depression. They went to our church, too. Nice family."

"Bullshit," said Matthew. "The Araignees were as fucked up as our parents. Don't you remember how they beat him? He'd come over with welts and bruises."

"He got work as an aide at the nursing home," said Luke. "He was always hanging around her room, even on his days off. I thought he was being a friend. After she died, he lost interest in the job. Came to work in my office."

"Told you there was something wrong with him, but you trusted him because he plays golf and listens to public radio." Matthew sneered at his older sibling. "You had him answering your phones, talking to those needy women, working on your precious suicide line."

"I didn't know," Luke rasped.

Matthew snarled into his brother's ear: "You've been his goddamn dating service."

"Oh my God," said Bernadette. It made sense.

"What?" asked Garcia, looking from Bernadette to the two handcuffed men. "Who are they talking about?"

"Wasn't enough you hooked him up with the women in town here," Matthew sneered. "You had to send him across state lines, to those classes in Wisconsin. How many girls there do you suppose he—"

"When?" interrupted Bernadette. "When was he in Wisconsin?"

Luke shook his head.

"July and August," Matthew said.

"The La Crosse murders," Bernadette said numbly.

"Who are they talking about?" asked Garcia.

"C.A." She pushed back her chair and stood up. "Snaky son-of-a-bitch."

Chapter 39

GARCIA STEERED THE PONTIAC BACK ON INTERSTATE 94 heading east and came to a dead stop as they neared the outskirts of downtown St. Paul. "Terrific," he said.

"There must be an accident," she said, trying to look around the minivan in front of them.

Traffic inched forward enough for Garcia to take an exit. "I'm getting off this parking lot."

The downtown roads were as snarled as the interstate. "Don't people stay in anymore?" Bernadette muttered, glaring through the passenger window at a knot of diners leaving a restaurant.

Garcia, screeching around a slow-moving compact, said, "Some folks have a life."

She relaxed a little when they finally got on the Wabasha Bridge, aiming for a St. Paul neighborhood just south of downtown. Bluffs dotted with trees overlooked downtown and the river. Beyond the trees were homes, including one belonging to Charles Araignee, receptionist moonlighting as a serial killer. She'd considered him a bit player in this drama—the doctor's errand boy—and now he was turning out to be the main attraction. The first time she'd even heard his last name was when the brothers uttered it at the kitchen table.

The spiders in her dream finally made sense: *Araignée* was French for "spider."

Unlike downtown, there were few cars on the road and no one on the sidewalks. On the right was a green tower containing steps that started at the top of the bluffs and led straight down to Wabasha. The structure reminded her of a forest ranger's fire lookout.

When they got to Prospect Boulevard, the street that topped the bluffs, Garcia pulled the Grand Am to the curb and turned off the engine. The agents silently surveyed their surroundings. A knee-high stone wall ran along the top of the bluff, and at one end of the stone barrier was a sidewalk that led to the green tower. The lighting in the neighborhood was like that around the rest of the city, with green poles topped by antique-looking lamps. While there was enough light to see down the streets and sidewalks, the wooded bluff beyond the stone wall was black. No homes were perched along the sides of the hill itself. At the very bottom were caves dug into the sides of the hill. They were once used for a variety of ventures (Bernadette remembered reading something once about a mushroom grower), but now most of them were filled in. It was a strange slice of St. Paul that seemed better suited to a wilderness area than to a city.

"What was the address again?" asked Garcia as he shoved his car keys in his coat pocket.

She fished a yellow square out of her pocket and tipped the note toward the light cast by the streetlamp. "The doc said Chaz doesn't live on the boulevard. He's on one of the streets running behind it."

Garcia reached under his seat and pulled out the *Hudson's Street Atlas*, flipped until he got to the neighborhood, and handed it to her. "We should have called for backup."

"We'll call when we get there," she said as she studied the map. After taking so many wrong turns in this case, she wanted to make sure Charles was indeed holding Regina Ordstruman at his home and not at another location. It'd be an embarrassment to the bureau and a humiliation to Garcia in particular if an army descended on an empty house.

"You know where we're going?" he asked.

"Yeah." She closed the book and dropped it on the seat between them.

"Okay." He reached past his coat and blazer, took out his Glock, and slipped it into his trench pocket.

She popped open the passenger door and reached inside her jacket pocket to touch her gun. "I'm ready."

As they stepped out of the car, Bernadette felt the nighttime scenery rock and tilt. She could have been standing on the deck of a boat. Waiting for the sensation to pass, she kept her hand on the open door of the Pontiac.

As he shut the driver's door, Garcia looked at her. "Are you okay?"

"Something's going on with this guy, and it's happening to me, too." She steadied herself and closed the passenger door.

Garcia came around to her side of the Grand Am with his cell in his hand. "I'm going to—"

"Don't call anyone yet."

"Are you going to be any good to me?"

"I'm fine."

"Your session with the scarf was hours ago," said Garcia, dropping his phone back in his pocket. "Why are you still picking up vibes from this asshole?"

"I have no idea." A gust of wind sent leaves tumbling down the sidewalk. Shivering, she snapped her jacket closed up to her throat and pulled her gloves tighter over her fingers. She swore her tolerance for the cold had diminished since her tumble into the river.

"How far?" asked Garcia as they crossed the quiet street.

"A couple of blocks," she said.

"Same drill as with the VonHader boys," said Garcia as they went down the sidewalk. "We'll scope it out before we make any big moves. If he's not home . . ."

"Then he's got her somewhere else."

"You're sure he's got someone?"

She hated hearing that doubt in his voice. No wonder he'd given up so readily on calling for backup. "If you don't believe my sight, believe the prof. Wakefielder's got a student missing."

After less than a block of walking, her chills turned into a hot sweat. She unsnapped her jean jacket and let the wind buffet her body. As the cold seeped through her shirt and hardened her nipples, another sensation invaded her body: lust. It had to be him again. She'd never had such an enduring and intense link to a killer. With previous murderers, she'd shared feelings so briefly. Why Charles was different dumbfounded her. Getting rid of him and his sick psyche was going to be a tremendous relief.

Reaching the corner, she scrutinized the street sign to make sure they were headed in the right direction. "One more block," she said, and they kept going.

After a few minutes of silence, Garcia blurted: "Your work on this case—"

She cut him off with a wave of her hand. "Don't go there, Tony. I know I screwed this up from the get-go."

"What are you talking about?"

"The prof did it. Matt did it. No, wait, Luke did it. Maybe they all three did it. Shit. It's none of them. The fucking butler did it."

"You nailed it in the end," he said. "The brothers are at the cop shop."

"Yes, but not for the dead girls. Plus the VonHaders' attorney will get them home in time for their morning Wheaties."

"But we're on our way to bagging the worst bad guy. It's all good."

"That's why you keep asking if I'm sure he's got another victim with him."

"I believe you."

He sounded unconvinced, but she let it go.

Every other home they passed had decorations in the yard or on the porch. Plastic tombstones. Rubber skeletons. Witches on broomsticks. Carved pumpkins. Bales of hay. Dried cornstalks propped against fences and dried ears of corn tacked to front doors. "When's Halloween?" she asked.

"I don't know; it's coming up."

"We don't have a life, do we?" They hung a right, both of them walking briskly while eyeing the houses around them and the collection of cars parked on the street. No one was out and about.

Charles's place was the last house on a dead-end street. The Von-Haders told them that he had inherited some money from an aunt and had used it to buy and refurbish the place. Unfortunately, they'd never been inside and couldn't give the agents a layout of the interior.

Standing at the top of a steeply graded lot, it was perched like a castle. In the valley on one side of Charles's place was a boarded-up house. In the dip on the other side was a patch of hardwoods and evergreens, a natural barrier that made up the dead end.

A sedan was parked on the street in front of Charles's house, and Bernadette figured it was his. It was an old gold Lincoln Town Car without a spot of rust on it, probably another inheritance from the aunt. She went over to the windows facing the sidewalk, pulled out a small flashlight, and looked inside. Immaculate. She punched off the light and dropped it back in her pocket.

They climbed the long steps leading up to his doorstep but stopped and crouched down before they reached the top. His home was one of the largest in the neighborhood, with an open porch stretched across the front. It was a two-story structure with a tower in front that could contain a third-floor room.

"A Victorian," she whispered. "Queen Anne style."

"Listen to the architecture expert."

"The windows in front are black," she observed.

"Let's go in around back, through the woods," Garcia said. "If we stay low, we should be good."

They took the steps down and darted into the woods, going from tree to tree until they could see Charles's backyard. A wooden privacy fence boxed it in, but there was a gate facing the woods. Planted on one side of the gate was a lamppost; Bernadette didn't like how bright it was. An alley ran behind the fence, and beyond that were the garages of the neighbors. Some of them had floodlights mounted over their doors. It looked like Charles didn't have a garage.

The pair hiked up the hill leading to the backyard and went to the gate. It was unlocked, and they slipped inside. A screened porch ran across the back, and a bright floodlight was mounted over the porch door. As the pair walked deeper into the yard, she could see that a small square and a large rectangle on the second story were lit.

"He's home," she whispered, pointing up.

Garcia nodded. They spotted a garden shed planted in a far corner of the yard and squatted down next to it. "Now what?" he whispered.

"Stay here," she whispered.

Before he could argue, she ran for the back of the house. She hadn't picked a lock in some time and hoped she could instead get inside the easy way. She spotted a doormat in front of the porch's bottom step and lifted it up. Nothing underneath. She retrieved a rock sitting to the right of the steps and checked the bottom but didn't find what she was looking for. The stone next to it was a dud, too, but the third rock she tried was the charm. She pried off a trap door in the fake rock and probed the compartment with her finger. "Good deal," she muttered, fishing out a key.

The screen door was locked, but it took only a few jiggles of the handle to unlock it. Holding tight to the door so the wind wouldn't slap it open, she went through and closed it behind her. She ran her eyes around the long, narrow space. Wicker chairs, couches, and coffee tables were neatly grouped, as if awaiting a party. Dried floral arrangements and candles topped each of the tables. Hanging from the ceiling, swaying slightly in the wind, was a chandelier containing tapered candles. Oriental area rugs covered the floor. The creep's porch was furnished more stylishly than her condo.

Bernadette went up to one of the windows and pressed her face against the glass. The curtains on the other side blocked her view.

Taking a deep breath, she stepped up to the door and inserted the key in the lock. She could feel the deadbolt turn. She put her hand on the knob and pushed the heavy wooden door open. A narrow band of white—the floodlight—followed her inside. She heard a creak behind her and turned to see Garcia stepping inside, carefully closing the porch door behind him.

They moved directly into the kitchen, a renovated galley. A butcher-block table was in the middle of the space, and modern glass-front cabinetry and steel appliances lined the walls. Heavy footsteps overhead made her freeze. She thought she heard music as well.

She closed the door behind her and turned the deadbolt; she didn't want to make it easy for him to flee. Garcia watched her hands but said nothing.

Moving carefully across the wooden floor, they headed for the door at the far end of the kitchen, with Garcia taking point. The kitchen's old-fashioned swinging doors opened into the formal dining area, a space with a long table surrounded by antique chairs. Then came a front room. Looking to the right through the parlor, they could make out the spindled railing of stairs leading up to the second floor. A bookcase was built into one side. The lace-covered windows at the front of the house had a dull glow from the streetlamps outside.

As they drew closer to the stairs, they could see a light at the top. Flattening themselves against the bookcase, they listened. Someone was singing, but she couldn't understand the words. It was an opera. She heard another voice; Charles was singing along.

Garcia slid closer to the foot of the stairs. They heard a thump at their feet and started. Garcia had knocked a fat book off the shelf. Reaching into their pockets, they pulled out their guns and waited for their quarry to come down the stairs, but he continued with his singing.

Garcia moved to the foot of the stairs, crouched down, and aimed up. She did the same. There was a landing, after which the steps took a sharp turn and continued their ascent. It was the vision from her session with the scarf. They were in the right place. Had they come soon enough to save Regina Ordstruman, or was she already dead?

Taking out her flashlight, Bernadette ran the beam around the floor near the front door. Dark splatters dulled the shiny wood, but there were no big puddles. If he'd stabbed her to death, he'd done it elsewhere. Garcia came up next to her, stared at the blood, and reached into his pocket. Bernadette put her hand up. She didn't want him calling yet; she wanted to find the girl first. With a hard-set mouth, he pulled his hand out of his pocket. She clicked off the light, and they went for the stairs.

She put one foot on the middle of the first step and winced at the creak. She took the second step by setting her foot on the left side of the stair. Silence. Garcia followed behind her, both of them hugging the left.

Squatting behind the potted palm, they looked up from the landing. Through an open doorway, light and music spilled into the hallway. He'd stopped singing. Had he heard them taking the stairs? There was a pause in the music. Perhaps he was switching CDs. She prayed for new tunes that would get him singing again.

Her prayer was answered. Miraculously, she even recognized what he was playing. It was the music from *The Phantom of the Opera*. He was singing along again and not doing a half-bad job.

Holding their weapons in both hands, they finished their trek up the stairs. They made a squeaky beeline for the hallway table. Squatting next to it, they heard a toilet flush and water running. He was in the master bathroom, a logical venue for his operatic performance. While Charles launched into "The Music of the Night," she thought about their next move. They needed information from him, but not at the expense of the girl's life.

The hallway in front of her started to blur and spin. The dizziness was back, and more intense than before. If she folded, she'd give them away before they found the girl. Reaching up, she clutched the edge of the hallway table for support.

"Shit!" he yelled from inside the bathroom. "Fucking razor."

Feeling something sting her cheek, she stifled a yelp. Something wet dripped onto her gloved fist. Behind her, Garcia lightly touched her arm. She turned her head and saw his eyes widen with shock. Using her teeth, she pulled off her right glove. Reaching up, she gingerly touched her cheek and examined her fingers. Blood. He'd cut himself—and she was bleeding. Their connection was growing closer by the minute, and she had to sever it soon before she lost herself in him.

Chapter 40

THUMPING OUT OF THE BATHROOM, ARAIGNEE WAS DRINK-ing straight whiskey—she could smell it out in the hallway—and it made her nauseous. She hoped her tolerance for the stuff was the same, glass for glass, as his. How could she use her gun when she was plastered? Garcia would have to do all the shooting.

Inside the bedroom, they could hear dresser drawers being opened and slammed shut at a ferocious pace. Garcia touched her arm, and she looked at him hunkered next to her in the hallway. They were both thinking the same thing: Chaz was getting ready to take a trip.

Suddenly something shattered in the bedroom.

"Shit!"

He'd dropped his bottle or glass. Hopefully, that would end his binge for the night.

"Fuck!"

A sharp sensation stabbed her right hand, and she inhaled sharply. She switched the gun to her left hand. Lifting her right palm, she was horrified to see deep cuts across her index and middle fingers. He'd sliced himself on the broken glass. While she wiped her bleeding fingers on the leg of her jeans, she sensed Garcia tense next to her. He knew what was going on, and it was scaring the crap out of him. She wondered if the same question came to his mind as to hers: If they shot Charles Araignee, would she be hit as well?

The music stopped. The next sounds made them stand straight, ready to charge the room. It was a moan, followed by Charles's response.

"Shut up, bitch."

Gritting her teeth through the pain, Bernadette pulled her leather glove back on over the injury. She turned her head and nodded to Garcia.

Suddenly their prey bounded out of the suite. They watched his back as he went down the steps barefoot, dressed in plaid pajama bottoms and a torn T-shirt. He held on to the banister with his left hand and carried the broken glass in his right. The hand with the tumbler was bandaged.

"I've got the girl," Garcia growled, and bolted into the bedroom.

Moving to the top of the stairs, Bernadette looked down and saw Chaz next to the bookcase, bending over something. He'd discovered the book Garcia had knocked off the shelf. She took a step back from the railing and held her breath, wondering if the fallen volume would set off an alarm in his head. After a minute of quiet, she peeked over the railing again and saw he was gone. A faint light was coming from the kitchen.

Her weapon pointed, she glided down the stairs, cut through the front room, and went into the dining room. Sidling up to the kitchen door, she saw light spilling out from the bottom of the door. On the other side, she heard cupboards being opened and closed. If he was hunting for whiskey, she prayed he'd find none. She was starting to snap out of the daze, helped in part by the sobering pain radiating from her fingers.

She heard silverware rattling. What was he looking for? Before he sliced himself again or unearthed another bottle of booze, Bernadette decided to make her move. Crouching down, she pushed the swinging door open an inch. At the far end of the kitchen, with his back to her, he was fiddling with something on the counter. She couldn't see what it was; a bread machine blocked her view of his hands. She closed the door and stood up. With her gun in both hands, she raised her arms out in front of her. She kicked the door open and went through. "Don't move, Charles!"

He spun around with a revolver in his hand.

Keeping her gun trained on him, she shouted, "Drop it!"

He took a step backward.

The look on his face told her Charles was panicked, and his anxiety was becoming her own. "Drop the gun!"

"All right!" He lowered the revolver.

"Drop it now!"

"If you kill me, you'll never know about them."

"The six girls in the river? The two in the tub? The one upstairs."

His eyes bugged out. "How?"

"I should give you a bullet for each of them. Nine bullets."

He swallowed hard. "There're more. Kill me, and you'll never know who they are."

Was he lying? Bernadette tried to get a read of his emotions, and all she felt was anger. She had no idea if it was his fury or her own. It didn't matter. Her violent urges and sexual overdrive had been from him. The cuts on the face and fingers, the drunkenness, and now the anxiety—all had been unwanted gifts from Charles Araignee. She wanted to free herself of him and his emotions. Without saying another word, she took aim from across the room and pulled the trigger. The window behind him shattered.

"Crazy bitch!" Covering his head with his arms, he ducked behind the far end of the counter. He popped back up with the gun in his hands.

She crouched behind the butcher-block table. "Don't do it!"

"Go to hell!" Two shots rang out, both slamming into the glass-front cupboards lining the walls behind her. Glass and wood and bits of china rained down like hail. He lowered his arm, spun around, and ran to the door. Pulled frantically on the knob and worked the deadbolt.

Even as she took aim at his back, she struggled to negotiate with herself. *Lower the gun. This isn't right. You can't shoot a guy in the back. You could be nailing yourself in the back.* An instant before firing, she raised her arms and aimed for the wall over the doorframe. Wood and plaster exploded, showering him with dust and splinters.

He looked up at the hole. "Jesus!" He spun back around with his gun in his hand. She dove behind the butcher-block table again while another set of cupboards and china took the hit.

He darted back to the door, yanked it open, and ran out onto the porch. He frantically jiggled and pulled on the handle until he remembered how to unlock his own screen door. He slammed it open, ran down the steps, and took the sidewalk at full gallop. Throwing open the gate, he bolted out of the backyard with his gun in his right hand.

Garcia ran into the kitchen. "What the hell?"

"He's on the run!" Bernadette dropped her Glock into her jacket pocket and ran outside.

"Cat!" Garcia yelled after her. "Wait!"

"Stay with the girl!" Bernadette took the back steps two at a time and flew through the open gate.

She chased Charles down the alley behind his house, the way lit by the security lights mounted on the back of neighbors' garages. As she was closing in on him, he glanced over his shoulder, and she yelled, "Stop!"

He paused long enough to tip a pair of garbage cans in front of her.

She dodged the cans and retrieved her gun from her jacket. "Stop!" she repeated to his back.

The alley spilled out into the street. The two of them ran down the middle of the road in a chase scene that could have been mistaken for a violent domestic dispute: a bandaged man in his pajamas, running barefoot from a bleeding blonde—both of them armed.

After two blocks, the road emptied onto the boulevard that followed the top of the bluffs. Her quarry was pulling away from her. "Stop now!"

Bounding onto the sidewalk that led to the green tower, he was going to take the steps down to Wabasha Street. From there it would be a quick dash to the Mississippi. If he made it to the river, she'd lose him for good. She followed him down the sidewalk.

After the sidewalk came a set of steps leading down to a wooden walkway, a fifty-foot bridge that spanned the gap between the bluff and the tower. Bernadette stopped before her feet hit the wood. Araignee was almost over the bridge and to the tower. She went down on one knee and took aim at the white T-shirt. "Charles!"

He spun around, saw her gun trained on him, and raised his own. He fired a wild shot over her head, lowered his revolver, and headed for the tower.

She lowered her arms and went after him, her feet thumping across the wooden walkway.

Instead of sprinting down the steps, he froze on the landing and glanced over the railing. She didn't know why he hesitated; perhaps the height intimidated him. Whatever it was, it gave her time to catch up to him. She stopped twenty feet from where he stood, but kept her gun down. "Charles!"

He pivoted around with his revolver in his shaking hands. "Get away!" he panted. "I'll tell you about the other one! Just get away!"

By her count, he had one bullet left. While he couldn't shoot worth shit, the bullet could ricochet around the top of the tower—a cage the size of a small bedroom. Equally hazardous were the gaps between the railings: they were large enough to fall through or get shoved through. It would be a six-story drop.

She moved toward him but stayed on the bridge. "Put down the gun, and let's talk."

He backed up, pressing himself against the bars while keeping the barrel pointed at her. "You don't want to talk! You want to blow my head off!"

"I could have taken you out in your kitchen. I just want to talk. Swear to God. Tell me the names."

He raised his shaking hands. She hit the boards while his bullet disappeared into the night. "Fuck it!" He threw the gun at her and the revolver bounced on the boards behind her.

She got up and went after him, entering the tower and cornering him in the cage. "Tell me who they are."

He raised his hands high. "Not until you put the gun away."

"No way."

His eyes darted from her gun to the hole in the platform on his right. The opening was where the stairs started their descent. "Why should I tell you? You're going to kill me regardless."

"I want to get out of this dog kennel." She tipped her head toward the walkway. "Come on. Move it."

Keeping his eyes on her weapon, he inched forward. "You kill me, you're never going to get to the truth."

"Slowly," she said, pressing her back against the railing so he could move past her. "Keep those hands in the air."

His eyes darted to the stairs.

"Don't," she said.

"Don't what?" He threw himself on top of her.

A shot vibrated the platform. She felt a flash of pain in her own gut, and then it evaporated. "Charles?" she panted.

He rolled off her and onto his back, clutching his stomach. "You . . . shot . . . me."

Crawling to her feet, she kept the gun on him. "I'll call for an ambulance."

Holding his stomach with both hands, he moaned. "Oh . . . God!"

He wasn't getting away from her; stomach wounds were bad enough, and this had been at close range. She pocketed her gun and pulled out her cell. Punched in a number. "Try not to move."

"Oh . . . God! Hurry!"

Turning away from him, she spoke into the cell in a low voice. "I need an ambulance on the West Side . . ." While she gave directions to the dispatcher, the man behind her coughed and groaned. She had no pity for him. She felt nothing at all, and the numbness was a relief. Finally, she was liberated.

She hung up and turned around to see that Araignee had rolled onto his side. "Stay still. Help is coming."

"Ruth," he wheezed.

Bernadette didn't give a shit about Ruth anymore. She pocketed the phone and went over to him, kneeling at his head. "Tell me about the other drownings. Names."

"Twins," he wheezed.

She shuddered. "Names."

"I'm dying."

She knew better. The most evil ones often pulled through, their innate cruelty carrying them to a full recovery. She bet Araignee was one of those lucky pricks. She should have put a few more into him and guaranteed him a trip to the morgue. She stood up and turned away from him. He disgusted her. Twins. She'd get the names while he was in the hospital.

"God, I'm dying," he moaned behind her.

"I wish," she muttered. Taking out her cell, she punched in a number and walked out onto the bridge to look up at the night sky. The wind had died down, but the stars remained obscured by the clouds.

It rang once before Garcia picked up. "Cat? Where are you? What the hell is going—"

"Did she make it?"

"She's going to live."

"Thank God." She glanced over at the man down in the tower and turned back around. "I shot the bastard, but he's going to make it, too."

"The cops are crawling all over the West Side. Where are you?"

"Those green steps on Prospect Boulevard. Top of the green stairs, on the bluff."

"I'll send an ambulance."

"Tony, he says he killed twins. I hope to God he's—" She heard a scuffling noise and a chilling wail. For an instant, everything in front of her went black. She gasped.

"Cat!" Garcia yelled from the cell. "What is it?"

"Charles," she breathed, and lowered the phone. Turning around, she looked at the tower platform. Empty. She ran across the walkway and looked down. He'd crawled to the edge and slipped between the bars. By the glow of the streetlamps, she could see his lifeless body sprawled on the sidewalk at the foot of the tower.

Had it been a desperate attempt to escape, or an effort to end his life his way? She didn't want to weigh the third possibility: that her emotions had for once taken over *his* psyche, making her death wish for him become a reality.

Chapter 41

YELLOW POLICE TAPE AND FLASHING SQUAD LIGHTS TOOK over the neighborhood at the top of the tower, as well as the sidewalks and street at the bottom. A few people were roused from their beds by the sirens, throwing on coats and jackets over their pajamas to go outside and check out the ruckus. Half an hour after the body was taken away by the ME's hearse, a television news van pulled up and then promptly departed. There were no photographers, reporters, or news helicopters anywhere in sight.

Bernadette and Garcia sat in the front seat of his car. Every once in a while, he thumped the steering wheel with his fist to punctuate a point. Her gloves were off and in her lap, and she fiddled with them as he spoke. Her jean jacket had been bagged, and she never wanted to see it again. It was covered with Charles's blood and some of hers. Another article of outerwear lost to this case. The cuts on her face and fingers hurt, but the paramedics had taped her up.

A couple of blocks away, yellow tape also trapped Charles's house. Bernadette and Garcia had gotten there just in time. Regina Ordstruman had nearly bled to death in Araignee's elegant claw-foot tub. She was a University of Minnesota senior with a major in American studies and double minors in anorexia and depression. She'd never been a patient at the VonHader clinic, but Regina had tried to commit suicide twice before her twentieth birthday. She'd met Charles through the Suicide Stop Line that he'd so enthusiastically staffed as a regular volunteer—the number provided by the unknowing but ever-helpful Professor Wakefielder.

The tub and river drownings would all be examined to see how Charles Araignee had first come in contact with his victims. Recent drowning cases in Minnesota and Wisconsin would have to be resurrected to see if any were the twins Charles had tried to use as a bargaining chip. The murderer himself would be studied postmortem to see how one man's childhood obsession could turn into a killing spree spanning two states.

Because her death didn't match the pattern, the toughest loose end could be Zoe Cameron. Even if her autopsy showed she'd died of an overdose rather than her eating disorder, Bernadette was uncertain of Charles's complicity. Araignee could have talked her into suicide while the girl sat in that oppressive waiting room, or Cameron could have done it all on her own—the tragic timing wreaking havoc with the investigation into Wakefielder. The prof's lawyer would probably sue everyone in sight, but Bernadette figured no one owed Wakefielder anything. He purposely and habitually surrounded himself with unstable women half his age. Maybe this mess would convince him to stop offering classes that attracted basket cases.

Bernadette wasn't at all certain she would be entrusted with tying up the loose ends, or be allowed to take credit for cracking the cases in the first place. Even if she and Garcia managed to keep the use of her sight out of the reports, there would be other questions raised about how she'd conducted her investigation. For starters, the cops and the ME were asking how her suspect, though shot through the gut, could have managed to crawl out of the tower and fall to his death.

"He was alive when I called you," she told Garcia for the fourth time. "I did not push him. He jumped. Crawled, actually."

"After you shot him."

"Yes." She glanced through the window, at the tower across the street. "What else do you want from me?"

"Your gun's been turned over. His revolver's been recovered. We'll have to wait for ballistics. The crime scene crew is crawling all over the shooting gallery that used to be his kitchen." He paused. "I have to ask . . ."

"What?"

"Do you need some more time on the gun range or what? Why couldn't you hit him the first twenty times?"

She flexed her injured hand, a reminder of all the weirdness that had taken place while she and Garcia were stalking their prey in the house. "I was afraid if I shot him, I would also be . . ." Her voice trailed off.

"Let's keep that out of the reports, shall we?"

"Good idea." She looked over at all the blue uniforms mingling with the black FBI jackets. "Who from St. Paul Homicide—"

"Ed has it all under control."

"Your cousin drew the short straw on this?" She sank back against the car seat. "I suppose he's got questions about this tower thing, too."

Garcia rubbed his face with his hand. "You could say that."

Her shoulders sagged. "I'm sorry if I've put you in an uncomfortable position."

"I want you to go home and get some sleep." He ran a hand through his hair. "Please stay put, Cat."

"I will."

"I mean it. This is serious now."

"I know it is," she said.

"Don't leave the house without talking to me first."

"I won't go anywhere."

"Don't even go downstairs to collect your mail without calling me."

She nodded. "I understand."

"I've gotta hang around," he said tiredly. "I'll have one of our folks take you home."

"Not Thorsson," she said. "He'll lose me."

Garcia's face lightened for the first time since they got in the car. "Not Thorsson."

EVEN THOUGH she felt as if she'd been trapped in Garcia's car forever, dawn was still a couple of hours away by the time she got dropped at home. She was pretty sure Charles's suicide had happened after the papers' deadlines, but there'd be something on the TV news later in the morning. She made a mental note to leave the television off for the day and stay away from newspapers for the rest of the week. She walked into the bathroom, flipped on the lights, and peeled off her clothes. She activated the shower and hopped in the tub. The hot water felt good. She heard her phone ringing and ignored it.

Tired and aching, she threw on a bathrobe and hobbled into the kitchen to grab a bottle of water. The phone again. She picked it up off the counter. "What?"

Garcia said, "Did you see the morning paper?"

"You told me not to pick up the mail."

"Meet me at the VonHader place. Don't go in. Wait for me."

"Both men are in jail," she said. "There's no one there."

"Their lawyer sprang them already."

"But why—"

"My turn. I got a bad feeling," he said.

She hung up and stared at the phone. She was rubbing off on Garcia.

BERNADETTE PARKED a block over from Summit and jogged to the mansion, instinctively feeling the inside of her jacket pocket before remembering her gun was gone. When she got to the front door, Bernadette raised her fist to knock but hesitated. She had no idea what this was about, and Garcia had asked her not to go inside. Reluctantly, she stepped off to one side of the porch to wait.

She heard a vehicle rumbling down the street, but it wasn't her boss; it was someone in a beat-up station wagon. She saw the driver slow in front of a neighbor's house and toss a folded newspaper from the car window. It landed on the front stoop. Not a minute later, an early riser came out in his sweats and picked up his morning read.

Bernadette wondered if the carrier was going to stop in front of the VonHader place. She stepped away from the porch windows and watched while a newspaper landed on the sidewalk leading up to the steps.

"Shit," she muttered. Afraid someone inside was going to come out for the paper, Bernadette took cover behind the army of statues. Several minutes went by, and she wondered if she was being too cautious. As she started to stand, the porch light flicked on. Ducking back down just in time, she heard the deadbolt slide open.

Peeking out from behind a statue, Bernadette saw the doctor step out onto the porch. "Damn paper boy." Wrapping his robe tighter around his body, he pushed the screen door open and went outside to collect the morning news.

Immersed in the headlines, he paused in front of the door. With the porch light directly over his head, Bernadette was able to get a good look at his face. His mouth dropped open, and he put his hand out to steady himself against the doorframe. Whatever he was reading, it horrified him. "God, no," he said under his breath.

The Dow is down, Bernadette thought cynically.

As he folded the paper in half and tucked it under his arm, his expression changed. Relaxed. It was almost one of surrender, and it disturbed Bernadette. He disappeared through the door, closing it and locking it behind him.

Something was wrong, and she was impatient to get inside. Abandoning her hiding spot, she went up to the porch windows to scan the street for Garcia's car. She fished out her cell to call and then dropped the phone back into her pocket. He'd be there soon enough. She left her post at the windows and sat down on a concrete bench to wait.

INSIDE, LUKE VONHADER sat in front of the fireplace with a cup of coffee and a yellow legal pad. Tucked between two burning logs, the morning headlines erupted in flames and quickly collapsed into ash. Already yesterday's news. Shuddering at the bitterness of his dark brew, he wished there had been cream in the house. He had meant to pick up a few groceries Monday, but the day had gotten away from him. Clicking his pen, he began to write.

> *Dear Liz:*
>
> *All of the documents are where you'd expect them. If you have any questions, call Chip or one of his assistants. Susan in particular is up to speed on our holdings, as she handled matters related to my sister's passing.*
>
> *I suggest you sell our Scottsdale and Twin Cities properties and relocate to the East Coast. The private schools are good, and your mother would enjoy having you closer. Of course, it is entirely up to you.*
>
> *DO NOT believe what you read in the papers and see on television. I know you will try to shield our daughters from the ugliness, but it will be difficult. Again, a move might be best for all concerned.*
>
> *Kiss Em and Mel for me and tell them to take care of each other. I apologize for leaving my girls like this, but you more than anyone understand these demons of mine. I have lived with them for so long, they have taken over. Forgive the heartache I have caused you and try to move forward.*
>
> *All my love, Luke*

He set the pen and pad down on the coffee table and finished his drink. He carefully tore the sheet out of the pad and folded it in half, running his thumb along the crease. He folded it two more times and stood up to tuck the rectangle into the front pocket of his robe. He'd thought about finding a fireproof place to hide the letter, but he was confident the fire department would douse the fire before his body was incinerated.

He stepped up to the mantel and reached for one of his mother's favorites, a tall Victorian pedestal oil lamp with a painted base and original crystal chimney.

Chapter 42

A POP INSIDE THE HOUSE MADE BERNADETTE JUMP TO HER FEET.
She went to the door, knocked twice. No response.

The smoke she smelled was too acrid to be coming from a fire-place. She went over to the windows to check. The lace curtains were enveloped in flames. "Jesus Christ!" she gasped, backing away from the glass.

She ran to the front door and put her hand over the doorknob. "Shit!" The knob was already too hot to touch, even with gloves on. She pounded on the wood with her fists. "Fire! Get out!"

Bernadette darted back to the windows but couldn't see anything past the flames. "Luke!" she yelled to the glass. "Matt!"

She ran back to the door, lifted her foot, and brought it down on the lower panel.

Garcia was bounding up the porch steps. "Cat!"

Taking a step back, she raised her foot higher and kicked the door next to the lock. "There's a fire!"

Garcia saw the flames through the glass. "Crap!" He flipped open his phone and called for help.

She brought her foot down on the wood a third time, and it bounced off. "You take this fucking thing!" she yelled.

He replaced her in front of the door while she ran to the other side of the porch. She lifted a bust off its pedestal and ran to the windows. Swinging the statue upside down by the neck, she heaved it through the middle panes. The sound of breaking glass was followed by a roar as flames rolled out of the hole. "God Almighty!"

Garcia cranked his foot back and brought it down against the middle of the door. The wood didn't budge. "Try the back door!"

Bernadette pushed open the screen door, jumped off the steps, and ran around to the rear of the house. She went up the back steps and jiggled the back door's knob. Locked. She pounded on the wood with both fists. "Fire! Get out!"

She heard glass breaking above her and ran down the steps and into the middle of the yard. A wooden chair came sailing out of a second-floor window and landed on the ground, exploding in a dozen pieces. Dressed in a T-shirt and boxers, Matthew VonHader stuck his torso through the broken window while smoke billowed out from behind him. "Help! Please help me!"

Bernadette heard sirens in the distance. "Help's coming!"

He started coughing. "The smoke . . . I can't . . . I don't want to burn!"

"Stay low! Close the door and stuff a rag in the bottom!"

He turned away from the window and returned a moment later, coughing harder. "I can't . . . see anything!"

"Jump!"

He looked down with saucer eyes. "No!"

"It's not that far! Jump!"

Coughing and shaking his head, he answered, "I can't!"

"Tie a sheet to something and climb down!"

He backed away from the window. Bernadette kept her eyes glued to the dark hole and became worried when he didn't immediately reappear. "Matt!" she yelled up to the window. "Matt!"

Bernadette swept the yard with her eyes and in a far corner spotted a birdbath perched on a concrete column. She ran over to it, shoved off the bowl top, picked up the pedestal, and carried it to the back of the house. Using the pedestal as a battering ram, she slammed the bottom end against the middle of the door. The wood didn't move. She raised the concrete as high as she could and brought the bottom of the column down on the doorknob. The hardware fell off. She set the pedestal down, caught her breath, and picked it up again.

Breathing hard with sweat dripping from his brow, Garcia materialized at her side. "Front door wouldn't give an inch. Fire's coming out of all the first-floor windows facing the street."

Bernadette slammed the pedestal against the door twice, with no results. "Then Luke is dead."

Garcia dragged his arm over his forehead. "He's downstairs for sure?"

Panting, Bernadette dropped her battering ram. "He came out of the house to get the paper before the fire started."

"Shit. Did you see him reading it?"

"Yeah. It pissed him off. Why?"

"Nothing," Garcia said. "I'll tell you later."

"Matthew is upstairs," she said.

"Rigs are coming up the block."

Bernadette bent over to retrieve the concrete column. "Matt will fry before they get here."

"Forget that thing." Garcia positioned himself in front of the door, cranked his foot back, and brought it down next to the busted lock. The door didn't give. "Son-of-a-bitch!"

Bernadette heard screaming overhead and then two cracks, one immediately after the other. She darted into the yard and looked up at the window. Fire was pouring out of the hole. She retrieved the battering ram and ran to Garcia with it. "Did you hear that?"

"I heard!"

She passed the concrete column over to him and pointed to a first-floor window. "Do it!"

Running and carrying the column like a pole-vaulter, Garcia

charged up to the window and released the pedestal. It sailed through the glass, and the flames instantly shot out. "Crap!" spat Garcia.

Bernadette looked up at the second floor. Cupping her hands around her mouth, she yelled to the broken window, "Matt!"

Garcia said, "Maybe he made it downstairs."

"He's dead. They're both dead." Bernadette turned away from the house and suddenly noticed the alley was filled with people. A man on a motorcycle. Two teenagers on bikes. An old lady wearing a down coat over her robe and slippers. A couple of construction workers. Where had they all come from? It wasn't even dawn. Why hadn't they tried to help? They were all wide-eyed and silent, staring across the fence at the burning house as if it were a horror movie. She marched over to the back fence and waved her arms around. "Clear out! There's nothing to see! Go on! Get away from here!"

The crowd didn't budge, its collective attention torn between the screaming blonde and the burning house.

Bernadette picked a rock off the ground and started to crank her arm back. Garcia came up behind her and took the rock out of her fist. "Are you nuts?"

"They're acting like it's a freak show!"

"Forget them!"

She looked past him at the mansion. Flames were shooting out of every window. "How could it spread so fast?"

Garcia ran a hand through his hair. "It's an old house."

"Filled with old stuff," she added. The brothers' inheritance had made a fine funeral pyre.

From the street, a ribbon of water arced onto the roof. Garcia put his hand on her shoulder. "We can pull back."

Her eyes traveled to the window where she'd last seen Matthew VonHader alive. "He was afraid to jump. It wasn't even that far."

"Come on," said Garcia, steering her away by the elbow.

They started walking together along the side of the house. "This is unbelievable," she said. "It started right before you got here. I was standing on the porch, and I smelled smoke."

"The doc didn't notice you when he came out for the paper?"

"I hid behind some of the junk on the porch. I didn't know why you sent me here, and you told me to wait."

"Now I wish I hadn't," he said glumly.

"You think he would have let me in? Poured me a cup of coffee?"

"No. Probably not."

They moved to the front of the house, navigating around hoses and men. The firefighters had busted down the front door, but flames were shooting out and keeping them back. Garcia flashed his ID to a burly fire captain. The man thumbed over his shoulder at the house. "Any idea how many we got inside?"

"Two adult males, one of them with a gun. He may already have finished his brother and himself. We don't know for sure."

"Dandy," said the captain, leaving them and joining his crew in front of the house.

The two agents stood off to the side. More onlookers lined up along the sidewalk across the street. Two more police squads and another fire truck were pulling up. A television crew was setting up a shot from a neighbor's front yard across the street.

With the back of her hand, she wiped the perspiration off her forehead. "Why did he do this?"

"The fact that they were jailed made it into the late edition of the news," Garcia said as he stared up at the engulfed house. "Front page. Shrink and his brother questioned in the death of disabled father. Not a long piece. Just enough."

"How'd the paper get the story so quick? Who dropped the dime to the reporters?"

Garcia answered both questions with a single shrug.

"Did it include the sick family background?" she asked.

"No, but he saw it coming. The water torture. Abusive parents. All of it would have been laid out. Intimate, embarrassing, private stuff." He paused. "At the same time, I'll bet money that the media misses the public circus at the tower."

"What makes a good news story?"

"This does."

"Why is that?"

"Neat pictures," he said as flames shot through the roof.

For twenty minutes, they stood and watched wordlessly while firefighters ran back and forth with their hoses and axes. The sun hadn't yet come up, but the entire block was bathed in light, an unearthly red glow cast by the blaze and the emergency vehicles.

"Do you believe in hell?" she asked, her eyes glued to the frantic ballet.

"Yeah, I do," he said.

"So do I," she said.

Chapter 43

TWO BODIES WERE CARRIED OUT OF THE SMOKING SHELL.
The agents intercepted the twin gurneys as they were being wheeled
to the Ramsey County medical examiner's hearse parked on the
street. Garcia whipped out his badge and showed it to the ME investigator. "Can we have a last look-see?"

"Sure thing." The investigator nodded to the men at the head of
the gurneys. They positioned themselves at the top of the carts, their
backs blocking the view of the photographers and nosy neighbors.
Each man reached down and slowly unzipped his bag partway.

Bernadette and Garcia looked from one sooty corpse to the other.
Luke had put a bullet through his own temple, but not before nailing
Matthew in the chest. The elder brother had looked after his younger
sibling to the end.

"We're good," Garcia told the gurney crew. "One of our people
will meet you over at the lab for the autopsy."

"You know about the letter?" asked the ME investigator.

"CSI showed us," said Bernadette.

While his men zipped the bags up over the bodies, the ME investigator took out his notebook and clicked his pen. "Can you help us
out on locating next of kin?"

"My agent tells me the doctor's spouse and children are at their Scottsdale place," said Garcia. "Elizabeth is the wife's name."

"Lucky for them they weren't home," said the investigator, scribbling. He shoved the pad and pen back into his jacket. "Wasn't the bureau involved in a bad deal last night, too? Some weird-ass business with a fella getting shot and then going off that tower on the West Side? I didn't get the call, but I heard one of your agents . . ." His voice trailed off as he got a good look at Bernadette's eyes.

Garcia and Bernadette stared at him, and he clamped his mouth closed. Without another word, he and the gurney crew turned around and finished their trek to the hearse.

"I wonder what he heard about 'one of your agents,' " Bernadette said out of the side of her mouth.

"Who gives a shit?" snapped Garcia.

"Right," said Bernadette, watching as Luke and Matthew were loaded into the hearse. They'd be sharing the morgue with Charles Araignee.

"NOW WHAT?" asked Bernadette as she and Garcia walked toward their cars.

He nodded to an empty bus stop. "Let's sit down for a minute."

They went over to the bench and dropped onto the wooden seat. "I'm beat," she said.

He stretched his legs out in front of him. "Me, too."

In a front yard across the road, a woman raked leaves into an orange garbage bag while a little boy in a cape ran circles around her. "When's Halloween?" Bernadette asked.

"Why do you keep asking that?" Garcia asked with irritation. "It's soon. A week or so."

"I guess I'd better get some candy."

"Don't bother," he said. "As far as I know, kids don't trick-or-treat downtown."

"That's too bad. I like Halloween. We used to go to a barn dance when we were kids, with costumes and everything."

"I don't have any hay on hand, but you can come over to my place and pass out treats if you want. Tip back a few beers and grill some brats while we're at it. Make a night of it."

"I'd like that," she said.

"Great."

"Do I have to wear a costume?"

"Not unless you really want to," he said.

She stretched out her own legs and smiled, resisting the urge to make a crack about coming as a French maid. She cleared her throat. "Uh, I hate to ask . . ."

"Go ahead."

"That thing at the tower. How much trouble am I in?"

"I'm gonna try like hell to keep this away from the OPR," he said, referring to the Office of Professional Responsibility. "The OPR gets its mitts on it, you could be talking some serious beach time."

"A suspension?"

"Do you want me to lie to you?"

"Yes, please," she said meekly.

"Let's talk about this later," he said.

She liked that strategy. Bolting up, she announced, "I'm starving. Let's go get something to eat."

He got up off the seat. "How about a joint on Grand Avenue?"

A gust of wind slammed her, and she hunched her shoulders against it. "I don't care where we go as long as it's heated."

"The one with the walleye basket on the menu. I can't remember the name of the place, but there's a neon fish in the front window."

"Tavern on Grand. It's between Dale and St. Albans, right?"

"Right."

"Meet you there," she said.

"My treat," he said, and dashed across the street to his car.

WITH ITS log cabin decor—made complete by a chandelier constructed of antlers—Tavern on Grand was the quintessential Minnesota restaurant. They were well ahead of the lunch rush, so she and Garcia had their pick of tables. They took a booth in a dark corner, with Bernadette's seat facing the wall. She practically ripped the menu out of the server's hands.

"I'll give you a minute," said the waitress, a pretty twenty-something with long black hair and wearing a short black skirt. She moved on to another table.

"What are you getting?" Bernadette asked Garcia.

"The walleye," he said, unbuttoning his coat. "It's the house specialty. Comes with the works: potato, coleslaw, roll. They have this jalapeño tartar sauce that is out of this world."

"I'll get the same," she said, setting down the menu.

He slid out of the booth, took off his trench, and dropped it onto the bench. "I've gotta use the head. Order for me if she comes back."

She unzipped her leather bomber jacket and pulled off her gloves. "What do you want to drink?"

"Pop. Any kind, as long as it's not diet."

After he left, she continued perusing the menu. She might want an appetizer. The crab artichoke dip sounded great, and so did the stuffed mushrooms and the potato skins. She turned in her seat and searched for the server. She was on the other side of the room taking orders from a table filled with flirty young men. Bernadette returned her attention to the menu. Maybe instead of the walleye, she'd get the ribs.

"The jalapeño tartar sauce is to die for."

"I know," she said, looking up from the menu at the man standing next to the table. As he slid into the booth to sit across from her, she inhaled sharply and felt all the warmth drain from her body. Leaning across the table, she whispered, "What are you doing here? How did you get here? How can you be here?"

Creed looked at her with mock innocence. "What do you mean?"

"This isn't your haunt. This is miles from downtown, nowhere near our office."

"I used to eat here. Our ASAC's right, by the way. The walleye is hard to beat." He nodded at the menu sitting on the table between them. "The New York strip isn't too shabby either."

"How can you be here?"

He threw his arms up and rested them over the top of the bench. "Haven't you figured it out? That pile of concrete on Robert Street isn't what's haunted."

Looking over at the waitress, Bernadette was relieved to see her still occupied with the other table. She turned back around and hissed, "What are you saying?"

He tipped his head toward her. "You're haunted, missy. You're my connection to the land of the living."

She didn't want to know anything more; all she wanted was for him to leave before Garcia returned. "Save it for the office."

"You don't seem very appreciative of the fact that this could open doors for you." He grinned slyly. "You've got a friend in high places."

"Please."

"Let me say one word. Well, a couple of words. Charlene Araignee."

She sat frozen.

"Write it down," he said. "You'll have to go back about thirty years or so."

She swiveled her head and saw Garcia heading to the table. Snapping her head back around, she whispered, "I'm begging you. Please go *now*."

By the time Garcia reached the booth, Creed was gone. Sliding onto the bench, Garcia scrutinized her face from across the table. "What's wrong?"

Training her eyes on the menu, she mumbled, "What? Nothing . . . nothing's wrong." She couldn't tell him what had just happened; a ghost in the cellar was one thing, but how could Creed be popping up in a bar in the middle of the day to chat?

Garcia retrieved his menu. "You okay?"

She looked away from him and glanced over at the server. "She hasn't taken our order yet."

Garcia raised a hand, and the waitress came up to the table. "What looks good, folks?"

"Cat?"

"You go first," she said, keeping her eyes down.

Garcia ordered the walleye and a cola. She went with a bowl of wild rice soup.

"Is that it?" asked the waitress.

"Yeah. Thanks." Bernadette wrapped her arms around herself.

"How about something warm to drink?" asked the server.

"Tea. Hot tea would be great."

"I thought you were hungry," Garcia said as the server left with the order.

Rubbing her arms over her jacket, she said, "I think I'm coming down with something. I've got a headache and the chills."

"Want to cancel the soup and take off?"

"No, no. I think I've got some Tylenol in my jacket." She made a show of digging in her pockets when under the table, she was writing down the name Creed had given her.

"Take the rest of the day off, Cat."

"I have one thing I need to do at the office, and then I'll go home," she said, folding the slip of paper on her lap and tucking it away.

"Find the Tylenol?"

"Uh . . . no. Don't worry about it." She put her hands on the tabletop and smiled.

"UNBELIEVABLE," SHE breathed as she set down the phone. Then she picked it up again to call Garcia.

"Why aren't you home?" he asked.

"Tony, I know who Charles drowned. It was one twin."

"Who?"

"His twin sister, Charlene."

"Holy crap."

"They would have been—I don't know—six or so. Charlene supposedly fell into their family's pool. Charles was found sitting frozen in a lawn chair, staring at her body. Didn't get help or anything. Police report attributed his behavior to shock."

"Was he really in shock, or did he let her drown? Do you think he even pushed her in?"

"Who knows?"

"How in the hell did you come up with this?"

"A hunch." She looked over at Creed's desk. He wasn't there to enjoy the moment, and she felt guilty for taking credit.

"So that was *before* he watched the sick stuff at the VonHader house?"

"Yeah. Watching Ruth nearly drown and getting off on it, that pretty much sealed the deal. It's a miracle he waited until Ruth died to start acting out."

"Well, we haven't gone over old drowning cases yet."

"Yeah. You're right."

"Good work. This should help soften the problems around the tower mess."

She smiled to herself. Creed had bailed her out again, the spooky SOB. "That might be why my connection to Charles was so strong," said Bernadette. "He was half of a twin set, like me."

"Makes sense, at least in Bernadette World," Garcia said. "Now go home. You've had a long day."

Chapter 44

AFTER SPENDING MOST OF TUESDAY NIGHT DWELLING ON everything that had transpired over the previous ten days, Bernadette welcomed Garcia's early-morning phone call as a surprise and a relief. "How about we play hooky and take out that bike of yours? There're some great trails south of the cities, near Faribault."

"I know all those trails," said Bernadette. "Problem is you don't have a bike, and mine would be too small for you. It's only a one-fifty."

"I've checked out this joint that rents."

She knew the place he was talking about, and it would be perfect for a novice. At the same time, she was worried about his safety. "How green are you? If you got hurt, I'd feel terrible."

"I had a motorcycle. Still have the endorsement on my driver's license." He paused. "Is your back up for it? I didn't think about that."

"God, you make me sound like an old lady. Back is fine. Give me an hour and come over. I'll have the bike loaded on the truck by the time you get here. Have you got any equipment?"

"A helmet, I think. Stored in a box in the basement."

"Dig it out and dust it off," she said. "And wear your worst pair of jeans. You're probably going to rip the hell out of them and get them all muddy. You need a pair of leather boots. Hunting boots or work boots. They need to be tough and tall. By that, I mean over the calf."

"Why so high?"

"Obviously any part of any bike that falls on you could ding you up pretty good."

"Right about that."

"Dirt bikes have these sort of menacing-looking foot pegs that allow for a better grip, so riders can stand on them. They're bare metal, as opposed to being covered in rubber like regular bikes. They have springs to lessen the damage if they fall on you, but good boots are essential."

"I've got a pair of shit-kickers that would work."

"Riding gloves are important, too. I have an extra set. They're too big for me. They'll probably be tight on you, but they'll work. I've got spare goggles. Those should fit fine; they're adjustable."

"Sounds like we're going to war."

WITH HER HONDA and a pile of riding gear rattling in the truck bed behind them, they rode down together in Bernadette's pickup. During the hour-long drive down south, they exchanged stories about home-maintenance headaches, with Bernadette bitching about her dishwasher and Garcia griping about the furnace that would have to be replaced before winter. She asked about his weight training. He told her about a couple of health clubs that were decent and warned her away from one that had scary showers. They both admitted to dreading the upcoming holidays. She didn't have close family to spend time with, and he felt crowded out by his clan and that of his deceased wife's.

"They still include you?" she asked as she checked the highway exit signs and saw that her ramp was coming up.

"It's as if having me at the table is keeping a part of her at the table." He glanced out the passenger window. "Makes it hard to move on."

Bernadette navigated the truck off Interstate 35. "I'll bet."

He turned his head back around and looked at her. "What about you? My wife's been gone six years and Michael's only been gone three. You must still keep in touch with his people."

"His *people* never liked me, and they blamed me. They said I should have been paying better attention."

"It wasn't your fault."

"Yeah . . . well."

"With all the, uh, folks you've seen—Murrick and Creed and I don't know who else . . . Have you ever wondered?"

She hung a right on a county road. "If I'll ever set eyes on my dead husband?"

"What would you do?"

She jerked the truck to a halt at a stop sign, braking harder than she intended. "I'd have a helluva a lot to say to him, and he'd probably never show his face again."

"He really pissed you off."

She checked both ways and rolled through the intersection. "He dumped me in the most permanent way possible."

"Maybe it wasn't about you."

She didn't know what to say to that, so she turned the conversation around and asked him a tough question. "If you could talk to your wife again, what would you say to her?"

"That I love her and miss her. That I'm sorry."

Bernadette frowned. "Sorry for what?"

"Sorry for the accident. Sorry for not getting the idiot who ran her car off the road."

She hung a left onto a gravel stretch, glad to get off the subject of dead spouses. "Ready to rumble?"

SHE WAS PLEASED there weren't many other people riding. Garcia had rented a big beater of a bike, and Bernadette didn't think he could do anything to the Yamaha that hadn't been done before. The trails were muddy and there were a lot of ruts, but the hills weren't unmanageable. She looked up at the slate sky; as long as there was no storm, they'd be good.

Made up of more than a hundred acres of rolling land, the private riding area belonged to a retired farmer who was making a second living running the dirt bike park and renting out vehicles. Some of the trail wound around open fields while other sections looped in and out of stands of trees. A creek bordered the southern swath, and Bernadette had no intention of taking Garcia there. With all the blind corners, an inexperienced rider could easily end up in the water.

They rode together through a wide, straight trail. When they reached the start of a modest incline, she gave him some tips and then stayed at the bottom to watch how he handled it. Keeping both feet planted on the pegs, he shifted into low gear and sped up before ascending. He stopped at the top and turned around, waiting for approval.

She gave him a big thumbs-up and followed him.

Garcia performed just as well descending the hill. He shifted into low gear and went down with the throttle closed, applying the brakes to reduce his speed.

The bottom of the incline was a mud puddle. Garcia's big bike began to bog down, and when he opened the throttle suddenly to maintain his momentum, the front end got out from under him. He fell off the back, and the bike tipped on its side in the mud.

She came up behind him. "You okay?"

He nodded, fired the bike up again, and kept going.

She was nervous when they faced climbing the steepest hill in the park. If Garcia didn't do it just right, the front wheel could lift on him again. "I don't think you're ready for this!" she hollered over the engines.

"I can handle it!" he yelled back.

"Don't forget," she said. "Ease up on the throttle while shifting, or you'll end up on your back—maybe with the bike on top of you!"

Garcia started up. He stood on the pegs and leaned forward over the front wheel. He got to the top, waved at her, and kept going. She went up after him.

When they got to an area with a lot of closely spaced humps—moguls—she knew he'd need help. They stopped their bikes next to each other. "Stand on the pegs when you take these, or you'll never father children!" she yelled.

He laughed. "I want to have children."

He bumped and bounced over the mounds, and she followed, going slow in case he took a spill. He didn't.

HE RETURNED the rental bike while she rolled her Honda up the ramp and onto the bed of the pickup. Garcia was so caked with mud, she wouldn't let him sit down until she'd spread an old blanket over the Ranger's seat.

Before they got back on the highway, she drove into town to use the self-service car wash. She pulled into the bay, plugged a fistful of quarters into the power spray, and used the hose to clean her machine while it was tied down on the bed of the truck. She climbed back into the truck and looked at her dripping Honda through the rearview mirror. "It'll be dry by the time I get home."

"Maybe you should've hosed me down," said Garcia, slapping his caked thighs.

AS SHE TURNED onto the freeway for the drive back to the Twin Cities, the subject of the tower mess finally came up.

"It's an FBI case, so we can color it any which way we want," said Garcia. "Araignee carved up a woman in his bathtub and fired at a federal agent, so it was a justifiable shooting. The part about him doing the high dive, we'll work that into something believable. It was a suicide."

"It was," she said.

"When it comes to that fire, if there're any follow-up questions from the cops or the fire department or the ME's office, I'll handle them."

"Do you really think it was just the publicity that pushed the doc's self-destruct button?"

Garcia threw an arm up over the top of the bench. "What do you think set him off?"

"All of it."

"What do you mean?"

"Think about it. If a guy had strolled into Luke's office carrying the baggage the VonHader boys were dragging around with them, the doc would have put the guy on meds and booked him for a lifetime of counseling. Remember his letter to his wife? That stuff about his demons?"

Garcia nodded. "But instead of seeing a shrink, Matt deals by becoming a party boy and Luke doesn't deal at all. He pretends his parents' bullshit was minor. Then one of them ends up pushing their bastard old man down the stairs, and the other covers for him. More ugly luggage."

"I'm done with this," she said. "Let's talk about something else."

Garcia pointed ahead. "There's a great greasy spoon right off the next exit."

She thought about the last time the two of them tried to enjoy a restaurant meal. The prospect of Creed sliding into a truck-stop booth wasn't boosting her appetite. "I can fix us something at my place."

THEY PULLED UP next to his car, parked on the street in front of her loft. He looked down at his muddy jeans. He'd kicked off his boots and was in his stocking feet; even his socks had managed to get muddy. "I've got a change of clothes in my car, but I'm filthy all the way through."

"Shower at my place."

"You sure?"

"Quickly grab your stuff out of your car and hop back in. I've gotta pull around and park the truck in the ramp for the night. You can help me roll out the bike and take it back upstairs."

He popped open the passenger door. "You really haul that machine inside with you every time?"

"Absolutely—it's my baby. Now get going. Take your gear with you. You can keep my gloves."

He jumped out, grabbed his helmet and gloves and muddy boots from the floor of the passenger's side, and went to his car. Bernadette watched him while he bent over and dumped his riding gear into the trunk and dug around for his clean clothes. Garcia, dirty and sweaty, was all smiles after an afternoon of playing in the mud. He looked like a little boy.

She carried his clean clothes and her riding gear while he walked the Honda from the ramp onto the elevator. They reached her floor, and the doors opened.

"The neighbors ever catch you doing this?" he asked, as he rolled the Honda down the corridor.

Bernadette stepped ahead of him, juggled the gear in her arms, and unlocked the door. She propped it open for him with her foot. "People bring their bicycles inside all the time. What's the difference? Wheels are wheels."

As he went through the door and steered the bike into its usual corner, he shot a look at her microwave clock. "No wonder I'm hungry. It's getting near dinnertime. Hope you have enough food."

Bernadette draped his clean clothes over a kitchen chair and dropped her helmet and gloves and goggles onto the floor. She sat down and pulled off her boots. "I have enough."

"Can I shower first?"

She scrutinized his jeans. The mud had turned to gray plaster. "Please!"

He started for the bathroom, crunching with every step he took. "Hot shower will be good."

She dug out a garbage bag from under the sink and tossed it to him before he closed the bathroom door. "For your jeans. Wash them or toss them when you get home. Just don't let them mess up my bathroom floor."

"Gotcha," he said, shutting the door.

She realized he'd forgotten to take his clean duds into the bathroom with him and reached to grab them off the kitchen chair. Too late. She heard the shower running.

WHILE GARCIA cleaned up, she pulled off her sweatshirt and smoothed the T-shirt she had on underneath. It was good enough attire for this casual evening. She opened up a bottle of wine and poured herself a glass. Sipping, she inventoried the refrigerator's contents. The chicken breasts could be broiled. Baked potatoes would take a while, but that might not be a bad thing. They could pop in a movie.

"Don't do it—you'll be sorry."

Startled, she put her hand over her heart and slammed the fridge shut. She pivoted around and saw him standing in her kitchen. "Ruben," she whispered. "Get out of my house."

"You're half-hoping he hits on you." The shower stopped, and Creed looked toward the bathroom door. "I've got a news flash. He's planning on it."

She set her wineglass down on the counter. "Baloney."

"Why do you think he *forgot* his clothes out here?"

Garcia wouldn't be that manipulative. Creed was trying to make trouble. "I invited him to dinner, and that's all."

"You should make *me* dinner for taking care of your two assailants."

Her eyes narrowed while she processed what he was saying. "The bums in the basement?"

"Do you think you fought them off by yourself? Why do you think they stayed in the basement?"

"How did you keep them down there?"

He raised his hands over his head. "Boo."

She stifled a laugh. "My hero. Thank you. Thanks for the tip on the Araignee twin, too."

He took a deep bow. Then he stepped up to her and put his bony finger in her face. "But if you continue this after-hours socialization with our superior—"

The bathroom door popped open, and Creed looked toward it. Vanished.

Bernadette retrieved her wineglass. She didn't know if she should laugh or scream.

Garcia stepped out wearing boxers and a tank top, with a towel draped around his neck. "You forgot to give me my . . ." His voice trailed off as he looked at her expression, and his eyes swept the loft. "He was here just now, wasn't he? That August Murrick character was here."

She gulped the remainder of her wine. "Creed."

"What?"

Cupping the empty wineglass between her hands, she propped her back against the edge of the counter for support. "Ruben Creed has been . . . accompanying me."

"Stalking you?"

"He showed up at the restaurant yesterday. That was the first time I'd seen him outside the office."

"That's why you looked ready to puke when I came back from the can."

"Yeah."

"Why didn't you say something then?"

She shrugged. "I didn't want you to think I was loony tunes."

"How can he be . . . offsite?"

She took some weird comfort in Garcia's businesslike description of Creed's behavior. Her dead partner was "offsite." "I'm what's haunted, not the office."

"Is that possible?"

"That's how Creed explained it. He says—" She looked down at the empty wineglass in her hands.

"Spill it."

She looked up. "He says he scared those bums away for me." She smiled weakly. "A good thing, right?"

Garcia went up to her, put a hand on her arm, and walked her out of the kitchen, taking the wineglass out of her hand as they went. "I'm staying the night."

Garcia's offer came too quickly, and it made her nervous. "No, you don't have to stay. I mean, not for protection . . . Ruben wouldn't hurt me. He's been helping me."

Garcia set the wineglass down on the coffee table. "You don't sound too convinced of that yourself."

Bernadette dropped onto the couch. "I don't know what to think anymore."

He pulled off the towel and rubbed his head with it. "I don't like this one damn bit. I'll get dressed and make us dinner. I can crash on the sofa."

"It's my own fault. I let him hang around the cellar. He even started helping me. Doing computer work on the case."

He sat down next to her. "Tell me everything, from the beginning."

"Don't be mad. I really need a friend right now. Believe it or not, you might be my best friend. How pathetic is that?"

He threw an arm around her shoulders. "I feel the same way, except not the part about it being pathetic."

Laughing, she looked up at his damp face and tousled hair. She opened her mouth to continue describing Creed's office appearances and suddenly felt Garcia's lips over her own. She put her hands on his chest to push him away but instead savored the feel of the hard muscles under his shirt.

Groaning, Garcia peeled his mouth off hers. "We shouldn't do this."

"Yes, we should," she said hoarsely.

Garcia kicked the coffee table away from the couch. Together, they slipped off the cushions and went down on the floor, with him on top of her. "Am I too heavy? I don't want to hurt you."

"I won't break," she said.

He cupped her breast through her T-shirt while his mouth went to the side of her neck. She put her hand over his and moved his fingers under her shirt. He trapped her nipple with his large rough palm. "You feel so good under my hands. So beautiful," he murmured, his mouth gnawing her breasts over the thin cotton.

Cradling the back of his head, she pressed him closer and arched her body into his. "Let's go to the bedroom."

Garcia's body tensed. He raised his torso off hers and looked down at her with half-shut eyes. "I am so sorry. This is a mistake."

"A mistake?"

He gently disengaged her arms and rolled off her. "Son-of-a-bitch," he said to the ceiling, and got to his feet.

She propped herself up on one elbow and watched him. "Where are you going?"

He scooped his clean clothes off the kitchen chair. "I'll get dressed and get out of here, if you feel safe. If you're sure Creed won't do anything."

She ran a hand through her hair and got to her feet. "I want you to stay."

"That's why I need to leave, before this turns into an even bigger mistake for the both of us. For our careers." Hugging his clothes to his chest, Garcia went into the bathroom and slammed the door behind him.

She sat back down on the couch, unsure of what to do. She hadn't seen this coming, but Creed had. Could he look into the future, or was he simply a good judge of the male character? Both possibilities were annoying.

The bathroom door popped open, and a fully dressed Garcia walked out carrying the bag of dirty clothes. "I'm so sorry this happened. This was my fault entirely. A big mistake."

She followed him to the door. "Stop calling it that. You're making it sound like a—a checkbook overdraft."

He spun around. "I want you so bad it hurts. I haven't had a serious thing since my wife died, and I have a feeling we could—"

"We could!"

"I gotta go home and take another shower." He turned around, opened the door, and left.

"We could," she said to the closed door.

Bernadette shuffled back to the couch, dropped onto the cushions, twined her arms around her torso, and bent in half.

"I told you so."

She didn't bother looking up at him. "I was hoping you'd say that. It's just what I need right now."

"You're going to get in trouble, missy. By becoming attached to each other—"

"We aren't attached. We're both lonely and in need of a good lay. Stop reading so much into it." She got up from the couch, marched into the kitchen, and opened the refrigerator.

"I could go for a beer," he said to her back.

She exhaled an exasperated surrender and reached inside for two bottles. "St. Pauli?"

"St. Pauli is great."

Blind Spot

By Terri Persons

Bernadette Saint Clare is an FBI agent with a difference: she has an unerring but uncanny knack for apprehending killers. Her ability makes her a dangerous maverick in the Federal Bureau of Investigations.

Her reward is a backwater posting to Minnesota, but on her very first day a mutilated body is found: the killing is the work of a vigilante killer intent on settling old scores. Soon more bodies appear up and down the Mississippi. All are evildoers who have preyed on the innocent.

Forensic investigation is too slow for the dizzying sequence of events that now take place. Bernadette is catapulted from the heart-stopping sequence of slayings into a chase where stalker and prey swap places and where she will be taken to the very brink of sanity.

'I loved *Blind Spot*, and can't wait for more books featuring Bernadette and her spirits' *Independent on Sunday*

arrow books

THE POWER OF READING

Visit the Random House website and get connected with information on all our books and authors

EXTRACTS from our recently published books and selected backlist titles

COMPETITIONS AND PRIZE DRAWS Win signed books, audiobooks and more

AUTHOR EVENTS Find out which of our authors are on tour and where you can meet them

LATEST NEWS on bestsellers, awards and new publications

MINISITES with exclusive special features dedicated to our authors and their titles

READING GROUPS Reading guides, special features and all the information you need for your reading group

LISTEN to extracts from the latest audiobook publications

WATCH video clips of interviews and readings with our authors

RANDOM HOUSE INFORMATION including advice for writers, job vacancies and all your general queries answered

Come home to Random House

www.rbooks.co.uk